*For Torin, Dac
and Jenn*

Rejoice, oh gifted ones

For magic and wonder spring from thee

Beware, oh gifted ones

For vanity and greed covet thee

Brace, oh gifted ones

For vice and fault tempt thee

Strive, oh gifted ones

For courage and patience find thee

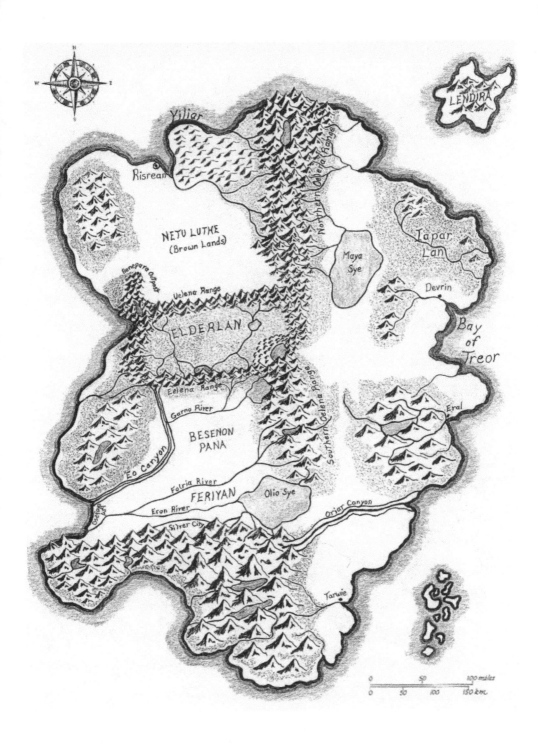

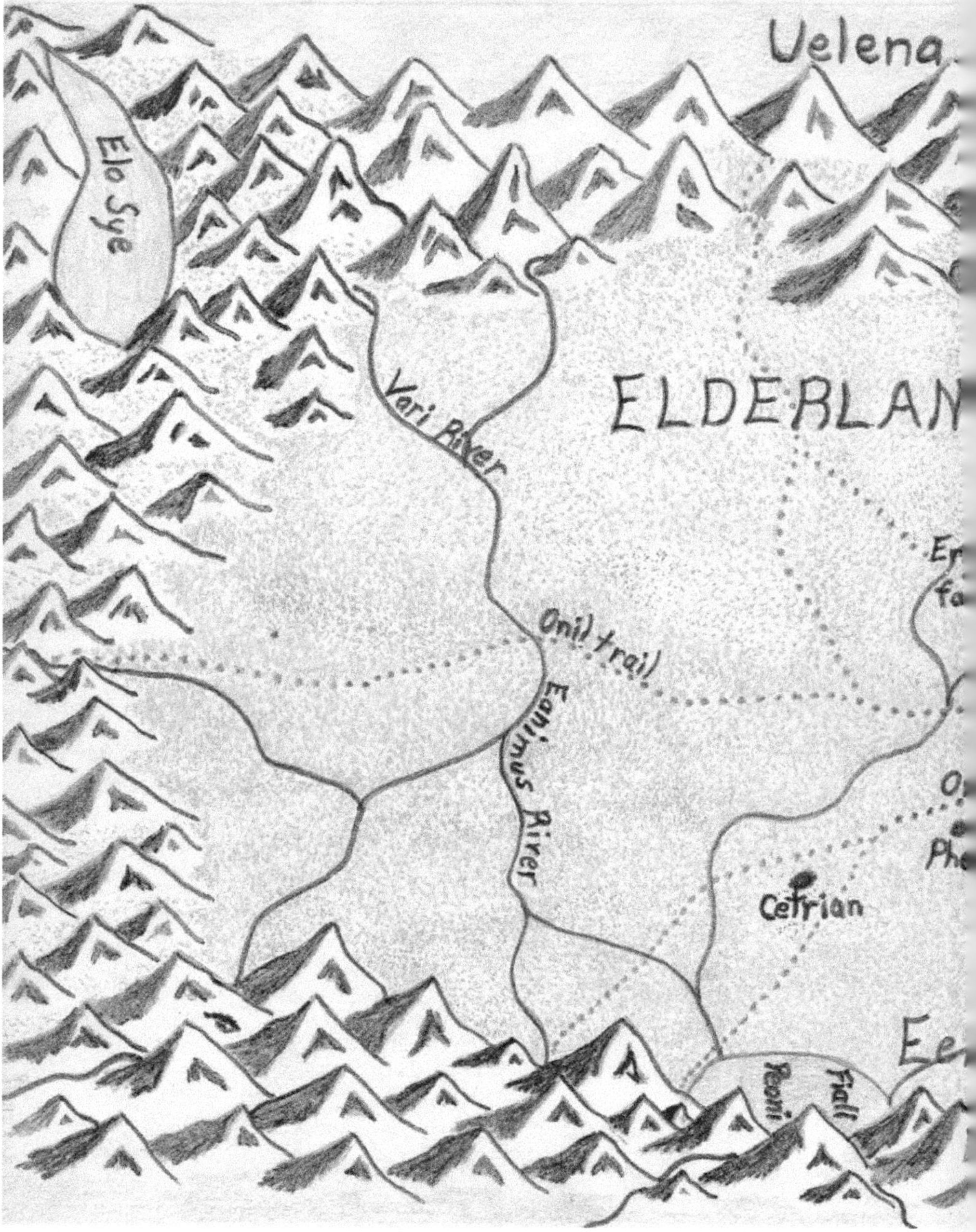
Velena
Elo Sye
ELDERLAN
Vari River
Onil trail
Eaminus River
Cefrian
Reoni
Fiall

ge
OREST
Taela River
Mai River
Meo Sye
Onil trail
Opal
en
Sara River
Yellow Beast
Gadressa
Fara Sye
Range

Contents

The Children
(in alphabetical order)

Name: Annie Perel

Age: 12 years   **Grade:** 7th

Eyes: brown   **Hair:** Auburn

Height: 5' 2"

Reader Notes: _____

_____

_____

Name: Bartholomew (Barth) Ricci

Age: 11 years   **Grade:** 6th

Eyes: Brown   **Hair:** Light brown

Height: 4' 8"

Reader Notes: _____

_____

_____

Name: Robert (Bobby) Forester

Age: 10 years   **Grade:** 5th

Eyes: Hazel   **Hair:** Light brown

Height: 4' 5"

Reader Notes: _____

_____

_____

Name: Celia (Cici) Miera

Age: 8 year   **Grade:** 3rd

Eyes: Cinnamon   **Hair:** Chestnut

Height: 4' 2"

Reader Notes: _____

_____

_____

Name: Corey (CPU) Pan

Age: 10 years   **Grade:** 6th

Eyes: Brown   **Hair:** Black

Height: 4' 6"

Reader Notes: _____

_____

_____

Name: Dylan Hester

Age: 9 years   **Grade:** 4th

Eyes: Brown   **Hair:** Black

Height: 4' 5"

Reader Notes: _____

_____

_____

Name: Emma Kadean

Age: 11 years   **Grade:** 6th

Eyes: Blue   **Hair:** Dark brown

Height: 4′ 7″

Reader Notes: _____

_____

_____

Name: Gabrielle (Gabi) Miera

Age: 11 years **Grade:** 6th **Eyes:** Hazel

Hair: Amber   **Height:** 4′ 7″

Reader Notes: _____

_____

_____

Name: Joshua (Josh) Hester

Age: 13 years   **Grade:** 8th

Eyes: Mahogany   **Hair:** Black

Height: 5′ 3″

Reader Notes: _____

_____

_____

Name: Mya Kadean

Age: 12 years   **Grade:** 7th

Eyes: Hazel   **Hair:** Blonde

Height: 4' 10"

Reader Notes: _____

_____

_____

Name: Rhea Morgan

Age: 12 years   **Grade:** 7th

Eyes: Gray   **Hair:** Dark red

Height: 5' 3"

Reader Notes: _____

_____

_____

Name: Sarah Mattus

Age: 10 years   **Grade:** 5th

Eyes: Green   **Hair:** Blonde

Height: 4' 5"

Reader Notes: _____

_____

_____

Name: Theodore (Ted) Wallis

Age: 13 years   **Grade:** 8th

Eyes: Brown   **Hair:** Blonde

Height: 5' 2"

Reader Notes: _____

_____

_____

Name: Timothy (Timmy) Davin

Age: 10 years   **Grade:** 5th

Eyes: Blue   **Hair:** Sandy blonde

Height: 4' 10"

Reader Notes: _____

_____

_____

Name: Wesley (Wes) Mattus

Age: 12 years   **Grade:** 7th

Eyes: Blue   **Hair:** Brown

Height: 5' 1"

Reader Notes: _____

_____

_____

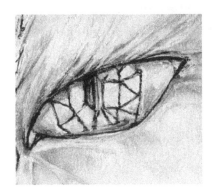

Prelude

Sarah awoke in the dark. She listened to the rain pitter-patter on the roof. She sat upright. Images from the dream filled her head. She had been lost in a forest at night. Her best friend, Timmy, was there. A burst of light shattered the darkness, then it was gone. She and Timmy moved slowly through the woods until they came to a field with a barn, and a cottage behind it. Lightning flashed. A tall man stood before them.

"You have a gift," the man said, "—a magical power. But with the gift comes a weakness. Beware of the gift and the weakness."

Sarah didn't understand the man.

The dream changed. She found herself in an immense field before a towering silver wall. A cat bounded up with long, shimmering silver fur and gleaming emerald eyes.

"You have brought a sapphire fruit," the cat said.

Sarah looked at her hands. A glittering blue object rested in them.

"What is this?" she asked.

"The fruit of power."

"What is it for?"

The cat didn't answer and bounded away.

Sarah awoke. She had dreamt the dream three times that night. She decided to tell her brother. She threw off the covers and jumped out of bed.

Chapter 1:
The Yellow Beast

Wesley Mattus strolled toward the yellow and red signpost, drawing his coat tight around him as wind scattered rain across the pavement. A crowd of kids waited at the sign, while the occasional car rushed down the road sending waves of water splashing into the air.

Ahead, the Kadean sisters stood side by side in matching blue parkas. Beside the girls squatted Barth Ricci; his eyes focused on a stream of rainwater rushing toward the curb.

The kids met there each weekday morning to catch the yellow beast, which everyone knew was the oldest, ugliest, and loudest school bus in Annaberry, New York. Although it looked like it would break down any minute, Ben, the bus driver, claimed it had run perfectly for thirty years straight. Wesley didn't believe that. He expected it would be going to the junkyard any day now.

Wesley twisted and called to his sister, who was crouched beside a hedge several houses back. "Come on, Sarah. The beast will be here any minute."

Sarah tipped her head and peered under the hedge. She was two years younger than Wesley and petite, with shoulder-length blond hair, an oval face, and bright green curious eyes. "Wait, Wes. Look at this," she cried. "It's a cat just like the one in my dream!"

Wesley rolled his eyes. He didn't want to hear any more about her dreams. She'd kept him up half the night talking about them. But Sarah was like that; when she got something in her head, she had to tell someone about it.

Engine roar filled the air, and the yellow beast rumbled around the corner. Dark yellow with a rounded front hood, the bus thundered toward the crowd of children and screeched to a halt at the signpost.

The door swung open. Wesley turned and called to Sarah again. She leaped to her feet and dashed down the sidewalk, her raincoat flapping in the wet wind.

As the other kids boarded, Wesley waited for Sarah. She bounded past him with a laugh and sprang into the doorway. At the top of the stairs, she gave Ben, the bus driver, a high-pitched hello!

"Morning," Ben replied with a mustached smile. "Don't get your seat wet."

Momentary confusion passed across Sarah's face.

Ben laughed. "Just kidding," he said. "That's not possible in this weather."

Wesley climbed the stairs feeling the heat from within sweep over him. At the top, he grinned at Ben and turned down the aisle. He passed several rows and dropped into the first empty seat, scooting over to the wall.

His friend Corey Pan lay on the bench in front of him reading a sci-fi paperback. Corey was a math and science wizard who had skipped a grade and could recite an endless array of scientific facts. He was so smart that everyone at school called him CPU after the chip that runs a computer. CPU was two years younger than Wesley and short for his age, with brown eyes, a broad face, and black hair that stood straight up, exposing his slightly oversized ears.

"You look out of it today," CPU said, using a finger to mark his place in the book.

Wesley sighed. "Sarah kept me up half the night, talking about a weird dream."

CPU grunted. "Glad I don't have a younger sister."

Wesley shrugged, thinking Sarah was easier to deal with than CPU's older sisters, who were so snooty and conceited that everyone called them the ice queens.

Wesley leaned forward and rested his head on his folded arms. He closed his eyes, hoping to get a few minutes of shuteye before the bus reached school.

When he opened his eyes, he saw Annie Perel across the aisle scribbling hurriedly in a binder. Annie was a slim girl with bony features, warm brown eyes, and shoulder-length wavy hair that always looked like it needed brushing.

She seemed to be working on her homework, which surprised Wesley because she usually finished hers at home and helped other kids with theirs on the way to school.

Wesley liked Annie. She had a big heart. If a kid fell on the playground, she was usually the first one there to help. And if someone forgot their lunch, she always offered to share hers.

Rhea Morgan sat behind Annie. Wesley knew better than to bother Rhea in the morning. Bad moods were normal for her, but mornings were the worst. Even a friendly hello could elicit a hostile glare. Rhea was tall for her age, with pale, freckly skin, gray eyes and thick red hair, which she parted on the left side. Today she wore blue jeans with a pale orange shirt peeking out from under her brown jacket.

Rhea's family had moved to Annaberry from South Carolina when she was ten, and she still spoke with a slight Southern accent. Although naturally pretty, Rhea's square jaw and permanent frown gave her a hard look that scared many kids away.

Annie finished her scribbling and set her binder down.

Rhea glanced up. "That's mine, you know."

Annie turned. "What's yours?"

"The binder."

Annie stared at the three-ringed folder. "No, it's not."

Wesley winced.

"Yes, it is," Rhea said firmly. "All my binders have orange borders like that one."

"So? Tons of binders have orange borders. It doesn't mean they're yours."

"Just saying," Rhea said. "If you borrow something, you should return it."

"I didn't borrow this!"

"Then you took it."

Annie's mouth tightened. "You want my binder?"

"No... I want what's mine," Rhea said.

"Okay, take the stupid thing."

Annie threw her math book down and grabbed the binder. She yanked it open and started ripping out the pages. "Ehh!" she cried, momentarily losing grip.

The bus slowed. Ben glanced over his shoulder. "Hey, what's going on back there?"

Annie tore out the last pages and threw the binder over the seat. Rhea caught it in midair.

Ben swung the wheel to the right and steered over to the curb, bringing the bus to a screeching halt. He leaped out of his seat and hurried up the aisle. "What's up with you two?" he shouted.

"She took my binder," Rhea said calmly.

"That's crazy!" Annie cried. "Everyone knows it's mine. But if she wants it, she can have it!"

"Okay, this needs to stop," Ben said. "This is the third incident with you two this month. If there's any more yelling or throwing things, I'll march you both down to the principal's office."

"I didn't throw anything," Rhea replied coolly.

Ben eyed the redheaded girl, his cheeks puffing, and his face flushed. Rhea stared back; her gaze steely.

"Last warning!" Ben cried. "No more trouble out of you two." He turned and strode back to the driver's seat. He jammed the key in the ignition and started up the engine.

CPU was hanging over his seat, watching open-mouthed. Wesley rolled his eyes. Something had happened between Rhea and Annie. They used to be best friends, but now they seemed to be mortal enemies. Wesley didn't know what had happened, but he guessed it was Rhea's fault because Annie was the nicest person he knew.

He scooted over to the window and stared out through the glass, watching as the bus rumbled through the old Eastwell neighborhood with its large homes and broad lawns. Brown and gray elm trees lined the streets, and leaves blanketed the grass and walkways, piled high in soggy mounds.

As the bus picked up speed, a car darted out from a side street ahead. Ben slammed on the brakes and hit the horn, which blared so loudly that pedestrians a block away leaped in fright.

CPU grabbed his stomach and bent forward, laughing. "Did you see that?" He hooted. "I love it!"

Wesley glared. He hated that horn. It was louder than the tugboat foghorns at Port Liberte. He remembered standing outside the yellow beast once when Ben blew on that horn. The sound had enveloped him like a wave, causing his brain to empty out and his muscles to jiggle like Jell-O in a thunderstorm.

As the bus neared the next cross street, Ben slowed and spun the wheel to the right. The yellow beast swung around the corner and screeched to a halt before another crowd of kids. Among them, Wesley spotted Josh Hester and Bobby Forester. Bobby's mother stood behind the boys gripping a big red umbrella above their heads.

Bobby climbed on first. He gave Ben a lopsided grin and started down the aisle, walking awkwardly like a toy with a couple of broken springs. Last summer, he'd had a terrible accident. He was playing in Newbury Park when a bolt of lightning shot out of the sky and struck him.

Bobby survived the strike but spent weeks at the hospital, then months at home recovering. He had only recently returned to school. He now walked with a limp and slurred his words when he talked.

The other children boarded one by one. Josh climbed on last, pausing briefly to talk to Ben before turning and striding down the aisle in his usual calm, confident way. Tall and slim, Josh had coffee-brown skin, and short hair cropped close to his head. As usual, he wore a black shirt beneath a long gray coat.

Josh nodded to Wesley as he passed and swung down in the seat behind him. Wesley nodded back. He admired Josh, who seemed to be good at everything. Josh was captain of the school's baseball team and soccer team. He was near the top in every class, and last year he had starred in the seventh-grade production of the Shakespeare play As You Like It. He and Wesley took art class together, and Wesley had seen Josh draw beautiful sketches of clipper ships crashing through ocean waves.

Despite his many talents and being popular at school, Josh rarely smiled. This seemed strange to Wesley, because he thought if he were Josh, he'd be the happiest guy in the world. Wesley knew Josh's mom had died when Josh was little, and Wesley sometimes wondered if that was the reason for Josh's melancholy.

Ben steered the bus into the intersection and swung the wheel to the right. He turned onto the old highway road. Soon they were passing fields and farmhouses. Wesley leaned against the window, watching tiny droplets of water slide down the glass and collect at the edges.

The rain stopped, and the air glistened. Wesley peered through the glass, spotting shimmering colors on the asphalt beside the moving bus. He watched the glittering colors curiously, then inclined his head, gazing up at the sky. High above, a pinprick of blue light darted down through the clouds like a luminous needle. He blinked at the strange sight and leaned back.

The brakes suddenly screeched. Wesley flew forward, bouncing against the seat back. Screams erupted as the bus slowed sharply. He raised his head and saw a blue wall of light—like the rolling surface of a swimming pool—rise out of the roadway. Ben slammed on the brakes, but it was too late. The bus barreled into the rocking blue wave. As light rushed down the rows, Wesley twisted, searching for Sarah. He caught her eyes for an instant, wide with fear. Then an electrical sensation stunned him, and everything went black.

* * * *

Wesley awoke on the floor beneath his seat, rolling back and forth as the bus bounced and lurched. He grabbed the seat bar and hauled himself up. Josh stood braced in the aisle a few feet ahead, while other kids lay sprawled unconscious on the benches and floor. At the front of the bus, Ben was slumped over the steering wheel.

Josh bounded up the aisle, but as he neared the driver's seat, Ben abruptly lurched upright and grabbed the wheel. Josh dropped into the seat behind him. Wesley glanced out the window. His heart thumped. They were rolling through a grassy field with no roads or buildings in sight. At the edge of the field, immense brown and gray trees towered into the morning sky.

The bus slowed, then hit a dip in the meadow and jolted to a stop, throwing everyone forward.

CPU raised his head above the seat back. "What happened?" he mumbled, touching fingers to his bleeding lip.

Wesley shook his head and twisted to look for Sarah, who was sprawled in the aisle. He called her name, and she sat up, gripping the seat cushion.

"You okay?" he yelled.

Sarah rubbed her cheeks as her eyes regained focus. "I think so."

Wesley nodded. He glanced back out the window. Above the field and trees, blue sky ran to the horizon, only broken here and there by puffy white clouds. The rain had stopped.

"Where are we?" CPU asked, sitting up straight.

Wesley exhaled and didn't answer.

Ben turned off the engine, and everything quieted.

9

A cry rang out. "Wuur huur!"

Wesley turned and saw Bobby Forester sprinting up the aisle, his eyes wide and his mouth hanging open like a fish. Bobby dashed past Wesley, but when he reached the driver's seat, Ben stuck out his arm and caught the boy. "Where are you going?" Ben asked in a shaky voice.

"Wuur huur! Wuur huur!" Bobby shouted breathlessly.

"What?" Ben grimaced. "I don't know where we are, but we're not where we should be. Go back to your seat, Bobby."

The words had no effect on the boy. Bobby squirmed and bounced in the driver's arms, his head swinging from side to side as he struggled to peer out the windows. But Ben didn't release him, and Bobby finally calmed down, meeting the big man's gaze.

"Whaa yoouu waanna, Beeen? Caana I goo oouut?"

"I'm sorry," Ben answered, clasping Bobby's shoulders. "No one's going outside. You need to return to your seat."

Bobby searched the big man's eyes, "Buut wuur huur."

Ben shook his head. "No, we're not where we should be, Bobby. We need to find out what happened. Go sit down."

Bobby shifted his weight from foot to foot. He nodded his head as if he wanted to say something to Ben but didn't. Then his shoulders slumped, and he shuffled back to his seat.

Ben rose and faced the children. "Is everyone okay back there?" he asked, wiping sweat from his face with a hand towel.

Annie leaned forward, pressing some tissues to her forehead.

"I think she hit her head," Wesley said, indicating Annie. Ben strode up the aisle and put his hand under Annie's chin, raising her face. He lifted the tissues away and grimaced at a nasty gash dripping blood down the bump of her nose and freckled cheeks.

"Ouch, we'll need a bandage for that," Ben said. "Let me get my medical kit."

After dressing Annie's gash, Ben checked on each of the kids. When he came to Wesley, he gazed at the boy worriedly, his breath coming in gasps, and his face red and puffy. "You alright?" he asked.

Wesley nodded, wondering the same thing about the big man.

The driver moved on to CPU. Wesley turned back to the window. Dense woods surrounded the field, but ahead of the bus, the meadow rolled for some fifty yards to a narrow opening in the trees that led toward a barren hillside rising beyond the meadow and the woods.

Ben returned to his seat and started the engine. The bus rolled forward a foot or two, then the wheels began to spin in the mud. Ben tried backing out, but again the wheels spun uselessly. After several failed attempts to go forward or backward, the driver turned the key, and the engine quieted.

With a sigh, he plucked a cellphone from his coat pocket, and tapped in a number. He listened for a long moment, then threw the phone down.

"Jeez!" he shouted. "Nothing works!" He turned to the kids, with a look of exasperation. "Okay, I want you all to call or text your parents. Let them know you're fine. My phone isn't working."

CPU had his mobile phone out and was keying in a number. Wesley saw the words "Network not found" flash on the screen. CPU grunted in surprise.

Wesley didn't have a phone, so he looked around at the other kids. Their phones all flashed the same message.

"No one has a connection," he shouted.

Ben frowned. He seemed to think for a moment, then he stood up. "All right," he said, "I'm going outside to check on the beast. You all stay in here. No fooling around."

Ben lumbered down the stairs and leaped to avoid the mud. He trudged around the yellow beast, stooping to his knees several times to examine the bus underside.

CPU leaned over his seat. "There's probably no damage," he said, pointing back along the field. "We didn't hit any rocks or stumps."

Wesley scanned the meadow. "But how'd we get here?"

11

CPU put his hand on his chin, then his eyes gleamed. "I know! We must have gone through a micro–black hole!"

"A what?" Wesley snorted.

"A micro–black hole. Don't you know what that is?"

"Yeah, but—"

"You have a better explanation?"

"Don't black holes destroy everything that goes into them?"

CPU shook his head. "Actually, no one knows what happens in a black hole. One theory is that it's a shortcut from one place in the universe to another."

"But I didn't see anything black," Wesley said, frowning. "There was a blue light. Are there blue holes?"

"No, that's stupid," CPU said, rolling his eyes.

Outside, Ben trudged to the tree line and studied the branches and underbrush. He walked along the woods, circling behind and to the left of the bus until he reached the opening in the trees leading toward the hillside. The driver gazed up the slope. After a moment, he turned and plodded back to the bus.

The kids were quiet as he climbed the stairs.

"Well, it appears we're stuck," Ben said, standing at the front. "I need to go get help. You all need to stay here. Any questions?"

The silence continued. Then Sarah timidly raised her hand. Ben nodded.

She ducked her chin without speaking.

Ben tapped his foot and frowned. "What is it, Sarah?"

"I have to go to the bathroom," she mumbled.

Groans and laughter filled the bus. "Your sister!" CPU said, slapping his forehead.

"All right!" Ben shouted over the noise. "Does anyone else have to go? 'Cause if you do, now's the time."

The kids all looked at one another, but no one else would admit to it.

Ben squinted at Annie. "Are you feeling better? Can you go with Sarah?"

"Sure," Annie said. She grabbed Sarah's hand and led her up the aisle and down the stairs. Ben followed the girls to where the meadow passed through the woods. Then Annie guided Sarah into the trees.

CPU's brow furrowed. "Even if we passed through a black hole, we must still be on earth. The air, vegetation, and gravity are all the same."

Wesley shook his head. He wasn't ready to believe they were anywhere but down some back road around Annaberry. CPU was smart, but black holes?

CPU crossed his arms. "Considering the temperature and climate, we must be in the Southern Hemisphere, maybe Africa or South America."

Wesley rolled his eyes.

Annie and Sarah appeared out of the trees and followed Ben back to the bus. As the girls climbed the stairs, the other kids hooted and laughed. Sarah blushed, but Annie shook her finger. "Yeah, we'll see how funny it is when you guys hear the call of nature."

After the bus quieted, Ben cleared his throat. "Okay, I'm going to go find help. If you get hungry, you have your lunches. I'll be back soon." He turned and clambered down the steps.

Wesley pursed his lips. "He's not supposed to do this."

"Do what?" CPU asked.

"Leave us alone. We should go with him."

"Did you see his face, all puffy and red? I don't think he's thinking too straight."

"Yeah, hopefully, he'll find some help and get back soon," Wesley muttered.

CPU nodded.

Ben passed out of the meadow and climbed the barren hill. At the top, he turned slowly, seeming unsure of what to do. Then he lowered his head and started down the far side, with each step disappearing further from view.

Chapter 2:
Cloud Games

Sarah puffed her cheeks and breathed out slowly. She tilted her head and stared out the window. What had happened to everything? Where were the roads and houses and cars? She remembered the blue light in the road and waking up on the floor of the bus as it bumped through this field. What had happened?

Tall trees circled the meadow. Thick underbrush hid the lower branches, but above the scrub, enormous limbs formed strange shapes, growing straight out and turning back at sharp angles, so the ends came close to the trunks. Beneath the scrub, wildflowers basked in the morning sunlight.

Sarah eyed her brother sitting several rows ahead and took a deep breath. She was glad he was there. Wesley was twelve—two years older than her—but he always seemed so calm and mature. She relied on him when things went wrong. As she watched, he pulled the band out of his hair and immediately wrapped it around his short ponytail again. That meant he was thinking. He always messed with his hair when he was thinking hard.

She hoped he'd figure out where they were and how they'd get home. He was pretty good at that kind of thing.

She remembered the time she got lost at the New York Zoo. Wesley found her, and together, they searched for their parents. Wesley located an information booth, where a tall lady with a warm smile paged their parents. A few minutes later, their mom and dad came running out of the crowd.

A scratchy voice brought Sarah out of her thoughts. "There's no present like the present," the voice said.

Sarah twisted and scrutinized her friend, Timmy Davin. Although two months younger than her, Timmy was almost a head taller, with sandy blond hair, freckled skin, and soft blue eyes that matched the cerulean scarf around his neck.

She and Timmy had been best buds since third grade. She liked him because he was different and smart. But he could also be airheaded and often said strange things that annoyed other kids. She didn't mind the things he said. They usually made her laugh and sometimes seemed to have a hidden meaning if you thought about it. However, today, she wasn't in the mood for his oddness.

"When do we reach the point?" Timmy asked.

Sarah scrunched up her nose. "Stop saying stuff like that. I'm feeling weird right now."

"Then how about a game of Crazy Eights?"

Sarah turned. Dylan Hester was standing in the aisle beside her with a deck of cards in one hand, and the other gripping the waist of his pants.

Dylan was Josh's younger brother, but nothing like his older sibling. Dylan was short and wiry, with a permanent smile that reminded her of a kid about to lick an ice cream cone. Dylan loved card games, and Crazy Eights was his favorite.

"What's wrong with your pants, Dylan?" Sarah asked, staring at his baggy jeans.

15

"My belt broke, and they keep slipping down. They were Josh's, but they don't fit him anymore, so my mom gave them to me."

"They don't fit you either." Sarah laughed.

"How about Crazy Eights?" Dylan asked again. "Celia's up for it," he said, nodding to the pint-sized girl with pretty, cinnamon eyes and olive skin standing behind him. Celia wore a pair of faded blue jeans beneath a yellow blouse with hundreds of shiny glitters sewn into the fabric.

Sarah flashed a smile at Celia whose face reminded her of a little elf.

Sarah thought cards would help pass the time. "Okay," she said, patting the seat. "Celia, you can sit with me."

Celia's eyes twinkled, and she hopped onto the bench, setting her pink flowered backpack beside her.

Sarah grinned at Timmy. "Sorry, no more room," she said, pushing him into the aisle. The sandy-haired boy shrugged and slid onto the seat across the way. Dylan began dealing the cards.

Sarah spotted a brush in a pocket of Celia's backpack and began tugging it through the younger girl's silky auburn hair.

As she brushed, Sarah noticed Bobby sitting by himself at the back of the bus. She wondered why he'd gotten so excited after they came to the meadow. They'd been in the same class for three years, and she remembered how smart and funny Bobby used to be before he got hurt. She visited him at the hospital. He was lying in a big white bed with machines hooked up to him. Tubes and wires ran to his arms and under his shirt. She tried to talk to him, but he couldn't answer, though his hazel eyes gleamed when she asked about his dog, Willow.

"Your brother's pretty out of it today," Dylan said.

Sarah looked up. "Huh?"

"Your brother," Dylan repeated, pointing up the aisle where Wesley lay snoring, his head hanging off the edge of his seat.

Sarah giggled. "That's because of me. I kept him up all night talking about my dream."

Celia raised an eyebrow. "A dream? What dream?"

16

Sarah rocked in place, remembering. "Yeah, it was strange. There was lightning and a forest and a tall man. He told me something about a magical power. Then the dream changed. A cat with beautiful emerald eyes and long silver fur ran up to me. The cat told me about a fruit like a sapphire. I didn't know what the cat meant. Then I looked at my hands and saw a shimmering blue object in them. After that, I woke up."

"Josh had weird dreams too," Dylan said. "He kept waking up and walking around the house. My mom tried to get him back in bed, but he wouldn't stay there."

Sarah leaned forward. "Just before the yellow beast picked us up this morning, I saw a cat under a bush that looked just like the one in my dream, with silver fur and green eyes."

"Wow," Celia said, clapping her hands. "Maybe it was the same one."

Sarah laughed. "I tried to talk to it, but it just gave me a snooty stare."

"I don't remember my dreams," Dylan said.

"I do," Timmy mumbled, flipping the end of his scarf over his shoulder. "And I feel like I'm in one most of the time."

"To us too," Dylan said, and all the kids laughed.

As time passed, the bus warmed. Sarah squeezed the handles of her window. The glass slid down, letting in a breeze carrying sweet smells from the meadow. She heard footsteps and turned. CPU was ambling up the aisle. He gave her a devilish grin and sat on the edge of Timmy's seat.

"Hey, CPU. Up for a game?" Dylan asked, hopefully.

CPU shook his head. "No, I have something better..." He pulled a chessboard out of his pack. "The game of kings!"

Dylan groaned. Sarah rubbed her forehead. She liked the little chess pieces, but she didn't know how to play.

"How about it, Dylan?" CPU said. "You be white."

Dylan shook his head. "Sorry. When there's no way to win, I don't spin."

They all knew CPU played in real chess tournaments and never lost to other kids.

CPU turned to Timmy. "Hey, buddy, how about it? I'll spot you four pawns."

Timmy shrugged one shoulder. "Sure. Okay." He scooted over on the seat and pulled the scarf off his neck.

CPU set up the pieces, leaving four of his pawns off the board. With this advantage, Timmy appeared to be winning until halfway through the game. Then in a few quick moves, CPU took Timmy's knight and his queen and put him in check. Three turns later, Timmy gave up. They played two more games, but those ended even quicker.

Sarah was tired of cards and had no interest in chess. She gazed out the window. Birds darted over the grass as it swayed in a light breeze. It seemed like summer, though she knew it was late November.

Timmy and Dylan moved to the front of the bus to play games on their phones with several other boys. Celia went to sit with her older sister.

Sarah tugged an apple out of her pack. As she bit into the fruit, she felt a tap on the shoulder. She twisted and found Josh gazing at her with his calm brown eyes.

"I heard you had a cool dream last night," Josh said.

Sarah swallowed the apple chunk. "Yeah, it was strange. I kept dreaming it over and over."

"Really? So, did I. Do you remember yours?"

"Uh huh, most of it."

"Was this place in it?" Josh asked, looking out the window.

Sarah squinted. "You mean this meadow?"

"Yeah, everything." He swept his hand through the air. "The meadow, the woods, the hill."

Sarah shook her head. "No, but I remember a cottage in a forest and lightning in the sky. Usually, lightning scares me, but this didn't frighten me at all."

"Anything else?"

Sarah stared out the window. "I remember beautiful fields and a silver wall running between two mountains. Then a cat with long silver fur ran up to me and started talking about a sapphire fruit." She laughed. "What was your dream?"

Josh tilted his head. "I don't remember everything, but at the beginning and the end I was standing in this field."

"Huh?" Sarah said, frowning. "This place? Have you been here before?"

Josh shook his head. "Never. But I talked to Bobby, and he dreamed of this place too."

Sarah blinked. "Bobby? You believe him?"

"Don't let him fool you. Bobby talks funny now, but he's still got it up here," Josh said, tapping his forehead.

Sarah's gaze clouded. "But if you've never been here, how could you dream about this place?"

Josh shook his head and stood up. Without another word, he turned and strode to the back of the bus.

Sarah's stomach felt queasy. She rubbed her tummy to try to calm it. She spotted Timmy at the front and climbed out of her seat.

"Hey," she said, plopping down beside the sandy-haired boy. "So, when do you think Ben will get back?"

"When he's finished with the finding," Timmy murmured without looking up from his game.

Sarah huffed and crossed her arms. "I shouldn't even ask you anything."

Across the aisle, Dylan lay on his back, reading a comic book. Celia sat in the row behind him beside her sister, Gabrielle. Gabrielle had the same olive complexion as Celia, but short brown hair that stuck out from under a New York Yankees baseball cap. As usual, she had on a gray sweatshirt, baggy blue jeans with holes in the knees, and black sneakers. At her feet lay a backpack with a skateboard sticking out of the top.

Sarah remembered the temper tantrum Gabrielle had thrown last week when the playground monitor called her "son." Of course, it was an easy mistake to make, since the playground monitor was new, and Gabrielle dressed like a boy. But Gabrielle also had a girlish side, which her long, curling eyelashes hinted at.

19

Gabrielle glared at no one in particular. "Are we gonna just lie around here?" she said. "I feel like a cat in a fish tank."

Dylan popped up in his seat and held his hand out. "Let's arm wrestle."

"No." Gabrielle snorted. "That's dumb." Her eyes flicked to the skateboard sticking out of her bag. "I need to work on my ollie."

"Try it up there," Dylan said, pointing to the hill rising beyond the meadow.

Gabrielle squinted at the hill. "Yeah, right. I'll hit a rock and do a nine hundred down the slope." She folded her arms over her stomach. Then she leaped out of her seat and pulled the door crank. The door swung out, and she bounded down the stairs, gripping her baseball cap to keep it from falling off.

Dylan dropped his comic book and jumped after her, clutching his pants. He caught Gabrielle in the meadow and ran along beside her.

Sarah glanced at Timmy. "You want to?"

"Yeah," he said grinning. Timmy pulled off his jacket and scarf and lay them on the seat.

Fifteen seconds later, Sarah and Timmy were jogging through the field with sunlight bathing their skin. Sarah breathed in the rich meadow smells. A breeze gusted. She bolted, and Timmy chased her. They caught up to Dylan and Gabrielle, and the four sprinted through the grass.

Dylan yelled and waved to the other kids on the bus. The door swung open, and children began piling out. Soon fifteen kids were romping through the grass. They started playing a game of tag with several kids it, but nobody seemed to care if anyone was caught.

Sarah ran until she was out of breath. She flopped down on the grass and tipped her face to the sky. Timmy, Gabrielle, and Dylan plopped down nearby. High above, scattered clouds floated through the blue.

Peering up, Sarah noticed a silver line running along the edge of a cloud. She squinted, following the line along the periphery of the whiteness. Her gaze flicked to several other clouds, and she noticed silver lines around them too. Then she saw one with a gold edge. The silver clouds floated in a crowd near the gold one.

"Look," she cried, pointing.

Several heads turned.

"Whoa. They look like fluffy Christmas tree ornaments," Dylan exclaimed.

The silver clouds began to billow and sway, floating away from the gold one. The gold cloud rolled and swelled in the direction of the silver ones, gradually gaining speed, though everything seemed to be happening in slow-motion.

When the gold cloud caught a silver one, their linings touched, and the colors transferred. The gold one turned silver, and the silver cloud became gold. The new gold cloud slowed and let the silver ones float away.

"Hey, they're playing tag," Dylan cried. "Just like we were."

Gabrielle frowned. Sarah's stomach felt queasy again.

"Look over there," Timmy said, pointing at the southern sky. Sarah spotted a gold cloud floating before a line of silver ones. The gold cloud changed shape, becoming a circle, then a square, then a diamond. At each transformation, it paused, waiting for the silver clouds to imitate the shape. Those that couldn't, left the line, while the others closed ranks.

The gold cloud morphed into a sail, then an hourglass, then a flower, and finally a wheel with eight spokes. Only one of the silver clouds could imitate the wheel. It moved forward and touched the gold cloud. The colors transferred, and the new gold cloud became the leader of the game.

Gabrielle grabbed her baseball cap out of the grass and sprang to her feet. "This place is wacked!"

Sarah sat up and watched Gabrielle march away. "I'm going too," she told Timmy. She leaped to her feet and followed Gabrielle toward the hillside. Ahead, Celia was picking flowers in the high grass.

As the girls approached, Celia smiled and pointed to clusters of red and blue blossoms. "Aren't they beautiful? Do you know what kind they are?"

"No idea," Gabrielle said, adjusting her cap. "I don't know a flower from a fruit loop."

"Do you want to make bouquets?" Celia asked in her sweetest voice.

Gabrielle rolled her eyes. "Why would I do that?"

"To put in the bus. They will smell so sweet."

"Sorry, sis. I don't do sweet," Gabrielle said, gazing up at the hill. "I need to practice my 180s."

Sarah followed her eyes. "You're going up there?"

Gabrielle nodded slowly. "Coming?"

"Yeah, I want to see where Ben went."

Gabrielle marched out of the meadow and started up the slope. Sarah followed. As they climbed the hillside, the grass thinned, and the dirt turned hard and clay-like. Near the top, they reached a plateau beneath an earthen mound.

"I'm gonna check this out," Gabrielle said. She scrambled up an incline to the left of the mound. Sarah waited beneath it, one hand shading her eyes from the sun.

Gabrielle disappeared behind the mound, then re-appeared at the peak. "Clutch," she shouted. "It's a natural ramp, with a landing where you are."

"It's kinda high," Sarah said, biting her lip. "What if you fall?"

"It's only dirt." Gabrielle shrugged. "Back home, I do most of my jumps on cement. This is no big."

Sarah nodded uncertainly.

"Let's go to the top," Gabrielle shouted.

Sarah eased along the plateau to where the incline was less steep and made her way up. When she reached the hilltop, Gabrielle was pulling her skateboard out of her pack.

Sarah gazed in the direction Ben had gone. She expected to see roads and farmhouses in the distance but observed only low brown hills rolling toward a far-off lake that shimmered in the sunlight. *There must be people by the lake,* she thought. *Ben will find someone.* A sense of relief filled her. She turned and gazed at the woods, stretching toward remote mountains.

"Where are we?" she murmured.

"Heck if I know," Gabrielle said. "And I don't really care. I just need to jump."

She took off her baseball cap and handed it to Sarah. "Hold this."

She dropped her skateboard in the dirt and tugged on her pads and gloves. She stared intensely at the mound. Then she exhaled noisily and stepped onto the deck.

She rolled right, then left, then straight down. When she neared the mound, she crouched, letting gravity do its magic. As the board reached the peak, she exploded into a standing position, and the board soared off the hilltop.

Moments passed as Gabrielle flew. Sarah sensed something strange. The board seemed to be gliding in a straight line. It wasn't falling.

Sarah scrambled to the top of the mound. "What's going on?" she shouted.

Gabrielle turned her head. Across the distance, their eyes met. Sarah sensed fear in Gabrielle's eyes. The board began to fall.

"No, no, no!" Sarah screamed as the board dropped out of the sky, plunging toward the earth a hundred feet below.

Gabrielle crouched and grabbed the ends of the deck, straining to keep it aloft. To Sarah's amazement, the skateboard slowed and became still—hovering in the air. Gabrielle leaned forward, and the board advanced in a smooth, straight line.

The wind gusted. Gabrielle pivoted. She swung the board up, bringing it perpendicular to the ground. She whipped around in a wide arc and glided back toward the hillside. Sarah straightened and rubbed her eyes, not believing what she was seeing. Gabrielle swiveled, and the board came back down beneath her. She cautiously rose to her feet, spreading her arms wide to keep her balance.

As the slope neared, Gabrielle crouched again. She kicked with her back foot, and the wheels landed together, but the right front wheel hit a hole, and the board flipped, sending her somersaulting into the dirt. She tumbled, banging her knee on a rock, and rolled back onto her feet. She stood trembling, dirt covering her from head to shoe tips.

"Are you okay?" Sarah hollered as she bounded down the slope.

Gabrielle exhaled and gazed skyward. "That was epic!" she yelled, shooting her arms over her head. She took a step, and her leg gave way.

Sarah scrambled over to Gabrielle, who was sitting in the dirt, blood streaming from a gash in her knee.

"Oh, no!"

"No big." Gabrielle grimaced. "I just need to wrap it up."

Sarah reached out her hand and brushed Gabrielle's thigh with her fingers. A tingle ran down her arm and through her hand.

"Whoa," Sarah said, jerking back.

Gabrielle stiffened. "What was that?"

"I don't know," Sarah said, staring at her hand. She turned it back and forth. "It felt weird."

Gabrielle took a deep breath, and her shoulders relaxed. "It was kinda cool. Do it again."

"Really?"

Gabrielle nodded quickly.

Sarah extended her hand and cautiously touched Gabrielle's lower thigh. The tingling returned, racing down her arm and out through her fingertips.

"Sweet," Gabrielle murmured, tilting her head back and closing her eyes. "It feels like sparks of electricity, but soft and gentle."

"Yeah, like the tingles you get when you do a perfect cartwheel."

Gabrielle grunted.

Sarah pressed her hand against Gabrielle's leg and crouched, closing her eyes. Gabrielle let out a yelp.

Sarah's eyes popped open.

"It's fixing it," Gabrielle hollered, pointing to her knee.

Sarah squinted. The gash had shrunken, and the bleeding had stopped. She jerked her hand back.

"No, keep it up," Gabrielle said. "It feels rad. It's fixing my knee."

Sarah dipped her chin. She cautiously set her hand back on Gabrielle's leg. The tingling returned, and the gash continued to shrink until it disappeared.

Sarah pulled her hand away. A wave of exhaustion swept over her, and her body became heavy.

"You fixed it," Gabrielle said.

"Okay," Sarah murmured, her mind fuzzy, and her vision blurred. "I'm tired now."

She lay back in the dirt and closed her eyes. The world spun, and everything faded away.

Chapter 3:
Fire in the Sky

Josh stretched his arms and squinted at the horizon. From the position of the sun, he guessed it was five or six o'clock in the afternoon, but there was still no sign of Ben. He frowned and gazed at the hill the bus driver had disappeared over. What happened to him? He wondered. Why hadn't he come back? And, where were their parents and teachers, or the police? Someone should be looking for them. It was weird that they were stuck all alone here in this field in the middle of nowhere.

Josh remembered the blue light in the road and the bus rushing into it. Then he blacked out. He awoke in darkness and silence. He sat up and stared out the window. A thousand stars shimmered in the dark sky. In the faint light he made out kids slumped on the seats and floor around him. Fear clutched at Josh. *Where are we?*

Then a crash shattered the silence, and the world burst into light. The bus landed in the meadow with a huge bounce, then it bumped and rumbled across the field.

Ahead, Ben lay slumped over the steering wheel. Josh leaped off his seat and bounded up the aisle. But before he could reach Ben, the driver bolted upright and slammed on the brakes. Josh fell forward but he grabbed a seat bar and held on.

Josh's heart pounded at the memory. He let out a deep breath and looked around, spotting Wesley leaning against the bus wall as he talked to his sister, Sarah. Wesley laughed as Sarah described some strange clouds she'd seen in the morning. Josh allowed himself a smile. When Wesley learned that Sarah fainted on the hill, he had panicked. Wesley was usually an easy-going guy, but he was close to his sister. Josh helped him carry Sarah down the slope. Then they lay her out on a seat in the bus. She had slept there for most of the afternoon.

Josh asked Gabrielle what happened, but she told him a crazy story about her skateboard flying through the air and crashing into the hillside. She claimed she tore up her knee in the collision, but that Sarah touched it and healed it. Then Sarah conked out.

Of course, Josh didn't believe this. He knew skateboards don't fly, and someone can't be healed by touching them. But when Sarah woke up, she said the same thing, so he didn't know what to believe. At least Sarah was okay, and Wesley could stop worrying.

Josh wandered through the field, noticing places where the grass had been beaten down during the day. The smell of meadow flowers filled the air. Josh noticed Dylan and Timmy collecting branches near the edge of the woods.

Despite their strange predicament, Dylan seemed as happy as a puppy at the beach. Dylan wasn't much of a worrier. Josh did that enough for the both of them. Though Dylan did ask if his mom—Josh's stepmom—would remember to feed their guinea pig. Josh thought she would.

Dylan was having too much fun to worry about anything. He wouldn't miss home until his stomach started growling around dinner time.

Barth Ricci's gruff voice rang out. He was shouting at Dylan and Timmy, who were helping him build a fort. Barth was two years younger than Josh, and a cool guy, but a bit funny looking, with a long body, short legs, and a head the size of a small watermelon. He had reddish, freckly skin and bushey brown hair cut short, exposing his large ears and prominent forehead.

Barth was smart. He could build almost anything. Last summer he'd constructed a three-story tree house in his backyard out of scrap wood from an old construction site. He'd also made several drones that flew, and a go-kart that he drove around the neighborhood. Once he'd dug a tunnel from his backyard down his driveway out to the front sidewalk, though apparently he'd gotten in trouble with the city for that.

Dylan and Timmy set large limbs at the corners of the fort. Then they laid crisscrossing branches for the roof. Boughs ran along three sides, and layers of leaves covered the top and walls.

Josh strode up next to Barth. "Looks good, dude."

"Yeah," Barth replied, lacing his fingers behind his neck with a satisfied smile. "If Ben doesn't come back today, we'll have a place to sack out tonight."

"You plan to sleep in there?"

"Uh huh, it'll be more comfortable than that tin can," Barth said with a glance at the yellow beast.

Josh nodded. He turned, noticing Rhea Morgan doing stretching exercises near the trees on the far side of the meadow. As she reached for the ground, her red hair bounced. Rhea was a mystery to Josh. She could do amazing things one minute and something crazy the next. He remembered the time she caught a kid copying her answers on a math test. She looked daggers at the dude. Then after the exam, she followed him outside. As the kid started talking to some friends, Rhea walked right up and punched him in the face. The guy fell with blood spurting out of his nose. Rhea jumped on him and landed several more blows before Josh pulled her off.

But Rhea could also do something wonderful. Josh had heard what she did when Bobby was hit by lightning. School was out for the summer, and Bobby was playing at Newbury Park with his dog.

It got cloudy and it began to rain. Suddenly, a bolt of lightning flashed down from the clouds and hit Bobby in a burst of white. He fell onto the grass, and his mom started screaming.

Rhea ran from the far side of the park and crouched over Bobby. She pumped on his chest and told his mom to breathe in his mouth. They did this until an ambulance showed up and paramedics carried Bobby away. Josh's dad said Rhea saved Bobby's life.

While Bobby was in the hospital, Josh visited him almost every day. When Bobby came home, Josh went over to his house after school while the therapists were helping him learn how to walk and talk again. On the days the therapists weren't there, Josh would do the same exercises with Bobby to help him recover.

During that time, Josh became close to Bobby's mom. Each day, she opened the door with a grateful smile. While he spent time with Bobby, she gave them chips and lemonade. He liked Ms. Forester. Josh's mom had died when he was young, and he wasn't close to his stepmom.

Josh rolled his neck and started back toward the bus. He came upon CPU and Annie sitting in the grass with a chessboard laid out between them.

Josh stopped. "How's the game going?"

CPU glanced up, then at his watch. "Not too bad—less than an hour."

Josh knew that Annie started games with quick moves, but as the game went on, usually slowed so that ten to fifteen minutes could pass between a turn. She had never beaten CPU, but she kept trying, and Josh admired that.

Annie took a deep breath and moved her queen out to the middle of the board. Without hesitation, CPU slid his bishop several squares forward to begin strangling her king. Annie gritted her teeth. CPU leaned back and gave Josh a confident grin. "What's up?" he asked.

"Sarah woke," Josh replied. "She told us the same thing as Gabrielle."

"You mean that Gabi's skateboard flew through the air and Sarah healed her knee?"

Josh grunted. CPU rolled his eyes and slapped his thigh.

Annie moved her king out of harm's way. CPU studied the board, then he slid his knight back several squares.

To Josh's surprise, Annie grinned and pushed her castle forward, putting CPU's bishop at risk. CPU blinked and straightened up. He moved his bishop safely away. Annie's smile grew. Without pausing, she brought her knight across the board to threaten his castle and queen.

"Hey, CPU. I think you haven't been paying enough attention." Josh laughed.

"Yeah, yeah," CPU muttered, sliding his queen back and leaving his castle vulnerable.

Instead of taking the castle, Annie shifted her bishop forward several squares and announced, "Check," putting both CPU's king and knight in danger.

CPU scrutinized the board. After a short pause, he slid his king away from peril. But instead of taking his knight, Annie sent another pawn forward. Josh nodded in admiration. In three more moves, CPU was back in check with a bishop and two pawns gone. Two moves later, CPU's shoulders slumped, and he conceded.

Annie leaped to her feet. "I just beat CPU!" she shouted, her voice rising higher and higher until it seemed to shatter the air, sending waves of sound surging through the atmosphere like tiny ripples on a lake. The wind stopped, the field went silent, and everything froze.

Josh shuffled back a step. "What's going on?" he said, glancing around.

Annie, CPU, and the other kids were as still as statues.

Josh's heart began to race. He grabbed CPU by the arm. "Hey, dude. What's wrong?"

CPU didn't react and continued staring straight ahead.

Josh turned toward the fort. Dylan and Barth were standing motionless there. Josh took a step, then the ripples faded, and the kids returned to life. Annie raised a shaky hand to her mouth.

CPU leaped to his feet. "What was that?" he hollered.

Annie's lips moved to speak, but no sound came out.

Josh stepped over and put his arm around her. "Are you okay? You screamed super loud. Is your voice gone?"

Annie bobbed her head.

Dylan bounded up, gripping his pants by the belt loops. "How'd you do that?" he shouted at Annie. "Everything froze, and we couldn't move."

Annie tried to speak but still couldn't. Dylan squinted and stuck his hands in his pockets. Gabrielle strolled over.

Dylan tipped his head and let out a cry. Gabrielle wheeled and clamped her hands over his mouth. They fell together laughing. Gabrielle's hat popped off and Dylan rolled away. He screamed again, but nothing happened.

"Hahaha, you can't do it," Gabrielle cried, grabbing her hat and adjusting it back on her head.

"You can't either," Dylan yelled, letting out a loud fart, which launched him into the air some three or four feet as his arms and legs swung frantically. He fell back into the grass, landing in a crouch.

There was stunned silence. Then Josh, Gabrielle, and CPU all burst into laughter. Dylan ignored them and farted again, shooting once more into the air and dropping back into the grass.

"I'm a rocket," he yelled.

"Yeah, a stinky rocket," Gabrielle laughed.

Dylan frowned and let off another fart. This one launched him some five feet into the air. He soared right over Gabrielle's head.

Josh stepped back in amazement. "Bro, how are you doing that?"

"I don't know," Dylan cried. "But I can fly."

Josh rubbed his forehead. Everything was crazy. He knelt beside Annie, who was sitting by the chessboard. "What's going on?"

Annie shook her head, raising her hands in bewilderment.

A cry rang out. Josh saw Wesley sprinting across the field and pointing at the woods on the far side of the meadow.

Josh rose and squinted at the trees. He spied someone on a branch high up one. It was Bobby. Josh started to run after Wesley. At the mid-point of the field, he slowed and cupped his hands to his mouth. "Hey, Bob, what're you doing up there?" he shouted.

There was a pause. Then Bobby swung his arms back and forth. "Yoouu seee, Joosh. Ii neeaar thee toop."

"Yeah," Josh answered. "But that's too high."

"Ii waanna see thiings!"

"What do you see?"

"Veerry beauutiifuul. Forresst and moouuntaaiins. Veery faarr!"

"It's dangerous up there."

"Ii noo affraaid. I cliimb gooot."

"Yeah, you climb good. But a branch could break."

Josh slowed up beside Wesley, who was standing some thirty yards from the tree. He spotted movement on a low limb, then red hair. Josh blinked in surprise. It was Rhea.

Rhea climbed rapidly through the branches, finally stopping just beneath Bobby's limb. She said something to the boy which Josh couldn't make out.

"Noo, I waanna staay," Bobby hollered. "I liike iit heeree. I fiine. Noo neeedd heelp."

"Hey, Bob," Josh shouted. "You should get down."

Bobby slid around to a limb on the far side of the tree.

Josh gritted his teeth and shared a look with Wesley. Bobby had been a good climber. But after he got hurt, he couldn't control his hands and feet well. Josh feared he would lose his balance.

"Hey, Bob, there's someone who would be really upset if she knew you were up there," Josh shouted.

Bobby became still.

"I don't want to tell her," Josh continued, a hint of warning in his voice. "But unless you come down, I'll have to."

The field became silent. Josh shared another glance with Wesley, who frowned and crossed his arms.

Bobby shifted his weight and coughed nervously.

"Joosh pleeaase doon teell mee moom. Yoouu knoow shee bee maad."

"Yeah, I know," Josh answered. "So come down now, and I won't have to."

Bobby straightened. He hesitated. Then he lowered himself onto the limb below.

On the near side of the tree, Rhea did the same. Without speaking, the two kids descended through the branches.

They hadn't gone far when a low rumble stirred the air. The ground began to vibrate like a road when a garbage truck passes by.

Josh scanned the field. He looked skyward. The rumble grew louder. Josh swung around. An orange glow was rising in the western sky. The vibration swelled. He yelled to Bobby and Rhea, but the rumble drowned out his voice.

Wesley motioned in a hugging gesture. Rhea nodded and wrapped her arms around the branch beneath her. But Bobby stood up on his limb, craning his neck to peer at the horizon.

Josh raised his hands in frustration. In the west, the orange glow swept upward. As it rose, the sky morphed into rich shades of red and yellow, reflecting an eerie radiance off the grass and the trees.

Rhea lay flat on her branch, gripping it tightly, while Bobby stood on his and reached for another.

A scream pierced through the rumble, and the world fell silent. The thunder stopped. The shaking stopped. Everything became still… everything, except Josh. He wheeled. Wesley and the other kids were as still as wax figures.

Josh squinted at the tree. He knew what he had to do. He sprinted through the shimmering ripples. He jumped, grabbing a low limb and swung his leg up and over, coming onto the branch.

In frozen silence, he climbed. Long moments passed as he rose toward Bobby and Rhea. Then, the silence ended and the air shuddered. He clutched the limb and raised his eyes. His heart pounded.

In the west, an enormous ball of fire hurtled across the sky. It thundered toward the meadow, passing overhead with a deafening roar, turning the sky into an ocean of orange and red.

A wave of heat washed over Josh. Then a hurricane-like wind slammed into the field, bending trees and grass, and knocking kids to the ground.

Josh clung to his limb as it swung wildly in the gale. The fireball roared past and shrunk into the east. The wind died down and the meadow quieted.

Josh relaxed his grip and sat upright. Some twenty feet above him, Bobby dangled precariously between two branches. Bobby's hold slipped, and he fell.

Rhea's hand shot out. To Josh's amazement, she caught Bobby's wrist as he dropped past. With a grimace, Rhea jerked the boy onto the limb and pulled him to her.

Bobby howled, "Hooot, hooot!" and shoved Rhea back, sliding away. "Yoouu huurtt. Yoouu huurtt."

"Suck it up," Rhea shouted angrily. "At least you're not in pieces on the ground."

The fireball disappeared over the eastern horizon, and the rumble died away. Sobs rose from the meadow.

Josh hauled himself onto Rhea's limb. "You caught him," he said, his eyes shining with wonder. "That was unreal."

Rhea shrugged and glanced away, seeming embarrassed.

Bobby cowered against the tree, cradling his left arm and frowning miserably.

"You alright," Josh asked with concern.

Bobby pursed his lips. Small tears appeared in his eyes. He stuck out his arm, pointing to a red welt that circled his wrist.

"What's that?" Josh asked in alarm.

"Ryeeaa. Shee hoot. Shee buurn mee!"

Josh shook his head in confusion and stared at Rhea. "What happened?"

"I don't know," Rhea said, rolling her eyes. "I just caught him."

Josh touched her arm. Her skin felt warm. "Okay," he said, "let's get out of this tree before things get worse."

Rhea lowered herself to the branch below. Bobby did the same. The three descended together. When they neared the ground, Wesley stepped under the tree. Josh swung off and landed in the grass. Bobby dropped down beside him.

"You okay?" Wesley asked.

"Yeess, but Ryeeaa hoott. Shee buurn mee."

"Look at that," Josh said, pointing to the welt on Bobby's arm.

"What happened?"

Bobby sniffled. "Ryeeaa hooot."

"She grabbed him there when he fell," Josh said. "I don't know how he got burned. I touched her. She wasn't hot."

Wesley's forehead wrinkled. He looked at Rhea in puzzlement. She reached the lowest branch, noticing his gaze. "What?" she said with annoyance.

"Bobby's burn?"

Rhea shrugged. "I don't know. I just caught him."

She hopped off the branch and landed a few feet away. Josh bent over and brushed off his pants, thinking if Rhea had burned Bobby, at least he didn't fall out of the tree. Josh didn't plan to tell Mrs. Forester about Bobby climbing. She would freak out. After he was hit by lightning, she became super protective, not letting him do anything remotely dangerous. She obsessed over the weather and wouldn't let him play outside if there was any chance of rain. She even wouldn't let him go on a school field trip to Myer's Lake because she thought he could drown.

Josh knew why she was scared, but he thought it wasn't right. Bobby couldn't avoid everything. There was always something dangerous, and Bobby complained he had no fun anymore.

"We need to check on the other kids," Josh said starting into the meadow. Bobby, Wesley and Rhea followed.

A loud fart sounded and Dylan shot into the air, soaring over CPU and Barth before landing back in the grass. Josh blinked and shook his head in disbelief.

As they neared the other kids, Josh sensed everyone was in a state of shock. He waved them over and they gathered around. Celia wiped her eyes.

"Is everyone okay?" Josh asked.

The kids looked at one another and nodded.

"Good," Josh said with relief. "That was crazy. I've never seen a fireball like that. I don't know what it was - a meteor or something. Freaky stuff keeps happening, like Annie freezing things and Dylan shooting into the air. Have you guys noticed anything else?"

"Like I told you," Gabrielle grumbled. "Sarah healed my knee".

"And Gabi's skateboard flew through the air," Sarah exclaimed.

"Strange things in a strange land," Timmy muttered.

CPU waved his hands around. "I know, I know what happened," he said.

Josh eyed him doubtfully. "What?"

"We must have gone through a micro-black hole."

Josh rubbed his cheeks as he considered this. "A black hole? Really? How does that explain the fireball and the crazy things you guys are doing?"

CPU bit his lip. "Well..."

"And what about Ben?" Rhea asked. "Where is he? He should have been back hours ago."

"It must have been further away than he thought," Sarah said, hopefully.

"No kidding," Rhea grumbled. "But he shouldn't have left us in the first place."

"He'll be back," Annie said. "I'm sure."

Barth cleared his throat. "I don't know about you guys, but I'd really like some spaghetti and garlic bread right now."

Everyone fell silent. They were all getting hungry.

A breeze picked up. Josh raised his head to look at the sun sinking in the west.

"It'll be dark soon," he said. "We may have to sleep here. Barth is building a fort that he can sack out in. The rest of us can stay in the bus. Hopefully, Ben or someone else will come by morning."

Barth's shoulders straightened and he grinned at Timmy and Dylan. "We got some work to do," he said.

The roof of the fort had blown away in the wind, but the frame still stood intact.

Dylan grabbed his pants. "Yeah, come on," he shouted and let off a fart that momentarily lifted him off the ground.

"Work and play for the day," Timmy cried.

"I'm coming too," CPU said, and hurried after them.

Most of the other kids wandered away. Some returned to the bus while others rested in the meadow.

Josh stood motionless. His eyes settled on the trees at the far side of the field.

Rhea leaned forward and stretched her arms, resting her palms on her feet. She straightened. "What's wrong?" she asked.

"Huh?" Josh said, "Nothing."

Rhea continued staring, and the frown on her lips flattened to an expressionless line.

Josh sighed. "I don't know what's going on."

Rhea chuckled. "Join the club."

Josh looked toward the woods. A faint mist floated out from the trees. A tingle ran down his spine. He sensed something there, something mysterious, something dangerous.

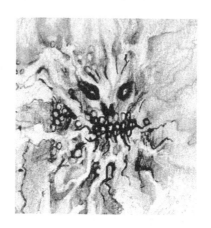

Chapter 4:
Mist above the Grass

As the last rays of sunlight reached out across the sky in vibrant yellows and reds, a breeze picked up, cooling the evening air. Rhea sat alone in the darkening field, listening to the hum of crickets and katydids. Distant voices reached her ears, carrying across the field from the fort near the trees. Wesley and Josh stood there, holding long gnarled walking sticks, while Barth, Dylan, and CPU jostled around inside the fort, trying to find a comfortable spot to sleep. Timmy had gone back to the bus.

Rhea stared at the night sky and listened to CPU complain about missing a soccer match between Brazil and Argentina. She groaned, wondering why anyone cared about things like soccer. She hated sports—unless you considered dance a sport which she loved. But what worried her was the science report due tomorrow morning in second period. She hadn't finished it yet. She had done the homework in her backpack, but the report was on her laptop at home. If it were late, her grade would drop.

Rhea puffed her cheeks and let the air out slowly. She rested her gaze on Wesley. Only the outline of his face was visible in the fading light, but she could picture his sweet smile and the short ponytail at the back of his neck. She adored his red cheeks and blue eyes and the thick curly brown hair covering his ears. She'd had a crush on him since forever, but she had never told him. Sometimes—like if he asked her a question or came too near—she would snap and say something mean. Not that she meant to exactly, but because being close to him just felt awkward. Still, watching him from a distance was nice.

He was the reason she and Annie had had a falling out. Annie had worked with Wesley on a booth for the autumn festival. He was so sweet and helpful that Annie crushed on him. She came over to Rhea's house that night and blurted out the news. Rhea was already stressed about her dad's birthday, and she couldn't handle her friend falling for the guy she obsessed over. She flew into a rage and said some mean things to Annie which she later regretted, but their friendship was severed.

Dylan scrambled out of the fort, swinging his hips and jumping around like he was letting off some more of his stupid farts. The other boys laughed, and the corners of Rhea's lips curled up into a smile. Dylan was different from Josh. While Josh was a cool customer, Dylan was a jokester and a wiry spark plug. At school, Rhea usually ate lunch by herself under the old oak tree near the athletic field. Dylan sometimes came over and talked with her. He wanted to get her to play cards or a game with him. Of course, she'd refuse, so he'd do handstands and pushups in the grass and mimic her accent.

Rhea stared at the evening sky. She couldn't find the moon, but the night seemed brighter than back home – as if the stars were closer. Their light bathed the field in a silvery glow like a thousand tiny lamps. She could make out the dark shapes of trees circling the meadow and could even see her own faint shadow in the grass.

She thought of Ben, and a quiet anger stirred in her. Where had he gone? Why had he left them and not come back? He had always seemed reliable, but now he was acting like as big a flake as any other adult - as her dad. She scowled, suddenly realizing Ben had the same reddish beard and deep, annoying voice as her dad.

Rhea hadn't seen her father in over a year, not since she and her mom's big fight. As usual, her dad had tried to play peacemaker and calm them down, but Rhea wasn't interested in being calm and screamed at him, blaming him for everything wrong in her life. That night he packed a suitcase, tucked her little sister into bed, and left the house. No one had seen him since.

The breeze had grown colder, and Rhea shivered. She rolled to her feet. To her right, the hill rose dark against the night sky. She swung her pack over her shoulder and strolled toward the yellow beast.

Sarah opened the door. Rhea climbed inside, pausing at the driver's seat to stare across the rows. Kids lay sprawled on the seats and floor, asleep or close to it. And at the back of the bus, Bobby sat by himself, his eyes shining in the darkness.

Rhea found an empty bench. She plopped down and scooted to the wall. Drawing her coat around her shoulders, she stared out through the glass. Across the meadow, Wesley and Josh were still talking to the boys in the fort. A gust of cold air blew against Rhea's cheek; her window was half-down. She shut it as the boys said their goodnights. Josh and Wesley ambled back across the field, dipping their heads together as if talking quietly. Wesley no longer had his walking stick.

Timmy opened the door, and the boys climbed inside. Josh followed Wesley to the back. Rhea's eyes drooped, and she dozed off.

She awoke in darkness and silence. Her watch flashed 11:38 p.m. She sat up, shaded the window with her fingers, and peered out. In the silvery starlight, the grass swayed, and the distant trees loomed dark and ominous.

Rhea heard a noise and twisted, spying someone creeping up the aisle. "Who's that?"

"Meee."

'Bobby? Why are you still up?"

"Iii scaareed," he whimpered, kneeling in the aisle beside her seat.

"Scared of what?" Rhea said with a snicker.

"Theerr baaad thiiing oouut theerre," he said, pointing to her window.

"What kind of 'baad thiing'?"

"Youu doona waana seee. Noo. Baad seee."

Rhea peered into the darkness. "I don't see anything."

"Itt coomee. Yoouu doont loook, Rheeaa."

Bobby reached out and covered her eyes with his hands.

"Get off me," Rhea cried, pushing him away. "What's wrong with you?"

Bobby withdrew across the aisle, raising his knees to his chest and ducking his head under his arms.

Rhea pursed her lips. Ghosts and such things didn't scare her. Horror movies just made her laugh. It was real life that frightened her, like being stuck on a bus in the middle of nowhere with a missing driver. She zipped up the front of her jacket and lay back in the seat.

Her gaze drifted to the window. In the darkness near the tree line, she saw movement. At first, it seemed to be mist floating over the grass, but the vapor swirled and formed into the shape of a bird with a long-feathered tail. The bird swayed and dissolved back into white fog.

Bobby moaned, and Rhea's pulse quickened. "What's wrong with you?" she snapped.

Bobby ducked his head but reached one hand toward her. "Noo loook, Rhheeaa. Veery baad thing."

Rhea ignored his pleas and kept her eyes fixed on the mist. The vapor drifted over the grass, and features appeared again. One end of the mist swirled into an oval shape with two black spaces like eyes. A black, jack-o-lantern mouth spread beneath them. Beyond the oval, the vapor narrowed into a rolling tail that swam through the midnight air.

Bobby's moans intensified, and fear crept into Rhea's heart.

"What is it?"

Rhea turned to find Josh's sharp eyes staring at her from two rows away.

"No clue," she said, her voice cracking. "Looks like some giant ghost fish or bird."

Josh pulled out his phone and set it against the window. The phone clicked as he snapped several shots. The vapor swayed, drawing closer to the bus. It slowed.

The mist rolled, and the oval head rotated, its black eyes swirling and the dark mouth widening. Then the head lunged at the glass. Rhea fell back into the aisle, her feet kicking up into the air.

The white face swept to the window, its swirling eyes growing to the size of hubcaps. Rhea's heart hammered in her chest. She wanted to scream, but her mouth wouldn't work. Then someone landed in her seat. The ends of a walking stick stuck out to either side of the figure – it was Josh.

Josh slammed the stick against the bus wall and shouted in a voice that woke all the other kids.

Rhea struggled onto her elbows and peered around Josh. The mist creature's face swelled, and its brow widened so that each eye stared through a separate pane of glass.

Josh yelled and slammed the stick again. The creature swung away, sliding toward the door. A shriek pierced through the noise. Ripples surged through the air. Rhea couldn't move.

The whole world became still. The mist creature froze. Nothing moved… except Josh. He leaped into the aisle and bounded toward the driver's seat. Yanking on the crank, he pulled the door shut.

The ripples faded away, and motion returned. The creature veered along the bus wall.

Gripping a seatback, Rhea struggled to her feet. She twisted and spotted Annie crouched down, one hand over her mouth. Rhea swung back around.

The creature reached the door and pressed against it before slithering onto the hood of the bus. There it rotated, and its skull-like features swelled out to the corners of the windshield. The children screamed and scrambled under their seats.

The creature stared down the rows. Rhea crouched low, while Josh stood near the driver's seat, his legs braced wide. He leaned forward and glared into the swirling eyes.

The mist slithered off the window and down the far side of the bus, its long tail rising and falling as it hunted for an opening in the metal and glass.

Rhea kept her eyes locked on the creature, but as it moved, the dark outline of Barth's fort came into view. She gulped, remembering that Barth, Dylan, and CPU were sleeping in there. Rhea pressed tightly on the seatback, hoping the creature wouldn't discover the boys. Her heart paused a beat as someone crawled out of the fort. The figure rose. Then Dylan's voice carried across the meadow. "What's going on over there?"

The mist swung toward the sound. Rhea and the other kids shouted. Dylan froze.

Josh's voice rose above the others. "Get out of there, Dylan. It's coming for you."

As the vapor rushed across the field, Dylan drew back a step, then let off a fart like an angry airgun shot and soared into the air, landing some ten yards from where he'd left the ground. The mist creature flinched and slowed, then it swirled toward him. Dylan spun and dashed away, clutching his pants and shooting off stinkers every couple of strides that shot him into the air and forward.

Josh pulled on the crank, swinging the door open. Rhea rushed after him with Wesley right behind her. Josh leaped down the stairs. The other two started after him, but Josh spun back in the grass. "You guys stay here," he said. "I just need to get Dylan."

"What about Barth and CPU?" Wesley cried.

Josh swallowed. "Okay, Wes, you get them. I'll try to distract that thing. Rhea, you stay here."

Rhea's mouth tightened, and she clenched her fists, but before she could protest, Wesley pushed past her down the stairs, and he and Josh were running.

Josh angled left toward Dylan, who was fleeing along the edge of the trees, while Wesley headed toward the fort.

Josh sprinted through the grass, running with his smooth, effortless stride, the long walking stick gripped tightly in his hands. Dylan bounded along the trees, farts exploding in the night, as the creature rushed through the air some twenty yards back.

Wesley reached the fort and stuck his head inside. A moment later he tugged Barth and CPU out. The two boys stumbled through the meadow, half asleep, while Wesley pushed them forward.

Josh caught Dylan at the southern end of the field. The younger boy sprang past his brother with a panicked cry, and Josh wheeled to face the onrushing creature. Rhea's breathing stopped. What's he doing? He's just standing there.

Josh raised the walking stick, gripping it at one end like a baseball bat. The mist elevated as it neared him, its black mouth spreading wide. The mist descended, and Josh swung, cutting up through the vapor as it swallowed him. Josh disappeared. Rhea gasped. The mist swayed and swirled, then the walking stick sliced back out of the fog.

Wesley hurried Barth and CPU around the front of the bus. Timmy opened the door, and Barth stumbled up the stairs. CPU followed.

"What is that thing?" Barth yelled as he staggered up the aisle.

"How do we know?" Rhea hollered.

Dylan bounded through the grass; his mouth wide open in panic. He angled toward the yellow beast and leaped, vaulting over the hood of the bus and landing with a thud beside the front wheel.

"Get inside," Wesley cried, pushing Dylan up the stairs.

Josh leaped out of the mist and turned, swinging the stick back through the swirling white. The fog rolled with the blows but seemed unaffected as Josh struck again and again.

44

Rhea tensed. "Get out of there, Josh," she murmured. She wanted him back on the bus. She turned to Wesley, standing at the door.

"Come inside. It's no use standing out there."

Wesley hesitated, glaring across the meadow at the churning vapor. His attention went to the fort, and his head swung up. "I forgot something," he yelled and bolted away.

Rhea heaved a sigh and pulled the door shut. She started down the aisle, keeping her eyes on the windows. Other kids cried and shouted around her.

The mist rolled away from Josh, leaving him alone in the grass. He planted the walking stick in the dirt and leaned forward, resting his weight on it. The fog edged along the trees. Then it veered back into the field. Rhea's heart thumped.

Wesley reached the fort and bent down, searching the grass. He leaped up with the walking stick in his hands.

"Is that it?" Rhea hollered. "You went back for that?" The mist came into view, rushing toward the fort. "Look out!" she shouted.

Wesley turned as the cloud of vapor came upon him. He swung his stick, then disappeared into the whiteness. Rhea gasped. She waited for long moments without breathing. Finally, the fog whirled and rolled away, leaving an empty field.

Rhea searched the darkness. "What? Where is he? C'mon, where is he?" She sprang up the aisle. Annie blocked her way.

"Where are you going?" Annie asked firmly.

"Out of my way," Rhea cried, pushing Annie back.

"Ow, that hurt," Annie said, rubbing her arm.

Rhea narrowed her eyes. "What hurts?"

"Your hands—they're hot. You burned me."

Rhea blinked and shook her head in confusion. "You're loopy. Get out of my way."

Annie gave a look of exasperation. She dropped into a seat. Rhea rushed past. As Rhea neared the door, Annie leaped back up. She scrambled down the aisle.

45

Rhea started down the steps, then turned, meeting Annie's eyes. "Stay here," Rhea said, her expression softening. "Keep the others safe."

Annie hesitated, then nodded.

Rhea sprang off the bottom stair and into the meadow. She dashed through the tall grass. Cold air rushed by her ears, drowning out all other sounds. To her right, Josh was jogging toward the fort. He shouted, but Rhea ignored him and angled toward the cloud of vapor.

The mist seemed to sense her movement and whirled, billowing back across the field. Anger swelled in Rhea as she rushed through the night air. Fear burned away in a blazing fury. She no longer felt cold or wind, only rage at this thing that had taken her friend. She careened toward the monster. The mist spread wide, and its dark mouth opened like a tunnel of blackness. Rhea leaped, floating for a moment. Then she fell through the fog with a deafening hiss, landing in the wet grass.

The bitter cold shocked her. Cold like she'd never felt before. But fog sizzled and steamed around her, and an echoing wail rose from the creature. The mist recoiled and swirled away. Rhea struggled to her feet. Her anger surged. She leaped again, spreading her arms as she fell through the icy whiteness. Steam bubbled up around her like water on hot coals.

She landed in a crouch, dripping wet from head to foot. The creature moaned and churned away, large gaps showing in the vapor. The holes closed, and the monster shrank as it floated toward the trees. Rhea's eyes blazed — the thing was hurt. She sprang again, water flying off her clothes. "I'll finish it. I'll kill it," she murmured, an avenging grin spreading across her face. Then a cry cut through her thoughts.

"Help, Rhea!"

The need in the voice stopped her. She turned. The cry came again – it was Josh. She hesitated, watching the mist rush toward the trees. Josh called again. Rhea spun and ran toward the fort, the night air cold on her face. As she neared the wooden structure, she saw him kneeling on the ground. Josh raised his eyes. "He's frozen."

Rhea gasped. Wesley lay still on the ground. Starlight glittered off crystals covering his body. Rhea bent down, resting her hand on his shirt. The ice vaporized in a cloud of steam. She jerked back.

"Whoa," Josh exclaimed. "It melted. Do it again. Melt more. Melt it all!"

Rhea opened her mouth as if to speak, and then closed it again. She set her hand on Wesley's shirt, running her fingers over the ice. Everywhere she brushed, the crystals steamed away. She touched lightly, afraid of burning him. On a pant leg, she lingered too long, and the scent of smoldering denim filled the air. She jerked back.

"No… keep it up," Josh said. "Don't be scared. Melt it all."

Rhea ran her hands up and down Wesley's pants and over his shirt. Everywhere she rubbed, the crystals liquefied into mist and melted into the grass. As the ice disappeared, she realized she had never touched Wesley before. A tingle ran down her spine, and she jerked away in sudden embarrassment.

Josh's eyes narrowed in confusion. "What's wrong? Keep it up," he said.

Wesley coughed and shuddered. Rhea stared at his gentle face. A thin sheet of ice covered his cheeks and forehead. She took a deep breath and set her hands back down, sweeping them over his shirt as the ice steamed away.

When she finished his front side, she leaned back. "Turn him over."

Josh grabbed Wesley by the shoulders and tipped him onto his stomach. Rhea ran her fingers along his legs and torso. Wesley groaned and shifted in the grass.

"He's lying in a puddle of water," Josh said. "Let me move him."

Rhea stepped back, and Josh hooked his hands under Wesley's arms, dragging him about ten feet away and laying him back down in the grass.

Rhea knelt and resumed her melting. When she accidentally brushed Wesley's arm, he flinched and opened his eyes. "Ow! That hurt."

Rhea's face tightened. "Sorry. I'm trying."

Wesley's eyes clouded, and he nodded.

Rhea ran her hands up and down Wesley's clothes until all the crystals had melted away. Then she sat back on her heels.

Josh leaned forward. "Are you okay, dude?"

"I'm cold," Wesley said, his teeth chattering.

"Yeah, and you're alive," Josh said, wiping his brow. "Let's get you back in the beast."

Josh hooked his hands under Wesley's arms and lifted him to his feet. Rhea stepped away. She heard footsteps and turned as Annie jogged up.

"What happened?" Annie asked.

"Wesley just learned what it feels like to be an icicle," Josh said with a laugh. "And, he'd still be one if it wasn't for Rhea."

Annie looked at Rhea, who avoided her gaze.

"I don't get it," Annie said. "What happened?"

"The mist froze him," Josh murmured.

Annie blinked in astonishment. "How?"

"I don't know, but it did," Josh answered.

"Where is it now?" Annie asked worriedly.

Rhea shrugged. "Probably off to lick its wounds. I burned some chunks out of it."

Josh put Wesley's arm over his shoulder. "Annie, can you give me a hand?" he said. "Let's get him in the bus."

Annie took Wesley's other arm and leaned under it. They moved slowly with Wesley through the field. Rhea followed a few feet back, afraid to touch Wesley again.

Annie glanced over her shoulder and cleared her throat as if she wanted to say something but didn't.

Thoughts turned through Rhea's head. *The creature was mist. It was ice-cold. Why did it attack us? Was it alive? Where did it come from?* She looked around warily. *Where are we?*

At the bus, Barth opened the door. Josh helped Wesley up the stairs. Sarah sprinted down the aisle and threw her arms around her brother.

"You're safe," she said, tears rolling down her cheeks.

"Yeah, but I'm tired..." Wesley mumbled.

"Come on. You can sit down," Sarah said, leading him up the aisle.

Rhea stopped at the driver's seat and scanned the bus interior. Half of the kids looked in a dazed stupor, while the other half seemed to be buzzing with nervousness.

Bobby was bouncing on his seat like a bear on a trampoline.

As Sarah and Wesley passed, Bobby grabbed Wesley and shouted, "I sooo haappyy yoouu saaffee."

"Me too," Wesley said weakly.

"Okay, okay," Sarah said, pushing Bobby back. "Let him rest." She helped Wesley to his seat, then she plopped down beside him. Sarah talked excitedly, as Wesley tugged off his wet shirt, then wrapped a coat around his shoulders.

Rhea returned to her seat. She slid up against the bus wall. She watched Annie and Josh near the front checking on each of the kids. They talked to the younger ones in reassuring voices, and Annie gave them each a hug. The kids slowly calmed down.

Rhea admired Annie's ability to comfort others. Rhea was strong and tough, but she couldn't do that. When she tried, it felt awkward and embarrassing. Watching Annie comfort others reminded her why they had been close once. Regret passed through Rhea. She decided to be nicer to Annie. Maybe they could be friends again someday.

Rhea pulled her coat tight and peered out at the field, silvery in the starlight. She wasn't tired. She decided to keep watch. If that creature came back, she'd finish it off.

Rhea leaned back in her seat and waited, her mind clear and ready.

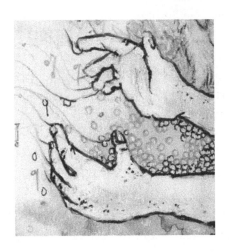

Chapter 5:
Barriers and Paths

After Annie talked to each of the kids, she returned to her seat and tried to calm herself down. She checked her watch—1:15 a.m. She had never been up so late. Her mind was fuzzy, and her muscles ached. A vision of the mist creature kept revolving in her head. She slumped in her seat and stared out the window, searching anxiously for any sign of white vapor. In the distance, the dark shape of the fort rose out of the grass. She held her breath, remembering Wesley disappearing in the fog there. It had attacked him. What was it? Was it alive? How did it freeze him? What about Josh and Rhea—why weren't they hurt? None of it made any sense.

Annie rubbed her upper arms. Then she smiled as she thought of Rhea melting ice on Wesley. She imagined how nervous and embarrassed Rhea must have been, but she'd done it. She'd saved Wesley's life. Along with her bad temper and moodiness, Rhea was fearless. Attacking the mist creature was crazy, but she had done it and survived.

Exhaustion finally overcame Annie, and she sank into a dreamless slumber. She awoke in the night to the sound of sobbing. She followed the noise up the aisle and found Celia crying in her seat. Annie took Celia in her arms and rocked her until the young girl drifted back to sleep.

In the morning, Annie awoke on the cold floor beneath her bench. She lay there momentarily, unsure where she was, then the events of the day before flooded back. She pulled herself onto the seat and peered out the window. Sunlight shimmered on the grass, and long shadows from the trees stretched lazily across the field.

She rubbed her tongue against her teeth. A sticky film coated her mouth. She had no toothbrush. She patted her hair. It was a mess, so she plucked a hairbrush out of her bag, and began tugging it through the tresses. She felt sticky and dirty and wanted to wash up. But what bothered her most was the deep ache in her stomach. She hadn't eaten anything since noon the day before, and it really hurt.

She wondered what Sheila—her Dad's girlfriend—had fixed for dinner last night. Sheila was a great cook. That was one thing Annie could say for her, but there wasn't much else. Annie wished her dad would show up. Was he looking for the bus? He must be. He'd be questioning the police, her teachers, the neighbors, everybody, while Sheila would be whining and complaining. Annie's mom probably didn't even know the bus was missing. She was at her new job in California, and her Dad would hate to tell her because she'd probably blame him.

But the person Annie missed most was her baby brother Pete. Though eight years younger than Annie, Pete was her best bud and followed her around like a puppy dog. Last week she'd taught him how to whistle with two fingers, which she quickly regretted. Even so, she missed his squealing laugh and their wrestling matches on the front lawn.

Annie stood up and stretched her arms. She saw CPU sitting near the front of the bus. She made her way up the aisle and plopped down beside him.

"How's it going, CPU?" she asked, crossing her arms.

CPU stared ahead without expression. "Could be better," he said in a flat voice.

Annie slouched. "Yeah, I know. Were you able to sleep?"

"Yeah, surprisingly, considering that I was half-starved and paranoid that the fog monster would come back and turn me into a popsicle. You?"

"Yeah, but I miss my bed."

"I hear that," CPU said.

"So, when is someone gonna find us?"

"No idea, but it's gotten harder." CPU raised his arm and pointed toward a thick wall of trees and underbrush running along the far end of the meadow.

Annie leaned forward and stared hard. She remembered an opening in the woods there yesterday, leading to the hill. Her heart thumped.

"What happened?" she cried. "The trees are blocking the way now—the way Ben went. Trees don't grow that fast."

"Apparently, they do around here."

Annie sprang to her feet and grabbed the door crank. She swung the door open and stumbled down the steps. The chilly air prickled her skin. She dashed through the field, her breath coming out in a fine mist.

When she neared the woods, she slowed and gawked at the thick greenery, searching for a way through. She pushed into the underbrush, but the growth was so dense that she couldn't get more than a foot inside. She backed away and stared at the trees in bewilderment, her heart thumping and fog spreading into her brain.

She heard footsteps and twisted as CPU came running up. She waved one hand at the new growth. "This is impossible."

"Yeah," CPU said with a baffled look and a shrug.

"When Ben comes back, he won't be able to find us. The trees are blocking the way. We'll be stuck here."

All expression disappeared from CPU's face. Annie's throat tightened. She crouched, covering her eyes, and began to sob softly, releasing the pent-up emotions from the past day. She cried until other footsteps reached her ears.

"Are you okay, Annie?"

Annie raised her head as Sarah came running up, with Timmy a few yards behind, his blue scarf hanging out of the pocket of his jacket.

Annie let out a moan. "We're trapped. These woods are blocking the way."

Sarah covered her mouth with her hand and scrutinized the trees. Then she folded her arms. "No, we're not trapped," she said firmly. "Someone will find us. If they don't see us, we can yell, and they'll hear us. Maybe they'll fly in a helicopter."

"But what's going on?" Annie asked. "It's as if the woods want to trap us here."

Sarah frowned. "It can't," she said, stamping her foot. "We'll find a way out, but we need your help, Annie. Us girls look up to you."

Annie gave a shaky smile. "I don't know about that," she said, brushing tears off her cheek. "There's at least one person who doesn't think much of me."

Sarah grunted. "Yeah, there's always a sour apple, but the rest of us know you're the best."

Annie pushed herself to her feet. "Okay, okay—no more moping."

Sarah wrapped her arms around Annie's middle and squeezed. "We can do it," she said.

Timmy tilted his head. "So, what're we gonna do, ladies?"

"Well," Annie said, "first we need to find some food."

Timmy nodded. "Something to eat would be pretty neat."

"Maybe, there are nuts and berries in the forest," CPU said.

"Let's get our packs and go hunting," Annie said. She started toward the bus, and the other kids followed her.

As they neared the yellow beast, CPU slowed and pointed to the far side of the meadow. "Hey, look. There's a path going into the woods."

Annie squinted but couldn't make out a thing. "What path? I was there yesterday. I didn't see anything."

"It's there now," CPU said, starting to jog.

"Paths and barriers everywhere but leading nowhere," Timmy muttered.

"You hush," Sarah said.

They followed CPU across the field. As they neared the trees, Annie spotted an opening in the woods.

"Hey, you're right, CPU."

CPU raised his chin. "Like I said."

"Why didn't we see this yesterday?" Sarah asked.

"Mice in a maze," Timmy muttered.

Sarah put her hands together. "Should we explore it?" she asked in a hopeful voice.

"Yeah, but we need to tell the others first," Annie said, "so they know where we went."

The children headed back to the bus. Annie led the way up the stairs and halted beside the driver's seat, surveying the jumble of sleeping bodies. "Hey, everybody," she said, clapping her hands. "Wake up."

Grumbles and groans filled the air.

"Sorry to bother you guys," Annie said. "We just found something."

Dylan pushed himself upright and rubbed his eyes. "You what?"

"We found a trail leading into the woods."

"So?"

"It wasn't there yesterday."

Dylan's brow knitted. "Why not?"

"I don't know, but we're gonna explore it. Who's coming with us?"

Celia raised her head. "But Ben told us to stay here."

"Yeah, and he also said he'd be back yesterday, but he wasn't. I don't know about you, but I don't want to spend another night in this place."

There were murmurs of agreement from other kids.

"Who's coming?" Annie asked again.

Dylan leaped out of his seat, gripping his pants by the waist, and hopped over to her. "I am."

Gabrielle and Barth said they'd go too.

A few minutes later, seven kids gathered outside the bus and started toward the far side of the meadow. When they reached the opening in the trees, Annie peered down the trail which ran straight for about fifty feet before angling left and disappearing. She hesitated, and her heart skipped a beat.

"What's wrong?" Dylan asked. "You scared?"

"No," Annie lied, shaking her head. "Of course, not." She took a deep breath and stepped onto the path. The other kids followed.

Annie walked cautiously at first, glancing from side to side at the dark woods, half expecting a strange creature to jump out at any moment. As the minutes passed, the trail gradually widened until all the kids could walk side by side. The trees grew strangely, arching away from the path like billowing sails, while sunlight sprinkled down through their branches.

After some fifteen minutes, the trail ended at a rocky field. On the far side of the field, a thick wall of greenery rose into the air. Annie heard a faint gurgling.

"Is that water?" she asked.

Sarah put her hand to her ear. "I think so."

"Let's go."

Annie sprang forward, and the others followed. Ahead, she spotted a break in the greenery and angled toward it. Several boulders blocked the way, so she scrambled over them. After pushing her way through thick foliage, she stepped out onto a sandy bank running along a stream the width of a neighborhood street. She let out a cry of delight and knelt at the water's edge. The other kids crouched nearby.

Lifting a handful of water to her mouth, Annie closed her eyes and drank until her thirst eased. When she'd finished, Annie spotted a small tree down the bank with large pink cherries growing in its dark green foliage. "Yum," she said, making her way toward the tree.

She picked one of the cherries and examined it. The fruit felt soft in her hands and glowed fluorescently. She sniffed it. It smelled like honey. "I hope this is okay to eat," she said to no one in particular. "But I'm really too hungry to care."

Annie bit into the fruit. A soft, sugary pulp filled her mouth. "Mmm... this tastes like cotton candy," she cried.

The other kids hurried over and began plucking off the fruit. Annie ate three more of the cherries; then she left to explore the bank. She found more fruit—a tree with oranges the size of cantaloupes, vines with juicy blue grapes, and a tree bearing hundreds of shiny purple apples.

After filling her stomach, Annie returned to the other kids, who were sitting on rocks along the water's edge. They had discovered a variety of other fruit, including some yellow peaches and polka dot pears.

Gabrielle was munching on an apple while Dylan kept popping grapes into his mouth, the blue juice dripping down his face and hands.

"Can't you wash yourself?" Gabrielle grumbled. "You look like a food fight casualty."

"Not till I'm done," Dylan said, flicking a grape at her. Gabrielle dodged the fruit and tossed her half-eaten peach, hitting Dylan in the stomach. Immediately, all manner of fruit was flying. But the fun ended abruptly when an apple conked Barth on his right temple.

"Ow... my head is pounding," Barth said, rubbing his forehead vigorously.

"Are you okay?" Annie asked, putting her hand on his shoulder.

Barth closed his eyes and leaned forward. The ground suddenly lurched, and a rumble swept through the forest.

"Whoa," Annie said, spreading her arms to keep her balance.

The rumble quieted, and Barth opened his eyes. "Okay, that's better."

"What's better?" Annie asked in a shaky voice.

"The pounding in my head," Barth said, blinking and frowning

"What about the earthquake?"

"Huh? What earthquake?"

"The one just now," Annie said, glancing around. "See. The trees are still swaying back and forth."

Barth pursed his lips.

Annie glanced at the other kids for confirmation. "You felt it, right?"

They all nodded.

"At least it was short," Annie said. "I hope we don't have any more." She rubbed her stomach. "Well, I'm full, and the kids back at the yellow beast must be hungry, so we should tell them about this place. Who wants to go?"

"I will," Dylan said, springing to his feet.

Gabrielle cocked her head. "Beat you back!" She grabbed her cap and sprinted off.

Dylan bounded after her, clutching his pants and shouting about unfair starts.

"Tell them to bring their packs." Annie laughed as they raced away.

"I'd like to get my pack," Barth said.

"Me too," Annie replied. The other kids agreed, and so a minute later, Annie, Sarah, Timmy, CPU, and Barth were walking back along the trail. Halfway to the bus, they caught sight of Dylan, Josh, and Wesley coming from the other direction.

"Like I said, it's all you can eat," Dylan shouted. "Fruit, fruit, and more fruit... right, Annie?"

She grinned. "Yeah, plenty. And it's yummy."

"Fruit for every delight," Timmy said.

Annie and the others continued. A minute later, Rhea appeared around a bend, striding toward the kids with her long forceful gait. To Annie's surprise, Rhea's face brightened when she saw them. Annie smiled back and gave a small wave.

"The stream's that way," Annie said, pointing back down the trail.

"I heard," Rhea said, her eyes shining.

When Annie reached the meadow, she saw Celia leaning against the bus, looking like a little Spanish pop star in her glittering yellow blouse.

Gabrielle was kneeling and tying Celia's shoes. Annie waved to the sisters, and Celia's face lit up.

"Come here, Annie. Look at this."

Annie jogged over.

"See," Celia said, sticking out her arms.

Annie saw a small blob of goo on each of Celia's wrists—the left one colored red and the right one white.

"What is that?" she asked frowning.

"I don't know," Celia said. "It was there when I woke up."

"It's rubbery," Gabrielle said, finishing her tying. "Watch." She pinched the goo on Celia's right wrist and stretched it out more than a foot in length. She held it there for a moment and let go. The goo snapped back with a slap.

"Ow," Celia cried, rubbing her arm. "That hurt!"

"Oh, that huurrtt," Gabrielle mocked. "Don't be a baby."

"I'm not a baby, and it hurt. You don't know because you don't have one."

"Yeah, I don't have blobs of bubble gum on my wrists."

Celia's eyes filled with tears. Annie put her arm around Celia. "It's okay. I think their cute," she said. "The colors are pretty. Do they come off?"

"No, they're stuck," Celia said, her eyes cast down and voice barely audible.

"Do you think it's tree sap?"

"No, I haven't touched any trees since yesterday."

At that moment, a sound like a dozen musical instruments all playing randomly at once filled the air.

Annie pivoted. "What's that sound?"

Celia giggled. "It's Ted. He's making music."

"He's what?"

"Go see." Celia pointed to the far side of the bus. "It's pretty funny."

Annie tried to figure out what Celia was talking about as she walked around the back of the yellow beast. There she found Ted Wallis standing alone in the grass and swinging his arms around like a symphony conductor as a stream of notes filled the air.

Ted was a big guy with a stomach like a walrus. He was a couple of inches shorter than Josh but weighed probably twice as much. He was wearing blue jeans, cowboy boots and a t-shirt with a picture of four long-haired guys.

"Where's that sound coming from?" Annie asked, covering her ears.

Ted's warm eyes twinkled. "Apparently me." He laughed, his big hands whirling and random notes pouring into the air.

"You?"

"I've always dreamed of being a musician. My mom signed me up for piano lessons once, but after three months, the teacher sent me home, saying I had no musical talent. Then my parents hired a tutor to give me violin lessons, but after two months the tutor quit, saying I had no coordination. I still wanted to play, so I begged my mom and dad to buy me a guitar. They did, and I watched guitar videos every day, but somehow, I never learned to play. I thought it was hopeless, and I would never be a musician, but now I can make music by just waving my hands around. It's amazing."

"No, it's crazy!" Annie said, sticking fingers in her ears.

"Not anymore crazy than you screaming and freezing everything."

Annie paused and nodded in agreement.

Ted dropped his arms, and the music fell silent. "So, hey, what did you find down the trail?"

"A stream and tons of fruit."

"Cool! I'm starved. Lead on."

"Okay, but I need to get my pack first."

Annie hurried around the bus. She reached the door as CPU, Timmy and Barth stumbled out, each holding several bags.

"Did you get mine?" she asked.

CPU shrugged. "We grabbed everything we saw."

Annie checked the packs but didn't see her blue one. She sighed and climbed the stairs.

Annie found her bag on the floor beneath her seat. She grabbed it, noticing the Kadean sisters sitting all alone at the back of the bus.

"Hey, aren't you two going to the stream?" she asked. "We've found loads of fruit."

Mya shook her head. "We're staying here, but could you bring us back something? We're hungry."

Annie's smile faded. Mya was twelve, the same age as her, and Emma was a year younger. Annie rested her hands on her hips. "No, sorry. I can't. But you can get some yourselves. Come with me."

Mya bit her lip. "Emma doesn't want to go, and I can't leave her."

Annie stared sideways at Emma, who was looking out the window with a pensive frown, her long silky hair flowing out from under a tan beanie.

"Really? But it's so nice there," Annie said. "Why would you want to stay here?"

Emma met Annie's eyes. "Ben told us to wait at the bus," she said.

"He wouldn't want us to go hungry," Annie replied.

"Yeah," Mya said. "I told her we could leave a note for Ben." She eyed her sister. "Emma's worried that if we leave, something bad will happen."

"What could be worse than being stuck in this meadow with no food or water?" Annie said, throwing up her hands.

Emma turned away. Annie strode up the aisle and dropped into the seat across from the girls. She liked the Kadean sisters, but

61

they could be annoying. Mya was friendly and easygoing, but once she started talking about something—particularly her beloved plants and animals—she could chatter on endlessly. Emma was sweet and a bit shy, but quite stubborn and fussy about things. Annie remembered the time she worked with Emma on a set for the fall musical. It took them twice as long as anyone else to finish because everything had to be perfect for Emma.

"You should come," Annie said. "It's so nice by the stream."

Emma bit her lip and pressed her face to the glass. Annie looked out too.

Ted strolled around the front of the bus, swinging his arms. CPU grabbed his stomach and laughed raucously as a shower of sound poured into the air.

"How about we go, and come back after lunch?" Annie proposed. "That way, we won't be gone long, in case Ben comes back."

Mya eyed her sister.

Emma inclined her head. "I guess we could go for a little while."

Mya smiled and gave Annie thumbs-up. Emma opened her binder and wrote a quick note for Ben. Then Annie led the girls down the aisle, snatching several empty soda bottles from behind Ben's seat.

As they stepped off the bus, CPU turned to face them. "Can you believe it?" he cried. "Ted's a one-man band."

"The music man with fancy hands," Timmy said.

"It's nutso." Barth glared. "It's impossible and wacked out."

Annie frowned slightly. It bothered her too. She didn't like things that made no sense. Was it magic? She wondered. Was there magic in this place? She scanned the meadow and tilted her head to gaze at the sky. It looked the same as back home.

"Ted, that noise is giving me a fat headache," Barth grumbled. "Shut it down?"

"Sorry guy, I can't," the large boy replied, laughing. "It's too much fun."

Barth's face tightened into a grimace.

Annie felt her hunger returning. She sighed and tried to push the worries out of her mind. "Let's go."

Chapter 6:
Strange Words

Wesley watched the sunlight sparkle off the gurgling water. A light breeze bent the plants nestled among the rocks and trees lining the stream. Most of the kids were gorging themselves on fruit. He'd tried several different kinds but preferred those that looked familiar, like the apples and pears. Still, he loved the pink cherries and couldn't stop popping those into his mouth.

After filling his stomach, Wesley sat down under an old willow tree that shaded the bank. He tried to relax but soon found his feet tapping restlessly and his fingers drumming the ground. He rose and wandered along the edge of the stream, clenching and unclenching his fists. He'd hardly slept during the night, lying wrapped in his coat and expecting the mist creature to return. After Josh and Annie calmed the other kids, everyone fell asleep, but him. He stayed awake until the morning light finally spiked above the treetops, then he drifted off for an hour or so before Annie woke everyone up.

A voice brought Wesley out of his thoughts. It was Mya. She was talking to her sister, Emma, as the girls gathered flowers in the meadow. Wesley's gaze drifted to Emma, and he caught his breath. She was so pretty he couldn't look away. She picked a blossom, moving with the grace of a cat on a windowsill. Wesley had wanted to talk to her since forever, but he never knew what to say.

Mya was different from Emma. She was warm and chatty, with shoulder-length blond hair, a round face, and hazel eyes. She was taller and heavier than Emma, and easy to talk to, though her obsession with plants and animals could get annoying. The sisters looked so different from one another that Wesley sometimes wondered if they were adopted.

Wesley knew their dad, who was a bigwig at an electronics company in Annaberry. Mr. Kadean was a friendly guy, who liked to wear business suits and shake people's hands so hard it hurt, but Wesley hadn't seen him around for a while. Their mom was a tall woman, with long dark hair and gentle, sad eyes. She often wore black high heel shoes and yellow dresses, but usually had a fixed smile that Wesley didn't entirely trust.

Wesley strolled to where Dylan was throwing rocks into the water. Timmy and Barth sat on a boulder nearby, staring intently at the flowing stream.

"What's going on?" he asked.

"There must be a million tiny fish in this water," Dylan said. "We should catch some for lunch."

"Those mini fish?" Timmy laughed. "Twenty-four won't make a dozen."

"How do you plan to catch them?" Wesley asked. "They aren't going to jump into your hands."

Dylan shrugged and rubbed the back of his neck.

"I know," Barth announced. "I need to find something." He strolled away.

Wesley climbed onto the boulder and gazed over the water, seeing hundreds of silver flashes moving through the current.

Barth soon returned gripping a long slender reed. He had tied a string to one end. Wesley was puzzled.

"A fishing pole," Barth declared.

"Where'd you get the string?"

"Some loose threads in my coat," Barth said, patting the brown cotton jacket tied around his waist.

"What about a hook?"

"I have an idea for that," Barth said. He stepped over to his pack and unzipped a side pocket. He scrounged around until he plucked out a paperclip. He bent one end of the clip and scratched it to a fine point against a rock. Then he tied the clip to the end of the string.

Wesley nodded. "Yeah, that might work."

"You bet it'll work," Barth said.

Just then, Bobby hurried over and stuck out his hand. "Hey, Baarf, heere yoouu aaree."

Barth scowled at the pronunciation of his name, but his irritation turned to delight when he saw what Bobby held in his palm—a tiny gold fishhook.

"Where'd you get this?" Barth asked, picking up the hook with his thumb and forefinger.

"Maade iit," Bobby said, puffing out his chest.

"You what?"

"Maade iit. Yoouu liikee iit?"

Barth studied the fishhook. "It's perfect. Much better than mine."

"Golden gifts from golden thoughts," Timmy said obliquely.

Bobby grinned and strolled away, hands in his pockets. Barth quirked an eyebrow at Timmy. Then he loosened the string from the paperclip and slipped it through the top of the hook, tying it back.

"What about bait?" Dylan asked.

"Maybe some fruit will work," Barth said.

Dylan held out a cherry.

"No, too sweet."

"How about some peach?" Wesley suggested.

The other boys nodded. Wesley used Barth's pocketknife to cut a chunk out of one. He stuck it on the end of the hook. Barth climbed onto the boulder and hung the pole out over the water, slowly lowering it into the stream. The other boys crowded around, watching eagerly as the line swayed in the current.

A crowd of tiny silver fish quickly gathered around the bait. Wesley's pulse quickened as the mass of fish closed in. Then he lost sight of the bait.

Barth started. "Hey, I felt a tug."

He lifted the line out of the water, but to the boys' dismay, there was no fish, bait, or hook on the end. Everything was gone.

"The string broke," Dylan said.

"Hmm." Barth raised the line to his eyes. "It looks like it was cut," he growled. "Probably by some tiny silver teeth."

He showed the boys where the end had been cleanly severed.

Dylan crossed his arms. "What do we do now?"

Timmy's eyes widened. "I know. Let's catch them the bear way."

"The what?" Wesley asked.

"The bear way. With our hands."

Wesley chuckled. "Those fish are too tiny. They'd slip right through our fingers."

"Then fruit's the meal," Timmy said.

Barth rubbed his forehead. "What we need is a net," he said. "Can you guys collect about a hundred sticks, each about a foot long?"

"What are you gonna do with them?" Dylan asked.

Barth winked. "Build a water cage."

The other boys stared at him as if he'd just said the sky was green.

Barth ignored their skepticism. "While you're doing that, I'll find something to tie them with." He hopped off the boulder and ambled into the meadow, eyes searching the ground.

"What's his plan?" Dylan asked.

Wesley shook his head. "I don't know, but Barth can build anything, so let's do what he says."

The boys began collecting sticks. They had a nice pile when Barth returned with several dozen long blades of grass. He sat beside the pile and started tying the sticks into flat squares. After he had six squares, he hooked those together into a box with one side swinging out like a hinged door.

Dylan dipped his chin. "What is that?"

"I told you—a water cage."

Timmy rubbed his chin. "A cage to catch the uncatchable."

Barth snorted. "Believe me; those fish are catchable."

"At least they can't bite through the box," Wesley said.

"Yeah, and maybe we'll have fish for lunch." Barth glanced around. "Now we just need bait."

Wesley tugged the peach back out of his pack and cut a couple more chunks out of it. He dropped them into the box.

"You ready?" Barth asked, his eyes gleaming. The other boys grinned. Following Barth's lead, they rolled up their pant legs and made their way into the water.

When they reached the center of the stream, they formed a line facing the oncoming current. Barth and Timmy each held a side of the box. While Dylan stood to the left of the boys—his baseball cap gripped tightly in one hand. Wesley waited on the right side.

A large school of fish appeared upstream. As the silver flashes neared, musical notes reached Wesley's ears. He glanced over his shoulder and saw Ted Wallis ambling down the bank, his arms swinging like a carnival juggler.

"Hey, you're sounding better," Wesley shouted.

"Yeah, I think I'm getting the hang of it," Ted hollered. He stopped on the bank, eyeing the boys in the water. "What are you flamingos doing?"

"Barth has made a box for catching fish," Wesley said. "We're testing it out."

Ted yawned. "Don't catch anything for me. My appetite has disappeared like a puddle on a hot day."

"They're coming," Dylan shouted, pointing to the school of fish which had moved closer. The boys got ready. Several of the fish glided near Dylan. He swooped his baseball cap into the water, scattering the silvery creatures.

"Whatcha doing?" Barth yelled. "We want them in the box."

"Sorry. They're super quick."

The school had vanished but soon reappeared. A small pack made its way toward the box. The boys watched breathlessly as five little fish darted inside. Barth and Timmy flipped the box up, trapping the tiny creatures.

"It worked!" Dylan yelled.

* * * *

Timmy peered down at the silvery creatures in the box. One suddenly sprang into the air. Timmy lunged, and a strange sensation came over him; the world seemed to slow like a sailboat in a fading breeze. The fish floated languidly upward, its tiny tail flipping gently from side to side in long-drawn-out motions.

Timmy snatched the shiny creature out of the air. Then he looked around. The sunlight had become a rainbow of flowing colors. The water moved like a sluggish dream. Ripples leisurely appeared and broke. Water drops slowly rose into the air. The wind murmured in the trees, and voices carried over the breeze in long vibrations.

Timmy peered down at the fish squirming in his hand, its green eyes staring blankly and its gills opening and closing in a futile effort to breathe. Timmy turned to Barth, who was closing the box more slowly than a snail inching along a branch. As the lid gradually came down, a second tiny fish leaped from the water.

Timmy stretched out his free hand and plucked the second one from the air.

The box closed and Timmy relaxed, gripping a fish in each fist, their tiny silvery heads sticking out above his thumbs and forefingers. The other boys started moving. Sounds and images accelerated.

"How'd you do that?" Barth cried.

Timmy tried to speak, but something was wrong. Air streamed past his face. Water rushed over the rocks. Voices morphed into high-pitched squeaks. Dylan, Wesley, and Barth moved around him in split-second jerks. Before he could get a word out, the other boys squeaked out a long series of sounds.

* * * *

Wesley watched Timmy in astonishment. A moment before, Timmy had moved with hummingbird-like quickness, but now he seemed slower than a sleepy turtle, his words coming out in long, low indecipherable tones.

Dylan tipped his head. "What's wrong with Timmy? It's like someone pushed his slow-mo button."

Wesley blinked, trying to clear the confusion from his brain. Then he heard voices above the gurgling water. "*Hithe mea. Feo doth ama dia.*" Wesley pivoted, searching for the source of the sound, but saw no one. He met Barth's eyes. The other boy shrugged.

"*Hithe mea. Feo doth ama dia,*" the shrill voices cried again

"Who's saying that?" Wesley asked. He did a slow turn and scrutinized the bank. There was no one there. His gaze dropped to Timmy's hands, and he noticed the mouths of the tiny creatures moving back and forth. The cries rang out again.

"It's the fish!" Wesley cried. "The fish are talking."

The little silvery heads flopped about, and the tiny lips moved, repeating the strange words. Timmy flinched and tottered. Wesley grabbed his arm, steadying him.

"What's the time?" Timmy asked, his eyes blank.

"Huh?"

"What time is the time?"

Wesley stared at the sky. "About one o'clock."

"Oh," Timmy said, his face relaxing.

"You alright?" Wesley asked.

Timmy shook his head and stared at the little creatures in his hands. Then he twitched and opened his fists. The fish dropped into the stream and vanished into the depths.

"They're gone," Wesley said, scanning the water.

"What about the box?" Dylan asked.

Barth lifted the lid, and the three fish inside sprang into the air, arcing over the sides of the box, and disappeared into the current.

"What kind of fish were those?" Dylan cried.

"I don't know, but I'm not catching anymore," Barth shouted.

Timmy squinted. "A silent strawberry beats a spouting sardine."

"What happened to you?" Wesley asked with concern.

Timmy shook his head. "When the fish jumped out of the water, I tried to catch it, then everything slowed—"

"It didn't slow," Dylan said frowning. "You started moving faster than a sparrow with a jetpack. We could hardly see you."

Timmy tottered again.

Wesley held his arm. "Let's get out of the water."

They moved toward the bank, Wesley supporting Timmy while Barth carried the empty box.

"How's lunch coming?" Ted asked as they neared the shore.

"Not good," Dylan said, "unless you want to talk to your chow."

Wesley and Timmy laughed. Ted's eyebrows rose into peaks. "Talk what?"

"That's the problem," Dylan said. "We don't know."

Wesley helped Timmy onto the bank. Then a splash rang out. At the center of the stream, a large green fish with gold dorsal and caudal fins raised its head above the surface. The fish glared at

71

the boys through silvery eyes, then swung its tail down with a loud slap, sending a spray of water high into the air. The fish's mouth opened, and Wesley heard a low gurgling voice. *"Feo doth luma dia. Rea sevi namo."*

The fish glowered. Wesley stared back in shock. The creature's mouth moved again, repeating the strange cry. Dylan sprang out of the water, gripping his pants and landing high on the bank. Barth also splashed ashore.

The green fish darted under the surface and reappeared close to the bank. Its tail swung and smacked the water, sending up a shower that splashed the boys.

A shout came from the far side of the stream. "What's that?" It was Josh. He jogged down to the bank.

The green fish wheeled and shot toward Josh. As it neared the other shore, the creature slowed and whacked its tail once more, sending a spray of water at Josh, who leaped to avoid it.

The fish spun around and glared at the other boys. Then it darted under the surface and disappeared into the depths.

"I think you must've upset a momma fish," Ted said, laughing.

"But it didn't speak English," Dylan objected.

"Why would it speak English?" Barth asked with a baffled frown.

"Because it talks."

"Fish don't speak English or any other language."

"It was speaking something."

Barth rolled his eyes and turned away.

"Timmy, let's find more talking fish," Dylan said.

Timmy nodded quickly, and the two headed down the bank.

Wesley stepped around to face Barth. "You still wanna catch something?"

Barth looked down. "No… No more fish for me." He turned and staggered toward the meadow. Wesley followed.

Barth stumbled to a boulder and plopped down. "You know," he said, raising his eyes, "I can usually figure stuff out, but nothing makes sense here. Fish don't talk, and you can't make music by waving your hands around."

"Yeah, everything's getting bizarre," Wesley said, rubbing his forehead.

"Wes, I have no idea what's going on. Do you?"

Wesley shook his head and crossed his arms. On the far side of the field, Mya and Emma stepped out of a grove of pine trees.

Mya's strong voice carried across the meadow. "Em, let's collect leaves from all the strange plants we find. We can study them when we get home."

Wesley couldn't hear Emma's reply, but his eyes met hers across the distance. She smiled, and he smiled back. Then his face flushed, and he turned away. He squinted at Barth, who was grimacing and pressing his fingers to his temples.

"Are you okay?" Wesley asked with concern.

Barth shook his head. "I've got a headache – it's pounding."

Barth clenched his teeth and closed his eyes. He tipped forward, resting his elbows on his knees. A rumble filled the air. The ground suddenly shifted, and Wesley stumbled forward. Narrow cracks opened in the soil around them.

Across the meadow, the girls screamed. The ground shifted again, and a roar echoed out of the forest. Then the shaking stopped, and the rumble quieted.

Barth sat up straight and opened his eyes. "That's better," he said.

"That was freaky," Wesley replied.

"What was freaky?" Barth asked.

"The earthquake."

Barth rubbed his forehead. "What earthquake?"

"The one just now. Didn't you feel it?"

"No," Barth replied in apparent confusion.

Mya and Emma hurried over, prancing nervously through the grass, as if afraid the ground would slip out from under them.

"Did you guys feel the earthquake?" Mya cried.

"I did," Wesley answered. "Are you guys okay?"

The girls bobbed their heads.

"That's the second one today," Mya said. "We felt the first one a couple hours ago."

"I did too," Wesley said.

"I didn't feel either one." Barth admitted. "My head was pounding both times." He ran his fingers through his hair.

Wesley rested his hand on Barth's shoulder. "Are you okay now?"

Barth nodded.

Wesley looked up at the blue sky and then across the field at the stream gurgling through the greenery. So many strange things kept happening. He sighed. He wondered what would happen next.

Chapter 7:
Humming

For the umpteenth time, Mya listened for a low rumble in the forest. She clenched her hands, which hadn't stopped trembling since the second earthquake an hour earlier. Fortunately, no one was hurt. A couple of trees had fallen, but everyone was okay. She now sat with Emma on a boulder in the center of the stream as the afternoon sun beat down through the trees. She dangled her feet in the current and relaxed her shoulders, listening to kinglets and robins singing in the branches.

A tingle ran up her spine. Despite the strangeness of this place, something about it thrilled her. She loved the weird plants and trees. Everything was different. A daisy was a daisy, but with an orange center rather than a yellow one. An aster was an aster, but with round petals instead of oblong ones. And the bark of trees was softer or rougher than back at home. She kept discovering plants she'd never heard of and jotted down descriptions of each one in her notebook to look up when she got home.

But even more than the strange plants, Mya loved the freshness of everything. When the bus first rumbled into the meadow, it was like they'd come to a new world, a different world—different from Annaberry.

A fly buzzed by Mya's face, and she slapped at it. A breeze twirled strands of her hair. She glanced up, hearing the flute-like call of a wood thrush. This place seemed to be a paradise, but something gnawed at her and kept her from relaxing and enjoying it—her parents. She knew her mom and dad were panicked. She and Emma had never been away from home for so long, and her parents didn't know where they were. Mya reached into her bag and pulled out her phone. She checked her messages. Nothing. The battery was dying.

She shifted and glanced at her sister, who had been quiet all morning. Emma seemed anxious and worried. Of course, Emma tended to be nervous, and a worrywart, but all the crazy things happening were exacerbating her natural inclination.

Mya watched Emma as she leaned forward, her long brown hair falling over her face. Mya had noticed Wesley watching her earlier. She had giggled, but she secretly envied her sister. She envied Emma's glowing skin, her soft blue eyes, and long silky hair. Some kids liked her sister just because she was pretty. Mya was pretty too and had tons of friends, more than her sister. But Mya enjoyed talking, while Emma was quiet and reserved.

Mya leaned down and lifted a handful of water to her mouth. It tasted sweet. She heard a splash and sensed someone walking downstream through the shallows. She squinted, trying to make out who it was. Today, her eyes were loopy. Everything seemed blurry. Earlier, she had asked Emma to confirm some plants and trees they'd passed, because she couldn't see them clearly.

Mya squinted at the oncoming figure, recognizing Annie from the way her shoulders swung from side to side with each step. Annie's backpack was slung over her shoulder, and her shoes were hanging from one hand.

"Isn't this place heaven?" Annie said

"Absolutely," Mya answered, blinking to clear the fogginess from her eyes.

Emma didn't comment.

Annie came to a stop in front of them. "I made you two a promise," she said. "So, despite this place being a paradise, I'm ready to go back to the bus if you want to."

Emma smiled and inclined her head. "Thank you, Annie. I'm ready to go. Mya, are you coming?"

"Of course," Mya said grumpily, wishing Annie hadn't remembered. She gathered her things and followed the other girls to the bank. As the three started into the meadow, Mya peered upstream and saw two figures rolling a tire sized rock into the water. She heard Barth's distant voice. "That's right. Put it there."

"Hey, Barth," she shouted, "we're heading back to the bus. You want to come?"

One of the figures straightened and shook his head. "Timmy and I are building a stepping-stone bridge to cross the creek," Barth shouted. "It's going to take a while."

"Okay, see you later," Mya said, disappointed that Barth wasn't coming. She liked to talk to him. Barth lived down the street from her back at home. She often hung out at his house after school. He was one of the few kids who didn't mind listening to her blabber on about the plants and animals she loved. She'd talk while he worked on his latest project. She occasionally wondered if he was really listening to her, so she'd ask him a question about what she'd just said. He usually had the right answer, but occasionally he gave her a blank stare and started talking about whatever it was he was working on.

Although they were good friends, she thought Barth's family was a bit odd. His mom liked to walk around the neighborhood in a pink bathrobe and slippers, chatting with everyone she met. Mrs. Ricci gossiped so loudly that people could hear her halfway down the block. Mya's mom frowned whenever Mya mentioned Ms. Ricci. Her mom thought Barth's mom was an embarrassment to the neighborhood.

Last spring, Barth's older sister had been a senior at Annaberry High School and captain of the cheer team when she suddenly left school and eloped with her college boyfriend. Barth's older brother was a junior at Annaberry High, but he kept getting into trouble, and she'd heard he'd spent several days in juvenile detention. Mya rarely saw their dad, who was a quiet man and an ex-marine, but not around much.

Mya leaned close to a large yellow and orange flower in the growth along the trail. She squinted, trying to make out details of the flower's petals, but everything remained fuzzy. She picked off the blossom and hurried to catch up to the other girls.

"What do you think this is, Emma?" she asked, showing the flower to her sister.

"It looks like a blanket flower to me. What do you think?" Emma replied.

Mya shook her head. "I can't tell... Something's weird with my eyes today."

"What do you mean?" Emma asked frowning.

"I just can't see clearly."

"I hope nothing's wrong."

"I feel okay, otherwise."

Emma pursed her lips.

"Did you guys feel the earthquakes earlier?" Annie asked.

"Yeah, I keep expecting another one," Mya said. "The second one was so strong; I thought the ground would open up and swallow us."

"Yeah, I felt dizzy," Annie said. "Then I realized everything was dizzy."

The girls all laughed.

"I saw you and Rhea talking earlier," Mya said to Annie. "Are you guys better now?"

Annie grunted. "I don't know... Maybe... It's been months since we really talked, but she was nice today."

"What'd you talk about?"

"She asked me how things were at home. I told her my mom was moving to California for her new job, and that Pete and I may go to live with her next year. She seemed almost sad about that, which stunned me. I asked her how things were for her. She said she hadn't argued with her mom much lately, but that she hadn't seen her dad in over a year."

"That's sad," Mya said, feeling genuinely sorry. "But I'm glad you two are friendly again. You used to be best buds."

Annie exhaled. "We were, but it's hard to be friends with some people."

Mya nodded.

They followed the trail for almost twenty minutes, when Mya began sensing something wrong—they should have reached the meadow by then. She was about to speak up when Annie halted and crossed her arms. "Did we go the right way? These woods look different. And where's the yellow beast?"

"Maybe we passed it," Mya said, turning in a slow circle. "Should we head back the way we came?"

Annie thought for a moment and shook her head. "No, let's go a little further just to be sure."

Mya didn't think it was ahead of them, but she saw Emma wrap her arms around herself, and knew her sister was growing anxious. Mya didn't want to upset Emma more, so she went along with Annie, and they continued down the trail.

After five more minutes, with no sign of the bus, Annie stopped and threw up her hands. "We definitely passed it. It can't be this far."

Mya eyed her sister. "What do you think, Em?"

Emma looked away and didn't answer.

"Let's go back," Mya said.

At that moment, cries rang out.

"Hey, someone's here," Mya said, peering up the trail.

"Yeah," Annie exclaimed. "Come on." She hurried forward.

Mya grabbed Emma's hand and tugged her along. The girls rushed around a bend and slowed to a stop, finding themselves at the bank of a stream.

"Another creek?" Mya asked.

"We'll need to tell the others," Annie said.

Suddenly a figure dashed out from behind a boulder. Mya squinted, trying to make out who it was. Then a second figure darted into view. The two raced across the sand, gripping long sticks in their hands. The nearer one grabbed his pants and shot into the air with a fart like a bear with bad indigestion. Mya immediately realized who it was. Dylan landed some twenty yards away and resumed his run.

"Stop that," the other figure yelled. Mya recognized CPU's voice. "You promised no jumping." He shouted, swinging his long stick.

"I can't help it." Dylan laughed, parrying the blow. "They pop out. I can't control them."

"What're you doing?" Annie yelled, bringing the boys to a halt. "What's going on?"

CPU and Dylan stared at Annie. "We're playing ninja warrior," CPU said.

"How'd you get here?" Annie asked.

Dylan thumped the end of his stick on the ground. "What? We came here with you."

Annie glanced around in confusion. "Huh? Where are we?"

"By the stream with all the fruit trees," CPU said, incredulously. "Remember?"

Annie raised her hand and covered her mouth. "Where's everybody else?"

"That way," Dylan said, pointing downstream.

CPU swung his stick around, and the boys launched into another exchange.

Annie turned to the other girls. "I don't believe it. We're back at the stream. We must have passed the bus and walked in a big circle."

A fog spread through Mya's brain, and her stomach felt queasy. How could they pass the bus without seeing it? She wondered. She gazed at her sister but couldn't read Emma's expression.

Annie sighed and started back along the trail, her arms swinging in frustration. Mya grabbed Emma's hand and followed. This time Mya didn't talk as they walked; she kept her eyes glued to the passing woods, searching for any sign of the bus or the meadow.

They walked for another twenty minutes with no sign of the yellow beast. Mya felt her breathing quicken. Sweat formed on her forehead, and her hands became clammy.

The girls rounded a bend, and a rocky meadow spread out before them. Mya heard a faint gurgling in the distance.

"What happened?" Annie cried. "We're back where we started."

"Where's the bus?" Mya asked in disbelief.

"The trail changed," Emma said quietly.

Mya turned to her sister. "It what?"

"The trail changed. It doesn't go back there anymore."

"That's impossible," Mya cried. "We followed it here this morning. How could it change?"

Emma frowned and shook her head. "We're being taken away."

"Taken away? From what?"

"From home," Emma said, sniffling.

Mya sensed her sister was about to break into sobs. She leaned forward and put her arms around Emma. "Don't be so gloom and doom. No one's being taken away. We'll get home soon."

"This is messed up," Annie exclaimed. "How could the trail change?" She jogged into the rocky field.

Mya grabbed Emma's hand and followed Annie. As they neared the far side of the meadow, Mya noticed several kids sitting together on the sandy bank. When she got closer, she could vaguely make out Sarah, Gabrielle, and Celia.

Ted sat a few feet away on a large rock, turning his hands and fingers back and forth to make soft chiming sounds, while Rhea sat under a tree reading a book. Mya couldn't make out Rhea's face, but she saw the red of her hair. Upstream, two kids were rolling a big rock into the water. She guessed that was Timmy and Barth.

"Where'd you guys go?" Sarah asked.

"We're not really sure," Annie said, pressing her palms over her eyes.

"Huh?" Sarah said.

"We tried to find the bus, but we couldn't," Annie said. "The trail doesn't seem to go there anymore."

"What? Of course, it does," Sarah replied, lines creasing her forehead.

"Go look for yourself. We can't find it."

The sound of a book slamming shut caused Mya to flinch. It was Rhea. The redheaded girl leaped to her feet. "Are you blind? You can't find a huge yellow bus?" she said glaring. Then she shoved her book into her pack. "I'm heading back. Who wants to come?"

"I will," Sarah said, hurriedly. She called to Timmy, who bobbed his head.

"I guess I'll go too," Annie said, in a tone of resignation. "It'll be nice to be shown how blind I am."

"Yeah, that'll be fun," Rhea said with a mocking smile.

Annie rolled her eyes. The three girls and Timmy started across the field.

Celia sat upright, holding a long stick which she'd been using to draw in the sand. "Where's everyone going?"

"To find the bus," Mya said.

"Why?"

Mya didn't want to worry Celia, so she just said, "They want to make sure Ben can find us."

"Oh, okay," Celia said, returning to her drawing.

Gabrielle snorted. "Ben's not coming back."

"What do you mean?" Mya said, tensing. "Of course, he's coming back."

"It's been twenty-four hours, and there's no sign of him. If he were coming back, he'd be here already."

"Something must have happened, and it's taking him longer than he expected," Mya said firmly. "He wouldn't leave us here." She glanced at her sister for support, but Emma averted her eyes.

Frustration welled up in Mya. She stomped her feet, suspecting Emma blamed her for their leaving the bus in the morning. She marched down to the stream where Barth was rolling another rock into position for his bridge.

"What happens if Ben doesn't come back?" she asked him.

Barth raised his head. "We have plenty of water and fruit here. We can build a shelter to sleep in. We should be okay until someone shows up."

Mya puffed her cheeks and let the air out slowly. Then she shuddered, remembering the terrifying mist creature of the night before. "But what if that fog thing comes back?"

"Oh..." Barth said with a pause.

Anxiety filled Mya like it had last spring when her parents were constantly arguing. At that time, she would go for long walks to calm down. It helped her relax and clear her thoughts.

Mya set her jaw. "I need to think," she said to Barth. "I'll be back in a bit."

Barth waved and adjusted his rock again.

Mya headed upstream, strolling along the sandy bank. After some fifty yards, the undergrowth blocked her way, so she turned and tramped into the woods. She soon found herself passing through groves of pines and beeches. The quiet of the forest comforted her. She was curious about the plants around her and stopped to study some, but everything looked fuzzy, and she couldn't make out exactly what they were. She sighed and continued walking.

A melody floated through her head. It seemed vaguely familiar, but she couldn't remember where she'd heard it. The tune was pretty. As she hummed, her worries faded.

A moment later, a sparrow landed on a branch ahead. Mya passed by the bird, and it hopped to another branch a few yards away. She soon sensed it was following her. Other birds joined the first, fluttering from tree to tree as she ambled through the woods.

A small animal peeked out from behind a dogwood bush. Mya stopped and peered at the little creature. She couldn't see it clearly but thought it looked like a shrew. She smiled at the little animal and resumed her humming. Just beyond the dogwood bush, a pair of squirrels scurried down a tree trunk. She watched them jump around playfully, then walked on, humming softly. To her left, a creature scrambled onto a dirt mound. It was a weasel. The weasel sat on its hind legs and stared at her. A moment later, a raccoon peeked out from behind an alder bush.

Mya shook her head in disbelief and came to a stop, falling silent. The animals watched her for some moments, then they quietly slipped away. Mya soon found herself alone. She shrugged and resumed her walk, humming the song again. The creatures reappeared in even greater numbers. Mya slowed and fell silent. The animals watched her, then drifted away.

Mya scratched her temple. Why do they keep appearing and disappearing? Then something occurred to her, and she let out a startled laugh. She started to walk again, swinging her arms freely and humming the song in a loud, clear voice.

* * * *

Back at the stream, Celia was drawing a picture of her dad and her abuela in the sand. They were standing near the big tree in their front yard. She drew her dad's pickup truck in the driveway and the sun above the house. She leaned back, tipping her head to the side and examining her work.

Gabrielle was juggling rocks a few feet away. "Ha, Abuela's head looks like a pumpkin." she laughed. "It's twice the size of Dad's."

"I know, I know," Celia grumbled, erasing that part of the drawing. "It's hard to get it right."

"Who's Abuela?" Ted asked.

"Our grandma," Celia said with a sigh. "I miss her so much."

"Not me." Gabrielle snorted. "If she were here, she'd be nagging us to do our homework or eat all the time."

Celia shrugged.

Gabrielle flipped several of the rocks into the air, but one soared out of reach. She lunged and caught it as she fell into the sand. "This is hard," she said, getting back up and brushing grit off her clothes. "Juggling two is easy, but three is like impossible."

Celia raised her eyebrows. She knew her sister. Gabrielle usually whined and complained when she was learning something, but once she got it, she'd walk around smugly for days showing off her new trick.

There was a rustling, and Celia peered over her shoulder. A pair of blue jays swooped out of the trees. Then a white-tailed deer suddenly pranced into the open with a pack of ground squirrels scampering at its hooves.

Celia sat up straight. A pretty melody reached her ears. She listened as the sound grew louder and clearer. Then Mya stepped out of the trees surrounded by a host of scuttling, scurrying, scampering forest creatures.

Celia squealed and sprang to her feet as the throng poured into the clearing.

Ted hopped off his rock and marched toward the chaos. "What's this?" he cried. "A critter soiree? Mya, are you the Pied Piper of the animal kingdom?"

Mya took a deep breath, her face beaming. "Maybe."

A booming fart sounded and Dylan suddenly soared through the air, landing amid the throng, his hands gripping his pants tightly. He lunged at a turkey, but the bird clucked away. The other animals scattered.

CPU ran up behind Dylan and dove at a rabbit. Dylan let off another stinker and launched into the air, touching down near a fawn which scampered into the trees.

* * * *

Mya stood stunned, not believing her eyes. "What're you doing?" she yelled. "You're scaring them."

"We're getting dinner," Dylan shouted as he and CPU surrounded the turkey.

"No! You can't eat them!"

"Why not?" CPU said. "We've been eating fruit all day."

"But fruit is good, and there's tons of it."

The boys ignored Mya and chased after the animals. Dylan leaped toward a pack of marmots, but two large ones bared their teeth. Dylan's eyes widened, and he leaped back.

Rabbits dashed through the grass. CPU readied himself and lunged at a small gray one as it bounded by. He snagged the creature by its hind legs. The rabbit struggled in his hands, breaking free and kicking CPU in the face before bounding into the woods.

"No, no," Mya screamed, her heart pounding. "Don't hurt them."

Barth strode up from the riverbank, waving his arms around. "Hey, guys, stop it. You're upsetting Mya. Even if you catch something, how're you going to eat it? We don't have a fire to cook with. Are you gonna eat it raw?"

This slowed the boys. Dylan turned toward Barth and groaned. "But I want a turkey dinner."

"Yeah, that would be nice, but you need to cook it."

Mya sighed and gave Barth a grateful look. She turned and discovered Celia tiptoeing up behind. Celia's eyes were as big as hen's eggs.

"Where did all the animals come from?" Celia asked.

"The woods," Mya said.

"They followed you?"

"Yeah, I think they liked the tune I was humming."

Celia blinked. "Can you teach me?"

Mya shook her head. "No. I don't want the animals getting hurt."

"I won't hurt them," Celia insisted. "I'll just play with them."

Mya smiled weakly and repeated, "No."

Celia dipped her head dejectedly. Mya put one hand on her shoulder.

"I know you won't hurt them, but someone else might," Mya said, scowling at Dylan and CPU.

A cry carried across the meadow, sounding like a bellow of pure frustration.

"What's that?" Celia asked, perking her ears.

"I think it's Rhea," Mya said with slight alarm.

"We're over here," Celia shouted.

Rhea strode into the clearing, her hands clenched, and her nostrils flared. Annie, Sarah, and Timmy followed close behind her, their shoulders slumped and faces long.

"This place is crazy, and it's all her fault," Rhea said, pointing back at Annie.

"How is it my fault?" Annie protested.

"You talked us all into coming to this stream, and now we can't get back."

"That's not fair," Sarah said. "It was CPU who found the trail, and we all decided to explore it. How could Annie know this would happen?"

Mya nodded firmly, glad that someone was sticking up for Annie.

Annie's eyes hardened, and she stood with her hands resting on her hips. "If we hadn't come down here, we wouldn't have found any fruit. At least now we won't starve while we wait."

Rhea pursed her lips and rolled her head. She glanced around, but when no one took her side, she grunted and strode back to the tree where she'd been reading earlier.

Annie glanced at Mya and shrugged.

Mya smiled wanly. Then she realized her sister wasn't with them. "Where's Emma?" she asked.

"We saw her walking along the stream," Annie said.

"I should go find her."

"I'll go with you," Annie said, brushing hair out of her eyes.

As they started up the bank, a splash sounded from behind them. Mya squinted, seeing Josh, Wesley, and Bobby wading into the water on the far side of the stream. She waited until the boys reached the near side. "Where did you guys go?" she asked.

"We followed the trail," Josh said as he stepped onto the bank. "It leads into a valley."

"Did you see any people?"

"No, but someone made that trail. If we follow it, it should lead us to them."

Celia hurried over. "Guess what, Josh?"

Josh bent down. "What?"

"Mya hummed a pretty song, and a whole bunch of animals followed her out of the forest."

Josh tilted his head to look at Mya. "What happened?"

"I don't know," she said. "I started humming this song, and the animals seemed to like it. They followed me until Dylan and CPU scared them away—the jerks."

"We were just trying to get some dinner." Dylan protested.

"What kind of animals?" Josh asked in bewilderment.

Mya rattled off a dozen of them.

"Whoa… more bizarre stuff," Josh murmured, glancing at Wesley in disbelief. "When's it gonna stop?"

"And, something else happened," Annie said, her mouth twitching.

"What? What happened?" Josh asked, seeming to sense something bad.

"We can't find the bus."

"Huh?"

"The yellow beast—we can't find it. We followed the trail back, but it doesn't go to the meadow or the bus anymore. Rhea couldn't find it either."

Josh turned and caught Rhea's eyes. She shook her head slowly and glowered. Josh's lips closed, and his jaw tightened.

Mya heard a rustling of branches and turned. Emma stepped out of the trees a few yards away, holding her beanie in one hand. Mya sighed and grabbed her sister's free hand.

Then Josh started to laugh oddly.

Mya eyed him doubtfully. "What's so funny?"

"Someone is playing a game with us," Josh said, straightening. "Should we play along?"

"Huh?"

"We're being led away. We found a trail this morning, we followed it, and now we can't go back. The trail continues on the other side of this stream. Should we keep following it? We've waited a day, and no one has shown up. We have fruit and water that'll last us for a while. But someone made this trail. If we stick to it, it should lead us to them."

"But if we leave, Ben won't be able to find us," Emma said, adjusting her beanie. "We should stay here. We came here on the yellow beast, and I think that's how we're gonna get home."

Mya gaped at her sister. "What are you saying, Em? The yellow beast is just a bus, and, anyway, we can't find it. We've waited long enough. I agree with Josh; this trail must lead somewhere. Let's follow it and see where it goes."

Wesley bobbed his head. "We can't sit around here forever. We need to do something."

"Yeah, I'm tired of waiting," Ted said. "I'd like to go with you all, but I won't get far in these." He pointed to the shiny new cowboy boots on his feet. "I bought these a week ago, and they're barely broken in."

Gabrielle leaned against a tree. "I don't know about staying or going. I just need a place to skate. There's nothing around here, so if it means going on a trek, I'm down for it."

"I want to go too," Sarah said, nibbling on her bottom lip. "But what about that mist thing. What if it follows us? We were safe inside the bus, but I don't want to be outside if it comes back."

There were quiet gasps and a wave of fear rippled through the children.

Rhea shook her head. "Don't stress about that fog thing. If it comes back, It'll be sorry for bothering us." She held out her hands, ten fingers spread and made a hissing sound. Dylan and CPU laughed nervously.

"If we leave," Barth said, straightening, "we need to bring lots of fruit with us. We may not find anything else to eat for a while."

The other kids agreed.

Celia raised her hand. Josh nodded, but she didn't speak, her eyes darting back and forth.

"Go ahead," Josh said encouragingly.

Celia hesitated, then she said, "Do you think there are unicorns around here?"

Gabrielle snorted, and the other kids started to laugh.

Celia stomped her feet. "It's not funny. I mean it. With all the magical things happening here, maybe there are unicorns too. Unicorns are my favorite animal!"

Josh knelt in front of Celia. "Maybe there are," he said with a grin. "We'll look for them."

"Will they like Mya's humming?" Celia asked.

The kids laughed again.

"Maybe," Josh said with a smile.

Mya stepped over to Celia and took her hand. "Sweetie, if you see a unicorn, you tell me, and I'll definitely hum that song."

Celia's eyes gleamed, and she bounced lightly on her toes.

Josh looked around at the other kids. "Anyone else?"

The children eyed one another, but no one said anything more.

"Okay," Josh said. "Let's have a vote. Who wants to stay here?"

Emma, Ted, and Barth raised their hands.

"All right, who wants to follow the trail?"

The rest of the kids raised their arms.

"It's twelve to three," Josh said. "So, we go. Ted will have a hard time with his boots—"

"And his blubber." Dylan blurted.

Ted grabbed his stomach. "That's right; this is gonna slow me down. But if we don't find more food, you guys are gonna wish you had some of this."

"Yeah, we probably will," Josh said, with a grin.

Dylan grabbed his pants and let off a fart like a bat hitting a baseball, launching him into the air. "Let's go!" he cried.

The kids filled their bottles and stuffed their bags with fruit. Then Barth led them across the stepping-stone bridge.

As they started up the far bank, Mya noticed Timmy hanging back, searching the water, his jacket tied about his waist, and his blue scarf hanging out of one pocket.

"So long fishies," Timmy said. "Sorry for bothering you. Maybe next time we'll learn your language." Then he spun and hurried up the slope.

Mya smiled, but as she gazed at the trees and water, she realized how fuzzy everything looked. A fear crept into her. *Am I going blind? Why's everything so blurry?* She clenched her jaw and shook her head. *I can't think like that. I have to be hopeful. I won't go blind.* She exhaled and turned to catch up with the other kids.

Chapter 8:
The Cage

Sweat dripped down Wesley's face and neck as he strode down the trail. He slowed and swung his pack under his arm, unzipping the top to tug out a water bottle. After a long gulp, he stuck the bottle back in his bag. Strange bird calls echoed through the forest, and a breeze rustled branches in the trees. He wondered where he was. They had walked for hours and still hadn't seen a single person.

He didn't feel tired, which surprised him. He'd hardly slept for a day and a half, though he usually needed seven to eight hours of sleep a night. He also felt strangely anxious. His hands were trembling, and he could hear his heart thumping. He glanced down at his shoes. His toes felt numb, and the numb feeling was moving toward the heels of his feet.

He pulled an apple out of his pack and took a bite. Josh was walking with Bobby some thirty yards ahead. As Bobby chattered on excitedly about a squirrel he'd seen jumping around in the woods, Josh glanced back and quirked an eyebrow. Wesley grinned.

The trail gradually descended into a wooded valley. Sunlight passing through the canopy gave the air a soft green glow, while the ground – which had turned hard and clay-like – crunched beneath Wesley's feet. Now and then the trees parted, and he saw distant foothills bordering the valley to the north and south, rising to snow-peaked mountains marching in parallel along the boundary of the valley. High above, popcorn clouds dotted the blue.

A loud fart echoed through the forest, and Wesley turned to see Dylan bounding up the trail. Dylan soared high into the air, ducking under a low branch in the canopy and landing beside Wesley with a loud thump.

They walked together, talking until a small bird with downy white breast feathers and wings striped like piano keys landed on the path ahead. Dylan slowed and clicked his tongue at the little creature, but the bird ignored him and began pecking the ground.

Dylan reached into his pack and tugged out a cherry, tossing it into the leaves near the bird. The bird nudged the fruit and split it open. Half of the cherry disappeared into its beak, and the rest fell back into the leaves. The bird pecked at the remainder until it was gone, then it raised its little head and stared at Dylan, its black eyes shining. Dylan gave it a lopsided grin and tossed another cherry.

Wesley heard footsteps and turned to find Mya and Emma strolling up behind them.

"Hey," he said.

Mya waved back while Emma smiled shyly.

"What do you have there, Dylan?" Mya asked. She peered at the little bird, then leaned close, squinting. Wesley noticed a faint whiteness in her eyes.

"That looks like a bay-breasted warbler," Mya said. "What do you think, Emma?"

Emma shrugged.

"It's definitely some kind of warbler," Mya murmured, still squinting.

"Yeah, I knew that," Dylan said, though Wesley knew he didn't.

Mya straightened and smiled. Then she and Emma continued on.

Dylan tossed another cherry into the leaves. The bird quickly devoured it.

"Let's get going, Dylan," Wesley said, stretching his arms. "We're falling behind."

"You go ahead," Dylan replied, his eyes fixed on the warbler. "I'll catch up."

Wesley nodded and started off. A few minutes later, Dylan came bounding by, with his fingers in his belt loops and farts shooting off like bubbles from a trumpet.

Wesley rounded the bend and found a crowd of kids resting in an open area beside the trail. He shrugged off his pack and plopped down near Annie and Celia, who were sharing an orange.

"How's it going?" he asked as he pulled out his water bottle.

"We're tired," Celia said, resting her head on Annie's shoulder.

"How long have we been walking?" Annie asked.

"About three hours."

"Can we camp out here?"

Wesley saw Josh pacing some distance down the trail and wearing an uneasy frown. "I doubt it. I think Josh wants to keep going until dark."

Celia groaned and stretched her arms. As she did, Wesley noticed the small blobs of goo on her wrists which he'd seen earlier – red on the right wrist and white on the left.

"You've still got those?" he asked, with surprise.

Celia shrugged. "They won't go away."

"They bother you?"

"Not really."

Wesley turned, seeing Dylan dealing cards to Barth and CPU for a game of Crazy Eights. As the game began, a small bird glided noiselessly up the trail and passed the kids. The bird swept around in an arc and flew back toward Dylan. Just before it reached the boy, the bird slowed and fluttered down on Dylan's shoulder, landing so gently that he didn't even notice.

Barth let out a laugh. "Hey, who's your friend?"

Dylan turned his head and jerked in sudden surprise.

"I think it's the bird you were feeding earlier," Wesley said, peering at the warbler.

The bird ruffled its feathers.

"Yeah, maybe it's still hungry," Dylan said, grinning. He reached into his pack and tugged out a cherry. He held the fruit out for the bird, but the warbler took no notice and drew in its wings, nestling down in the folds of Dylan's shirt.

"Hey, it likes you," Barth said.

The other kids crowded around. The bird paid no attention to them, instead burying its head under its wing.

"I didn't know warblers were so friendly," Mya said.

Dylan flashed a smile. "Yeah, 'cause I'm irresistible."

Celia tapped Mya's leg to get her attention. "Can you sing for it?"

"Sing what?"

"Sing the song you were humming."

Mya frowned. "No, sorry. I'm not going to sing or hum that song anymore."

Celia frowned with obvious disappointment.

"What're you going to call the bird?" Barth asked.

Dylan inclined his head. "Hmm... It likes cherries, so maybe I should call it Cherry."

The other kids approved. At that moment, Ted came striding around the bend with Sarah and Timmy in tow. As the three kids approached, Ted spotted the little bird and did a double take, causing Timmy to bump him from behind.

"Look at our little friend," Ted cried. He swung his hands through the air, producing a shower of musical notes, which the warbler completely ignored.

Sarah hurried over to the little bird and peered intently. The warbler raised its head and chirped softly, then it tucked its beak back under its wing. Sarah laughed.

Timmy smiled at Dylan. "Birds of a feather fly together," he said.

After several minutes, the boys returned to their card game, and Wesley sat down with Annie and Celia. He ate an apple and some grapes but soon found his fingers drumming his thighs and his feet tapping the ground. He rose and strolled down the trail, passing Josh and the others.

As he walked, his heart began thumping faster, and his hands trembled. A fog seemed to fill his brain, and his vision blurred momentarily. He slowed, one hand pressed to his chest, and breathed in and out deeply. Gradually, his vision cleared, and his pulse slowed. He resumed walking. A minute later, he spied a narrow path veering off to the right of the main trail. He blinked and stepped onto the path. He peered down it, following the course as it wound into the trees. Where does that go? He wondered and cautiously stepped forward.

As he passed into the woods, Wesley glanced back to make sure he could remember where he had left the main trail. He followed the path until light around him faded, and a buzzing sound filled the air. He slowed and looked about. Thousands of tiny bugs covered the leaves and branches around him. He listened. The buzzing grew louder. His palms dampened, and his heartbeat quickened. Something about this place made him anxious. He decided to head back.

When he reached the main trail, his anxiety eased. He wiped the sweat off his forehead, wondering why he'd felt nervous at all. The darkness didn't scare him, and he didn't usually mind bugs. He frowned and headed back to find the other kids.

He saw CPU first, who was standing by himself and staring up through an opening in the canopy.

"What's going on, CPU?" Wesley asked. CPU didn't seem to hear him. Wesley tapped on his shoulder.

CPU twitched and turned in startled surprise. "Oh, hey, Wes. I didn't know you were there… Look at this. A bird. It's huge!"

"What? Where?"

CPU pointed at distant mountains visible through the canopy. "There," he said, "flying between those two peaks."

Wesley squinted, but he could only make out blue sky and snow-covered slopes. "Where? I don't see a bird."

"Right there," CPU said. "It's enormous and nasty looking."

Wesley gazed again but saw nothing. He stepped back and studied his friend, sensing something different about him. "Hey, where are your glasses, CPU?"

CPU rubbed his forehead. "In my pack. They were giving me a headache, so I took them off."

"Huh?" Wesley said, thinking CPU was joking. "Aren't you blind without them?"

CPU rolled his shoulders. "Yeah, I thought so, but I can see great now. I can see each tree on those mountains. Look, there's a fox chasing a rabbit in the snow. Ha! The rabbit dove into a hole."

Wesley squinted at the distant mountains. "I don't see any trees or rabbits – just blobs of green and white. It's too far away."

"Yeah, it's weird," CPU said, "my eyes seem great, but my ears are stuffed up. Everything sounds faint and distant like I'm trapped in a pipe under the ground."

"Have you tried yawning?"

"Yeah, many times – it doesn't help."

Wesley's brows furrowed. "Are you sick?"

"I feel fine," CPU said.

Wesley shrugged and continued on to the other kids. He found Celia sitting beside Annie with her arms extended, and her forearms pressed together as a pink object swelled from her wrists.

"What's that?" Wesley asked, his voice rising in surprise.

"A bubble," Celia said, glancing up.

The blobs of red and white goo Wesley had seen previously on her wrists appeared to have mixed into a pink liquid that was swelling to the size of a cantaloupe.

Wesley blinked in amazement. "How are you doing that?"

"I'm not. It's doing it," Celia said.

Wesley called Josh over, and the other kids crowded around.

Josh knelt beside Celia. "It's like a little balloon," he said. "What happens if you move your arms apart?"

"It shrinks. See..." She separated her arms, and the bubble collapsed, returning to a blob on each wrist – one red, the other white.

"That's cool," Josh said softly. "Can you put your arms together again?"

Celia did, and the bubble puffed out once more, quickly expanding to the size of a watermelon. As the sphere swelled, Celia blinked and wobbled unsteadily.

Wesley grabbed her shoulder. "Are you okay?" He asked.

"Yeah, just a little tired," she said, her shoulders sagging.

"Okay, that's enough. You can stop," Josh said gently.

Celia separated her arms, and the goo returned to two small blobs. She yawned and lay back, resting her head on Annie's lap. A moment later, she was snoring softly.

"That was quick," Wesley whispered.

Josh grunted. "Yeah, it's been a long day."

"Should we camp here?" Wesley asked.

"No, let's go a little further before it gets dark. I'm still hoping to find some people, so we don't have to sleep outside."

A sudden moan caused Wesley to catch his breath. He turned and saw Bobby lying on the ground, curled up like a ball.

Josh strode over and knelt beside the boy. "What's wrong, Bob?"

"Myy stoomaach huurt."

"Your stomach?"

"Yeeaah, baad... Baad thiing coommiing."

Josh's eyes darted. "What's coming? What's bad?"

Wesley remembered the bird CPU had seen and wondered if it was still there. He jogged back to the opening in the canopy and stared at the northern sky. Far off, a dark object moved through the blue.

He called CPU over. "Is that the bird you saw?"

CPU strolled up and peered through the canopy. "Yeah, do you see it now! It's humongous and headed our way."

Wesley watched the dark wings rise and fall. "Maybe that's what's scaring Bobby."

CPU grimaced. "Yeah, probably. It scares me!"

"Hey Josh, come look at this," Wesley shouted.

Josh joined them and peered at the sky where Wesley pointed. "A bird?" Josh said doubtfully. "I don't think...." His voice trailed off. "Whoa... that thing's a truck."

"I told you," CPU said, slapping his thigh.

"Hey, everybody, crowd around together," Josh yelled to the other kids. "We're safer as a group."

The kids crowded together. Wesley picked up Celia, pressing her to his chest. Josh grabbed a gnarled walking stick he'd found earlier in the afternoon. Wesley frowned, wishing he had kept his from yesterday.

The bird continued moving in their direction. As it drew near, Wesley inhaled sharply. Its wings spread some twenty feet from wingtip to wingtip, and its chest looked like that of a lion.

The winged creature swept overhead and arced in a wide circle above the trees. Wesley's heart pounded. The bird slowed. Then without warning, it pitched forward and plunged toward the children. Screams erupted, and Josh raised his walking stick like a baseball bat. Wesley crouched, holding Celia tight.

The bird plummeted for what seemed an eternity but was probably several seconds. Then with a powerful thrust of its wings, the winged creature broke out of its fall and started back up into the sky. Dazed, Wesley watched as the bird wheeled and soared northward, slowly shrinking into the blue.

"What just happened?" Annie asked, rubbing her forehead in bewilderment.

"Maybe we didn't look so tasty up close," Dylan said.

"It was like some mutant condor," Mya muttered. "It could easily carry off a sheep or deer, let alone one of us."

"Cherry was spinning like a Disney teacup," Dylan said, glancing at the warbler on his shoulder.

Josh looked around. "All right, we need to stay close together. We don't want something like that finding any of us alone. Let's hike a little further. I want to find a well-hidden place."

There were grumbles, but all the kids gathered their things. Wesley zipped up his pack and lifted it onto his shoulders. Then he remembered what he'd seen further up the trail. "Hey Josh, a little ways ahead, there's a path that leads off the main trail."

Josh quirked an eyebrow. "Really? Did you check it out?"

"Yeah, but I didn't go far. I can show you."

Josh nodded.

The kids all started out, glancing around nervously and huddling close to one another. Only Bobby smiled happily; his pain apparently vanished. Celia was still asleep, so Wesley carried her.

When they came to the place where the narrow path left the main trail, the kids peered into the woods. The warbler sat up on Dylan's shoulder and chirped sharply. Then the little bird ruffled its feathers and took flight, gliding to a branch directly above the narrow path some twenty feet into the trees.

"Look... maybe Cherry wants us to go that way," Dylan said.

Josh glanced at Wesley. "How about you?"

"It gets a little creepy, but I'm curious to see where it leads."

"Then let's explore," Josh said. "You lead the way, Wes."

The children started single file down the path, with Wesley at the front holding Celia in his arms and Josh bringing up the rear. As they passed under Cherry, the little bird hopped off her perch and landed back on Dylan's shoulder with a happy chirp.

Wesley walked cautiously, scrutinizing the woods for anything strange. As before, the foliage quickly thickened, and the light dimmed. A buzzing sound filled the air. Wesley glanced back to make sure everyone was with him and pointed out bugs crawling on the leaves and branches.

After some ten minutes, the buzzing quieted and the darkness faded. Wesley quickened his pace. He rounded a large elm tree and froze in wonder at the edge of a clearing. Before him, a wrought-iron structure towered some four stories into the air.

Wesley stood at one end of the rectangular structure which looked at least fifty feet wide and two hundred feet in length. Within the structure, five enormous trees grew in a single line from the front of the enclosure to the rear. In the branches of the trees, thousands of shiny objects glittered in the sun.

Knee-high grass covered the floor of the clearing, and a narrow creek wound its way out of the woods to the right of the structure, passing between the second and third trees before disappearing into the forest to the left of the clearing.

As other kids stumbled out of the woods, there were gasps and shouts of astonishment. Wesley made his way along the front of the structure toward an iron door, which appeared to be the only entrance.

"Holy blue monkeys," Dylan shouted in wonder as he stepped into the clearing. "How did this get here?"

Cherry gave a sharp tweet and spread her wings. She hopped off Dylan's shoulder and flew through the iron bars, gliding to the nearest tree. The little bird landed on a high branch and promptly began singing as if she'd come to her favorite place in the world.

"Hey, Cherry," Dylan yelled. "How can we get in there too?"

The bird chirped twice, then resumed singing. Dylan rolled his eyes.

Josh was the last to step out of the trees and at the sight of the iron structure, his jaw went slack.

"I guess we found something," Wesley said with a grin and shifted Celia in his arms.

"Yeah, it looks like some giant cage. Well, at least we know we're not alone," Josh said. "Someone built this."

"Let's go inside," Dylan cried, bounding over to the entrance. He pushed on the bars of the door, then pulled, but they didn't move. He stepped back frowning. "How does it open?"

"Let me have a look," Barth said. He plodded over to the door and squatted, studying the bars. Wesley knelt beside him.

Wesley saw two large hinges which fastened the door on the left side, but nothing fixed it to the structure on the right.

Barth's brow creased. "There's no lock," he said, pushing on a bar. "The door should swing right open."

Josh joined the boys. He examined the door, resting his hand on a bar. The gate shifted. He jerked his arm back.

"Hey, it moved," Dylan cried.

Josh stared at his hand, then set it back on the bar and pushed. The door swung smoothly inward.

"How'd you do that?" Dylan cried.

Josh shook his head. "I applied pressure, bro."

"So, did I!"

"Me too," Barth said frowning.

Josh shrugged and stepped through the doorway. The others followed cautiously.

Inside, Dylan glanced around and bounded into the air. "What're those shiny things in the trees?" he cried.

"Ii waannaa seee," Bobby exclaimed.

Dylan and Bobby started toward the first tree. Wesley followed. As the three came under the branches, a breeze gusted causing the shimmering objects in the trees to spin like thousands of tiny mirror balls.

Wesley strode to the trunk of the tree and settled Celia in the grass. Sarah, Timmy, and Rhea came up behind him. Wesley inclined his head. The lowest limbs of the tree were some ten feet above the ground, extending out from the trunk like giant gnarled arms.

Dylan bounded into the air and touched the nearest limb before dropping back into the grass. "You want me to get some of those shiny things?"

"Can you?" Wesley asked, leaning against the tree trunk.

"Just watch."

Dylan crouched, gripping his pants with one hand. Then he sprang, letting off a loud stink bomb as he shot up into the air. He grabbed a limb and swung himself around and onto it. He grinned at the kids below and sat upright, eyeing the many shimmering orbs around him.

Cherry hopped off the branch high in the tree and landed back on Dylan's shoulder. Dylan nodded to the bird and slid forward toward the nearest shimmering orb. He took the object in his hands and leaned close, eyeing its glittering surface. "It feels soft and spongy," he said, "like a bathtub toy."

"Is it some kind of fruit?" Sarah asked.

"Hmm..." Dylan said, studying the shimmering object. "Yeah, but I wouldn't eat it. The edges feel hard, like little crystals. It might break your teeth."

He turned the fruit over in his hands as the light played off his face. Then he tugged the stem until it snapped. Unzipping a pouch in his pack, he dropped the fruit inside and slid out on the branch toward the next shimmering orb.

After collecting a half dozen of the fruit, Dylan swung off the branch and landed in the grass. Wesley and the other kids crowded around. Dylan pulled one out of his bag, and to everyone's surprise, the fruit had turned a dull yellow.

"Noo moore liiight," Bobby said, pursing his lips in disappointment.

Dylan frowned and stepped out from under the tree. He held the fruit up in the sun as if expecting it to resume sparkling, but it remained the same dull color. He pulled several more of the objects out of his bag, but they all looked the same.

Dylan's shoulders slumped. "Sorry," he said as he handed a fruit to each of the kids. "They don't shine anymore."

Wesley studied the surface of his fruit. Like Dylan said, it felt soft and spongy, except it was covered in a pattern of five-sided crystals whose edges were hard. He was hungry but didn't dare bite into it.

Sarah let out a yelp. "Mine's sparkling," she cried, lifting her orb, which was glittering again.

"Miiinnee tooo!" Bobby exclaimed. His fruit was pulsing a soft white light.

"Ow… this is hot!" Rhea cried, juggling her fruit around like a bun fresh out of the oven. Her orb glowed brightly orange, then yellow. She dropped it, and the fruit rolled. The grass around it burst into flame.

"Whoa! Put it out!" Wesley hollered.

All the kids jumped over and stamped on the ground, quickly extinguishing the flames.

"Man," Wesley said, turning his shoes over to check the blackened soles. "That could have burned this place down."

He eyed Rhea's fruit which had returned to a dull yellow but otherwise lay unscathed in the charred grass. He picked it up and offered it to the redheaded girl, but she waved him off.

"No, thank you. I don't want that now."

Wesley shrugged and dropped the fruit into his own pack.

"This is pretty," Sarah said, rolling the orb in her hands as it glittered brilliantly.

"Why does yours do that?" Timmy asked.

"Because I'm special," Sarah said, laughing.

Wesley cleared his throat and tugged out his water bottle. It was empty, so he headed to the creek. After filling the bottle, he took several gulps and wiped his mouth. His heartbeat slowed from the excitement moments before.

He turned and noticed the Kadean sisters a little ways down the bank. Mya was pointing to trees beside the clearing and speaking to Emma, who was gazing at the water. Wesley caught his breath. Emma's silky brown hair and exquisite profile always stunned him. How could someone be that pretty?

Fingers snapped before Wesley's eyes. He blinked and turned to find Josh standing behind him.

"Hey, Romeo," Josh said with a laugh. "Come with me. I want to check something out."

"Huh?" Wesley said, his face flushed.

"Let's check out the path on the other side of this clearing," Josh said, leaning on his heels. "Maybe we can find something else cool."

"Okay," Wesley said distractedly. He glanced one more time at Emma, then took a quick drink from his bottle and capped it. He jammed the bottle back in his bag and hurried after Josh, who had started toward the gate.

"I went all around the inside of this cage," Josh said, "and there's no other way out." He stepped through the entrance. Wesley followed. The boys strolled around the front of the iron structure and along the side, heading toward the rear of the clearing.

"The path continues at the far end," Josh said, pointing ahead.

They found the trail and followed it as it snaked through dense woods and small clearings. Finally, it came to the shore of a small lake. The water glittered in the afternoon sun. Wesley picked up a stone and tossed it, watching the rock skip a half dozen times. "Is this what you were looking for?"

Josh shook his head. "Let's hike around and see if the path starts up again."

They circled the lake but found no other trail. When the boys returned to where they had started, Josh clasped his hands behind his neck and grimaced. "This is it?" he asked. "I thought there would be something else... another sign of people."

"That cage thing is cool," Wesley said. "We can camp out there tonight."

"Yeah, let's head back."

The boys returned to the path. As they neared the clearing, they heard shouts and hurried forward. When they came into the open, they saw the other kids gathered at the far end of the iron structure.

"What's going on?" Josh yelled.

"It's locked," Dylan cried. "We can't get out."

Wesley and Josh jogged up. They saw Barth, Timmy, and CPU leaning on the iron door. The boys were pushing, but it wasn't budging.

Josh rolled his eyes. "With all that noise, I thought it was something serious."

"It is! We're trapped in this thing," Dylan said.

Josh approached the iron door. The other boys backed away. Josh grabbed the bars and pulled. The door swung out like someone had greased its hinges. The other kids gasped.

"How did you do that?" Dylan demanded.

Josh shook his head. "C'mon. It was nothing." He strode through the open gate and waved the other kids over. He knelt and scanned their faces. "How about we make camp here?" he asked. "There's water, and this cage gives us protection from things like that giant bird."

Relief filled the eyes of the kids, and they all nodded.

"Good," Josh said. "Find a comfortable spot to sleep." He rose and strolled away. Wesley followed.

"How did you open that door?" Wesley asked.

"Anyone could."

"No, they all pushed, but it wouldn't move."

Josh shrugged. "I don't know. It's another one of the million things that don't make sense here."

Wesley grabbed Josh's shoulder and stopped him. "A lot of things seem different for you." Wesley peered hard at his friend. "When Annie screamed yesterday, no one could move except you. And when that mist thing attacked, it froze me, but it didn't hurt you. Now you're the only one who can open that door. Isn't that weird?"

"Uh huh," Josh said quietly. "Really strange." He lifted Wesley's hand off his shoulder. "Are you hungry? I'm starved. Let's get something to eat."

They headed over to their packs, which were lying beside Celia. She was still asleep. Wesley tugged out an apple, and Celia opened her eyes. "Where are we?"

Wesley shrugged. "Who knows, but we found a good place to make camp."

"Oh," Celia said, sitting up.

Just then Sarah's high, warm laugh reached Wesley's ears. He twisted toward the sound. Sarah was standing directly in front of Timmy and holding a crystal fruit in each hand. She tossed one to

Timmy, and he caught the shimmering orb, but the light immediately faded, and the fruit turned a dull yellow.

Timmy frowned. "The light doesn't shine, so it's not mine." He tossed the fruit back. Sarah caught it, and the orb began glittering again. Celia gasped.

A quiet rumble stirred the air. The ground vibrated. Wesley scanned the sky. Along the western horizon, an orange glow rose into the blue.

"Another fireball?"

Josh checked his watch. "Six twenty-five, same time as yesterday." He leaped to his feet and shouted, "Everybody head for cover. Our friend, the flaming meteor is making another pass."

Wesley leaned against the tree. Celia sat beside him while Sarah parked herself on his far side.

"I'm scared," Celia said, her voice quivering. Wesley put his arm around her and Sarah.

As the rumble grew, Wesley heard a gentle humming. He tipped his head back. Above, the crystal fruit had begun spinning in the branches.

"Hey," Wesley cried, pointing to the fruit. The other kids gazed, their eyes widening and mouths opening in wonder.

Orange and yellow streaks swept up into the western sky. Then a red dot appeared on the horizon, hurtling east at a terrible speed. The crystal fruit whirled faster, and the humming swelled. Then a white light shot out from each fruit in each tree to a single point above the iron structure. The light burned there for a moment in a brilliant luminescence, then swept out over the top of the structure and down the sides like a single pane of glass.

Wesley pressed Sarah and Celia down and leaned over the girls, shielding them from the coming heat and wind. With a deafening roar, the fireball swept by. The ground shook, and the thunder drowned out all other noise, but Wesley felt no heat or wind. He raised his head. The trees at the edge of the clearing were bent like in a hurricane-force gale, but the air around him was calm and still.

He closed his eyes and waited. When he reopened them, the white light from the fruit had faded, and the humming had ebbed to a quiet murmur. The fireball shrank into the east, and peace returned to the meadow.

Wesley caught Josh's gaze. Josh opened his mouth without speaking and closed it again.

Annie sprang to her feet and threw up her arms. "Did you see that?" she cried. "The fruit protected us! The light blocked the fireball!"

Dylan bounded skyward. "It was a force field - like in the movies!"

"Light protecting the gifts from the height," Timmy said.

Wesley scanned the clearing. He felt dazed, and cautiously rose to his feet. He stepped out from under the tree and gazed west at the sun drifting beneath the horizon. In the east, a carpet of stars climbed into the sky.

Celia ambled over and clasped his hand. "Aren't they beautiful," she said, staring at the stars.

"Yes," Wesley murmured.

Celia tipped her head. "I wish my dad was here. He'd put me on his shoulders so I could see better."

"I can do that," Wesley said, squeezing her hand. He swung her up and set her on his shoulders. "Is that better?"

"Yes," she said, patting his cheeks. "Thank you."

"Hey guys, I need to talk to everyone," Josh shouted, waving all the kids over.

Wesley set Celia back down in the grass.

"I've been thinking something," Josh said, "and probably most of you have been thinking the same." He studied their faces. "What just happened has convinced me – we're not in Annaberry anymore, or New York, or maybe even America." He paused, letting his words sink in. "When the yellow beast drove through that blue light yesterday, I think it took us to a different place, a different land, maybe a different world."

"A micro black hole," CPU murmured.

Josh nodded. "Whatever it was, we're a long way from home. We've been walking all day, and we haven't seen a single person or building. We're in a strange place – a place where fireballs shoot across the sky, where fish talk, where mist creatures can freeze you, and where light shines out of fruit. And, some of us are doing some crazy things – things that seem magical."

There was silence. The kids looked around. Wesley heard Celia sniffle. He put his arm over her shoulder.

Rhea cleared her throat. "I've been thinking the same thing since the fireball yesterday. This is definitely not Annaberry or New York."

"What should we do?" Sarah asked, her lips trembling.

"We need to find someone to help us," Josh said. "Somebody built this cage. And, someone made the trail we've been following. We need to find out who."

"We should never have left the yellow beast," Emma said grimacing.

"What good would have staying there done?" Mya asked. "If we're not in Annaberry, no one would have found us anyway."

"Ben would've," Emma said firmly.

"We waited," Mya said, "but he didn't come back."

"We already argued about this," Annie said.

"Right, what are we going to do now?" Wesley asked.

Ted raised his head and smiled at the night sky. "I don't know," he said, "but I think I love this place. Except for that freaky mist creature, it's been wonderful. We have food to eat, water, good weather, and music."

Ted moved his index and middle fingers, and the sound of piano keys filled the air. Celia leaned against Wesley. Ted raised his left hand and moved three fingers, adding a light horn-like resonance. Then his pinky finger twitched, producing a bell note.

"That's cool," Wesley said. "What is it?"

"Sea of Glass," Ted said with a wide grin.

"Sea of Glass?" Annie asked.

"Yeah, a song by Tom Middleton, a DJ. He's the bomb."

Ted swept his arms from side to side, and music filled the air. Then a quiet humming joined in.

Wesley inclined his head. "Do you hear something?"

Ted slowed. His music quieted, and the humming grew clearer. He raised his eyes and shuffled back a step. "The fruit… they're making sound."

Wesley glanced up. The crystal fruit in the trees were turning slowly.

"They're humming," Wesley said. "They're playing along with you."

Ted laughed. He listened, then he swung his hands from right to left. Music flowed out in a shimmer of sound. The crystal fruit whirled. The humming swelled, spreading through the clearing. Ted raised his arms and flung them down. The sound roared, and the humming surged. Ted swayed and rocked. The music rose and fell, and the humming washed through everything, filling the spaces between each note, and weaving a great tapestry of sound.

Ted slowed, and the music quieted. He swung his arms, and the sound thundered, exploding into the night. He played on and on. The kids listened spellbound.

Finally, Ted dropped his arms and bent over, beads of sweat rolling down his face. The crystal fruit slowed, and the clearing quieted. The last rays of sunlight flickered over the horizon.

There was silence. Wesley began to clap, and the other kids joined in.

Ted pushed his hands through his hair and straightened. "Thanks, guys, but I'm more tired than a bear in December." He staggered to the nearest tree and flopped down, laying spread eagle in the grass.

"I'm sleepy too," Celia said, "Can we sit down?"

Wesley nodded, and they seated themselves near Ted.

"I miss home," Celia said. "I miss my dad and Abuela. Do you miss your parents?"

Wesley nodded. Celia closed her eyes and was soon snoring softly.

Wesley wasn't tired. He stared at his sneakers. The numbness in his toes had spread up to the balls of his feet. He untied the laces and tugged his shoes off. He rubbed his toes. There was no feeling.

He sighed and sat back. He thought of home and his mom and dad. A well of longing filled him. He wished he was home. He looked down at Celia. "Yeah... I miss them," he said quietly. Then he closed his eyes and leaned against the tree.

Chapter 9:
Light in the Dark

Celia sat upright and blinked in the sunlight, pouring down through the branches. The field about her was a jumbled puzzle of sleeping kids. She rose, feeling stiff and a sore from the day before. A breeze brushed her face. She squinted at the sky. The morning sun was still hidden behind the trees. She stretched her arms and strolled through the grass to the end of the enclosure.

With stalks swaying above her waist, she squatted and took care of business, thankful that Abuela had left a packet of tissue in her backpack. A few minutes later, she started back, noticing points of light moving over the grass. The shimmering fruit were rotating slowly in the branches. High above them, a sea of clouds floated eastward.

Two sparrows startled her when they swooped by her face. She laughed and tilted her head to watch them dart and dip above the grass. They chased one another, sweeping past the trees and through the iron bars, disappearing into the dark woods at the edge of the clearing.

As Celia strolled up to the tree where the rest of the kids were sleeping, Dylan turned his head and opened his eyes. He stared at her for a moment and then stretched his arms, disturbing Cherry, who'd been resting on his stomach. The little bird ruffled her feathers and raised her head.

Celia crossed her arms. She wanted a little bird. She didn't know why Cherry liked Dylan so much, more than any of the girls.

"Where'd you go?" Dylan asked.

"For a walk," Celia said with a half shrug.

Dylan sat up, and the warbler hopped off his stomach. "Where's Josh and Wes?"

Celia looked around. She hadn't noticed they were gone. "I don't know."

Dylan leaped up and jogged to the entrance of the enclosure. Someone had left the door propped open.

Celia tiptoed among the sleeping kids. Gabrielle lay curled up between CPU and Barth. Gabrielle was a late sleeper. On weekends she'd snooze until noon, while Celia liked to wake up with the dawn.

On the far side of Barth, Bobby lay on his back, staring at something he held in his hands. Celia headed over.

"Hey, Bobby, whatcha got there?"

The boy blinked at her slowly a few times. "Hiii Ceeliiaa. Itt aaa doomiinoo."

"A domino? Where'd you get that?"

"Maaddee iitt," Bobby said, grinning.

Celia squinted. "Can I see it?"

Bobby held out the small object. It felt smooth and cool in Celia's hands. She studied the surface and counted the dots—ten on one side, seven on the other.

"If we had more of these, we could play a game," she said.

Bobby nodded. "Neeed mooree time."

Celia didn't understand what Bobby meant and handed the domino back. Her throat was dry, so she pulled her water bottle from her pack. Resigned to fruit for breakfast, she tugged out some cherries too.

A few feet away, Annie rolled over. "Good morning, senorita," Annie said with a wide smile. "How'd you sleep?"

"Good," Celia said,

Annie rolled onto her back and stared up at the tree. "Me too. This place is so peaceful. And the weather's nice. What a strange November." She sat upright and slowly surveyed the clearing. "Where's Josh and Wesley?"

Celia shrugged. "Dylan went looking for them."

"Mmm, speak of the devil," Annie said.

Celia followed her gaze and saw the two older boys coming out of the woods with Dylan hopping behind them. They passed through the entrance to the iron structure and strode over to the tree.

"Okay, everybody, wake up!" Josh shouted. "We can't sleep all day. Our food won't last long. We need to find more. Let's get moving."

Celia groaned and rubbed her forehead. She didn't want to walk more. They'd gone so far yesterday. Annie smiled sympathetically and hugged her around the waist. "Come on, senorita. You're tough. You can do it."

Celia washed her face at the creek and filled her water bottle. Then she stuffed her things in her bag and pulled it over her shoulders.

When everyone was ready, they made their way single file through the gate, while Josh held the door open and Wesley led them into the woods.

The canopy quickly thickened, and the light faded. Strange sounds echoed through the forest. Celia began to tremble. "I'm scared," she whispered.

Annie took her hand. "I know... Me too. But if we stick together, we'll be okay."

Celia gave Annie a grateful smile. Annie was her favorite of the girls, except for Gabrielle of course. Annie noticed little things, like Celia's hair clip being crooked or her shoe untied. She reminded Celia of her mom, though Celia didn't remember much about her mom. It had been three years since she'd last seen her.

Celia remembered that day – a summer afternoon at their home in Honduras. She was playing with her cloth dolls in the driveway when a black van stopped in front of their house. Four men climbed out and strode across the yard. One of them glanced at Celia through dark glasses. Another one rapped hard on the front door.

Celia's mom answered and stood in the doorway with her arms folded. She talked calmly at first, but gradually, her face reddened, and her voice rose as she argued with the men. She stamped her feet and pointed at the van, telling the men to leave, but one of them pulled out a gun, and two others grabbed her. They dragged her from the doorway.

Celia screamed and ran across the yard. She dodged the men and threw her arms around her mom's legs. The men let go. Her mom picked Celia up and held her close. "Hush, little Cici," she said. "Be brave for me." Then she set Celia down and walked with the men to the van. She climbed inside, and they shut the door. As the van drove off, her mom gazed pensively through the window. Celia waved goodbye.

When Celia's dad came home several hours later and learned what had happened, he clenched his fists and stomped around the yard, swinging his arms and shouting. This scared Celia, and she ran to the shed and hid in the back. Her dad found her and carried her out as tears rolled down his cheeks. He set Celia down on the front lawn and headed into the house. A minute later he came out lugging a pile of clothes. He dropped the pile in the back of his truck.

Gabrielle appeared at the front door; her brow knitted. "What's going on, Cici?"

Celia shrugged.

Their dad told the girls to put their favorite clothes and toys in a pile on their beds.

As the sun sank below the horizon, Celia carried her favorite yellow blanket outside. She lay the blanket on the grass and played on it with her dolls until she fell asleep. She awoke in the back seat of the truck as it bumped along a dirt road. Gabrielle sat beside her, and her dad and Abuela were in the front seat.

Celia jerked upright. "Where are we?"

"Guatemala," her dad answered in a flat tone.

"Where's mama?"

"She can't come with us," her dad said, his jaw tightening.

"Why?"

He didn't answer, but she later learned that bad men had taken their mom away. Her dad feared the same thing would happen to the rest of the family, so he was taking them to a safe place.

They drove for days, sleeping in the car. After they crossed the border into Texas, they stopped at the home of a family friend. The next day they continued to New York City, where they stayed with some of Celia's cousins. After two weeks, they arrived in Annaberry.

It had been three years since they'd driven out of Honduras. Celia thought about her mom sometimes, but less often than before. Her dad and Abuela took good care of them. On weekends, they had picnics in the park. In the evenings, her dad would tell them stories about their mom. Celia thought her mom was a saint, but once when her dad was describing something her mom had done, Abuela shook her head and muttered, "If she was so good, why isn't she here with her daughters?"

This caused Celia's dad to pound his fist on the table, but Abuela just stuck her chin in the air and shuffled out of the room silently.

Later, when Celia was alone with Gabrielle, her sister tried to explain.

"You're too young to remember Cici, but when we were little, mom wasn't around very much. She was always at some strike or protest or other thing. She didn't have time for me or you. Abuela took care of us."

As these thoughts drifted through Celia's mind, the trees parted, and she stepped onto the main trail. The kids stopped and counted heads. Then they started out. Concealed by the thick forest canopy, they relaxed and spread out along the path.

A feeling of happiness welled up in Celia, and she began to hum a song which she'd learned many years before.

"That's pretty," Annie said. "What's it called?"

"*Veo Veo*," Celia replied. "It means 'I See, I See' in Spanish. My mom used to sing it for Gabi and me when we were little."

"Can you teach me?" Annie asked.

"Don't," Gabrielle shouted from behind them. "It's a dumb song."

"No, it's not," Celia protested, looking over her shoulder with a frown. She smiled at Annie, her eyes twinkling. "I don't remember all the words, but the beginning goes like this '*Veo veo que ves una cosita y que cosita es.*'"

Annie tried to sing along, but it sounded so funny that Celia couldn't help but laugh. She sang the words several more times until Annie finally got them. Then they sang together.

As the morning passed, Celia noticed a change in the woods. The trees became narrower, soaring high into the air with thick brown vines winding up their trunks and large S-shaped leaves growing thickly on their long spindly branches.

With each gust of wind, clouds of leaves tumbled through the air and settled on the forest floor. While in the foliage along the side of the trail, clusters of long-stemmed purple flowers grew among daisies and waves of small red blossoms.

Strange sounds rang out in the forest—long bird calls and rapid, shrill shrieks of unseen creatures—causing Celia's heart to flutter. But as the morning drew on, the sounds quieted, and she calmed.

Just before noon, they rounded a bend, and Celia noticed to her left a faint light shining deep in the woods. She inhaled sharply and tugged Annie to a stop. "What's that?" she asked, pointing.

Annie leaned forward. "Hmm... Looks like some kind of lamp."

"Should we go see?"

Annie adjusted her pack and shook her head. "We shouldn't leave the trail."

"But it doesn't look far. Maybe there're people there," Celia said.

Another voice shouted. "Hey, what's up, ladies?"

The girls turned to see Barth ambling up behind them.

"We see a light in the woods," Celia said.

Barth halted next to the girls. "Where?"

Celia pointed.

Barth peered into the dark forest. "Geez... what's that?"

"Let's go see," Celia said, bouncing on her toes.

Barth's brows drew together, but he didn't say anything.

"Maybe we'll find someone who can help us," Celia suggested.

Barth stared at the faint light. "Hmm... I guess we could go a little ways in to get a better look."

Celia grabbed Annie's hand, pulling her into the trees. Barth followed. Celia walked cautiously, glancing now and then at the trail receding behind them. As they neared the light, a sweet fragrance filled the air.

"What's that smell?" Celia asked.

Annie sniffed. "Maybe jasmine."

"Jasmine?"

"It's a plant with pretty white flowers that smells wonderful."

The children made their way until the trees parted, and they found themselves in a glade with a tall, spindly plant at its center rising almost five feet into the air. In the foliage of the plant nestled a dozen egg-shaped purple fruit, and at its top bloomed an enormous golden flower with long curving petals that glowed in the dark woods.

"This is it," Celia said. "This is making the light." She crept up close to the plant. Annie and Barth stood beside her. Barth tugged off a purple fruit.

"I wonder if it's edible?" he said, eyeing the fruit's smooth surface.

Celia peered up at the blossom. "It's so beautiful. Annie, can you give me a boost?"

The older girl nodded and lifted Celia by the waist until she was eye level with the flower petals. The fragrance enveloped Celia, and a fog whisked into her brain. She closed her eyes and felt the world slowly spin. "I feel kinda strange," she said. "Can you put me back down?"

Annie set Celia down on the soft dirt. The young girl's legs went limp, and she collapsed to the ground. Annie knelt beside her.

"I feel weird too," Annie said, rubbing her forehead.

Celia took a deep breath and lay back in the dirt. Annie reclined next to her. Barth joined them a moment later.

Celia's worries drifted away. She closed her eyes and floated into a dream. She found herself in a lush meadow. Above her, a purple sky spread from horizon to horizon like a watercolor painting. She strolled through tall grass until she found a quietly flowing stream that shimmered orange and yellow. She laughed at the beautiful colors, wondering what made them.

A note rang out, then another, piercing the quiet. The vision faded away. Celia opened her eyes. The golden flower towered above her. More notes rang out like water gurgling down a stream. She shook her head and struggled to sit up. "What is that?"

Barth raised himself on his elbows. "It sounds like Ted – his music."

Celia shook Annie's shoulder. The older girl sat upright, blinking, and yawning. The three rose and made their way toward the sound. As they walked through the trees, Celia caught glimpses of the trail ahead. Ted came into view, standing with his feet apart and his arms swinging exuberantly.

"What's going on?" Annie asked.

"That should be my question," Ted said. "I came around the corner just as the three of you stepped into the trees. I figured you'd be back in a moment and decided to wait, but then I lost sight of you. Ten minutes must have passed, and I began to worry that you were lost, so I started making music. I thought you might hear your way back."

"That was smart," Annie said. "It was weird. We found this lovely flower that smelled amazing, but then we got sleepy, and all of us conked out. You woke us."

Barth chuckled. "So, you finally found something useful to do with your music."

"Yeah, it's good for preventing sleep," Ted said, with a laugh.

Celia stared at her hands, remembering the beautiful dream. "I felt so happy there. Can we go back?"

"No," Annie said sternly. "That was scary. We shouldn't fall asleep like that in the middle of the day. Who knows how long we would've been out? And now we've fallen behind everybody else."

"Yeah, I was bringing up the rear," Ted said.

"Okay, let's catch up," Annie said.

"Sorry, you're not getting me to rush," Ted replied. "I like rambling at my own pace."

"Me neither," Barth said. "I'll keep Ted company."

"Suit yourselves," Annie said. She smiled at Celia. "Come on, let's see how fast we are."

Celia grinned, and they started to jog, their backpacks bouncing as they left Ted and Barth behind.

The girls jogged until several kids came into sight, including Rhea, Dylan, and Wesley. Celia slowed, and Annie eased up beside her. As she caught her breath, Celia noticed Rhea walking a few steps behind Wesley and staring at him strangely.

"What's Rhea doing?" she asked Annie.

The older girl covered her mouth, but Celia heard a laugh slip out. "I don't know," Annie said after a moment. "Maybe she has a secret."

Celia leaned close. "What secret?"

Annie inclined her head and shrugged.

Celia wondered what Annie meant by a secret. Then she noticed the little bird sitting on Dylan's shoulder, and her resentment flooded back. She huffed angrily that he had a bird and she didn't. But a moment later it occurred to her that Dylan had stopped jumping and making his annoying farts ever since Cherry started sitting on his shoulder. She tipped her head and smiled, deciding it was probably a good thing that Dylan had found a little bird.

The children walked on until Josh called a halt for lunch. Celia gratefully swung off her pack and sat down in the leaves, blanketing the trail. She was hungry and pulled out a peach. As she took a bite, she noticed Wesley standing a few feet away, his arms crossed over his chest.

"Aren't you tired?" Celia asked.

Wesley unfolded his arms. "No, I'm okay."

Annie squinted. "Give your feet a break. We probably have a lot more walking to do."

"Yeah, I know, but I feel fine."

"Really?" Annie said skeptically. "The rest of us are pooped."

Wesley shrugged and rubbed his upper arms.

"Stop bothering him," Rhea said. "If he says he's not tired, he's not tired."

Annie chuckled. "Okay, but at least I'm not spying on him."

Rhea stiffened, and her face flushed. "What did that mean?"

Annie gave her a half smile. "Nothing."

Rhea's eyes grew flinty. "No, you said, 'spying.' What did you mean by that?"

Annie laughed. "I was just kidding."

Rhea jumped up; her hands clenched. Annie rose too, her smile gone.

Josh stepped between the girls. "Okay, cool it. Things are bad enough without any more fights."

Rhea glared at Annie, but Annie ignored her gaze. Annie nodded to Josh and sat back down. Celia nervously pulled on a strand of her hair. She hated it when Annie and Rhea fought. She liked them both. Rhea could be nice. On Celia's first day of school in Annaberry, the vice principal asked Rhea to show her and Gabrielle

121

around. Rhea seemed proud to do it and made her feel welcome. A couple of days later, when two fifth grade boys stole Celia's lunch money, Rhea found out and caught the boys. She took them behind a classroom and stuck their heads in a trashcan. They never bothered Celia again.

Celia decided to change the subject. "Aren't those flowers pretty, Annie?" Celia asked, pointing at some small pink ones in the underbrush.

Annie tipped her head. "Yeah, they're nice." Her eyes went to the peach in Celia's hand. "You have any more of those?"

"Uh huh, a bunch."

Celia pulled another peach out of her bag. As she handed it to Annie, the small blob of red goo on her right wrist jiggled. Celia watched it wiggle back and forth. She glanced at her left hand; the white goo was still there. She wondered if she could make another bubble. She hurriedly finished her peach. Then she pressed her forearms together, causing the red and white goo to mix. The tingling sensation returned, and the goo became a pink liquid which quickly swelled into a bubble the size of a grapefruit.

"Look at what I did!" she cried.

"Whoa," Annie said. "That's so strange."

"Yeah, and fun."

Celia pressed her arms together more firmly, and the bubble expanded to the size of a watermelon. As it grew, the world began to swim before Celia's eyes. "I feel dizzy," she said weakly.

"You felt that way last time," Annie said, frowning. "Maybe you should stop."

Celia didn't want to stop, but her fatigue swelled so that she could barely keep her eyes open. Finally, she separated her arms, and the bubble collapsed, returning to a small blob on each wrist again.

Celia lay down sideways, resting her head on Annie's thigh. She closed her eyes and listened to the other kids talk. Ted's music started playing. It sounded like violins.

Annie suddenly stiffened, causing Celia to open her eyes. "What happened?"

"Did you see that?" Annie replied.

"See what?" Celia asked.

Annie pointed at the woods. "There... Something flew between the trees."

"A bird?"

"I don't think so. It sparkled."

Celia peered into the dark forest. "I don't see anything."

"It's gone now."

Dylan bounded over. "You saw something sparkle?"

"Yes"

"Was it red?"

"No, yellow," Annie replied.

Dylan's shoulders slumped. "Aw, when I was walking with Wesley, I saw something sparkle in the woods. It flew out of a bush and was red. It darted behind a tree, and I didn't see it anymore."

Celia's weariness faded. She heard laughter. Bobby was standing at the edge of the trees with a wild look in his eyes.

"Theey huurr! Theey huurr!"

Dylan twisted, and Cherry hopped off his shoulder. "Who's "huurr," Bobby?"

"Theey aaree!" the other boy cried, sweeping his arms through the air.

"What?" Dylan asked.

Bobby ignored the question and leaned forward, peering into the forest. He took a step into the trees.

"Whoa, whoa," Josh hollered, striding over. "You don't want to go in there, Bobby."

"Buut ii goo seee theem," the younger boy protested.

"You shouldn't go in the forest all alone," Josh said. "You could get lost." He put his arm around Bobby, but the younger boy pushed him back.

"Ii noot loost! Theeyy heeree!"

"Who's here?" Celia asked, her brow furrowing.

"Theeyy woondeerfuul." Bobby beamed. But his smile faded, and he hunched over moaning.

"What's wrong?" Josh asked, leaning down.

"Itt huurt... Itt hurt."

"What hurts?"

"Myy tuummyy."

"Okay, sit down," Josh said, helping Bobby to the ground. "You got too excited."

Bobby leaned forward, breathing heavily, and pressed his arms to his stomach. Josh tried to calm him, but Bobby continued to moan. Then Bobby straightened with a panicked look in his eyes. "Noo. Noo. Baad thiing coomee. Hiidee eeveeryoonee."

The kids glanced around in concern.

"What's coming?" Wesley asked.

Bobby's mouth moved, but no words came out. He hunched over and let out another moan.

Murmurs spread among the kids. Celia's heart thumped. She heard a distant flapping sound. She stopped to listen. The noise grew louder. Then it swept overhead.

"What's that?" she asked in a whisper.

"A bird—I think," Annie said, her face pale. "A big one."

"Baad biird," Bobby groaned.

"Maybe it's the one we saw yesterday," Wesley said.

The flapping sound came back, but louder. As if several winged creatures were flying together, the noise grew and then faded away.

"Let's get off the trail. It's too easy to spot us here," Josh said, pointing to gaps in the canopy.

The children hurried into the woods, with Josh carrying Bobby in his arms. Gabrielle grabbed Celia and rushed her forward. The children found a grove of cedar trees and crouched under their branches which concealed the sky.

The flapping sound returned, and everyone froze. It quieted. After several minutes of silence, Gabrielle became restless and crept out from under the trees. Ted moved his hands, and soft notes carried through the woods. Josh signaled for quiet.

Wesley climbed one of the cedars. As he made his way up, Bobby moaned and clutched his stomach again.

"Itt huurt. Theeyy coomiing baack."

Celia waved urgently to her sister, but Gabrielle remained crouched by a bush, staring up through the branches.

Ted continued playing. Josh edged close to him and locked his hands over Ted's fingers. "Stop," he said in a low voice.

The flapping sound returned. Celia shuddered and huddled close to Annie. Gabrielle scurried back under the cedar trees, plopping down next to Dylan. The flapping sound grew, then faded away.

Wesley descended from the tree. "There were five of them," he said, his eyes wide.

"Birds?" Dylan asked with an audible gulp.

"Yeah, like that huge one we saw yesterday. They were flying together."

"But predator birds are solitary," Mya objected. "They shouldn't do that."

"Tell them," Wesley said, shaking his head.

"Where'd they go?" Dylan asked.

Wesley pointed south.

Bobby sat up and smiled cheerfully.

Josh knelt beside him. "Feeling better?"

"Yeeaah, beetteer noow. Mooree saafee."

Josh chuckled. "If you're right, we have our mine canary."

Wesley nodded with a faint laugh.

"What's a 'mine canary'?" Celia asked Annie.

The older girl leaned close and whispered. "It's a bird that coal miners take underground to warn them of danger."

"Oh," Celia said, not sure how a bird could warn someone of danger.

"Bobby's feeling better," Josh said. "Let's get moving. We're getting low on water. Hopefully, we'll find another stream soon."

Celia grabbed Annie's hand and struggled to her feet. She exhaled, trying to stay relaxed, but her heart kept thumping, and her hands quivered. She breathed in deeply and glanced around.

"Come on, Cici," Gabrielle said, waving her forward. Celia followed her sister and Annie.

As they neared the main trail, Celia saw a flash out of the corner of her eyes. She spun and glimpsed a magenta sparkle in the dark woods – her favorite color – but it vanished instantly, and she couldn't tell what it was. She tugged on Annie's hand. "I saw one."

"Saw what?"

"A sparkle. Like you did."

Annie peered into the trees. "There's something out there. I don't know what it is, but I want to find out."

Chapter 10:
Silver Blades

A light mist moistened Celia's clothes—leaving tiny droplets on her skin—as she strolled with Annie down the trail in the early afternoon heat. Since spotting the magenta sparkle in the woods, she hadn't seen any others, but now and then she spied small creatures scurrying through the undergrowth or scampering along branches in the trees.

Annie had borrowed Celia's hairbrush and was tugging it through her wavy tresses as she talked about a crazy math teacher who liked to teach songs with mathematical equations.

Some twenty feet ahead of the girls, Sarah was walking with Timmy. Celia eyed Sarah's clothes – a cream-colored blouse with frilly sleeves and striped blue Capri leggings. She liked Sarah's clothes. She decided to ask her dad to buy her a blouse and leggings just like that.

Timmy strolled next to Sarah with his long legs kicking forward and his head rolling from side to side with each stride. Timmy's blue scarf was stuffed into the pocket of his gray jacket which he had tied about his waist. The end of the scarf hung out of the pocket so that it almost touched the ground as he walked.

Timmy leaned toward Sarah and whispered something in her ear. Celia couldn't tell what he said, but it seemed to anger Sarah because she spun and punched him right in the shoulder. Timmy snickered and backed away, while Sarah went after him. Timmy dodged behind a tree, but Sarah chased him, cuffing him several more times before halting and crossing her arms. Timmy rubbed his sore arm, and Sarah grinned.

Annie chuckled and rolled her eyes.

"Why is Sarah hitting Timmy?" Celia asked.

"He probably said something annoying. He tends to do that."

Celia frowned. She didn't think Timmy was annoying.

"I'm starved," came a voice from behind the girls. Celia turned to see Barth stride up. He unzipped his pack and scrounged around until he pulled out the purple fruit he'd found at the flower in the morning. "I almost forgot about this. I wonder what it tastes like."

"You dare to eat that?" Annie asked, dipping her chin in disapproval.

"Why not? All the other fruit around here tastes great."

"But that flower was weird. It made us sleepy. I wouldn't—" Annie started to say, but Barth took a bite.

"Yummm." He said, licking his lips. "Tastes just like brown sugar. Do you want some?"

Both girls shook their heads. Annie reached into her pack and pulled out an apple.

"Do you have any more of those?" Celia asked. She was all out.

"Yeah, a couple. Do you want one?" Annie asked. Celia nodded, and Annie pulled a second apple out of her bag.

Barth took another bite of the purple fruit, then gave the girls a sour look. "Geez, this is too sweet, it's making me feel sick." He examined the remainder of the purple fruit, then tossed it into the bushes.

A breeze picked up, twirling Celia's hair and rustling branches along the trail. Celia finished the apple Annie had given her and pulled out her water bottle. Josh and Bobby walked up.

"A food break?" Josh asked.

Celia and Annie nodded.

"I feel kinda weird," Barth said, tottering slightly.

Josh reached out to steady him. "Are you okay?"

"Everything's spinning," Barth said, holding his hands over his eyes.

"Okay, sit down," Josh said, helping Barth to the ground. "Bob, you run ahead and tell the others we're gonna stop here for a bit."

Bobby started away.

"I'm so tired," Barth murmured. He slumped over; his eyes closed. A moment later, he was snoring softly.

"That happened fast!" Josh said.

"I wonder if it was the fruit?" Annie replied, frowning. "He shouldn't have eaten it."

"What fruit?"

Annie told Josh about the glowing flower and the purple fruit.

"Okay, no one else eats any more of that," Josh said. "And we'll stop here until he wakes up."

Bobby returned with Sarah, Timmy, Wesley, and Dylan in tow. The other kids were still behind them and caught up in ones and twos.

Celia sat down and idly gazed at the canopy above the trail. She noticed small gaps in the foliage and wondered if the black birds could see them through those holes. Her heartbeat quickened, and her hands trembled. She tried to forget her worries. She thought about school and her nice third-grade teacher, Mrs. Fanhouse, who read stories to the class every day after lunch. She thought of Ben and wondered if he'd returned to the bus. *Did he find anyone to help? I wish he were here.* She thought. *Josh is a good leader, but he's just a kid. Ben is a grown up and can take care of us.*

Celia reached out for Annie's hand. As she did, she heard a painful moan. She glanced toward the sound and saw Bobby curled up on the ground; his arms pressed against his stomach. Annie rose and went to Bobby. Josh and Wesley joined her.

Josh knelt and spoke quietly to Bobby. Then he raised his head. "I don't hear any birds, but Bobby thinks they're coming back, so let's get off the trail."

Annie helped Josh carry Bobby behind an azalea bush on the left side of the path. Wesley and Rhea lugged Barth to the same spot. As they lay the boys down, a flapping sound filled the air.

Mya grabbed Celia's hand and tugged her toward the underbrush to the right of the trail. As she headed into the bushes, Celia saw Dylan run down the path and leap into the air. He grabbed a branch high in the canopy and pulled himself up into the foliage.

Celia ducked behind a laurel bush with Mya and Emma. She looked around for Annie but didn't see her. Sarah and Timmy were crouched under a tree a few feet to her left. She peeked up; eyeing bits of blue sky visible through the foliage. The flapping grew louder. Then the blue disappeared in a rush of black. Celia froze, her heart pounding as the rushing darkness swept by.

The blue returned, and the sound of wings faded. Celia's heart eased. She peered across the trail, catching a glimpse of brown hair in the thicket. She guessed it was Annie. She rose and started out of the underbrush. Mya grabbed her arm. "Don't go. It's not safe."

"But I have to," Celia said, tugging out of Mya's grip. She had to get to Annie. Celia crept to the edge of the trees and peered across the trail. She sensed movement in the bushes. Annie's profile came into view. Celia smiled and took another step. Annie spied her and motioned to stay put. Celia hesitated, not sure of what to do. Then her determination returned, and she stepped into the path.

Leaves rustled. She paused and listened. She trod slowly forward, noticing patches of sunlight here and there on the dark soil. She neared the far side of the trail and exhaled, the hint of a smile forming on her lips.

Then a crash shattered the calm. Celia stumbled. Something fell from above, landing on the trail in a shower of broken branches and leaves.

She turned. A creature rose from the ground, great wings hunched to each side of its immense black-feathered body. Fierce yellow eyes peered out from its feather-bare head, and powerful leathery claws ripped the dark soil beneath its breast.

The creature beat its wings and rose. Celia stumbled, adrenaline surging through her. She raised her hands desperately to fend off the creature. Then a cry pierced the air, rolling out like ripples on water – freezing everything in its path. The world became still and silent.

The bird froze, suspended in midair, its wings spread across the width of the trail. Its talons outstretched toward Celia.

Something burst from the woods, and a gnarled stick came crashing down on the winged beast. The bird collapsed in a crumpled heap. Josh leaped over the motionless creature, clutching the long walking stick in one hand. He rushed to Celia and lifted her as the cry faded away.

Celia found she could move again. "Josh... I'm so...," she started to say.

"Don't talk," Josh said in a hushed voice. He started toward the woods.

Then another crash shattered the quiet. Celia screamed as a second winged creature crashed through the canopy and landed on the trail floor.

Josh set Celia down. "Run!"

Celia dove into the thicket and Josh swung around to face the great bird. Celia pushed her way through the underbrush, twigs, and branches scratching her skin. Out of the corner of her eye, she glimpsed Wesley leap into the trail. Then Annie's arms closed around her and pulled her down.

"I'm so sorry," Celia said, tears running down her cheeks.

"Shush," Annie said, pressing her hand over Celia's mouth. "It's okay."

Celia twisted. Through the foliage she glimpsed Wesley and Josh standing together in the trail, facing the second giant bird. The creature nudged its fallen companion and gave a piercing cry. The cry was answered from somewhere above, and another crash splintered the canopy. Two more winged monsters dropped to the trail floor in a shower of broken branches.

Josh sprang—swinging his stick like a baseball bat. He slammed the branch into the nearest bird, and the creature collapsed to the ground. Wesley rushed past Josh, whirling a long stick at the other birds, which retreated hastily.

With the second bird lying prone in the dirt, Josh joined Wesley, and they advanced on the two remaining winged beasts. Then a long stretch of canopy behind the boys shattered, and a half-dozen winged monsters crashed to the trail floor. Dylan fell among the splintered branches, landing smack-dab in the middle of the flock. He grabbed his pants with a panicked look and somersaulted high over the birds toward Wesley and Josh. As Dylan soared through the air, Cherry left his shoulder and swooped down among the huge winged creatures. Dylan landed with a plop behind Wesley, and Cherry glided over, landing back on Dylan's shoulder.

The flock fixed their yellow eyes on the boys. Then one let out a screech, and the rest advanced, their wings beating and their claws tearing the dark soil.

"Go!" Josh yelled to his brother. Dylan bounded toward the trees and dived into a thicket.

Wesley and Josh stood side by side as the huge birds advanced. Then one of the winged creatures rose and swooped at Wesley. He swung his stick, but the bird dodged the blow and ripped the limb from his grip, hurling it up through the shattered canopy.

Wesley backed up, fear in his eyes. A cry rang out, and Rhea sprang from the trees directly behind the birds, her eyes burning like fiery coals, and her skin pulsing a deep red color. Rhea rushed toward the winged beasts, grabbing the backside of the nearest one. The bird screeched in fright and bolted away as its rear feathers caught fire. Rhea straightened and laughed menacingly. Then a fierce cawing cut through her laughter.

Celia tipped her head back. Above the trees, a great flock of winged creatures circled, one among them dwarfing the others. Charcoal black, with silver streaks running front to back on its enormous wings, the largest bird fixed its swirling eyes on Rhea and let out another terrible cry. Three of the winged beasts swept toward the redheaded girl, their talons outstretched.

Rhea whirled her arms, and flames flickered in the wake. She slowed… waiting… fire dancing off her bare skin. One of the birds grasped Rhea in its great claws and lifted her from the ground. But suddenly the bird shrieked and released the girl, smoke rising off its scorched talons. Rhea fell to the ground and rolled to her feet, laughing darkly as the birds wavered above her.

The leader of the flock let out another cry, and the winged beasts turned, diving toward Celia and Annie's thicket. The creatures crashed into the foliage. Annie's voice rang out. Everything froze again. The world became silent. Nothing moved… nothing, except Josh. The boy sprang among the birds, striking with terrific speed, bringing down five of the beasts in seconds. Then Annie's cry faded, and the world became motion. A creature burst through the undergrowth, seizing Celia in its terrible grip. It lifted her into the air.

As the ground dropped away, Celia screamed. The winged beast rose into the flock above the trees. Celia twisted and saw Annie across the way, struggling in the talons of another bird.

Something flashed by Celia's eyes. She swung her head and spotted Cherry darting beneath the winged creature. The warbler nipped at the huge bird's feathers, and the winged beast beat its wings to rid itself of the nuisance.

Cherry zipped in and out, avoiding the powerful thrusts of the great bird. A symphony of sound filled the air. Celia turned and saw Ted standing some distance down the trail, his arms swinging vigorously as an orchestra of notes poured into the air. The giant birds slowed and fell silent, momentarily transfixed by the beautiful sound. Then a note rang off-key, then another. The melody broke. The birds stirred from the spell. The lead bird gave a piercing cry, and two winged monsters dove toward Ted. He shouted and stumbled back.

Celia heard a thump. Her captor pitched, swinging her wildly. Celia cried out in fright. Then she saw Gabrielle's skateboard falling toward the ground. She blinked in surprise; then her jaw fell open as the board slowed in the air and shot back up toward the winged beast.

As the skateboard rushed toward the bird, another winged creature plunged and knocked the object away, sending it spinning into the underbrush. The board disappeared for a moment, then it popped back out and glided to Gabrielle's outstretched hands.

Gabrielle shrugged off her pack and jumped onto the board. She crouched, gripping the deck. She rose into the air. Several birds swung toward her. Gabrielle darted and ducked, avoiding their attacks, then one plunged at her from behind. Celia screamed, but it was too late. The bird slammed into Gabrielle, knocking her off the board. Gabrielle fell into the trees, disappearing in the foliage.

The bird gripping Celia rose higher. Below, other winged creatures hunted the children, catching them one by one. Celia's heart sank. Then something flashed out of the woods. A black bird screeched and fell. More flashes swept from the trees in a swarm of colors quicker than the eye. The scene turned chaotic as panicked birds lashed out at the tiny sparkles engulfing them.

One of the flashes slowed, and Celia stared dumbfounded. It was a tiny figure—about six inches tall—hovering in the air. It wore a long orange gown and had shimmering black hair, delicate features, and wings quicker than the eye.

"A fairy," Celia murmured. A shiver ran down her spine.

The fairy leveled its gaze at the flock circling above and raised a needle-like blade in its tiny hand. The fairy let out a cry and swept into the moving stream of sparkles rushing toward the bird holding Josh. The fairies swirled around the winged beast, attacking and cutting with their tiny blades. The huge creature squawked and swung at the flashes in desperation, but the fight ended in moments, and the creature crashed to the ground. Josh leaped away unhurt.

More sparkles poured from the woods, swarming the birds. The fairies darted and sliced with their tiny blades, and winged creatures dropped from the sky. As the birds fell one by one, the fairies caught the children and slowed their descent, setting them down safely.

Celia's captor beat its enormous wings and rose away from the flashing throng. Annie's bird did the same, while the remaining winged creatures battled the stream of flashes with talon and beak.

The largest of the birds let out a fierce cry. Celia and Annie's captors soared away. With tremendous thrusts, the winged beasts powered through the air, hurtling northward toward distant mountains. Celia shouted to Annie, and Annie shouted back, but the rushing wind drowned out their voices.

The birds swept upward and headlong. As the mountains reared closer, Annie's captor fell behind. Celia watched in fear as Annie shrank into the distance. She shouted again and stretched out her arms, but there was nothing she could do.

Her bird rose higher and powered across the sky. Below, the woods spread out like a green carpet dotted with blue lakes and meandering streams. Tears welled up in Celia's eyes, and she shivered in the cold wind. The winged beast bent its great head and gazed down at her. Celia froze. The creature studied her, then something softened in its eyes, and it raised its head, concentrating on the looming mountains.

Celia looked behind her. Annie's bird had vanished. She was alone. Tears blew away in the rushing wind. Her shoulders slumped. Then behind her, something twinkled in the distant blue.

She squinted and spotted five tiny shimmering points of color. The colors grew, and Celia's heart pounded. It was the fairies. They were coming!

The great bird sensed the danger. Its yellow eyes peered back at the glittering hunters. The bird swung forward, powering higher and faster in a race away from the tiny blades.

The wind roared in Celia's ears, and the forest flew by below. The bird inclined its wings and arced left, heading toward a pass in the looming mountains.

Celia twisted. To her dismay, the fairies had shrunk into the blue. She shouted, but the wind carried her voice away.

As the mountains neared, Celia shivered in the cold air. Beyond the peaks, an empty brown land came into view. Celia looked back. One sparkle remained in the sky, a golden one, shimmering like a tiny flame.

As the shadow of the winged beast crossed the mountain slopes, the tiny golden sparkle grew brighter, and Celia's heart thumped with hope.

The great bird hurtled through the mountain pass and into the brown lands spreading northward. The shimmering fairy grew closer. It was a girl fairy in a glittering golden gown, with steely eyes, clenched jaw, and long blond hair streaming in the wind.

The fairy closed on the great bird, and Celia's eyes met hers. For a moment, time seemed to stand still, then the fairy's hard face softened into a smile, and Celia's fears flew away with the wind.

In a final burst, the fairy crossed the remaining distance. Her silver blade whirled and sliced into a powerful talon. The winged beast screeched in pain and swung away. The fairy rolled with the bird and slashed again. Dark drops oozed from the great creature's flesh, splashing Celia's clothes.

The bird tipped its wings and arced right. The fairy pursued. The blade cut again, tearing into muscle and tendon. The winged beast squawked forlornly and opened its talons, surrendering its prize.

For a moment, Celia remained still in the roaring wind. Then she fell. The bird soared away.

Celia turned and gazed down at the brown plain spreading out beneath her. It all felt like a dream. She wondered if she would wake up. Then a golden sparkle flashed by her eyes. The fairy hovered there for a moment, her golden gown billowing in the wind. Then her wings became still, and the two fell together.

Celia rolled onto her side and gazed at the tiny creature. The fairy was smaller than a Barbie doll, with delicate features, glowing skin, and piercing green eyes. Celia had never seen anything so beautiful.

The fairy darted to a belt loop beside the front button to Celia's jeans. The little creature pushed up the edge of Celia's shirt, exposing a loop on the other side of the button. She wrapped her tiny arms through both loops and braced herself against Celia's pelvis. Then closing her eyes and clenching her jaw, the fairy set her wings humming.

Celia let out a scream as her middle was yanked up, and her shoulders and feet dropped down, leaving her in a horseshoe position. She trembled uncontrollably and hyperventilated, but as her falling slowed and the wind quieted, she calmed back down. With some effort, she righted herself.

The tiny fairy's face reddened as she strained to slow their descent. Then a flash buzzed by Celia's eyes, darting around in quick hummingbird-like movements. It was another fairy—a boy. He was dressed in a shimmering blue tunic tied at the waist by a silver belt. Silver hair fell to his shoulders, and ocean blue eyes glimmered in his intelligent face.

The golden fairy motioned to a belt loop on the side of Celia's pants. The blue one glided to the loop and fixed his arms through it. As his wings whirled, Celia suddenly tipped sideways. She let out another cry, her heart pounding, and her breath coming in gasps.

The golden fairy's eyes flashed angrily, and the blue fairy winced, but he slowed his wings so that Celia leveled out in the air and began floating comfortably again. Celia's heartbeat eased, and her breathing relaxed.

The golden fairy smiled approvingly. The blue fairy rolled his eyes. Together they halted Celia's falling and began slowly carrying her upward. As they ascended the mountainside, other fairies appeared and found places to latch onto Celia's clothes. Celia watched them anxiously, worried that they would tip her again, but they worked well together, and she stayed steady in the air.

After a sixth fairy appeared, the golden one eased away to let the others do the work. They bore Celia up toward the mountain pass, chatting noisily in high, pure voices as their wings whirred like tiny fans. Celia listened to their conversation. The language was strange, but the sounds were pretty, and she wanted to learn them.

As they passed over the mountains, the golden one darted here and there among the fairies, giving directions. Then she slowed and hovered close to Celia's face, gazing intently. Celia stared back, unsure of what to do. Then she got her nerve. "Thank you," she said. "You saved my life."

The fairy tipped her head, and her brow wrinkled slightly. "*Anea feo maya, nari hanu?*"

Celia cleared her throat. "I'm sorry, I don't understand. Do you speak English? Hablas español?"

The fairy blinked several times, and said, "*Anea movae. Feo anea iwa meandu.*" Then she shot away, disappearing into the blue.

As they crossed the mountains, the forest came into view, extending out like a green blanket to the horizon. Celia let out a deep breath, hoping she would be back with her friends soon. Her shoulders eased, and her eyelids grew heavy. She shook her head to fight off the fatigue, but exhaustion overcame her, and she fell asleep.

She dreamt she was standing at the base of a grassy hill. She started up the slope, climbing until she reached a spring that gurgled out of the soft soil. She cupped her hands and drank the water, but it had no taste. She gazed up the hill, shading her eyes from the bright sun, then she continued climbing. At the top, she found a big rock and sat on it.

Below, the valley spread out in all directions. High above, white birds circled. Then a black-winged creature appeared on the horizon, and the white birds fled.

"Don't go," Celia shouted as the birds disappeared into the blue.

"Hey Cici, wake up!"

Celia recognized her sister's voice. She turned. "Where are you, Gabi?"

"Down here."

Celia glanced from side to side. "I don't see you."

"Open your eyes."

Celia did. Several fairies were gazing at her inquisitively. "Gabi?" she asked.

"Look down."

Celia twisted. Her sister was gliding on her skateboard some twenty feet below—just above the treetops.

"Gabi! What're you doing?"

"What do you think? I'm riding."

"But you're in the air!"

"Yeah, it's rad! My board flies. Except if I look down, I'll freak out, and it falls. I guess I'm scared of heights now."

"Are you scared?"

"No, because I'm just above the trees, but if I went up to where you are, I'd spaz."

Gabrielle bent her knees, causing the board to rise slightly and glide over a treetop sticking out above the others. "I tried to chase that bird that grabbed you, but it was too fast. I couldn't keep up. Lucky those fairies did. They fly like bullets."

"I saw you fall," Celia said. "Did you get hurt?"

"No, I'm cool. I landed in some branches. I got scratched up, but I'm good. How about you? Did that bird rough you up?"

Celia shook her head. "I'm okay. The fairies protected me."

Gabrielle nodded.

"What about Annie?" Celia asked, her heart thumping with worry.

"The fairies caught her bird first. They went postal on it. They carried Annie back to the trail."

Celia peered ahead and spotted shattered parts of the forest canopy where the birds had crashed through to the trail floor. As she neared the gaps, several kids came into view, standing among hundreds of tiny sparkling figures.

"See you on the ground," Gabrielle shouted and darted down through the broken canopy.

The fairies bore Celia down through the trees and gently set her on the trail floor. Relief passed through Celia as she felt firm earth beneath her feet. She crouched and touched the ground.

"Welcome back, senorita."

Celia raised her head as Annie walked out of the trees, her arms outstretched. Celia leaped up and ran to Annie's embrace.

"It's okay," Annie said, hugging her tightly. "You're safe."

Celia tipped her head, tears swimming in her eyes. "Is everyone else okay?"

Annie tensed and glanced around. "Yeah, except we can't find Sarah and Timmy."

"What happened?"

"We don't know. We didn't see birds catch them. We think they're hiding in the forest."

Celia stared into the trees, wondering where Sarah and Timmy were. Then a sound like bees streaming out of a hive filled the air. A line of fairies poured out of the woods, but these fairies looked different. Their expressions were solemn. They wore copper-colored garments with little coats that reminded Celia of a marching band. On their shoulders, they carried tiny bows and quivers of arrows.

A gray-bearded fairy dressed in a long purple gown glided among the copper ones. The copper fairies halted together, and the purple one swooped down among the children, studying their faces as he passed. When he reached Celia, he hovered for a moment, searching her eyes. Celia stared, blinking several times and not knowing what to do.

She waited, noticing tiny silver triangles stitched into the top corners of the fairy's gown. The purple fairy dipped his head and spoke to her. "*Mello sette mi feo beala?*"

The color drained from Celia's cheeks, and she looked around in confusion. The other kids shrugged. Celia took a breath and said in the sweetest voice she could manage, "I'm sorry. I don't understand."

The fairy's expression hardened, and in an annoyed tone, he said, "*Runi mi feo ba seve ineo mora?*"

Celia frowned, wondering if she'd done something wrong.

The purple fairy waved his hand sharply, and the copper ones moved with lightning quickness to the children's bags, lifting them high into the air.

"Hey, what are you doing?" Annie cried. "That's our stuff!"

"*Feo humi seva mulah grea,*" the purple fairy said coolly. Then he pointed toward the woods to the right of the path.

"I think he wants us to go that way," CPU said.

Josh stepped forward. "Okay, little man. If you want us to go, we can, but we need to find our friends first. They're somewhere in the woods around here."

The fairy peered hard at Josh and repeated. "*Feo humi seva mulah grea.*"

Rhea stepped alongside Josh. She scowled, and her skin turned a dark reddish hue. "Sorry, dude, we don't understand you, but we have to find our friends. We're not going without them."

The purple fairy lowered his chin, and his eyes passed from Rhea to Josh.

Celia spotted a girl fairy in a pink gown who had helped carry her over the mountains. The fairy had smiled warmly at her in the air. Now she frowned and avoided Celia's eyes.

"It's no use," Rhea said. "They don't understand. Screw them. Let's go find Sarah and Timmy ourselves." She turned to Wesley. "Ready?"

"You guys wait here," Wesley said to the others. "We'll search the nearby woods. If we get lost, we'll shout, and you guys yell back." He and Rhea started toward the trees.

The purple fairy whirled and raised his hands, pointing toward the two kids. He spoke in a severe tone. *"Feo humi ba doth!"* Then quicker than a snapping rubber band, an arrow was set in every bow of every copper fairy in the clearing.

"Careful, guys," Josh shouted. "They're ready to shoot."

Wesley stopped and stared in puzzlement at the fairies. Rhea halted too and exhaled sharply. "Okay," she said, "let them fire their toothpicks. How much can it hurt?"

A bow twanged, and a tiny arrow quivered in Rhea's upper arm.

She laughed. "I didn't even feel it."

Wesley plucked the dart out. Another bow twanged, and an arrow quivered in Wesley's neck. He tugged that out too and turned toward the purple fairy, his eyes angry. "Why are you doing this?"

Rhea stumbled, confusion in her eyes. "I feel weird."

"Whoa," Wesley said, staggering. He collapsed to the ground. Rhea fell beside him.

"Oh no," Annie cried, rushing toward Wesley and Rhea.

"Feo wanna beile runos pena!" the purple fairy barked.

The other kids froze.

Out of the corner of her eye, Celia spied her sister cautiously stepping onto her board. Gabrielle started gliding toward the trees. The fairies swiveled toward her. Celia screamed in warning. Gabrielle crouched and shot forward. Arrows flew. Gabrielle dove and ducked from the flying needles. More bows twanged. Gabrielle disappeared into the trees. Celia heard a thump. She leaped forward. "Gabi!"

"No," Annie yelled. Something pricked Celia's arm. She twisted. A tiny dart quivered there. The world spun, and everything went black.

Chapter 11:
Pools and Stones

Gabrielle opened her eyes. Before her a mist rose off the surface of a pool. She stared at the water, blinking as she tried to get her bearings. A thin blanket of wool-like material covered her. She pushed the blanket off and sat up. Her skateboard and backpack lay at her feet.

She glanced around. She was in a clearing about the size of two front yards. Mossy grass covered the ground, sweeping to a line of saplings that marked the edge of the glade. Beyond the saplings, trees rose high into the air, branching out in a wide canopy that shaded the pool and the grass.

The pool was pear-shaped and stretched some fifteen feet across. Other children slept under blankets in scattered bunches around the pool. Gabrielle counted the kids. There were thirteen, including her. Sarah and Timmy were missing.

She rubbed her forehead and felt a bump the size of a robin's egg. The bump was warm and tender. She remembered riding her skateboard into the woods to escape the fairies. She felt a pinprick in her leg. A tiny arrow had pierced her blue jeans. The world spun and went dark.

Gabrielle's jaw tightened in anger. The fairies didn't need to shoot arrows. They just wanted to find Sarah and Timmy.

Fitful snoring brought Gabrielle out of her thoughts. Dylan lay beside her. She tugged on his arm. "Wake up, kangaroo. I need someone to talk to."

Dylan opened his mouth and ran his tongue over his lips. He rolled over. "Where are we?"

Gabrielle grunted. "How should I know? We're in some forest."

Dylan pushed the blanket off and sat up. "Where's Cherry?" The warbler was nowhere to be seen.

Gabrielle shrugged. "Maybe it flew home."

Dylan groaned, and his shoulders slumped.

Gabrielle grabbed her pack. "At least we have our stuff."

She stuck her hand into a pouch and pulled out her phone. She switched it on and waited. The battery had drained to forty percent. She couldn't find a signal. Gabrielle tossed the phone back into her bag.

"How long have we been out?" Dylan asked.

Gabrielle had no idea. She stepped over to CPU and glanced at his watch. It said 7:05 am. "What time was it when those fairies found us?"

"It was the afternoon," Dylan said.

"Then we must've slept overnight."

Gabrielle's throat was parched. She strolled over to the pool and cupped her hands in the water. It was warm. She lifted a handful to her mouth.

"You gonna drink that?" Dylan asked scowling.

"Why not?"

"It's green."

"I'm too thirsty to care," Gabrielle said and swallowed a mouthful. "Mmm..."

Dylan shrugged and joined her at the water's edge. He drank several gulps.

Gabrielle stretched her arms. "We should explore this place."

"Okay."

Gabrielle headed toward the woods to the left of the pool. Dylan followed. As they neared the trees, a dozen fairies in copper garments glided out of the underbrush. The fairies formed a line with bows drawn.

"Not these dudes again," Gabrielle said.

A copper fairy wearing a bright red belt advanced out of the line and gazed sternly. *"Feo humi lene ba methe."*

"What's he saying?" Dylan asked.

"How do I know?" Gabrielle said. "Probably something like, 'Stop, or we'll shoot our dinky arrows.'"

"We're prisoners?"

"I guess so… Let's try the other way."

Gabrielle turned and jogged toward the opposite side of the clearing. Dylan bounded after her. They passed Bobby, who was sitting upright, a blanket covering his legs. He watched them with curious eyes.

As Gabrielle and Dylan neared the far trees, another line of fairies hovered out of the bushes. The two kids slowed.

"This is a joke," Gabrielle said, turning and starting back toward the pool.

Dylan remained standing by the line of fairies. He bounced lightly and clasped his hands over his head.

Bobby jumped up and jogged toward Dylan. "Soo meeny pooiinty," he cried. "Doon't shooot. Wee friieennds."

The fairies stared at Bobby blankly.

Gabrielle grunted. "I don't think they get the friends part." She grabbed her pack and pulled out her skateboard.

Wesley rolled over and stared at Gabrielle sleepily. "Are Sarah and Timmy back?"

Gabrielle shook her head, feeling her anger returning.

Wesley grimaced. "They're out there somewhere, probably scared and hungry."

Josh stirred. "They're not back?"

Wesley nodded grimly.

Josh sat up. "We're gonna need the fairies' help."

"Yeah, but they don't understand."

"We'll figure it out. Don't stress. We'll find Sarah and Timmy."

Barth yawned and sat upright. He rubbed his forehead. "Where are we?"

"Everyone keeps asking that," Gabrielle said. "How do we know?"

"What happened?"

"You snoozed through all the fun," Gabrielle said mockingly.

"The what?" Barth asked.

Gabrielle told him how the birds attacked them, and fairies rescued them.

Barth seemed to think she was joking until Gabrielle pointed to the line of sprites hovering at the edge of the clearing. Barth blinked and got up. He walked toward the copper clad fairies.

Gabrielle dropped her skateboard and stepped on. It drifted forward, floating about an inch above the grass. She caught up to Barth and swooped around him. She accelerated and headed toward Bobby, who was sitting cross-legged near the trees with his head bent forward, and his hands clasped together.

"What's up, dude?" Gabrielle asked as she glided up.

Bobby opened his eyes. "Ii maakiing suumeething."

Gabrielle hopped off her board. "Making what?"

"A suurpriisee foor thee faairiees."

Gabrielle saw he had something in his hands. "What's that?" she asked.

"Suurpriisee."

"Let me see."

Bobby leaned away. Then he opened his palms, revealing a tiny glass figurine.

Gabrielle peered closely. It was a little glass dog. "Mmm... Where'd you get that?"

146

"Maaddee iit," Bobby said, his eyes gleaming.

"Made it? How?"

Bobby grinned. "Itt haard, buut fuun."

Gabrielle frowned and took the figurine from Bobby's hands. She raised it to her eyes. It reminded her of Bobby's dog, Willow.

"I recognize this. It's your dog. Where'd it come from?"

"Toold yoouu. Ii maadee iit," Bobby said with an impatient sigh. He snatched the figurine back. "Ii maakee iit foor thee faairiies."

Gabrielle rolled her eyes. Birdcalls rang out. Gabrielle turned. A dozen copper fairies glided into the clearing carrying a large wooden crate. A second group bore a large crystal basin with glass cups hanging from the sides and a clear liquid splashing around within.

The fairies set the crate down near the pool and lifted off the lid, revealing a large mound of tiny golden cakes. They placed the basin down beside the crate.

"Food and drink," Dylan shouted.

The other kids hurried over. Gabrielle grabbed several cakes and popped one into her mouth. It had a tangy flavor, like orange loaf bread. She gobbled down the cakes and picked off a glass from the side of the basin. She dipped it into the liquid. It tasted sweet and cool. She gulped the liquid down thirstily.

After satisfying her appetite, Gabrielle strolled back to the pool and sat near Annie and Celia. Her anger at the fairies was fading. "This is alright," she said, leaning back in the grass. "If they keep feeding us, I may forgive those arrows."

"Not everyone is okay," Annie said, staring across the clearing, where Wesley was pacing worriedly.

Gabrielle frowned. She was concerned about Sarah and Timmy too, but she didn't know what to do. No one knew where they were, and the fairies wouldn't help.

Music suddenly filled the air. Gabrielle twisted. Ted was whirling his arms and fluttering his hands. Beautiful sounds carried

147

through the clearing, entrancing the fairies who loosened their bows and gazed raptly at Ted.

Gabrielle laughed. Her eyes went to Emma and Mya. The sisters were sitting together on the far side of the pool. Emma whispered something in Mya's ear and waved her hand around. The light near her seemed to warp and twist like a kaleidoscope. Gabrielle lost sight of the girls. She blinked to clear her vision. A moment later, the light changed, and the girls reappeared.

Gabrielle stood up. "Hey, what happened?" She shouted.

Emma giggled and waved her hand again. The light warped, and the sisters vanished for a second time. Gabrielle looked around to see if anyone else had noticed.

At that moment, a birdcall rang through the clearing, and three colorful fairies flew into the glade, followed by a dozen copper ones. One of the three fairies – a girl, dressed in a shimmering red gown – glided up to the children.

"*Mette meandu*," she said in a soft voice.

The kids looked at one another.

"I'm sorry, we don't understand," Josh replied.

The red fairy flashed a warm smile and pointed to the trees. "*Honna seva mulah grea.*"

"I think she wants us to go that way," Annie said. She waved to get the fairy's attention and pointed to their backpacks. "We need to bring our stuff."

The red fairy winked cheerfully and motioned to the copper fairies, who swept around the children and flew to the bags, lifting them into the air.

"I guess they're going to carry them," Gabrielle said.

"Okay by me," Dylan replied, hopping into the air. "Let's go."

The children followed the fairies into the woods. They walked for about twenty minutes, winding back and forth through the trees until Gabrielle lost all sense of her direction.

Finally, they came to a large clearing dotted by dozens of pools like the one they had woken up at. A light mist floated off the pools, and glittering crystalline rocks protruded from the ground around the clearing. At the far end of the glade, an enormous crystal rock rose into the air, its peak piercing the thick canopy above.

Slender-trunked trees grew among the pools and rocks, their branches soaring and spreading out like enormous umbrellas, concealing the glade from the sky. While thousands of golden acorns hung in the branches, reflecting sunlight from the pools and crystal rocks below, bathing the glade in a golden glow.

The fairies led the children into the clearing. As they passed a pumpkin-sized crystal rock jutting out of the soil, Barth leaned over and blew on it.

"Whoa," he said. "There's no condensation."

"So?" Gabrielle replied.

"It must be a diamond," Barth said. "Diamonds are perfect conductors of heat, so when you blow on one, you don't see any steam."

"No way. That's too huge to be a diamond," Gabrielle said, rolling her eyes. "If it's a diamond, what's that?" she said, pointing to the enormous crystal at the far end of the clearing.

Barth's mouth closed. He stared hard at the massive crystal. Gabrielle chuckled, thinking he was clueless.

As the children made their way through the clearing, hundreds of fairies streamed out of tiny holes in the gigantic crystal rock. The fairies formed lines running through the clearing. They danced and sang. The atmosphere reminded Gabrielle of colorful festivals in Honduras. She decided to join the party. She pulled out her skateboard and stepped on.

Suddenly, a dozen copper fairies surrounded her with bows drawn and faces fierce. The dancing and singing stopped, and a thousand tiny eyes fixed on her.

Gabrielle glanced from side to side and raised her arms in bewilderment. "What? What's wrong with me riding my board?"

The copper fairies gave no answer but continued staring sternly with bows pulled tight. Gabrielle's anger returned, and she glared defiantly. Then a fluttering sound reached her ears, and she looked up. Above, a beautiful fairy in a golden gown descended from a peak high on the soaring crystal rock.

"That's the one who saved me," Celia said in a hushed voice.

Gabrielle scowled, no longer trusting the fairies. The crowd parted for the golden one as she floated down. When the fairy neared the children, she turned to the copper sprites and spoke. *"Seta, beao anea eril plena."*

The sprites relaxed their bows and backed off.

The golden fairy turned and met Gabrielle's eyes. With a slight bow, she said, *"Honna vothe meau wente."*

Gabrielle stared back awkwardly, having no idea what the fairy had said.

"This is my sister," Celia said, beaming proudly.

The golden fairy blinked and smiled at both girls. Then she glided up close to Gabrielle's face and inspected her.

Gabrielle felt awkward. Her cheek twitched, and she had a sudden itch on her lower back. She reached around to scratch with one hand and adjusted her baseball cap with the other.

Before today, Gabrielle hadn't believed in fairies, and the idea of tiny people with wings seemed absurd, but now one hovered inches from her face, while hundreds more floated nearby. It was crazy but amazing. A tingle ran down her spine.

The golden fairy touched the curving ends of Gabrielle's right eyelash. Then she turned to the crowd and said, *"Ana roya sevi danu, ipa beo ava nari."*

The throng burst into laughter, and the golden fairy gazed back at Gabrielle with a wide smile.

Gabrielle had no idea what was funny, but she laughed along.

After some moments, the crowd quieted. Gabrielle cleared her throat. "This is cool," she said, glancing around and nodding.

The golden fairy tipped her head and said, *"Feo anea netalu."* Then she swooped away, making a wide arc around the children.

Bobby trembled as she passed and stamped his feet. "Sooo preeety."

The fairy slowed and hovered up to Bobby's face. Her smile flattened to a narrow line. She peered into his hazel eyes and spoke as if to herself, *"Feo cyano. Feo jien."*

Bobby grinned impishly. The fairy descended to his left hand, touching it softly. Bobby quivered. The fairy glanced around quickly; then she glided toward the towering crystal rock. She motioned for the children to follow.

Gabrielle stuck her skateboard under her arm and strolled along with the others. When they neared the soaring crystal, the golden fairy flew up to a ledge high on the rock where a white-bearded fairy in a long, silver robe waited. The silver fairy gazed down at the children. When his eyes found Gabrielle, she felt shy and reached up to rotate her hat so the brim would hide her face.

The golden fairy landed on the ledge and dropped to one knee before the silver one. The silver fairy touched the golden one's forehead. A light pulsed there and vanished. The golden fairy rose and embraced the silver one. Then the two stood side by side on the rim of the ledge. The crowd cheered.

After a minute, the throng quieted and resumed their festivities. The two fairies beat their wings and rose off the ledge, gliding down to the children. When they neared the ground, the golden one slowed and followed the silver fairy. The silver fairy floated by the children, pressing his palms together in a praying manner as he passed.

At the last one, which was Josh, he stopped and turned his head from side to side. He cleared his throat, then said in a halting, grainy voice, "Welcome to Oriafen, gifted ones."

Gabrielle's jaw dropped. For a moment, she didn't believe what she'd heard. The silver fairy studied their faces, then he continued. "I Theralin, chief of Panishie. Long I not speak your tongue. Little I remember but try I will put your hearts at peace."

The children stood stunned; then Bobby started bouncing on his toes. "Thaat goood," he cried. "Thaat goood."

The other kids burst into laughter.

151

Josh stepped forward. "We're happy to meet someone who speaks English," he said. Then he introduced himself and the other children.

When Josh finished, the silver fairy spoke again. "We honor receive gifted ones our land. Long we fear none return. I send news to old friends who help you."

"That's cool," Josh said. "We'll take any help. But we're worried about our friends who are lost in the woods. We need your help to find them."

The silver fairy spoke to the golden fairy in a quiet voice. Then several copper sprites glided over and joined in the conversation. Then, the silver fairy turned back to the children.

"Your friends safe. Elderlan takes them another path. You not fear."

"Huh?" Josh said, his brow creasing. "Who is Elderlan? I don't understand."

"Elderlan everywhere," the old fairy said, sweeping his hands through the air. "Elderlan bring you Oriafen and take your friends another path."

"Oh, no, no," Rhea said, stepping forward. "They shouldn't go on another path. They should be with us. One of them is his sister." She pointed to Wesley. "We need to find them."

"No you fear," the old fairy said, shaking his head. "Elderlan protect them."

Rhea's face reddened, and her fingers clenched. "You keep talking about 'Elderlan.' What is that? Is it the forest? If so, there are strange things out there. It didn't protect us. If you can't help us, we'll help ourselves."

Josh shot Rhea a glance. "Let's keep this cool," he said in a quiet voice. "We don't want to piss them off."

"But they're ignoring us," Rhea said. "They aren't listening."

The silver fairy shook his head. "We listen. You not understand, child."

Rhea tensed and shot the old fairy a cold stare. "Please don't call me 'child,'" she said. "I'm thirteen years old, and I do understand."

Josh raised his hands and faced Rhea. "Okay, okay. Chill out. We need their help."

Rhea stamped her feet and wheeled toward Wesley. "What do you wanna do? It's your sister."

"I know," Wesley said, his face grim. "But having a temper tantrum won't help!"

Rhea clenched her jaw. Annie touched Rhea's arm and leaned close, whispering in her ear.

CPU shot a glance at Gabrielle. He whispered, "Psycho girl."

Gabrielle snorted.

Josh turned to the silver fairy. "I'm sorry. We're upset, but we're worried about our friends. If you can help us in any way, we'd appreciate it."

The old fairy nodded. His wings pulsed, and he rose away from the crowd.

The golden fairy glided after him to the plateau, and the two disappeared through a hole in the crystal. The other fairies resumed their festivities, while the copper sprites withdrew to the edge of the clearing, hovering there like silent sentries.

Josh spoke quietly to Wesley, while the other kids eyed one another.

"I need some music," Ted said. He swung his arms and notes poured into the air.

Gabrielle set down her board and stepped on it. "I want a better look at that rock," she said, gazing at the massive crystal. She wove her way forward, riding inches above the grass.

As she neared the stone, her board jerked to a stop, and she stumbled forward, almost falling off. She twisted. Dylan was gripping the back of the deck. "Hey, doofus, let go," she cried.

"Sure, but I'm coming."

Dylan grabbed his belt loops and leaped, flipping over Gabrielle and landing on the front of the board. A crowd of fairies burst into laughter.

"No room for two," Gabrielle said, pushing Dylan off and swooping away. Dylan bounded after her, somersaulting through the air as fairies cheered and clapped.

Gabrielle reached the huge rock and started up, tacking close to the surface to keep her fear of heights at bay. Dylan followed, leaping from outcrop to outcrop up the rock face. As they ascended, Gabrielle spied narrow passageways spiraling into the stone, leading to chambers in the clear rock where fairies lived and worked.

Gabrielle glided higher and higher until she passed into the canopy. Clutching her cap with one hand and the board with the other, she ducked and darted through the foliage until she burst out above the tree cover. The sunlight momentarily blinded her, and she covered her eyes. Everything was quiet. The sun felt hot on her skin.

As her vision adjusted, the roof of the forest came into view, stretching out in endless rolling green waves. To her right, the point of the crystal jutted out above the trees like the tip of an iceberg. Gabrielle darted up the rock and balanced at the peak. Whirling on her board, exhilaration filled her.

A band of fairies swarmed out of the canopy. "*Mealo wanna! Mealo onno!*" they cried, tugging on her clothes and pulling her down toward the greenery.

Gabrielle resisted until Dylan poked his head above the branches. "The fairies are freaking out," he said. "They think it's dangerous up there. They want you to get back under the trees."

Gabrielle sighed and yielded to the fairies, gliding down through the foliage. Beneath the trees, she whirled and coasted along the face of the rock, descending the stone in long sweeping arcs like a snowboarder down a hillside. Dylan followed, shouting and laughing as he bounded from outcrop to outcrop in a zigzag descent.

At the forest floor, Gabrielle skidded to a stop and observed other kids lounging by pools among crowds of fairies. She made her way toward a pool, noticing the fairies near Celia all had pink gowns, while those by Annie were dressed in orange, and the ones surrounding CPU and Barth wore brown and gray gowns. She wondered why different colored fairies had gathered around different kids.

Barth and CPU were arguing, so she headed toward them.

"Of course, they have thermochromic properties," CPU cried. "That's why you only see the colors when they touch their skin."

"Yeah, but the colors get darker and lighter depending on their mood, so something else is going on," Barth said.

Gabrielle came to a stop. "Thermo what?"

CPU blinked. "Thermochromic... It's when heat affects DNA, causing it to change color."

Gabrielle frowned. "DNA... what?"

CPU waved his hand dismissively. "Never mind, but we think it's why the fairies' clothes change color."

"But they have many different colors. How could that happen?" Barth asked.

"Good question," CPU said, his voice trailing off. He rubbed his chin.

Gabrielle didn't wait for an answer. She spun and glided toward her sister, who was sitting cross-legged at the edge of a pool, her hands in her lap and red and white goo slowly oozing from her wrists.

"What are you doing, Cici?" Gabrielle said as she slid to a stop. "That's freaky."

Celia grinned. "Yeah, but it's fun, and it tickles."

"It makes you tired."

"I know, but not if I do it just a little."

Gabrielle frowned. Celia shrugged and turned her arms, pressing them together. The goo mixed, forming a pink bubble that rapidly swelled to the size of a cantaloupe. Gabrielle quivered, feeling curious and repulsed at the same time. She knelt and cautiously touched the pink sphere. It felt smooth and soft, like the surface of a ripe nectarine.

"It's not sticky."

"No, it feels nice," Celia said.

Other fairies crowded around Celia, watching spellbound as the bubble swelled.

Celia turned her wrists, and a gap opened in the pink surface. As the sphere expanded, the gap widened to several inches in width.

"Why doesn't the air blow out?" Gabrielle asked in puzzlement.

Celia shrugged. "Maybe it's magic."

Suddenly, a boy fairy darted through the opening in the bubble. He fluttered around inside. The other fairies clapped and laughed. A second fairy zipped through the opening. Others quickly followed until half a dozen sprites were hovering around inside the sphere. Gabrielle laughed as the fairies bumped and jostled one another.

Celia's eyes began to droop, and her head nodded forward.

Gabrielle reached out to prop up Celia's shoulder. "Stop it, Cici. You'll zonk out."

"Yeah, I'm pooped," Celia replied, waggling her head to shake off the fatigue. She spread her arms apart, and the goo vanished into her wrists, pushing the fairies out into the open air.

The sprites complained at the sudden end of their game, but Celia was oblivious and tipped on her side. She curled up and closed her eyes.

Gabrielle leaned over her sister. "You sleep, Cici. I'll wake you if they bring more food."

"Thanks, Gabi," Celia said softly. A moment later, she was snoring.

Gabrielle folded her arms. She wondered why Celia became so tired when she made a bubble. A voice rang out. She turned and saw Dylan standing among a crowd of fairies near the trees on the right side of the glade. Gabrielle hopped on her board and rode toward the commotion.

"Back off!" Dylan yelled, swinging his arms around and karate chopping the air. "She's my friend. Stay away."

Gabrielle slowed. A half-dozen copper sprites hovered around Dylan with bows drawn, while the little warbler sat perched on his shoulder in a defensive stance.

"What's going on?" Gabrielle cried.

Dylan turned; his face flushed. "I don't know. They don't like Cherry. They want her to leave… or something."

A clear cry rang out, and the copper sprites relaxed their bows. Gabrielle saw the golden fairy gliding down from high on the great crystal.

As the golden fairy neared the crowd, she swept around in a wide circle and fluttered down between the copper sprites and Dylan. Turning first to the sprites, she spoke in an admonishing tone. This caused the fairies to back off.

Then she wheeled and glared at the little bird. Resting her hands on her hips, she scolded the warbler with sharp chirping sounds. Cherry raised her beak and answered with defiant peeps. Then Cherry dipped her head and nestled down in the folds of Dylan's shirt.

The golden fairy glared at the little bird in exasperation. Gabrielle covered her mouth to hide a laugh.

The fairy motioned for the crowd to leave and turned to Dylan, staring at him reproachfully. When he frowned back, she let out a sigh and flew back to the great crystal rock.

Gabrielle strolled up to Dylan; her board tucked under her arm. "That was nuts."

"Yeah," Dylan said, shaking his head. He leaned toward Gabrielle. "Have you noticed there aren't any other birds around."

Gabrielle made a quick scan of the trees and listened but didn't hear any chirping.

"They must hate birds," Dylan continued. "But they can't push Cherry around. She's staying with me."

"Definitely," Gabrielle said with a sympathetic grin. She stepped back on her board and headed toward a pool where the ground sloped and rolled around the water. She glided along the bank and did cuts and turns. It felt just like riding on the ground, but smoother and faster. She practiced her accelerations and stops until she got bored. Then she hopped off and plopped down on the bank.

Lying back, she gazed at slivers of blue-sky peeking through the canopy. Ted's music floated through the glade. She felt sleepy and nodded off. When she awoke, the ground was vibrating like a tree in a steady wind. The fairies were streaming back to the towering crystal.

Ted strolled over. "It appears our favorite fireball is making its fly-by."

Gabrielle groaned and strolled toward the edge of the glade, where most of the kids were already waiting. As she neared the woods, frustration swelled in her. *Why are we hiding? I'm not scared.* She thought. She spun and jumped on her board, ignoring a shout from Dylan. She knelt and glided up toward a sparse spot in the canopy.

Gripping her cap with one hand and the board with the other, she darted through the branches and broke out above the trees. The western sky was a sea of yellow and orange. She slowed, watching waves of color ripple up through the atmosphere. A dot appeared on the horizon. She lingered as the point swelled into a swirling, fiery sphere.

Her heart raced. It was time to get below. She angled down, darting into the tree cover. She shot through the branches and into the glade, but before she reached the ground, a blast of heat and wind slammed the clearing, tossing her like a rag doll into one of the pools.

As she sank beneath the surface, she gripped her board and baseball cap. Under the water, everything was quiet. It felt calm, peaceful. Then she remembered she couldn't swim, and panic set in. As oxygen vanished from her lungs, she kicked frantically and burst out above the surface. Splashing wildly, she touched the bank and pulled herself onto shore. The roar of the fireball faded into the east.

Celia and the other kids ran from the trees and grabbed Gabrielle's arms, pulling her fully out of the water.

"That was nuts!" Annie shouted. "Are you crazy?"

Gabrielle rolled onto her back and spread her arms, letting out a huge laugh as the water drained off her clothes. "That was so worth it!"

With the sun sinking in the west, fairies brought blankets for the children. Gabrielle wrapped herself in one and tugged off her wet clothes. She laid the wet clothes on the grass and huddled under the blanket.

In the deepening darkness, fairies lit candles around the clearing. Tiny flames shimmered off the pools, and mist floated from the water like wispy clouds.

The fairies joined hands and circled the clearing, their gowns glowing in the night air. They danced and sang, their soft voices filling the darkness. Dylan curled up beside Gabrielle. Celia lay a few feet away, her head resting in Annie's lap. The voices quieted, and the fairies returned to the great stone, while the copper sprites resumed their sentry positions at the edge of the glade.

Here and there, tiny stars peeked through the canopy. Gabrielle watched as they twinkled in the darkness. She thought of home. She missed her dad and her bedroom. She let out an involuntary yawn, then shook herself to stay awake. She didn't want to sleep, but exhaustion finally overcame her, and she slipped into slumber.

She found herself at the window of her room in Honduras, drawing a picture of the ceiba tree in her backyard. A shadow appeared. She glanced over her shoulder. Her mother stood behind her with one arm bent and her face bruised. Gabrielle flinched.

"Do you remember me, Gabi?" Her mother asked. The words came out in a gravelly voice.

"Yeah, I do, mama. I always will."

Her mother sat down. Gabrielle continued drawing, but the tree looked strange. She grew frustrated and turned toward her mother, who was staring off into the distance with an expressionless look.

"Don't you want to see me draw?" Gabrielle asked, but her mother didn't reply. Gabrielle reached out to touch the woman. She felt nothing and awoke… It was a dream – like she'd had many times before. She didn't understand it.

Gabrielle sat upright. She listened. The night was quiet, except for a rustling far off in the trees and the snoring of children around her. Gabrielle counted bodies – twelve, including herself. Someone was missing. She glanced around and sensed movement at the edge of the glade. She squinted and recognized a figure with a short ponytail. It was Wesley. He was pacing.

She sighed. Wesley was worried… about Sarah. What had happened to her and Timmy? *Where were they? Had the birds taken them, or some animal eaten them?* Gabrielle shivered at the thought. Her fatigue evaporated. She decided to stay up for a while.

Chapter 12:
Lightning and Fire

Timmy gripped Sarah's hand as she pulled him through the underbrush. Behind him, the great bird thrashed and tore through the dense growth, but Timmy felt strangely calm.

"Come on," Sarah said. "We have to find a place to hide."

The underbrush gave way to open woods, and they sprinted through the trees. Ahead of them, a massive sequoia loomed.

"In here," Sarah said, tugging Timmy into a damp hollow at the base of the tree. They scrambled to the back of the hole and waited in the shadows, their heavy breathing muffling other sounds.

Outside, the thrashing continued as the bird hunted the children. Then the noise stopped. Timmy heard the distant cries of his friends. Sarah leaned against him, covering her mouth. Timmy did the same. Although the bird couldn't see them, it could still be listening.

Minutes passed, and Timmy heard no more noise. He relaxed and motioned toward the entrance of the hollow.

Sarah shook her head and whispered, "No, let's stay here. It may not be safe yet."

A piercing squawk shattered the quiet, and a great beak swung through the opening of the hollow. Sarah shrieked as the bird forced its way into the hole. Timmy slid back, pulling Sarah with him, but the creature reached out with a sinewy talon and closed its claws around the Sarah.

A surge of adrenaline coursed through Timmy, and the world slowed, becoming almost still. Sounds spread out in long, drawn-out notes, and light moved around him in silky, flowing waves of color. He leaped forward and rammed the enormous bird with all his strength. The creature tipped back through the entrance, still clutching Sarah in its mighty talon.

Timmy grabbed one of the claws and pulled but couldn't pry it loose. He set his feet against the wall for leverage and yanked again. The claw finally sprang free. He did the same for the other three, and Sarah dropped out of the bird's grasp, falling slowly toward the ground. Timmy easily caught her.

Holding Sarah in his arms, he stared at the bird's dark, musty plumage filling the entrance to the hollow. There was a narrow gap above the creature through which they could squeeze. Raising Sarah over his head, he slid her onto the bird's oily back. Then climbing onto its wing, he shoved her forward so that Sarah slid halfway through the gap. He pushed her from behind, and she slipped down the bird's backside and into the dirt outside the tree. Timmy took a deep breath and pulled himself forward, then slid down after her.

He stood up, his heart pounding like a gorilla on a drum set. He had no idea where they were or which way to go. Strange, soft sounds carried through the forest – the distant cries of his friends. He listened but couldn't tell which direction they came from.

Slinging his pack over his shoulder, he lifted Sarah into his arms. He made his way forward, searching for any sign of the trail or his friends. He walked until his arms grew weak. He stopped and laid Sarah down in leaves beneath a maple tree.

He glanced back but saw no sign of the bird. His heartbeat slowed. He plopped down in the dirt, and his body relaxed.

Sounds quickened, and the world accelerated. Sarah sat upright and said something, her words coming out in high-pitched squeaks. He tried to answer, but before he could finish a word, Sarah screeched out a long series of sounds. She raised a finger to her lips, and her eyes flashed in warning. He became quiet.

The world gradually slowed. Sounds morphed into ordinary noises. Sarah gave him a worried look. "You okay?"

He rubbed his forehead and nodded.

"I don't hear the bird," she said, glancing around. "What happened? It grabbed me, then suddenly we were here."

"It's back there a ways," Timmy said, peering over his shoulder. "When it grabbed you, everything slowed. I got you free. I tried to find the other kids, but I couldn't."

"What do you mean slowed?" Sarah asked.

Timmy shrugged. "I don't know. The same thing happened at the stream yesterday. I got scared, and everything slowed down. Then when I wasn't afraid, everything sped up and became normal again."

Sarah peered at him. "I think it's you who is speeding up. You were moving so fast that everything else seemed slow. Then you slowed down, and everything seemed fast."

Timmy shrugged, not sure what was going on.

Sarah tipped her head back. Timmy did the same, seeing bits of sky visible through the canopy.

"The sun is over there," Sarah said, pointing back the way they'd come, "so the trail should be that way." She pointed to the right.

Timmy scratched his nose, still feeling light-headed. He tugged his pack over his shoulders and followed Sarah. They walked for about twenty minutes but saw no sign of the kids or the trail.

Sarah halted and crossed her arms. "Now I'm not sure where we're going."

But the wrong way may be right if the right way isn't. Timmy thought. He almost said this out loud but realized it would just annoy Sarah. He waited as she considered their options.

She threw up her hands. "We should have found the trail by now. This must be the wrong way. But if we head back, the bird might find us." She looked from side to side. "We could go right or left instead and hope we run into the trail. What do you think?"

Timmy shrugged.

Okay, let's go to the right," Sarah said, turning.

Timmy followed.

They walked and walked but saw no sign of the kids or the trail. The woods thinned and stretches of sky became visible through the branches. Staring up, Timmy wondered why the sky looked the same, but everything below kept changing.

After about an hour, the land began sloping down, and Timmy heard a gurgling sound ahead. "Is that water?" he asked.

Sarah listened, brushing hair out of her eyes. "I think so."

They were both thirsty and hurried forward. The ground steepened until they were sliding through leaves and soft dirt. As they slipped down the slope, they grabbed vines and roots to slow their descent. They skidded to a stop at a shallow creek at the bottom of the ravine.

Timmy cupped his hands in the water and swallowed. He drank and drank. Then he lay back. Something about this place felt familiar, even safe. He exhaled deeply.

After resting for some minutes, he rose and strolled along the bank, following the creek as it wound through the ravine. He happened upon a patch of berry bushes and plucked several berries. They tasted juicy and sweet, so he plucked more. Then he headed back to find Sarah.

She was sitting on a rock along the bank. He shared his berries with her. She loved them and wanted more, so he led her to the bushes he'd found. They ate dozens of berries and stuffed more into pouches in their packs.

They followed the creek for some minutes when Timmy began to feel dizzy. Fog seemed to cloud his brain. Sarah felt the same, so they sat down. Timmy lay back and closed his eyes. Within moments he was sleeping. When he awoke, it was dark. He sat up with a start. He could see nothing, but he heard the gurgling of water and Sarah's soft breathing.

"Phew, what a nap," he said, rubbing his eyes.

His stomach ached, so he reached into his pack and grabbed more berries. As he chewed, he listened to the night sounds. A branch broke and fell nearby. An owl hooted.

The sleepiness returned, and he curled up beside Sarah. When he awoke again, the sun was shimmering through trees at the top of the ravine. He heard a rustling and raised his head. A doe and two fawns were sipping at the water's edge just ten feet away. The doe raised her head and met his gaze. He smiled hopefully. The doe nudged her fawns. The three bounded across the water and rapidly ascended the far side of the ravine.

Timmy brushed leaves and dirt off his clothes. He tugged on Sarah's arm. "Hey, golden hair... Time to rise and sparkle."

Sarah propped herself on one elbow and scratched her nose. "Huh? Did I fall asleep?"

"Yeah, we both took quite a nap. It's tomorrow already."

Sarah tilted her head and rubbed her neck. "I'm starved."

"Me too, but don't eat more of those berries. I think they're sleepy-time fruit."

"What do you mean?"

"After we ate them, we both conked out."

"Oh, yeah." Sarah frowned, then she tugged an apple out of her pack. "I only have a couple more of these."

Timmy grabbed two pears from his bag and gave her one. They tossed the berries away and ate pears and apples instead. Then they started off.

As they walked, the land leveled out, and they found themselves passing through dense forest. They made their way through the forest until the sun rose high in the sky, and the creek widened to a slow-moving stream.

They stopped at a shady spot along the bank and shared a cantaloupe-sized orange. Timmy sighed, again feeling strangely relaxed and safe in these woods. Dragonflies skimmed over the water. He spotted a beaver climbing onto a rock upstream. It dove into the current and disappeared beneath a mound of mud and sticks.

They rested for almost an hour and then resumed the trek, following the stream through the afternoon. As the sun sank in the west, the underbrush grew thicker, and they had difficulty making their way forward. Timmy didn't mind, but it bothered Sarah. "We aren't getting anywhere," she grumbled.

Where is anywhere, when we're nowhere? Timmy thought though he didn't say this out loud.

In the fading light, the ground began to tremble, and a rumble reached Timmy's ears. He glanced at his watch. It was six twenty-five in the afternoon. "I think we should sit," he said.

Sarah's brow creased. Timmy pointed to the sky. "The fireball."

"Oh," Sarah said, pausing to listen. She plopped down next to a tree stump and drew her knees to her chest. Timmy knelt beside her. The rumbling grew, then faded away.

"It wasn't so loud," Sarah said.

"Why?"

"We must be further away."

"Should we change direction?"

Sarah stared at her hands and shook her head. "No, I think we would just get more lost."

The children followed the stream until it ended at a lake. They stood on the shore, staring across the water at trees on the far side some two hundred yards away. A breeze rippled the surface. In the west, the sun dipped beneath the horizon, causing the lake to shimmer in yellows and reds.

A flapping sound came from the west. Timmy stared at the horizon, but the sun obscured his view. As the flapping grew louder, his heart pounded. Then a winged creature landed on the water's surface. A moment later, two more birds joined the first. Timmy's heart slowed as he recognized the white plumage and graceful necks of swans.

Four more of the beautiful birds joined those already on the water. The swans dipped their heads beneath the surface and raised their backs, shaking droplets off their glistening plumage.

"It's magical," Sarah murmured.

Timmy nodded. The air began to cool. He tugged on his jacket and wrapped his scarf around his neck, letting the ends hang down his front.

The swans floated together in a turning semicircle. Then one left the circle and glided toward the children. It drew near and bowed its neck, peering at Timmy and Sarah through large round eyes. It held their gaze for a moment, then glided away, staying close to the shore. The swan slowed and glanced back, then rolled its neck as if beckoning to them.

"I think it wants us to follow," Sarah said, starting toward the bird.

Timmy doubted that but went along.

The swan glided smoothly through the water. Timmy and Sarah walked along the bank about ten feet behind the creature. They came to a muddy area on the shore where a path seemed to lead away from the water. Timmy saw footprints in the mud. "Someone's been here," he said.

"Yeah, and they have big feet," Sarah replied, setting her shoe beside the footprint. Her shoe was less than half the size.

The swan floated away to rejoin the flock. The children watched for a moment and then started down the muddy path. As they walked, the sun disappeared beneath the horizon, and darkness descended. They were soon stumbling in almost total black.

Sarah bumped against a tree. "Ow," she said, rubbing her arm. "I can hardly see anything."

"Like the walking blind," Timmy said.

"We should stop."

Timmy agreed. In the dim light, he saw an open area in the woods just ahead. He took Sarah's hand and led her forward. It was a small glade. He crouched, touching the grass, which was dry. Then he shrugged off his pack and plopped down. Sarah sat beside him.

Timmy felt hungry and pulled out a peach. As he bit into the fruit, a blast shook the air. He flinched.

"What was that?" Sarah asked in a hushed voice.

Timmy had no clue. "A falling tree?"

"It sounded more like dynamite!"

A second blast rang out, followed by two more in quick succession.

Sarah jumped up. "Snap, we have to check this out." She grabbed his hand and pulled him to his feet.

"But it's so dark," Timmy said. "We can see hardly anything."

"I know, but we can hear."

Do ears replace eyes when the light is dear? Timmy thought.

Sarah tugged Timmy forward, stretching out her free hand to feel for any objects ahead.

As they crept through the darkness, the explosions grew louder, and Timmy's anxiety increased. He tugged on Sarah's shirt. "Let's stop. I'm scared."

"No… no," Sarah whispered. "We need to find out what this is."

Timmy gulped, trying to swallow his fear.

The woods ended at a meadow. They crept to the edge of the trees. Another flash lit up the sky, and a stone structure came into view as big as the barn on his grandpa's farm. To the right of the building, a low wall ran south, bordering a wide pasture.

Sarah's eyes glimmered, and she whispered, "I've been here before."

Timmy blinked, not understanding what she meant. "Huh?… When?"

Sarah paused and frowned. "I can't remember."

Two more blasts shattered the quiet. Sarah grabbed his hand and pulled him through the trees running left along the field. As they hurried through the woods, a burst of light erupted ahead. In the momentary flash, Timmy saw a man at the center of the meadow jumping around like a confused clown, his arms flailing back and forth as jagged bursts of light whipped into the sky. The man slowed and raised his hands; then two bursts of light shot out from his fingertips.

Timmy froze in astonishment. Sarah turned, her mouth in the shape of a donut.

The man danced around manically, shooting off more bolts of electricity. Several minutes passed, and finally, he dropped his arms and stopped. Timmy heard his heavy breathing.

Sarah leaned close and put her mouth to Timmy's ear. "I remember now," she whispered. "This place was in my dream. I wasn't scared. It was safe… I think we should go talk to him."

Timmy shook his head. He had no intention of talking to a guy who was shooting electricity out of his fingertips. He backed up. Leaves crunched under his feet. A growl rose from across the field.

The stranger turned and spoke in a low, gravelly voice. *"Setha luma heri nea? Verana feo ita mia."*

Timmy froze. Then a burst of light shot from the man's hand, racing toward the trees where he and Sarah were hiding. Timmy's heart pounded like rocks in a landslide, and everything slowed. Sounds turned to low moans, and the light racing across the field decelerated to a trickle of water leaking into the darkness.

Sarah became still. Timmy lifted her into his arms and clutched her so that her head hung over his shoulder. He stumbled through the woods, hurrying away from the field. He staggered for some thirty yards until he could carry her no further. Then he set her down beside a tree.

He crouched and stared back. In the distance, the burst of light advanced slowly across the meadow, its white glow revealing two animals moving almost unperceptively through the grass.

The light inched toward the trees and then disappeared in a low, drawn-out explosion several feet from where he and Sarah had been hiding. Timmy realized the electricity wouldn't have reached them, and the pounding of his heart eased. He plopped down beside Sarah and leaned against the tree, ready for what would happen next.

Everything gradually sped up until Sarah was flitting about him in quick, sudden movements like a hummingbird around a petunia bush. She spoke in a high-pitched whisper, but the sounds came so fast that Timmy could understand nothing. He waited. Finally, the world slowed again.

"Are you okay?" Sarah asked.

Timmy hugged his arms. "Yeah... I think so."

"Let's go talk to him."

"He scares me."

"I know. Me too, but he's the only person we've seen for days. Maybe he can help us."

The low, gravelly voice carried through the woods again. *"Ana kella quon. Metoha... Bonjour...* Hello?"

Sarah raised a hand to her mouth. "Did he just say hello?"

Timmy nodded, not quite believing his own ears.

"We should answer him."

Timmy frowned, feeling confused.

The stranger made his way to the edge of the trees and peered into the woods. The children stared back. Sarah cleared her throat. "Who are you?" she shouted.

There was a pause; then the man let out a gravelly laugh. "Who am I?... Perhaps I am one you seek; one you should find."

Sarah gave Timmy a puzzled look. "What does that mean?"

Timmy shrugged.

Sarah stood up. "We don't understand you."

The man folded his arms. "I see. Well, what I mean is that perhaps I am someone who can provide you help."

Sarah cleared her throat. "The light and explosions scare us."

"Of course."

"Will you stop?"

170

"Yes, they are only for my amusement."

Sarah crouched and met Timmy's eyes. "Let's go," she whispered.

Timmy held his breath and nodded.

He and Sarah made their way to the edge of the clearing. The stranger stood a few feet from the trees, his arms crossed. He looked taller than Timmy's dad, who was six-foot-three. The man had wide shoulders, thick arms, and hands almost as big as dinner plates. A scraggly beard covered his prominent jaw and chin, and a long, dark cloak draped over his shoulders.

"You are young," the man murmured as the children stepped into the open. "To be alone in this forest, you must be gifted ones. What are your names?"

Timmy hesitated, but Sarah said hers, so he did too.

The stranger's face softened. He knelt eye level with them. "When did you come to this land?"

Sarah glanced at Timmy and squinted as she tried to count. "Three days ago, I think," she said. "We came on our school bus."

"A bus," the man chuckled. "I haven't ridden one of those for forty years."

"Oh," Sarah said. "You used to ride a bus too?"

"Yes, to school. Everyday. A long time ago."

Sarah gave the man a penetrating look. "What is your name?"

"I am called Eredel, though once I was known as James." He turned and pointed behind him. "This is my home. Forgive me, but I don't often receive guests, and my hospitality is out of practice. You must be tired and hungry."

"Yes," Sarah said. "All we've been able to eat is fruit."

Eredel rose. "Then come," he said. "I can offer you a hearty meal and a place to rest." He started toward the building. Sarah nodded to Timmy.

As they stepped out of the trees, two dogs rose from the grass several yards away. Timmy wavered.

Eredel noticed his hesitation. "Don't be afraid. They won't harm you. They're my companions, Gala and Lela."

Timmy smiled cautiously at the dogs, which reminded him of his uncle's border collies. The dogs stared back, their eyes shining and tails wagging in the moonlight.

Eredel led the children around the large stone structure which he called his barn. They headed toward a cottage, where candlelight flickered in the windows and smoke rose from a chimney. A wave of relief swept through Timmy. He didn't want to sleep outside another night.

Eredel led the children into a low-ceilinged room with a large wooden table at its center. A cooking pot simmered on an open fire to the left, while bookshelves and cabinets lined the walls. On the far side of the room, Timmy spotted two doors in the wall.

"Please sit," Eredel said, pointing to chairs by the table.

Sarah plopped down in one, and Timmy sat in another. Eredel tugged off his cloak and hung it beside the door. Beneath the cloak, he wore a light brown shirt, dark pants and leather sandals on his bare feet. In the candlelight, Timmy could get his first good look at the man. He had a long, slim face, lined with wrinkles and clear, piercing eyes. Thick, gray hair fell to his broad shoulders, and his skin appeared strangely translucent. Although he looked as old as Timmy's grandfather, he moved with the power and grace of a much younger man.

Eredel fed kindling into the fire, so it blazed hotly. Then from a cabinet, he withdrew a loaf of bread and a small butter urn. He sliced the bread and set it on the table with the urn.

Timmy grabbed a piece eagerly. As he spread the butter, he noticed a squirrel perched on a windowsill at the back of the room. The squirrel peered at him through quivering eyes, while it chewed on a nut held in its tiny paws.

"Hey, look," Timmy said, pointing to the window. Sarah twisted and blinked as the squirrel grabbed another nut from a pile on the windowsill. She laughed. A squawk filled the air.

Timmy's eyes followed the sound. He saw a crow hop off a dresser. The bird glided over the floor and snatched up a mouse scurrying across the room. The crow swept to the fireplace and dropped the mouse in a ceramic bowl on the ground.

"Cenio, enough of your games," Eredel said as the bird returned to its perch on the dresser. "Let the little creature be."

The crow squawked and ruffled its feathers. Sarah smiled. The mouse peered cautiously out from the bowl. Then it scampered up the side and leaped to the floor before vanishing through a crack in the wall.

The squirrel was now munching on the last nut from its pile. The squirrel finished chewing, then squeezed through a narrow opening in the window and disappeared into the night. Timmy caught Sarah's eye, and they both laughed.

Eredel set steaming bowls of soup and wooden spoons on the table. Timmy leaned forward, inhaling the broth's rich aroma. He felt light-headed with hunger and was glad to have something other than fruit to eat.

Sarah tasted the soup. "Yum. It's delicious."

"Eat your fill," the man said as he removed three cups from a cabinet and poured water into them.

Timmy stirred the broth with his spoon. He saw lots of vegetables, but no noodles or meat. "What kinda soup is this?"

"Tomato, asparagus, and herbs from my garden," Eredel said as he set cups on the table.

Timmy stared at his bowl, trying to hide his disappointment.

"Taste it, young Tim," Eredel said encouragingly. "It may be to your liking."

Timmy lifted the spoon to his mouth. He swallowed. The broth had a surprisingly thick, rich flavor. He hungrily ate spoonful after spoonful and sopped up the last of it with his bread.

Eredel brought a chair over and joined them at the table. The three ate quietly until Sarah raised her head and peered curiously at the man. "When you first saw us, you called us 'gifted ones.' What did you mean?"

The hint of a smile crossed Eredel's lips. "Each living being who passes from your world into this one receives a gift, a magical power. Have you discovered yours yet?"

Timmy thought for a moment. He glanced at Sarah, and they nodded together.

"So, you are gifted ones," Eredel said.

Sarah tugged on the crust of her bread. "Does everyone in this world have magic powers?"

"No, this is a land of wonders and mysteries, but its people possess no inherent magic. Only those who come from your world – our world – receive a gift, a power. But be warned, along with each gift comes a weakness. Sometimes the weakness is silly or funny, but often it is terrible and frightening. I received a gift. It is a fantastic power, but it came with a weakness that I must struggle with each day."

"Power that reaches beyond the narrow," Timmy muttered.

The crow squawked, and Eredel's eyes flashed. "Why do you say such words, young Tim?"

Timmy flinched.

"Oh, don't mind him," Sarah said quickly. "He often says silly things like that."

"But those are words of power," Eredel declared, standing up. "Where did you learn them?"

Timmy shifted uncomfortably in his chair. "I don't know. They just popped into my head."

Eredel swung away and appeared lost in thought. In the silence, Sarah mustered up the nerve to ask another question.

"You told us your name was James once, but now it is Eredel. Why is it different?"

The man sat down. "I was born with the name James, but Eredel was given to me in this land."

"Who gave it to you?" Timmy asked.

"That is a story for another time, but now please tell me how you came to this world and your journey?"

Timmy glanced at Sarah, preferring to let her talk. He wasn't very good at describing things. When he tried, he usually jumped around to the important parts and confused everyone who was listening.

Sarah told Eredel how their bus had passed through a blue light in the road and driven into the meadow. She told him about Ben leaving and what happened that day. When she described the mist creature, Eredel's face darkened. He rose from his chair and strode around the room. Sarah became quiet and shifted her chair closer to Timmy's.

Eredel opened a cabinet and removed a thin silver chain. He set the chain around his neck and adjusted his collar, so it disappeared under his shirt.

Sarah cleared her throat. "Do you know what that mist was?"

"That was a friend once," Eredel said haltingly, "but he succumbed to his weakness."

Sarah's hand went to her mouth. "Your friend. That mist was your friend?"

"When I knew him, we were boys. He received a special gift. We shared adventures, but his weakness consumed him until there was nothing left but cold dark hunger."

"Hunger that consumes and is never gratified," Timmy said as if in a trance.

The crow squawked again, and Eredel's eyes grew flinty. "Again, you speak words of power. Why do you say such things, young Tim?"

Timmy hunched in his seat. "I'm sorry, I don't know. They just come to me."

Eredel stroked his beard. "Hmm... Perhaps this is your gift."

"Actually, I think his gift is something else," Sarah said. "When he gets excited or scared, he moves super fast."

"Everything slows down," Timmy said, "like a sailboat in a fading wind. Then it all speeds up again."

"So that's how you disappeared into the woods," Eredel said with a chuckle.

Timmy nodded.

"Where do these gifts come from?" Sarah asked.

Eredel folded his arms. "I can't say. There are things in this world beyond my understanding." He took a sip from his cup and wiped his mouth. "Please continue with your story."

Sarah described how they found the fruit at the stream and followed the trail until the black birds attacked.

"Rarewar," Eredel murmured.

The crow screeched and vaulted off its perch, swooping across the table. Timmy jumped back.

Sarah twisted, watching as the bird landed back on the dresser. "What's wrong with your crow?"

"He's scared," Eredel said with a sigh. "Rarewar frighten him. They are the great birds of Hiapana. Sidtarr captured a few many years ago and bred them to serve him."

Sarah's brow creased. "Sidtarr? Who's that?"

"The usurper of Risrean. He covets your gifts and commands the rarewar to bring you to him."

"What about our friends?" Sarah asked, her face ashen.

"I fear they have been taken," Eredel said.

"What will happen to them?"

"He won't hurt them at first. He wants their gifts. He'll indulge and pamper them to gain their trust. However, if they resist, his anger can be fierce."

"What should we do?"

"We'll find your friends and bring them to the only safe place in this land."

"Where is that?"

"The Kingdom of the Silver Cat."

"A cat has a kingdom?" Timmy asked doubtfully.

Eredel chuckled. "Yes, he's a special cat and an old friend."

"That's funny," Sarah said. "I dreamed about a cat with silver fur the night before our school bus came to this place."

Eredel smiled. "Your dream was touched by this land."

"Can the silver cat help us get home?" Sarah asked.

"Perhaps he can," Eredel said, "but he'll need something, something special… a sapphire fruit."

"A what?

"A sapphire fruit… the fruit of power. It was thought they all were lost, but some must exist. It's what brought you to this land. If we find one, we can use it to send you home."

All this talk of fruit, kingdoms, and cats made Timmy's head swim. His eyes drooped, and he slumped in his chair.

Eredel rose.

"It's late, and you should rest, Sarah and Timmy. Come with me." He strode to one of the doors at the rear of the cottage and opened it. He led the children into a room. More bookshelves lined the walls. Beds of straw and woolen blankets covered the floor. Stars twinkled in a window high on the back wall.

"Simple accommodations," Eredel said, "but I hope you find them comfortable."

"Comfier than sleeping in the forest," Timmy said.

The children thanked Eredel, and he left the room.

Timmy dropped his pack into a corner and plopped down on a bed. It sank beneath his weight. He lay back, stretching his arms. Exhaustion swelled through him, and he closed his eyes.

"I don't think I can sleep," he heard Sarah say. "I'm too worried about Wesley and the others. Did you get what he said about the sapphire fruit and the silver cat?"

Timmy was too tired to answer and drifted into a dream.

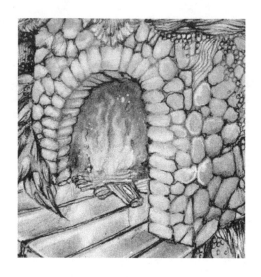

Chapter 13:
The Farm

Sarah blinked in the sunlight streaming in through the window. She turned on her side. Timmy lay sleeping on the bed across from her. Behind him, books and trinkets filled shelves along the wall. Sarah peered at the books but couldn't read any of the strange symbols on the bindings.

She sat up on one elbow and looked through the doorway. Eredel stood at the hearth, with the crow perched on the table behind him.

Sarah scratched her cheek and stood up. She smoothed her hair back and stepped through the doorway. Eredel smiled. "Young Sarah, did you sleep well?"

"Yes," she said yawning. "The best in days."

"Good. Are you hungry?"

Eredel pointed to pancakes simmering in a pan on the hearth.

"Yes, I am, but I'd like to use a bathroom first."

Eredel pointed to the door. "There's a privy outside to the right."

Sarah said thanks and stepped outside. She spotted a wooden shed with an old rickety door. When she opened the door, Sarah blanched at the stink that poured out. Waving around her hands to clear the air, she took a breath and stepped inside.

Quickly finishing her business, she hurried back out, slamming the door behind her. She stopped and glanced around. An orchard extended behind the privy and beyond that a vegetable garden. The woods began some fifty yards back, and a creek ran along the edge of them.

On the other side of the cottage, a stone wall enclosed a large pasture where horses and cows grazed. The smell of grass and a faint scent of manure filled the air.

Sarah studied the scene, a smile slowly spreading on her face. Everything seemed so beautiful and peaceful. She thought Eredel must be happy living here.

She spun on her heels and headed back to the cottage. As she neared the door, Eredel's dogs appeared from behind the barn. She remembered their names and called to them. "Hey Gala. Hey Lela."

The dogs trotted over, their tails wagging like happy metronomes.

Gala brushed her nose against Sarah's leg. Sarah knelt and rubbed the soft fur on the dog's neck, noticing gray speckles in his black coat and a white patch on his stomach.

Lela held back for a moment and then came forward, moving with a slight limp. Eredel had told Sarah that Lela was the mother, and Gala was her four-year-old pup. Sarah rubbed Lela's soft brown fur. Then she hugged both dogs around the neck and went inside.

A steaming plate of pancakes lay on the table. Timmy was standing in the doorway of the room where they'd slept, rubbing his eyes. Eredel said, "Good morning" to Timmy and motioned for Sarah to sit, handing her a cup of milk.

Timmy shuffled over to the table, staring hungrily at the pancakes. When Sarah told him about the privy, he nodded quickly and hurried out the door, returning a few minutes later.

As the three ate, Eredel probed Sarah and Timmy with more questions about their journey. Sarah did most of the talking. When she mentioned, they couldn't find their bus after they went to the stream, Eredel rubbed his chin in a way that reminded Sarah of her teacher, Mr. Schmidt.

When Sarah described the huge iron cage they had found and slept in, Eredel's eyes widened.

"You passed through the door of Opal?" he exclaimed, slumping back in his chair.

"What door?" Sarah asked. "What's Opal?"

"The iron structure which surrounds the sieli moni trees."

"You mean the trees with the shiny fruit?"

"Yes. The Ancients bound the door with a spell so none could enter."

"Why did they do that?"

"To protect the trees."

"Who are the Ancients'?" Timmy asked.

Eredel took a drink from his cup, then said, "They are a people who once lived in this land but are gone now."

"Where did they go?" Sarah asked.

"They sailed into the western sea."

"Why did they do that?" Sarah asked.

"I don't know… I am curious how you opened the door to Opal."

"We couldn't get it to budge at first, but then I think Josh opened it. Right, Timmy?"

"Yeah." Timmy nodded.

"Who's Josh?" Eredel asked.

"He's one of our friends," Sarah said. "Kind of our leader. He's tall and smart and nice, but super serious."

"How did he open the door?"

"He pushed on it; I think." Sarah glanced at Timmy for confirmation. "That's it. He pushed on it. We all went inside. Then Dylan jumped up into one of the trees and pulled off a bunch of the shiny fruit. He gave one to each of us, but they all stopped shining... except for mine."

"Yours still shines?" Eredel asked.

Sarah bobbed her head and went to the back room to get her bag. She brought it to the table and rummaged through it until she found the soft fruit. As she held it up, a tingling ran through her fingers, and the fruit began to sparkle like a diamond in sunlight.

Eredel's mouth opened, and he stepped back. "You're a healer."

"A what?"

"The sieli fruit perishes when it is plucked from the branch. The light dies. But when you hold it, the light returns. You're a healer. A life giver. That's a rare gift."

Sarah paused. "When I hold it, my hands feel kinda tingly, but it also makes me tired. After I get that tingling, I usually fall asleep."

"That's your weakness," Eredel said solemnly.

Sarah inclined her head. "Huh?"

"As I told you, each gift comes with a weakness. Your gift is to heal, and your weakness is the weariness you feel. I don't want to tire you, so please set your fruit down. We have much to do today."

Sarah put the fruit on the table. It again faded to a dull yellow. Eredel picked it up.

"It's been years since I held a sieli fruit," he said, running his index finger over the smooth surface. "The trees you found are the last remaining ones in Hevelen. The others were destroyed many years ago."

"I'm sorry," Sarah said. "What's Hevelen?"

Eredel grinned. "Let me show you." He stepped over to a dresser and pulled out a long roll of paper, which he spread on the table. It was a map.

"This is Hevelen," he said, indicating a body of land covering most of the map. "And Elderlan is here," he said, pointing to a forested valley surrounded by mountains near the center of the map. "You began your journey in eastern Elderlan and followed the Onil Trail to Opal, where you discovered the sieli trees."

Sarah peeked quickly at Timmy. He was trying to pay attention, keeping his eyes on Eredel, but she knew—like her—that the names were confusing.

Eredel moved his finger about an inch along the map. "This is my farm."

Sarah sighed. "We've only gone that far? But we've been walking for two days."

Eredel chuckled. "The world is much larger than you imagine, young Sarah."

Sarah's eyebrows drew together. "Where is the Kingdom of the Silver Cat you talked about?"

Eredel moved his finger down the map, "Here," he said. "At the base of the Hiapana Mountains."

"That's far away," Sarah said. "How long will it take to get there?"

Eredel tapped his fingers on the table. "We must find your friends first, who have been taken to Risrean." He pointed to a spot on the northwestern coast of the map. "Then we will go to the Silver City."

"How do we get there?" Sarah asked. "I've never walked that far."

"Can you ride?"

"Ride what?"

"A horse."

"No, but Timmy can."

"I like horses," Timmy said, eagerly.

"My horses can bear you on this journey," Eredel said. "But after we reach the Silver City, we must find a *cenarri moni*?"

Sarah's brow knitted. "What's that?"

"The sapphire fruit I told you about—the fruit of power."

"You mean this?" Sarah said, pointing to the pale, yellow fruit on the table.

Eredel shook his head. "That's a sieli moni. It's a sister fruit to the *cenarri moni,* but not as powerful." He drummed his fingers on the table. "Tomorrow, we begin our journey, so today, we must prepare."

"What about the rarewar... those black birds?" Sarah asked. "What if they find us?"

Eredel smiled. "You need not fear the rarewar when you're with me. Those birds will avoid us, yet other creatures may not. Your clothes reveal that you are a gifted one. It's best that you change them... Though first, you should bathe."

"Bathe?" Sarah and Timmy said at the same time.

"It'll be your only opportunity for some time."

"Okay," Sarah said, excited by the idea of getting clean.

"I don't need one," Timmy said, frowning.

"Yes, you do!" Sarah cried, wrinkling her nose.

Eredel laughed, and Timmy rolled his eyes.

After they had finished their breakfast, Eredel led them to the large stone barn. Inside, stalls ran along one wall, and a chicken coop—housing scores of clucking hens—occupied the other wall.

At the rear of the barn, Eredel opened a large chest, revealing a mound of clothes. "I have some garments that may fit you." He dug through the chest, pulling out different clothes and handing them to the children.

Arms full, Sarah and Timmy followed Eredel out of the barn and across the field to the creek running along the edge of the woods. They stopped where the creek formed a pool within a ring of boulders sticking out of the ground. Towels hung from a post beside one of the boulders, and a bar of soap lay in a nook carved into the post.

Eredel motioned toward the pool. "After you've washed up, try on the different garments until you find something you like." He headed away toward the orchard.

Timmy glanced around awkwardly. "You can go first."

"Thanks," Sarah said, with a firm stare. "Now, goodbye."

"Oh," Timmy said. He hurried away in the direction of the cottage.

With Timmy safely out of sight, Sarah knelt behind a bolder and undressed. She wrapped a towel around her and stepped into the pool. The water was cold but felt good in the warm sun.

She relaxed, letting the water soothe her until loud barking disturbed her serenity. She peered over the top of a boulder and blinked in surprise. An ox was pulling a plow through Eredel's garden, but she saw no one behind the plow. Gala and Lela, however, were barking and nipping at the oxen's hooves. The dogs seemed to be urging the large animal down a long furrow. The ox wasn't too pleased by the dogs' prodding, showing its displeasure with a kick every few steps. The dogs easily avoided the kicks as they guided the large creature to the end of the furrow. They turned it around and started up the next row.

Sarah let out a little laugh and dipped back into the water, again thinking how amazing it would be to live in this place. Timmy said he wanted to move to the country someday. His grandpa had a farm in Kentucky, where they raised pigs and chickens. Timmy had spent a couple of summers there, helping his grandpa with chores. In his free time, Timmy fished and swam in a river running along the edge of his grandpa's property and caught frogs in marshes along the riverbank. It sounded wonderful.

After soaking for fifteen minutes, Sarah heard Timmy call her name and ask, "Are you done yet?"

"Almost," she yelled back and reluctantly climbed out of the water. She dried herself and rummaged through the clothes Eredel had left, finding a loose-fitting shirt and gray pants which she put on. She tugged a brush through her wet hair, then headed back to find Timmy.

He was leaning against the cottage wall, watching horses and cows graze in the pasture.

"That was nice," Sarah said, smoothing her wet hair. "Your turn."

"Finally," Timmy said, with a small snort. He hurried across the field, skirting the orchard and disappearing behind the boulders.

Sarah stared out at the pasture, shading her eyes from the bright sunlight. Two horses grazed among a half-dozen cows. She had never seen a horse in real life. She strolled to the pasture wall to get a closer look. The nearest horse had a beautiful golden coat and a snow-white mane. It raised its head as if listening to something. Then it shook away a couple of flies and resumed chomping on the grass.

The second horse was dark gray with several large white marks on its back and flank.

A breeze picked up. The gray horse trotted across the pasture to a lusher area and resumed grazing.

After several minutes, Sarah headed over to the orchard, where Eredel was kneeling at the edge of the garden with the crow perched on his shoulder. He extended his hand toward a small animal crouched on a furrow. It was a ground squirrel. The squirrel scampered up, took something from Eredel's hand, and popped whatever it was into its mouth. Another ground squirrel did the same, while others scurried up and down the furrows.

"What are they doing?" Sarah asked.

"Planting," Eredel said. He reached into a bag at his feet and brought out a handful of seeds. Another ground squirrel scurried up and offered out its paws. The crow let out a sharp squawk. The squirrel flinched.

"Hush, Cenio," Eredel said, snapping his fingers at the bird, "or you're going inside."

Eredel dropped a pinch of seeds into the squirrel's outstretched paws. The little creature popped the seeds into its mouth and scampered away.

Eredel brushed off his hands and straightened. In the sunlight, his skin looked slightly transparent to Sarah. Muscles and tendons were faintly visible on his face and arms.

Eredel smiled. "I don't know how long our journey will take, so I'm planting early and hoping we don't get a spring frost."

"Spring? But it's almost winter."

"In this land, the seasons are different from those you know. Here, a year is twice the length of yours back home, so we are still in mid-spring."

"No wonder the weather is so nice," Sarah said, watching the ground squirrels. "How do you get them to help you?"

"It's not hard. They enjoy seeding the soil. It's in their nature to prepare for winter."

"But squirrels back at home don't do this."

Eredel laughed. "Creatures are different here."

Sarah had already figured that out. The animals seemed to understand so much. Some could even talk. She surveyed the garden. The squirrels ran up and down the rows, dropping seeds into the dirt and covering them with fresh soil. Their eagerness reminded Sarah of the mice in the movie Cinderella.

After some minutes, Sarah headed back to the creek to check on Timmy. She shouted to make sure it was okay. He hollered that he was getting dressed, so Sarah waited a little longer and strolled over to the boulders. She found Timmy drying his hair with a towel. He had on a pair of brown pants and a dark green shirt.

"How was the bath?"

"Cold," Timmy said, with a shiver. "It feels good to have clothes back on."

Sarah smiled and circled the pool. Timmy followed her. They walked along the creek to a shady spot under a tree. They sat with their feet in the water.

"This place is peaceful," Sarah said, staring up into the branches. "I'd love to stay, but I keep worrying about Wesley and the other kids. What if they're in some terrible place?"

"They could be worried about us too," Timmy said.

"Maybe..." Sarah's voice drifted off, thinking she and Timmy were lucky to have found Eredel's farm. She sighed. "Did you see the squirrels helping Eredel plant seeds?"

"Yeah, no wonder he likes it here. But it must get lonely sometimes, being all by himself...," Timmy said quietly.

"Except for the animals. He probably has friends too who visit him sometimes," Sarah said. She lazily kicked at the water.

Sarah heard footsteps and glanced over her shoulder. Eredel was striding across the field. She rose and waved. Eredel waved back and headed over.

"Now that you're all cleaned up," he said, "I must ask for your help. We need to prepare food for our journey."

Sarah and Timmy nodded eagerly. They followed Eredel back to the cottage, where he put them to work baking a pancake-like bread. They cut the cooled bread into pieces and packed it into leather pouches. They worked busily until lunchtime.

Eredel set out cheese, bread, and fruit for them. Sarah broke off a chunk of bread and sat down. As she chewed, she noticed several mice nibbling on a piece of cheese in the corner of the cottage. Cenio eyed the rodents sourly and hopped up and down on his bookshelf perch. The mice glanced at the bird warily but continued eating.

The crow let out a shrill squawk, and the mice started. The little creatures looked to Eredel, who shook his finger at Cenio. "Quiet," he said. "They are my guests. No more complaints from you."

The crow squawked and ruffled its feathers brusquely. Then it glared at the rodents and turned away.

After lunch, Eredel asked Sarah and Timmy to help him prepare food for the animals to eat while he was away. That took most of the afternoon. By the time they finished, the sun was low in the sky.

With her chores done, Sarah strolled to the stone wall enclosing the pasture. She sat on the wall and watched as a half-dozen hens pecked at the ground. Timmy sat beside her, and they talked until Gala trotted over and began herding the chickens toward the barn. Sarah smiled at the cleverness of the dog as it rounded up the uncooperative birds and guided them through the big doors. With all the chickens safely inside, Gala trotted into the yard and began barking at Sarah and Timmy.

"What's wrong with him?" Timmy asked.

Gala barked again and pointed with his snout toward the barn doors.

"I think he wants us to go inside," Sarah said with slight puzzlement.

"Eredel went in there earlier," Timmy said. He hopped off the wall. "Let's see what he's doing."

They passed through the large wooden doors and found Eredel kneeling beside a cow lying prone on the floor. All the other cows – eight in number – were inside the barn, plus several ponies, dozens of chickens, and Gala and Lela.

Eredel raised his head as the children entered. "Come sit. It's time to be indoors."

"Huh?" Sarah said.

"Find a comfortable place to rest. This one will be giving birth soon, and its calf is in an awkward position."

"Where should we sit?" Sarah asked.

Eredel pointed to a pile of hay in one of the stalls.

Sarah looked at Timmy and shrugged. They sat in the stall, the hay sinking softly beneath their weight. Sarah bounced and pushed Timmy, who rolled onto his stomach. She lay back and stretched her arms behind her head. The ground began to tremble. The shaking intensified, and a low rumble filled the air. Sarah realized what was coming. She sat upright and drew her knees to her chest. Her heart thumped rapidly, but the animals in the barn seemed undisturbed by the shaking.

Eredel continued with his work as the rumble grew. The sound swept overhead with a terrible roar. Then the noise faded away. Sarah caught Eredel's eye. "What is that?"

"Dragon fire," he replied casually.

"That fireball?" Sarah asked. "We've seen it every day since we've been here."

"Yes, it's dragon fire."

"From a real-life dragon?"

Eredel nodded and resumed his work.

"Why does it fly across the sky?"

"It's a warning from a distant enemy," Eredel said without looking up. "He's reminding us of his power."

"Who?"

"I'll tell you another time. For now, don't be afraid. It is no danger to us."

Despite Eredel's words, Sarah's heart continued to patter rapidly. She tried to calm herself, but it didn't work. Gala trotted to the barn door and nudged it open. The chickens began wandering out, but the other animals remained inside. Sarah glanced at Timmy. "Should we go out?"

He shrugged. "If the chickens aren't chicken, why should we?"

Sarah laughed and stood up, brushing hay off her clothes. She and Timmy walked through the doors. Blinking in the sunlight, Sarah gazed across the pasture, where Eredel's two horses were grazing.

Eredel strolled out, carrying a pail in each hand.

"Why didn't your horses come in the barn?" Sarah asked.

"They are stubborn," Eredel said. He handed a pail to each of them. "Can you help me fill the trough?" He pointed to a large wooden tub in the pasture where the cows and horses drank. The children nodded.

It took five trips from the well beside the cottage to fill the trough. With water nearing the rim of the tub, the horses trotted over and began to drink.

Sarah and Timmy returned to the cottage, where they found Eredel lifting a steaming pot of stew off the fire. Lela and Gala lay on a rug to the right of the door, watching their master with calm, intelligent eyes. Eredel set the stew on the table.

All the hard work had roused an appetite in Sarah. She ladled the stew into three bowls. She handed one to Timmy and took one for herself. As she ate, she wondered who would take care of the farm while Eredel was gone. She asked Eredel.

"Oh… Lela will be in charge," Eredel said, as he sliced a piece of cheese. "She can handle everything fine."

"Your dog will take care of your farm?" Sarah asked, almost spilling her spoonful of stew.

Eredel chuckled. "Yes, she's done it before."

Sarah glanced at Lela with newfound admiration.

After dinner, Eredel withdrew to his room. He reappeared several minutes later dressed in the long black cloak they'd seen him wearing the first night. Cenio sat perched on his shoulder.

"Are you going somewhere?" Sarah asked.

"I'll just be outside, engaging in my nightly indulgence," Eredel said, his smile tight and slightly pinched. "Tomorrow, we begin our journey, so you may want to rest in your rooms." He strolled through the door. Gala and Lela followed with heads down and tails unmoving.

Sarah looked at Timmy. "What do you think he's gonna do?"

Timmy shrugged. Sarah didn't feel like going to her room, so she stepped to the cabinet along the wall across from the hearth and examined the dusty books lining the shelves. Strange symbols ran along their bindings. One read *"Beles Cenarri Moni."*

Sarah tugged out the book and thumbed through the pages. The words were written in a mysterious language. At the back, she found a picture of a tree with dozens of beautiful blue fruit in its branches. The fruit glittered like jewels.

As she peered at the drawing, Sarah heard buzzing like a swarm of bees, then a loud explosion. She glanced at Timmy, who was fiddling with a metal gadget that whirled silently when he pushed it.

Timmy met her gaze. "He's doing it again."

Sarah crept to the door and cracked it open. Timmy ambled up. Gala and Lela lay crouched on the far side of the door, their snouts tucked under their paws.

Eredel stood in the center of the field. He extended one arm and a jagged line of electricity shot out from his open hand, racing over the grass in a brilliant burst of light before disappearing in an echoing boom. He swung his other arm into the air, and an electrical charge cut up into the sky, illuminating the meadow before vanishing in a ground-shaking blast.

Sarah's heart thumped. Eredel looked taller now, his shoulders thrown back and his eyes gleaming. He swung from right to left, firing electrical charges again and again into the night, leaving behind faint smoky lines and a burning smell. He continued firing charges for some ten minutes. Then he bent over gasping for air, his arms hanging toward the ground. He rocked from side to side, his face a mixture of joy and exhaustion.

Sarah glanced at Timmy. "I think he's done," she said in a hushed voice.

Eredel remained bent over for several minutes, but then he straightened and raised his arms again. An electrical charge raced into the sky, then another. The shots grew in volume and brilliance. He laughed crazily, shouting nonsensical words. Charges fired again and again until his exhaustion returned, and he tottered, almost falling. He dropped to his knees and leaned forward, resting his palms on the ground.

After some time, Eredel tried to rise again, but he couldn't and collapsed in the grass. Sarah cried out and pushed open the door. She started toward Eredel. He rolled over and raised his arms but seemed oblivious to her. Electricity shot into the night. Sarah slowed to a stop and watched. Eredel cackled in a crazed voice. It sent shivers down her spine. She turned and returned to the cottage.

Inside, Sarah looked at Timmy. "I can't watch this," she said. She headed to the back room and lay on the straw, her hands trembling and her stomach in knots. Timmy entered and sat across from her.

"Can we trust him?" Sarah asked. "He seems crazy."

"What else can we do?" Timmy said, crossing his arms.

The explosions continued but grew weaker and sporadic until they ended entirely. Sarah listened for several minutes but heard nothing more. She rose and went to the cottage door.

Outside, Eredel lay face down in the grass. Gala and Lela were crouched beside him. Sarah pushed the door open and made her way across the field.

"Are you okay?" she asked, kneeling beside Eredel.

He groaned.

A breeze gusted. Sarah shivered. "It's getting cold. You should come inside."

Eredel rolled over. "Young Sarah, now you have seen my disease. Beware of your gift, as its weakness may burrow into your soul."

Sarah didn't know what to say. She helped Eredel to his feet and walked with him slowly through the grass. He moved weakly as if an old man. The dogs trailed behind silently.

Inside, Eredel staggered to a chair and collapsed into it. He raised a shaky hand, brushing away wisps of gray hair.

Timmy stepped out of the back room. Eredel didn't meet his eyes.

"Why did you do that?" Timmy asked.

Eredel looked down at his hands. "I needed to," he said. "It's part of me."

"We don't understand," Sarah said. "Why couldn't you stop?"

Eredel coughed and wiped his mouth but didn't answer.

Sarah sighed. She returned to the backroom. Timmy followed her. They sat across from one another.

"We need to be careful," Sarah said. "There's something wrong with him. Maybe he can help us, but there's something wrong too."

Timmy peeked at the door before murmuring, "Where storms come, they will come again."

Sarah lay back on the straw and tried to calm down. She heard noises in the kitchen. Eredel was working. She wondered what he was doing, but she was too tired and drifted off to sleep. She awoke with a faint light flickering through a crack in the door. She peered out. Eredel was sitting at the table reading a large book. A candle burned beside him.

In the morning, Timmy's snoring woke Sarah. She rolled him onto his side to quiet him. Then she rose and stepped out of the room. Eredel was standing at the hearth, stirring something in a large pot.

"Morning," she said with a strained smile.

"Good morning, Sarah," Eredel replied with a slight stammer. "I'm sorry for last night, but now you have seen my weakness. Each day I must struggle with it. Some days, I succeed. Other days, I fail. Last night, I failed. I must be stronger, and I will be. We have a long journey ahead. You will not see my disease again until you and your friends are safe. The horses and ponies are ready. We will start this morning." He stirred the pot again.

Sarah woke Timmy. They ate breakfast, then packed food and gear onto the backs of the ponies, while Eredel led the two horses from the pasture and saddled them.

"Have you ridden before?" Eredel asked the children. Timmy said he had, but Sarah shook her head.

Eredel smiled. "That's fine. Marigo's an excellent tutor."

"Which one is Marigo?" Sarah asked.

Eredel led the children to the gray horse with white spots. "She's frisky but gentle and tireless."

"Can she carry both of us?"

"She's carried me many times. I think she can easily carry the two of you," Eredel said.

Sarah rubbed Marigo's neck. The mare dipped her head and fixed a gentle eye on Sarah. A warm feeling spread through Sarah. She liked this horse.

Eredel helped Timmy into the saddle and then lifted Sarah on behind him. He handed Timmy the reins and adjusted the stirrups, so Timmy's feet reached them. Eredel explained how to use the reins and stirrups, then he patted Marigo on the neck and said, "Okay, lady. Show them how it's done."

The mare set out, circling the meadow at a bumpy trot. Sarah almost fell off twice, but she held onto Timmy, and they returned safely to where they'd started.

"You are quick learners," Eredel said with a laugh. Then he mounted the golden horse, which he called Osa and whistled for the dogs. Gala and Lela came running.

"Gala, you're coming with us," Eredel said. "Lela, I trust you to take care of the farm while I'm away."

Lela gave a happy bark.

"Wonderful."

Holding a rope, Eredel led the three pack ponies behind Osa. Marigo followed the ponies, and Gala brought up the rear. They trotted to the northern corner of the farm, where Eredel guided Osa and the ponies across a shallow place in the stream. Marigo and Gala followed, and they started into the woods.

Sarah glanced back as the trees swallowed her view of the farm; the only place where she'd felt safe since coming to this land. She turned and stared ahead, wondering what dangers lay before them, and when they would find another safe place.

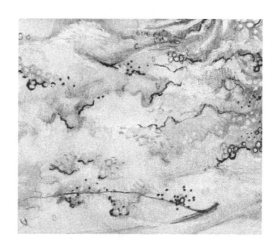

Chapter 14:
The Anolari

Josh sat up and pushed the blanket off his shoulders. A patchwork of kids lay sleeping around him. He took a slow breath. It was now the third day since ariving at Oriafen. Back home it was Sunday. He'd missed two soccer practices. His coach would be pissed. He was sweeper, and the district championships were next Thursday. If he weren't back, his coach would play Raymond Mont.

Josh missed the team, but he also liked it here. Despite all the strange things happening, he felt at home... like this was where he should be.

Still, something gnawed at him – guilt. His parents must be freaked. Everyone at school, all his friends and teachers probably thought the bus had been highjacked and kidnapped. It would be huge news back home, but no one knew the truth. Who'd believe that they'd driven through a blue light and been transported to a strange land? It was crazy.

Yesterday the fairies had led them to a waterfall so they could bathe and wash their clothes. Washing off the dirt and grime from the days outdoors felt good. After the bath, the fairies gave them each a towel and a colorful gown to wear. Only Celia, Annie, and Emma put on the gowns. None of the boys would. They just wrapped themselves in the towels until their clothes dried out.

Josh rubbed the sleep out of his eyes. He squinted, spying Wesley on the far side of the clearing doing sit-ups. Josh rose and headed across the clearing.

"Hey dude, it's too early for a workout," Josh said, as he strode up.

"I know," Wesley replied, "but I couldn't sleep. I started walking around last night. The copper sprites probably thought I wanted to escape or something and followed me like little stalkers. But when the sun came up, they went back to their posts. I still wasn't tired, so I started doing these exercises."

Josh eyed his friend and his natural frown deepened. Wesley looked gaunt, with dark rings under his eyes and brown splotches covering his skin. Josh knew Wesley hadn't slept for six nights... not since the night the yellow beast drove into the meadow.

"Don't stress about things," Josh said. "You should relax. I know it's hard with your sister gone and all, but you need to take it easy. You need to rest."

Wesley lay back. "I'm trying, but I feel weird, and this numbness in my feet is bothering me."

"Huh? Numb?" Josh asked.

"Yeah, it started a couple of days ago in my toes. Now it's spread up above my ankles."

"Whoa..." Josh said, shaking his head. "One more strange thing," He rested his hand on Wesley's shoulder. "Take it easy. If the numbing gets worse, let me know."

Wesley nodded and resumed his sit-ups.

Josh made his way toward the middle of the glade, passing several pools with mist floating off the water. *What are we going to do?* He wondered. *We can't stay here forever.* The old silver fairy said he had a friend who could help them, but so far no one had shown up.

Josh slowed to a stop and stared at the enormous crystal rising at the end of the glade. Barth had said it was a diamond. Josh shook his head. He couldn't believe that. It was too big – a thousand times larger than the biggest diamond he'd ever heard of.

A fairy darted out of an opening high in the crystal rock and drifted down toward the pools. As the tiny creature neared, Josh recognized the shimmering gown and blond hair of the golden fairy. He'd learned her name was Sirie – short for Siriena – and she was the daughter of Theralin, the chief of the fairies.

Sirie landed on the grass beside Celia. She tapped the young girl's cheek and whispered something in her ear. Celia opened her eyes, and her face lit up. She began talking excitedly, her fingers twirling as she spoke. Sirie listened, a smile playing on her face.

Celia spoke in English but also used a few fairy words she'd learned. Josh listened, wondering how much Sirie understood. When they'd first met, Sirie didn't speak any English, but in the few days since she had picked up a surprising number of words.

Josh had learned a few words by listening to the fairies and talking to Sirie, but Annie was picking up the language even faster and could already hold long conversations. Most of the other kids were struggling to learn a word or two. Josh smiled, remembering yesterday when Ted tried to tell the fairies how much he loved music. He said something wrong because several of the fairies turned bright red, and the others laughed hysterically.

Celia's high-pitched voice filled the air. She was singing a song the fairies had taught her. This woke several of the kids, who sat up and began talking while the Panishie laid out cakes and fruit by the pools.

Josh was hungry and headed over to the chow. As he stuck a cake in his mouth, he felt a tap on the shoulder. He turned to find the golden fairy perched there.

"Hey," he said, through a mouthful of cake.

"Hey," Sirie replied with an impish smile. "Happy morning."

Josh swallowed. "Yeah, happy… so happy, I'm bored," he said. "There's nothing to do around here but eat and play."

"Yes, you rest and have fun," Sirie said, her expression turning serious. "Later, hard things."

"What?" Josh said. "What kind of hard things?"

"Long walk."

"Walk to where?"

"Silver City – safe place."

"Silver City?" Josh repeated. "Where's that?"

"Far away. Long walk."

Josh's brow creased. He wondered how far she meant. He took another bite of cake. As he chewed, fairies gathered around the other kids, talking and laughing. The fairies asked questions and joked, though none, other than Sirie, came near him.

"Why are you the only one who talks to me?" Josh asked.

Sirie pursed her lips. She gave him a mischievous grin. "They afraid you."

"Why?"

"You different."

"Different from what?"

"Different from others."

Josh stared at Sirie skeptically. "Are you afraid of me?"

She tipped her head back and laughed. "No."

"Why not?"

"Because we same," she said as if it were a silly question.

He was confused. "How are we the same?"

"Many ways," Sirie said. She hovered close to his face and tapped his cheek lightly with her fingers. "We lead."

He wasn't sure what she meant. Sirie floated up to his forehead and touched strands of his hair. Then she ran her fingers along his skin. Josh blushed, and he heard Annie and Celia giggle.

"Stop that," he said.

Sirie floated back a few inches and tipped her head to the side. "Why?"

"Because it feels weird."

"Okay, but you pretty."

"Huh?" Josh's mind went blank. "Oh," he finally stammered, "so are you."

"I know," she said matter-of-factly. "But why you not smile?"

"What?" Josh said. He coughed to clear his throat.

"You pretty, but you not smile."

"I smile," he said frowning.

Sirie laughed. "Not much. And now you..." She hunched her shoulders and screwed up her face, "...that."

Josh couldn't help but smile. "You've seen me at the wrong times," he said, rolling his eyes.

Sirie shrugged. There was an awkward silence, then Josh remembered what he'd wanted to ask her.

"Why do the fairies keep hurting my brother's bird?"

Sirie's smile faded, and she let out a deep sigh. *"Beo doth dia moya."*

Josh knew those words. *Doth* meant to break, and *dia* meant law.

"How could a bird break a law?"

"You not understand," Sirie said with a dismissive wave of her hand.

"I know... That's why I'm asking you."

Sirie closed her mouth and glared. She darted away.

Josh shook his head. For three days, the fairies had ignored Dylan and bullied his little bird. They darted over when Dylan wasn't paying attention and struck Cherry with the blunt ends of their silver blades. Then they'd dash away. Cherry would screech. Dylan would chase the tormentors, but they were too quick for him.

Josh heard a fart like the punching of a pillow. He turned to see Dylan hopping over with Cherry fluttering beside him. Dylan landed in front of Josh and glowered. "Why do you even talk to her? She's just like the rest of them."

Josh knew he meant Sirie. "She's not bad, Dylan. There's been some kind of misunderstanding."

"No, it's really simple – she and the rest of 'em hate my bird, and they want Cherry out of here, but she's not going anywhere. She's staying with me!"

"Good," Josh said, "she should stay. But something's strange. Look around... You don't see any other birds. And you don't hear any in the trees. Why?"

"Because the fairies hate them. They chase them away," Dylan said, his hands closing into fists.

Josh thought Dylan might be right. He changed the subject. "I hear you're making a cool hideout."

Dylan grunted; his face still flushed with anger. "Yeah," he said after a moment. "We're almost finished digging. It's deep. When it's done, we're going to lay branches and leaves on top so no one can find it."

"Awesome," Josh said. "I'd like to see it when you're done."

"For sure," Dylan said, a smile returning to his face. He bounded toward Rhea, who was sitting alone at the edge of a pool.

Rhea shared Dylan's loathing of the fairies. She hadn't forgiven them for refusing to search for Sarah and Timmy. She ate the fairies' food but wouldn't talk to them or participate in any of their games. She spent her time reading and exercising. The fairies avoided her and didn't bother Dylan or Cherry when they were near her.

A tapestry of sound filled the air. Josh saw Ted waving his arms around as if he were trying to catch a dozen butterflies. Josh listened to the music. It seemed to be getting better every day. The fairies loved it. Hundreds would follow Ted around as he played, some fairies even joining in with their own curious instruments.

Ted made music happily, but Josh was worried. Ted didn't seem to eat much, and he was losing weight. His clothes hung loosely on his large frame. When Josh asked him about it, Ted laughed and said he was on a "music diet."

Some distance from Ted, the Kadean sisters sat by a pool with a dozen fairies hovering around them. Emma whispered in Mya's ear and giggled. Josh's brow furrowed. The recent change in Emma unsettled him. Before they'd come to Oriafen, Emma was nervous and worried all the time. Now she was happier than a bee in a bed of flowers, laughing and chatting with the fairies and the other kids.

Mya seemed as surprised by her sister's change as Josh was. She watched Emma with a confused, befuddled look.

There was also something strange about Mya. Even from this distance, Josh could see her eyes were different. There was a faint white film covering her pupils. Yesterday, when they walked to the waterfall, Emma had to hold Mya's hand and lead her through the woods, to keep her from bumping into things. When Josh asked Mya what was wrong, she said things looked fuzzy and a muddle of colors.

This troubled Josh. CPU didn't hear well either. Was it something about this place? Had they gotten sick? He didn't know. CPU was getting worse. Josh had to shout now for CPU to hear anything.

Josh finished his cake and washed it down with a glass of the clear liquid, which the kids called fairy juice. He strolled among patches of flowers. He passed Annie, who was chatting with several fairies. She had learned the fairies called themselves the Panishie, which meant "prism creatures." They first came to this glade after a shower of fire from the sky left crystal stones buried in the ground.

Josh stared at the towering crystal rock, which the fairies called Oriafar, as hundreds of tiny winged creatures streamed out of openings. The fairies danced and sang in lines circling the glade. When they finished their singing, a band of copper sprites brought three small chests out and set them on the grass. One chest contained green garments, another had red garments, and the third held tiny silver gloves.

The colorful fairies separated themselves into two groups. One group slipped on the green garments over their gowns, while the other group donned the red garments. Then each fairy tugged on a pair of silver gloves.

The groups formed two lines—one green and one red—facing each other above a pool at the center of the clearing. Leaders were chosen for each side. A fairy in a gray gown led the red team, while Sirie led the green side.

Elderly copper sprites gave instructions to each team. Two fairies in the green line began to tussle. One touched the other with a silver glove, and the other fairy fell out of the air, splashing into the water below. Three copper sprites darted down and fished out the fallen fairy, who appeared unconscious. They carried the fairy and lay him down on the grass, while the other troublemaker was scolded by the elderly copper sprites.

After the commotion died down, the clearing fell quiet. Josh caught Wesley's eyes and sensed he was eager to see what was going to happen.

A whistle sounded, and the lines launched at one another. The fairies moved so quickly that Josh could hardly see them. The goal seemed to be to knock out members of the other team using the silver gloves.

The fairies dodged and darted as the lines rolled back and forth. Soon more than half of the participants were lying on the grass. Sirie was a blur of motion at the head of the green team, battling red opponents and knocking one after another out of the air.

The red line weakened until the greens broke through and divided them. The greens surrounded both groups, and the skirmish continued until a handful of red fighters remained. A copper sprite blew a whistle, and the match ended. The greens celebrated the victory. Sirie hugged each of her teammates. Then her eyes found Josh, and she glided over.

"You see? We fast and win," she exclaimed, waving her hands around excitedly.

"You mean you're fast," Josh said. "I saw who was taking out most of those red fairies."

Sirie grinned. "You watch more. See how good we are." She darted away.

After a short rest, the fairies reassembled into red and green teams. Then an argument broke out, which wasn't settled until Sirie moved to the red team, and several red fairies joined the green side.

The teams readied for another skirmish. The red side massed in a pyramid shape with Sirie at the point, while the green side formed into a cube.

A whistle rang, and the reds attacked, leading with their point. To Josh's surprise, both sides kept their formation as the fighting intensified.

Sirie was a blur of motion, and the pyramid rapidly cut through the cube, dividing the green team. The greens retreated and formed into a pair of walls that closed back on the pyramid, squeezing it into the shape of a ball.

The fighting raged until only five of the red fairies remained, surrounded by twice their number in green. Sirie led the red fairies, while a boy in a blue gown under his green uniform led the greens. Sirie extended her hand to the blue one, saying something which sparked laughter among her comrades.

"I know that blue fairy," Celia said. "He was the one who helped Sirie save me."

The blue fairy spread his arms to each side and said something which generated laughter and clapping from his teammates. Sirie frowned and launched at the blue one. They fought one on one as the other fairies skirmished among themselves, but soon Sirie lost all her teammates, and she alone faced six greens.

The green fairies circled warily, seeming hesitant to attack. Sirie gave a shrill cry and struck in a whirlwind. One by one the greens dropped into the pool until only the blue fairy remained.

Sirie paused to catch her breath.

"So, who's gonna win?" Josh asked Celia.

"Sirie, of course," Celia said confidently.

Quicker than a hummingbird, the golden fairy attacked, becoming a blur of motion. The blue fairy defended himself desperately. The attack raged for long minutes until Sirie drew back, her face red and her shoulders slumped.

The blue fairy studied the golden one warily. Then he darted forward with lightning quickness. Sirie became still. She fell out of the sky, dropping into the waiting arms of three copper sprites.

The green team celebrated, and a mass of fairies swarmed the clearing. Josh lost sight of Sirie and the blue one. Copper sprites gathered the uniforms and gloves, then carried them away.

The celebration turned into a festival, and fairies brought out platters of fruit and cakes. After grabbing some fruit, Josh searched for Sirie. He spotted her resting on the grass at the edge of a pond near the towering crystal. She was surrounded by a dozen colorful fairies and looked groggy.

As Josh neared, the blue fairy flew up and landed beside Sirie. She tried to push him away, but the blue one dodged the move, and she fell over. The other fairies laughed, and the blue one leaned down to help her up. Sirie grabbed his arm and pulled him to the ground. They rolled until she was on top. She pinned his arms and said something. Then, to Josh's surprise, she leaned forward and kissed his cheek. Josh turned on his heels, heading back the way he'd come.

Later in the morning, the Panishie hurried about in what seemed to be nervous excitement. Hundreds of fairies poured out of the great crystal stone, joining those already in the clearing. The fairies assembled in rows by color. As order formed out of the chaos, everything quieted.

Josh spotted movement in the woods west of the clearing. He angled himself to get a better look. A dozen short figures stepped out of the trees. The figures strode into the glade with an air of authority. They stood about two feet in height and wore dark cloaks over brown tunics tied at the waist. Their faces had the bronzed, weathered look of those who spent much time in the sun. Slender blades hung from their belts, while bows and quivers rested on their shoulders.

To Josh's surprise, the newcomers marched right past the rows of Panishie and continued trudging along the perimeter of the clearing. As they circled the glade, Josh noticed short wings protruding from their backs. He inhaled sharply in surprise. They were fairies, though much larger than the Panishie.

The small band circled the clearing, bowing to the copper sprites as they passed. Finally, they returned to the rows of Panishie and halted there.

A horn sounded. Theralin, the old silver fairy, glided down from Oriafar surrounded by a dozen copper sprites. The newcomers dropped to one knee and bowed their heads as Theralin alighted on the grass. The silver fairy floated up to eye level with the leader of the newcomers and extended his hands, palms facing the sky. The other did the same, palms facing the earth. Their hands rested together for a moment, then they both laughed and began chatting like old friends.

With surprised looks at one another, the kids waited along with the rest of the fairies. After several minutes, Theralin motioned to the other newcomers, and they rose. Josh counted fifteen in all. Theralin extended his hands palms up to each of the newcomers as he had their leader, and they returned the gesture palms down.

Then Theralin introduced Sirie and soared back to Oriafar. After a brief conversation with Sirie, the newcomers marched over to the children. The leader scanned their faces. Then he said, "I am told you speak the English language."

The children gasped.

"Yes, we do," Josh said hurriedly.

"Good," the leader replied. "I am Leoku, and these are my companions. We are the Anolari, though some call us ranger fairies."

"It's awesome to meet you," Josh said excitedly. He introduced himself and each of the kids.

Leoku scrutinized the children. "It is a wonder that so many gifted ones have come to our land. This is a cause for celebration. A cenarri moni has been found."

"A what?" Josh asked.

"A cenarri moni... the fruit of power," Leoku said. "In your language, it is the sapphire fruit. But we will speak of that later.

Now, you must prepare for your departure. The danger is near. Your enemies will return, and the Panishie cannot protect you.

A wave of fear passed through the kids.

"You mean the black birds?" Josh asked, clearing his throat. "The fairies handled them pretty nicely."

Leoku shook his head. "Their master has other servants and more powerful. They will come for you. You are not safe. You must go to Feriyan, the Silver City. Only the silver cat can protect you."

There was murmuring among the kids.

"What master do you mean? And why does he want us?" Wesley asked.

"He is Sidtarr, the usurper of Risrean. He covets your gifts — your powers. When you came to this world, you each received a power. Perhaps you have discovered it." Leoku glanced around. "Sidtarr covets your powers. He seeks them for his own ends."

The children became quiet.

"You mentioned a place called Feriyan," Josh said. "Where is that?"

"A kingdom many days journey to the south. At the heart of Feriyan is the Silver City, where the silver cat resides."

"A cat?" Dylan asked.

"He is not an ordinary cat. He can protect you."

Celia stepped forward. "But we want to go home."

Leoku gave her a gentle look. "I'm sorry, child. We cannot take you home, but we can lead you to a safe place."

Celia rubbed her cheeks, and tears welled up in her eyes. Josh wrapped his arms around her and said to Leoku, "Two of our friends are lost in the woods. We need to find them before we can go."

The ranger fairy frowned and spoke to the Panishie. Josh couldn't understand most of what was said, but after some back and forth, Leoku turned to the kids. "Your friends have taken another path," he said. "They have found a protector. Do not fear for them."

"That's what Theralin said," Wesley cried, "but one of them is my sister. We need to find her and Timmy. We need to get them back with us."

Leoku's eyes narrowed, and he shook his head. "I'm sorry. You may find them one day, but you must follow your own path."

"What do you mean?" Rhea cried, her face reddening. "We've been following paths for days, and we're no closer to home. Don't play word games with us. We need to find our friends."

Leoku's face turned expressionless, and he did not reply.

Ted stretched his arms and crossed them over his chest. "Guys, I'm sorry, but I'm not going anywhere," he said. "My feet can't do any more walking. Besides, this place is a paradise. I'm staying put unless we find a way to go home."

Emma pushed into the space next to Ted. "Yeah, this place is wonderful. How can we think of leaving?"

"But we're in danger," Annie said. "That Sidtarr guy is hunting us."

Several kids started to speak at once. Josh raised his voice and quieted everyone. "Okay, we need to talk about this among ourselves."

He led the children across the clearing and crouched before them. "So, what do you want to do?"

"Gooo," Bobby said, bobbing his head vigorously. "Daangeer heeree. Muust goo."

Wesley sighed. "I can't leave without Sarah and Timmy."

"But you heard Leoku," Josh replied. "Someone is protecting them. Maybe they're okay."

Wesley grit his teeth.

Emma nodded. "We should find them first. Mya can't go anyway. Something's happened to her eyes. She can barely see."

Mya frowned at her sister. "I can go if everyone else does. I just need someone to help me."

"You heard Leoku say it's dangerous here," Annie said. "I think we should go to that Silver City he talked about."

"But how can we trust him?" Rhea countered.

"He's a friend of the Panishie, and the Panishie have helped us."

"Yeah, and they also took us prisoner, and won't search for Sarah and Timmy."

"They hate birds," Dylan cried. "They're cuckoo! I'm getting out of here."

"I'm down to go," Gabrielle said. "Things are pretty chill here, but it's getting to be a snooze."

"I miss home," Celia said, sniffling.

"I'm staying put," Barth declared. "CPU and I are almost finished with our hideout. If the birds or something else comes, we can hide there."

Josh eyed CPU, who was staring off into the distance. "How about it, CPU? What do you want to do?"

CPU didn't hear Josh, so he repeated the question louder. Barth tapped CPU's shoulder. CPU turned, looking surprised that everyone was staring at him. "What? What happened?"

"Do you want to go or stay?" Josh asked.

CPU pointed to Barth. "Whatever he decides."

Josh grimaced. "Okay, some of us want to stay, and others want to go. But we should stick together, so we need to agree on this."

The arguments grew more heated. Minutes passed, and no one changed anyone's mind. Josh rubbed his temples, feeling a headache coming on. He needed to think, to clear his thoughts.

"I'll be back in a bit," he said to Wesley. He strolled into the trees. He walked until he happened upon a creek gurgling over mossy rocks. He slumped against a granite boulder and took a deep breath, watching the sunlight shimmer on the water.

He didn't know what to do. He believed what Leoku said… that they were in danger. But many of the kids wanted to stay. He was worried about Mya and CPU, and he didn't know how far Ted could walk.

A buzzing tickled his ear. He turned. Sirie was hovering there. She eyed him with concern.

"Anea feo dath?"

Josh's gaze dropped. "No, I'm just frustrated."

"*Dimu feo grea?*"

"Yes," he said, nodding, "we need to go. We need to get to a safe place and find our way home."

Sirie stared hard at him and said, "*Mea jui owali.*" Then she darted off.

Find it together? Josh thought, translating her words. *What does that mean?*

A breeze rustled branches. Josh tipped his head. He reached into his pocket and tugged out a thin leather wallet. Inside, he found a faded picture of his mom. She was walking with him through a park on a winter day. He was probably three years old. She was holding his hand and gazing at him lovingly. When he felt down or confused, he liked to look at this picture. It made him feel better.

He thought of his friend, Artie Reynolds. What would Artie say? He'd say, "Josh is a doer." Artie's favorite word. "Doer."

Josh nodded to himself. He stuffed the picture back into his wallet. He had to get the kids to a safe place. He couldn't force them, but he had to try. And, he needed help. He needed Wesley and Annie and Rhea. Together they'd get it done.

A gleam returned to Josh's eyes. He rose and started back through the woods, feeling hopeful again. When he reached the glade, everything was strangely quiet. The kids had drifted into scattered groups. Few of the Panishie could be seen, and the Anolari were sleeping in a circle beside one of the pools.

Dylan jogged over. "Where have you been?"

"I needed to think."

"Those Anolari are so cool! They like Cherry. They stroked her feathers and talked to her. They kept saying 'brave' and pointing to her. They're not like those psycho rainbow fairies."

"Why are they all asleep?"

Dylan shrugged. "After eating, they all lay down. Now they're snoring like lawn mowers."

"Where's Wes?"

"Don't know."

Dylan grabbed his pants and bounded away. Josh strode through the clearing, passing colorful flowers and dark pools. He spotted Wesley sitting under a tree.

"Hey, dude, how're you feeling?" Josh said as he strode up.

"I'm okay," Wesley said, with a slight wince.

Josh put his hand on his friend's shoulder. "We need to get the kids to a safe place, and I need your help."

Wesley rubbed his forehead. "But I can't leave Sarah and Timmy behind… Would you leave Dylan?"

Josh knelt and met Wesley's gaze. "Not if there was any way possible. But think about it. We don't know where they are. We don't know how to find them. We only know someone is protecting them. Waiting around here won't help Timmy and Sarah. But we've got other kids we need to get to a safe place. The ranger fairies will take us to the Silver City. Leoku says that silver cat will protect us."

Wesley closed his eyes. He tipped his head back. "Sarah had a dream about a silver cat the night before we came to this place. She dreamt it over and over. Now there's a silver cat who people say can protect us. Isn't that weird?"

"Yeah, it's quite a coincidence. Maybe it means something. Maybe that's why we should go there." Josh rose. "Think it over, man. I'll be back in a bit."

Wesley nodded. Josh headed away. He passed a crowd of fairies talking in hushed voices. Sirie flew down from Oriafar with four copper sprites trailing her. She glided up to him, her face flushed.

"What's wrong?" Josh asked.

"*Beao wenna ana,*" Sirie said, her eyes flashing angrily.

"Why are they following you?"

"*Metia ana geo grea iwa feo cien Anolari, ipa ana Theralin mana ba.*"

Josh's brow knitted as he tried to translate the words. "You want to go with us, and your father says 'No'?"

Sirie nodded.

"He's right. This is your home. And, some of the kids want to stay here, anyway. You can help them."

Sirie's expression hardened. "I do what I want. No one stops me."

Josh pointed at the copper sprites. "Those guys might try."

Sirie's wings whirled in a blur. "They useless," she said, almost spitting the words.

"Okay, okay. It's up to you," Josh said, raising his hands.

Sirie's face softened, and she darted to his shoulder. "You nice, Josh. You good."

The four sprites eyed Josh warily. He shrugged, knowing Sirie was happy because she got what she wanted.

He turned. On the far side of a nearby pool, Emma and Mya were sitting among a crowd of fairies. Emma seemed in a good mood, laughing and chatting with the crowd. He wondered what she and Mya would do. Emma wanted to stay, but Mya was torn. Mya wanted to go to a safe place but didn't want to leave her sister.

Emma moved her hands, and the light around her seemed to crease and fold. The sisters vanished. Josh took a sharp breath. A moment later, the light unfolded, and the girls reappeared. A crowd of fairies broke into excited clapping. Josh shook his head. He'd seen Emma do this several times over the past couple days. She seemed to be able to warp and twist light with her hands.

"Did you see that?"

Sirie followed his gaze. "Setha hia?"

"Emma and Mya disappeared. Then they reappeared."

Sirie frowned. "What?"

"Emma. Watch Emma."

Sirie fixed her eyes on the girl.

Emma said something to Mya and turned her hands again. The light creased, and the lower half of her body momentarily vanished. The fairies cried in delight again.

"Stop it, Em," Mya said. "You're making them crazy."

"I know. It's fun," Emma said, rocking her hands and making her body disappear up to her shoulders.

211

Sirie squinted. Then she recoiled, her eyes wide. "It her! It her!"

"What? Who?"

"Emma. She like her. Now I remember."

Josh blinked, feeling confused.

Sirie clapped her hands eagerly. Her wings fluttered.

"Who's she like?" Josh asked.

"My sister."

"You have a sister?"

"Yes, I go now. Bye."

Sirie darted off with the copper sprites hurrying to keep up. He stared at Emma. There was something about her. She had a calm, cool beauty. She wasn't his type, but he knew why Wesley had a huge crush.

Josh remembered he wanted to talk to Annie. He headed across the clearing and found her with Rhea, Gabrielle, and Celia. The girls were sitting beside a crystal stone sticking half out of the ground.

"So, have you decided?" he asked.

Annie smiled. "Yeah, we're going," she said, glancing at the other girls for confirmation.

"Great," Josh said with a sigh. "But you guys know it won't be easy. That Silver City is far away. We'll be walking for many days."

"For sure," Annie said.

"Yeah, we'll pull our weight," Rhea added.

Josh felt relieved. He headed back toward the Kadean sisters. As he neared them, a band of fairies glided down from Oriafar, including Sirie and Theralin. The fairies flew up to Emma and Mya and hovered there.

"I tell my father to see you," Sirie said to Emma, "so he come."

"Okay," Emma replied with apparent confusion. She smiled at the old silver fairy, who stared back somberly. Emma bit her lip and tugged on Mya's sleeve. Mya coughed and didn't seem to know what was going on. Josh doubted she could see the fairies clearly.

There was an awkward silence. Emma cleared her throat. "We love it here," she said. "Thank you for letting us stay."

Theralin stared. Mya turned to her sister, sensing something amiss. She started to speak but stopped when Theralin turned and floated away. Sirie shrugged and followed her father.

Josh strode over to the girls. "What was that about?"

Emma shook her head. "We don't know."

Josh paused for a moment, watching the fairies leave. He asked. "Have you decided if you're going to the Silver City?"

Emma frowned. Mya gazed at her sister skeptically.

"It feels safe here," Emma said. "This is the only place that's felt safe to me since we left the yellow beast. I know if I leave, I'll get scared again."

"But feeling safe doesn't mean you are safe," Josh said.

"Will we be safe walking on our own to the Silver City? I'd rather stay where the Panishie can protect us."

Josh glanced at Mya. Her eyes seemed unfocused, and a white film covered her pupils.

"I'd like to go," Mya said, "but it would be hard. Someone would need to guide me. And I can't leave Emma."

"I understand," Josh said, "but most of the kids are going, and I was hoping to keep everyone together. Please keep thinking about it."

The girls said they would. Josh headed off to find Barth and CPU. As he guessed, they were working on their hideout. Josh found them lugging dirt out of a big hole. He talked to them for several minutes, but they were determined to stay. He left, feeling more discouraged.

As he stepped into the clearing, Josh spotted Theralin fluttering aimlessly along the bank of a pool. Sirie hovered nearby. The old fairy landed on a stone protruding from the bank and sat with his hands clasped under his chin. Sirie alighted beside him and whispered something in his ear. Theralin waved her away. Sirie rose into the air. She saw Josh and rolled her eyes. Then she glided back to Oriafar with the four copper sprites shadowing her.

Josh didn't know what to make of Theralin; something had upset the old fairy.

Josh spied Wesley sitting beside a shallow pool with his feet hanging in the water and made a beeline toward him.

"Hey dude, I talked to Annie and Rhea. They want to go to the Silver City. Dylan, Celia, Bobby, and Gabrielle will too. After we get those kids to a safe place, you and I can go looking for Sarah and Timmy. Okay?"

Wesley stared back. "You'll do that?"

"Absolutely," Josh said.

Wesley nodded. "I keep thinking about Sarah. She dreamed about that silver cat over and over. There must be a reason. Maybe it's at that Silver City... I think I'll go."

A smile spread across Josh's face, and he leaped forward, giving Wesley a tight hug. "Alright man, we'll leave tomorrow. Get some sleep tonight."

"I'll try," Wesley said, with an uncertain smile.

Josh patted his back.

Josh was suddenly thirsty and went to find his pack. He pulled out his water bottle and drank. Then he lay down, resting his head on the bag, and closed his eyes. He awoke sometime later to a low rumble. The ground was trembling beneath him.

Josh sat up. The Panishie were flying to the great stone, and the kids were hurrying into the woods. The Anolari sat in a circle beside a nearby pool, seeming unconcerned with the rising noise.

The sound rose to a roar, and the fireball swept across the sky. Josh ducked and covered his face with his hands as a hot wind slammed into the clearing. Everything quieted. Josh strolled over to the ranger fairies

"What is that thing?" he asked Leoku, pointing at the sky. "Why does it keep flying by?"

"It is a reminder," Leoku said, his face solemn. "A reminder from a distant power."

"What do you mean?"

Leoku shook his head. "We will talk of it later."

Josh tipped his head and looked away. He ambled over to a tree and leaned against it. The glade was beautiful in the early evening light. He heard a faint flutter. He saw Sirie gliding down from Oriafar dressed in strange clothes… brown pants and a gray shirt. Her golden locks were tied back in a bun.

"What's going on?" he asked as she flew up. "Why are you dressed like that?"

"*Metia feo*," she said.

"Huh? What did I do?"

"I go with you."

"Your father said 'yes'?"

"Yes, he at peace now. So, I go."

"What changed his mind?"

"Emma."

"Emma?" Josh asked. "Why Emma?"

Chapter 15:
Departure

Annie rubbed the sleep from her eyes as the Anolari noiselessly emerged from the woods. At the far end of the pool, Wesley paced. Annie frowned. Wesley looked gaunt and pale like he was sick or hadn't eaten for days. He seemed tense and worried. She wondered what had happened to the easygoing, happy guy she knew. Annie rolled over in the blanket. Celia lay asleep beside her. Annie gently pushed strands of hair off the younger girl's face. Celia opened her eyes.

"Good morning," Annie said with a wistful smile.

Celia sat up. "Do we have to go?"

Annie sighed. "We do. It's dangerous here. We have to go to a safe place."

"But what about Barth and CPU? Aren't they going?"

"No, I don't think so," Annie said, grimacing. She was furious at Barth. He had the silly idea that he could dig a hole in the ground and hide there from the huge birds. Did he really believe they wouldn't find him? And of course, CPU went along with the idea like a good little lemming.

"What about Mya and Emma?" Celia asked.

"They don't want to go either," Annie said, with a deep frown. "Ted neither."

"Why?"

"They've made up their minds, and they're too stubborn to change them. They like it here and want to stay even though they know it isn't safe. Josh thinks we should go. I trust Josh."

Annie tugged on her shoes and helped Celia with hers.

A few minutes later, they were eating breakfast with Bobby and Gabrielle. Josh strolled up. "Be sure to pack as much food as you can into your bags," he said. "The ranger fairies say there won't be much to eat on the other side of the mountains."

Celia caught Josh's eye. "I'm scared," she said quivering. "What if we don't have enough food? What if we starve? What if those black birds find us?"

"I think we'll have enough food, and we'll be with the Anolari," Josh said. "They'll guide us. Rhea and Wesley are going too. Together, we'll be okay."

Josh looked away. Annie thought she sensed uncertainty in his eyes. She wondered if he believed his own words.

After breakfast, Annie helped Celia pack. As they stuffed their belongings into their bags, Ted's music carried through the clearing. Annie turned and saw Ted sitting at the edge of a pool, lost in his beautiful sounds.

She walked over and tapped his shoulder. "Hey, big guy. Won't you come with us? We're going to miss your music."

Ted dropped his arms and peered up at her. "I'm still hoping you'll all come to your senses. There aren't many pastures greener than this. I don't see how leaving makes sense."

"Yeah, this is a wonderful place, but it's not safe here," Annie said. "The fairies told us so."

Ted shrugged. "Are we safer walking for days on our own to some strange city?"

"Teedd," Bobby shouted and jogged over. "Ii soorry saay gooodbyye. Thiis foor yoouu."

Bobby stuck out his hand.

"What have you got there?" Ted asked. There was a thumb-sized silver whistle in Bobby's palm hanging on a thin silver chain. Ted picked up the whistle. "Where'd you get this?"

"Iii maadee iit."

"Huh?... How'd you make it?"

Bobby extended his hands and cupped them together.

"Don't joke with me, Bob. You can't make a whistle with just your hands."

"Ii doo," Bobby said, nodding emphatically. "Ii shoow you."

Bobby cupped his palms together and closed his eyes. He leaned forward. His face briefly flushed. It returned to normal. He opened his hands. A silver coin lay in his right palm.

Ted snorted. He reached out and picked up the coin.

"So, you've learned a magic trick!"

"Noo, ii maadee iit!" Bobby cried.

Ted examined the coin. "You made this? And the whistle? How did you do that?"

Bobby grinned and folded his arms over his chest.

"Well, that is talent," Ted said, slapping Bobby on the back. "You'll never be short of cash and always be ready to ref a game."

Annie chuckled, wondering where Bobby had found the whistle and coin.

"Itt prooteect yoouu," Bobby said, raising his hands and shaking them about like there was magic in them.

"What will protect me?"

"Thee whiistlee!"

"Really? What does it sound like?" Ted said, putting the whistle to his lips.

Bobby's eyes widened in alarm. He reached out to stop Ted, but the large boy leaned away and blew. Annie heard nothing, but suddenly every fairy in the clearing dropped out of the air or crumpled to the ground.

Ted flinched and pulled the whistle out of his mouth. "Uh-oh... what just happened?"

Before Annie could reply, a dozen ranger fairies sprang to their feet and charged at Ted with bows drawn.

"Hey, hey," Ted hollered raising his hands in the air. "Didn't mean to upset."

Annie was about to scream to freeze the ranger fairies when Leoku barked an order, and the Anolari halted, their bows aimed at Ted. Leoku strode over, his jaw tight.

"That object is dangerous," he said, indicating the whistle. "The sound harms Anolari and other creatures."

"I'm sorry," Ted said, with obvious concern. "I had no idea. I definitely won't use it again." He threw the object to the ground.

Leoku picked it up and handed it back to Ted.

"No, keep it safe," he said. "It may be useful someday." He turned and led the ranger fairies away.

Annie let out a sigh.

Ted glared at Bobby. "Is this some kind of dog whistle? Are you trying to get me killed?"

"Itt foor prooteect yoouu. Noot plaay wiith."

Annie suppressed a laugh.

"Well, give me a heads-up next time," Ted said scowling.

"Yoouu keeep iit?"

"Yeah, I'll keep it."

Ted dropped the chain around his neck, and the whistle disappeared under his shirt.

After everyone had packed up, Josh led the kids to the south side of Oriafen, where the Anolari had assembled. Hundreds of Panishie hovered there.

Sirie flew out of the crowd of fairies dressed in the different clothes Annie had seen her wearing the night before. Four copper sprites flew along behind her.

"Why is Sirie dressed like that?" Celia asked.

"She's coming with us," Annie said with a wink.

"Yay!" Celia said grinning and bouncing on her toes.

A bell rang out, and a band of fairies flew down from the towering crystal rock. They were led by the blue fairy who Annie had seen in the scrimmage the day before. The blue fairy spoke quietly to Leoku. Then Leoku turned to the children.

"The Panishie have gifts for their departing friends."

The blue fairy went first to Josh and gave him a small green pouch. He gave other pouches to Wesley, Rhea, Gabrielle, and Annie. Annie peeked into hers and saw silky gray material.

"Use care," Leoku said. "Those are *filia dio*, which means silence gloves. Do not touch the silvery edge."

"Why are they called silence gloves?" Annie asked.

"Because they cause silence," Leoku said with a curious smile.

Annie stuck her fingers into the pouch to pull out the material. She avoided the silvery edge but couldn't get a good grip and pushed her hand deeper into the pouch. Suddenly her arm went numb. The numbness spread through her body, and she fell to the ground. Annie heard cries and Celia squatted in front of her.

"Are you okay?" Celia asked with a worried expression.

Annie couldn't speak.

"Do not fear," Leoku said, kneeling beside Celia. "The needles of the *filia dio* have pierced her, but the effects are temporary."

"Can you hear me?" Celia asked, peering into Annie's eyes. Annie stared back, unable to talk or even blink.

Josh plucked the silky material from his pouch and shook it out. It was a thin fabric in the shape of two gloves with a silvery surface on the palm and the underside of the fingers. It looked like a big version of the gloves the fairies had worn in their game the day before.

Josh gently tugged one of the gloves onto his hand. "Hey, Dylan," he said. "Come over here, bro. Let's test this out."

"No way. Stay back!" Dylan shouted and bounded away with a stinker like a nervous goat.

Josh laughed.

Sensation crept back into Annie's limbs, and she sat upright. She watched as the Panishie gave silver rings to Bobby and Celia. Both rings were set with a stone of midnight blue.

"Those are owli far," Leoku said as Bobby and Celia put the rings on their fingers. "The stone takes in light during the day and shines it at night."

"It's beautiful," Celia said quietly. She held up her hand so everyone could see.

"If I'd known they were giving away stuff that nice," Ted said with a chuckle, "I might be going with you guys."

"It's not too late," Josh said, hopefully.

Ted shook his head and smiled at Bobby. "No, I have my silver whistle. That'll do."

Josh helped Annie to her feet. "You okay?"

"I'm fine," Annie said, brushing off her clothes. "But I'm not touching those gloves unless I have to," she said, tying the pouch to her belt and lifting her backpack to her shoulders.

"Time to go," Dylan cried. He bounded over to Ted and gave him a big hug.

While the kids said their goodbyes, Annie noticed Sirie gliding over to the blue fairy. Sirie took the boy fairy's hands in hers and pressed them to her cheeks, gazing tenderly into his eyes. Annie elbowed Celia and nodded. Both girls grinned.

Annie heard her name called and turned. Mya was staring her way, but her eyes seemed unfocused, and her pupils were a whitish gray color.

"Is that you, Annie," Mya asked.

"Yes," Annie said, stepping over and wrapping her arms around Mya's neck. "It's me. I'm going to miss you."

"Me too," Mya said, her voice quivering.

Annie took a deep breath and wiped tears from her eyes. Emma stepped over, smiling warmly, and moved in for a three-way hug. Annie was surprised to see tears in her eyes too.

"It's okay. I'm sure we'll see each other soon," Annie said, hopefully, but not confidently.

"Come, children," Leoku cried. "Our journey is long, and time does not wait."

Annie let go of Mya and Emma. She took Celia's hand and followed the ranger fairies into the trees. Glancing over her shoulder, she waved with her free hand at the kids staying behind – Mya, Emma, Ted, Barth, and CPU – who were standing among hundreds of hovering Panishie.

Annie felt an aching sadness. Ted raised his arms and swung them in two wide arcs. Notes poured into the air, and the fairies began to sway. Annie's eyes grew damp again. She wiped her cheeks and glanced down at Celia, glad at least that she was coming.

Bobby and Wesley led the way, strolling at the front of the troop surrounded by a half-dozen ranger fairies. Despite their height, the Anolari easily kept up with the kids, bouncing along with each stride. Now and then, one would flutter its wings and rise into the air, causing Annie to wonder why they walked at all.

Bobby talked non-stop to the ranger fairies, but they rarely responded, listening but remaining silent. This didn't seem to bother Bobby, who chattered on happily as if he were having a delightful conversation.

As the morning passed, the air warmed. Patches of mist floated through the trees, leaving tiny droplets on Annie's skin and clothes. She and Celia started a game to see who could spot and name the most flowers. Annie spied a cluster of lupines and a patch of asters, while Celia pointed to some daisies and poppies in a meadow they passed. To the girls' surprise, Rhea joined in the game, spotting a cluster of primroses and some purple snapdragons.

Now and then, Gabrielle zipped by on her board, practicing her cuts and turns as she wove in and out of the procession of kids. She sometimes darted into the woods but didn't go far because Leoku had warned her it wasn't safe.

Sirie glided near the back of the troop with the four copper sprites hovering close by her. She chatted with Celia for a bit but spent most of her time talking to Josh. Annie listened as Sirie described strange forest creatures, such as red-haired squirrels that sang in the starlight and huge tortoises that crawled to a distant sea every summer.

When Josh mentioned the talking fish that they'd seen at the stream, Sirie laughed, telling him it was a good thing they hadn't eaten the fish, because that would have violated the *ama dia*. Annie wasn't sure what *ama dia* meant, but she suspected it was some kind of law.

At midday, the party came to a stream winding through a grove of fruit trees. Sirie said the trees had been planted for travelers. The children rested in the shade and ate lunch.

After eating, they resumed the trek and happened upon a field dotted with enormous stone ruins and a cobblestone path that led to a dilapidated temple. Leoku said the ruins were built by the Ancients but abandoned when they left Hevelen.

"Who were the Ancients?" Annie asked.

"A great race who ruled for a millennium until they renounced power and wealth and came to Hevelen to live in peace and solitude," Leoku said. "They made their home in Elderlan for many generations but sailed into the west after the Cirelyon wars. Some believe they took the cenarri moni with them,"

"Do you mean the sapphire fruit?" Annie asked.

"Yes," Leoku said, studying her face. "It gives the wielder great power. It brought you to this world."

"Did it make the blue light in the road?" Annie asked.

Leoku nodded. "You saw the radiance of a cenarri moni. It was thought they all were lost, but your arrival reveals that some still exist in Hevelen."

"The Ancients must have been giant people," Dylan said. "Their houses are huge."

"Yes, they were," Leoku said. "Powerful, wise, gentle, and beautiful, with golden hair and emerald eyes. The Anolari mourn the day the Ancients departed Hevelen."

Leoku glanced up, and his eyes darted. "We must return to the woods," he said with a worried expression. "I fear your enemies are hunting for you."

Leoku led the children back into the trees, and they continued walking until late in the afternoon when Leoku called a halt.

The kids gratefully swung off their packs and plopped to the ground. Then a soft rumble rose from the west. The ranger fairies flew up into the trees, leaving the children and the five Panishie fairies below.

"What's going on?" Annie asked, looking around. "Is it the fireball?"

"No, be calm," Leoku answered from his perch. "Remain still, and it will pass."

The clamber rose, and Annie pulled Celia to her. Gabrielle hopped on her board, while Rhea positioned herself in front of the girls. Josh put his arms around Bobby and Dylan.

"What's that noise?" Wesley asked. Leoku stared into the distance and didn't answer.

The sound continued to grow. A tiny bear-like creature bounded out from behind a bush. Then another appeared and another. The little bears bounced toward the children, tumbling through the bushes on four paws and two, looking like stuffed toys with joyful smiles.

The bears tumbled pell-mell toward the children, and Leoku shouted again for calm. Gabrielle angled her board up and rose above the heads of the kids, while Annie gripped the straps of her pack and watched the furry faces bouncing toward her.

The first creatures hopped by. Annie felt their soft fur brush against her skin while a sweet aroma like pancake syrup filled the air.

Celia squealed. "They're grabbing my bag," she cried, clutching the straps of her pack.

"Stop it!" Rhea yelled above the din. She spread her arms out, pushing away the passing mass of creatures. Growls erupted from the bears, spreading through the herd.

"No!" Leoku shouted. "Don't hinder them. They are gentle creatures and won't harm you unless angered. Let them pass."

The growls rose to a roar as the furry animals turned on the redheaded girl. Rhea raised her hands above her head, and the bears quieted. After several tense moments, the creatures resumed their forward movement, flowing past the kids.

Annie felt dozens of tiny tugs on her pack, but she held fast to her bag until the last of the bears disappeared into the woods behind them.

"That was freaky," Gabrielle said, floating lower.

"They were like little teddy bears, only alive," Celia said.

Leoku hopped out of the tree he'd been perched in. "They are immi," he said. "They live in the forests of Hevelen and move in herds, searching for food. They smelled something in your bags and were curious, but they are docile creatures and will not violate what isn't theirs."

"Why did you jump into the tree?" Annie asked, frowning. "It wasn't cool leaving us on the ground."

"You are larger creatures, so the immi will pass without harming you. But smaller ones, such as the Anolari can be carelessly injured."

Annie wasn't satisfied with this explanation, but all she said was, "Really?"

Leoku didn't reply.

With the woods quiet again and the syrupy smell fading, the party resumed the trek. They descended hillsides through groves of aspen and birch to the banks of a lake spreading south toward snow-capped mountains.

"This is the Fiali Peonie," Leoku said, pointing to the lake. "We have traveled enough today and will rest here for the night."

Annie heaved a sigh of relief and dropped her bag. She sat under a tree near the water's edge. The lake surface shimmered in yellows and reds, reflecting the setting sun. Celia and Rhea sat on either side of her, and the three girls shared fairy cakes and fruit.

With her stomach full, Annie leaned against the tree and rubbed her upper arms. Celia rested her head on Annie's shoulder and closed her eyes. Soon Annie heard Celia softly snoring. She caught Rhea's eye. "You trust those ranger fairies?" Annie asked in a hushed voice.

"No," Rhea said matter-of-factly. "You?"

"I did until that stampede of little bears earlier. I couldn't believe they flew into the trees and left us on the ground by ourselves."

Rhea shrugged. "Get used to it. Everyone lets you down. Expect it, and you won't be disappointed."

"Not everyone. You can count on some people."

"Like who?"

"Like our moms."

"Not my mom," Rhea said with an edgy laugh.

Annie was incredulous. "What do you mean? She's always there for you."

"Yeah, she's there to yell at me when I screw up," Rhea said with a sullen laugh.

"That's not true," Annie objected. "She works her job and then comes home and cooks dinner. She nags, but it's because she loves you. You guys argue. The problem is you're too much alike. You're both stubborn and quick-tempered. Though when you need her, you can count on her, just like I can count on you."

"Maybe," Rhea said softly. She wrapped her coat around her shoulders.

Annie smiled to herself.

As the evening cooled, Josh and Wesley helped several of the ranger fairies build a fire. Annie pulled Celia's blanket out of her pack and laid it over the sleeping girl. The ring the Panishie had given Celia began to glow a beautiful soft blue. Annie covered her hand with the blanket to hide the light. Bobby had fallen asleep several feet away. His ring began to glow too, so she covered that as well. Then she joined the others by the fire.

Sirie and the copper sprites had vanished. "Where's your BFF?" Annie asked Josh.

"She's visiting some place in the woods," he said.

"She will share the night with the one who brought her into this world," Leoku murmured.

"You mean her mom?" Annie asked in surprise.

"Yes, her mother passed into the shadow world when Siriena was a child, but her spirit lives on in the woods of the Fiali Peonie."

"Oh," Annie said, feeling sad for Sirie.

"Did you know her mother?" Josh asked.

"Yes, Theralin and I were like brothers then. Celione was his queen and a beauty of the Sienshie tribe. All who knew her fell under her spell, but in the end, she drowned in the Esante Trea."

"How?" Annie asked.

"The war of betrayals—the Palon Zum—shattered her heart. It took her brothers and her firstborn."

"You mean Sirie's sister? The one Emma resembles?"

"Yes, Fioena."

"What was the Palon Zum?" Josh asked, leaning forward.

"It is an unhappy story. Are you sure you want to hear it?" Leoku said.

Josh nodded firmly.

"There are five fairy tribes. The greatest are the Panishie and the Gadreshie. The Gadreshie are known as the black fairies because they dress in black garments and live a life of work, training, and warfare.

"Each year, warriors from the five tribes compete in the Micherian Festival. When Siriena was young, Fioena accompanied her father to the festival. There a Gadreshie prince lost his heart to Fioena. The prince competed in the games with such passion that he overcame all challengers and earned the Micherian cloth. Upon victory, he offered the cloth to Fioena to express his love."

"That's romantic," Annie said.

"But the prince's actions caused disquiet among the tribes," Leoku continued. "The Gadreshie and the Panishie are long-standing rivals. Fioena declined the gift, but some Gadreshie suspected she'd bewitched their prince. Others claimed she'd driven him insane. Fearing for his daughter's safety, Theralin spirited Fioena away and brought her to Oriafen. He forbade her from contacting the Gadreshie prince."

"That was stupid," Rhea said, rolling her eyes.

Leoku winced. "The prince's passion burned. He and his comrades journeyed through Elderlan until they found Fioena gathering herbs with other Panishie maidens. The prince revealed himself, and the two spent time together.

"They met secretly again over the following days, and their love bloomed. The prince knew his tribe would never accept a Panishie princess, and Fioena knew her people would never trust a Gadreshie prince, so they fled together.

"News of the lovers' escape reached the ears of an enemy, and he sent his servants to hunt them down. The servants found the lovers and murdered them in a manner that it appeared to be a crime by fairies. The Panishie and Gadreshie tribes each accused the other of the killings and vowed revenge, sparking a terrible war.

"Only after the Anolari learned the truth and informed the other fairy tribes of the true killers, did the war end, but many lives had been lost, including those of Celione's three brothers. In despair, she drowned herself."

"That's so awful," Annie said, feeling a wave of sadness.

Everyone was quiet for some time. Then Josh said, "A Panishie dressed in blue gave us gifts when we left Oriafen. Is that Sirie's brother?"

"No. He is her cousin, Tarian. When his father, Malon, died in the Palon Zum, Theralin brought Tarian to Oriafen. He and Siriena grew up like brother and sister. Tarian is a fine warrior and a wise prince. Only he among the Panishie can match Siriena in combat. Some say he will be chief of the Panishie someday, though others say he cannot because he is of the Sienshie tribe."

"What about Sirie?" Annie asked. "Won't she become chief after her father?"

"The Panishie do not have female chiefs," Leoku said, matter-of-factly.

"Why?... That's not fair," Annie said, feeling a flash of anger.

"But not surprising," Rhea said, rolling her eyes.

"That is the way of the Panishie," Leoku said. "You cannot change it."

"But why do they hate birds?" Dylan asked.

Leoku let out a deep breath. "They believe birds aided the Gadreshie in the Palon Zum. So, they banned them from Oriafen." Leoku eyed Cherry, "Your friend is the first to breach the ban."

"Cherry isn't afraid of anyone or anything," Dylan said grinning. He tipped his head and eyed the little bird on his shoulder proudly.

"Did they really help the Gadreshie in the war?" Annie asked.

"Different creatures aided each side, but most avoided the war. I see no truth in the Panishie claim, and the ban has done more harm than good."

The children nodded. Josh peered at Leoku curiously. "You and the other Anolari have wings, but you don't often fly. Why?"

"We are creatures of the earth," Leoku said. "We can move through the air, but we prefer the ground. We are nourished from the soil."

Annie wasn't sure what Leoku meant by nourished, but she had a question. "Do you think Emma resembles Sirie's sister?"

Leoku laughed for a moment. "Yes, it is a wondrous thing. She speaks and moves with Fioena's grace and beauty."

Annie whistled lightly and glanced at Wesley. Rhea frowned.

"What do you think of the Panishie?" Josh asked.

Leoku raised one brow.

"I mean, do you like them? They seem uncomfortable around you."

Leoku chuckled. "Maybe they are. We are the guardians of Elderlan forest and decide who may live here. The Panishie have been warned. If they cannot exist in harmony with other creatures, they must leave." Leoku put his hands together at his waist.

"That would be sad," Annie said. "Oriafen is a beautiful, wonderful place."

Leoku met her eyes. "The Panishie are moody and changeable creatures. They are like air and light, but they must learn to live with earth and water."

Annie nodded, not quite sure what Leoku meant. As the conversation continued, she felt a wave of exhaustion pass through her. She almost tipped over and struggled to her feet. "I'm really tired. I think I'll go to sleep."

"Yes, it is late, and our journey tomorrow will be long," Leoku said. "You should all rest."

Rhea walked with Annie back to where Celia slept. Annie tugged out her blanket and curled up next to the younger girl, with Rhea on Celia's other side.

Annie sank into a dreamless sleep but woke while it was yet dark. She heard Rhea's breathing and the crackling fire but felt something had woken her. On the far side of the fire pit, a figure stood in the darkness. She sat upright suddenly. The figure moved, and she recognized Wesley.

She went over to him. "Hey, you scared me," she said. "Why are you still up?"

"I couldn't sleep," Wesley said, rubbing his forehead. "I'm tired, but I haven't been able to sleep for days. It's like I can't relax."

"Are you worried about Sarah?"

"Yeah, but it's more than that."

"Try to stop thinking about it. Just take it easy."

"I can't."

Annie was silent for a moment. Then she said, "Have you ever meditated?"

"No."

"You should try it. My mom meditates every day, and she says it really helps. She has a job at a big computer company, and it's the only way she can handle the stress."

"How do you do it?"

"First you sit down with your back perfectly straight," Annie said. She plopped down and showed him. "Then you close your eyes and focus on your breathing. You don't want to think about anything else. If your mind starts wandering, focus on your breathing again. Keep doing it for a while. When you open your eyes again, you should feel better."

"Okay, I'll try," Wesley said, shrugging.

"I hope it helps. Now I'm going back to sleep."

Rubbing her eyes, Annie returned to her blanket. She lay her head on her pack and watched Wesley in the darkness. She hoped the meditating would help but wasn't sure it would.

Her thoughts drifted to the other kids who had stayed behind at Oriafen. She wondered how they were. Oriafen was a wonderful place. She understood why they wanted to stay. But were they in danger? Would something take them away? The Panishie were good fighters. They defeated the black birds easily. But Leoku said something else—more dangerous—would come. What was that? Annie's heart quickened, and her palms grew damp. She breathed in deeply. She hoped her friends would be safe.

Chapter 16:
The Sound

When Barth awoke, for a moment he didn't know where he was. Then CPU's snoring brought him back. He sat up and tugged off the blanket. He studied the walls of the hole and grinned in satisfaction. The hideout was almost done. They had finished the digging two days ago, and yesterday he and CPU set rocks into the walls to keep the dirt from falling back in. Then they cut bamboo stalks and laid them into the floor. Today they planned to do the roof.

He climbed the ladder. Peering over the top of the hole, he watched morning mist float through the trees.

It was hard to see the other kids go. He had hoped they would stay together. He thought it was safer to stay with the Panishie. He was glad CPU hadn't gone, but he worried about him. CPU's hearing was getting worse. Barth now had to look him in the eye when they talked so CPU could read his lips. They'd invented some hand signals to communicate quickly, but Barth wondered what would happen when they got home. Would CPU's hearing get better? Would he be normal again? Hopefully, this was something temporary—like an ear infection—that would go away.

As CPU's hearing worsened, his eyesight seemed to improve. Yesterday, Barth lost his pocketknife while gathering branches for the roof of the fort. By the time he noticed the blade missing, the sun had gone down. CPU searched for it in the dark, and - to Barth's amazement - found the knife in leaves thirty feet from the hideout.

Barth climbed out of the hole and headed to the glade. The fairies had laid out bowls of cakes and fruit beside a pool. Barth grabbed a bit of everything, then he sat down near the Kadean sisters, who were sleeping beside a bed of flowers.

Mya opened her eyes and squinted. "Is that you, Barth?"

"Yeah. The fairies put out breakfast if you want some."

"No, I'm still sleepy," Mya said, rolling onto her back and pulling the blanket over her head.

Barth liked Mya. She reminded him of his sister. Some kids said Mya talked too much, but he didn't mind; he liked her voice. She also seemed cheerful most of the time. They had been friends since third grade. She often came over to his house after school to do her homework while he worked on his latest project. While he liked Mya, he wasn't as fond of her sister. Emma was too quiet and snooty. She seemed to worry a lot, which annoyed him. Although, since they'd come to Oriafen, she'd been in a pretty good mood.

Barth admired the Panishie. Oriafen was beautiful. The glade was a little paradise. Their fighting also impressed him. The fairies had easily handled the black birds. That was why he had stayed. He felt safer with the Panishie than trekking to some far-off land.

Barth bit into an apple and watched Ted amble over to the food. Ted grabbed a couple of peaches and a half-dozen cakes, then headed Barth's way.

"Howdy."

"Hey, big guy," Barth said, noticing that Ted's clothes looked baggy on him. "You hungry?"

"Absolutely," Ted said. "I always have an appetite before I start my sounds. But once the music begins, the hunger goes away, so I need to eat now." He paused to stuff a cake into his mouth, then he continued. "How was it sleeping in that hole?"

"Great. Comfortable."

"Claustrophobic?" Ted asked, quirking an eyebrow.

"Not a bit. And when we finish the roof, it'll be a good place to hide."

"Right," Ted said and bit into a peach. Before long he'd finished off the cakes and all the fruit he'd grabbed. He wiped crumbs off his lap and waved his hands around. Music filled the air.

Barth grit his teeth. The music annoyed him. It wasn't the sound—which wasn't so bad— but the fact that Ted made it without any musical instrument. He just swung his hands around, and notes poured out. It was nuts!

Barth had tried waving his own hands, but no music came out. He hated things that didn't make sense. He glared at Ted, almost wishing the guy had gone off with the other kids so he wouldn't have to hear his crazy music all day.

As Ted made his melodies, fairies gathered around the large boy. Some sang along, while others played their own instruments.

Mya groaned and rolled onto her side. "Who can sleep with all that racket?" she said, staring in Barth's general direction. He winced slightly. The whitish film in her eyes was more apparent than yesterday, now entirely covering the black of her pupils. It reminded him of the eyes of his dog, Mosho, after she went blind with cataracts.

Mya nudged Emma, and the two girls headed for the woods with Emma leading Mya forward.

Hundreds of fairies streamed out of Oriafar and began their morning exercises. Barth watched the fairies do their dance-like calisthenics until CPU stepped out of the woods and stretched his arms. Barth waved to CPU, and the boy headed over.

"You ready to finish the roof?" Barth asked, enunciating the words so his friend could read his lips.

"Yeah, just let me eat something. I'm starved," CPU said, picking out a handful of cakes and plopping down beside Barth. The two ate and talked until Mya and Emma returned arm in arm.

"Morning," Emma shouted with a wave of her hand.

Barth tapped CPU's shoulder and pointed to the girls. CPU's face flushed, and he glanced away hurriedly.

Emma noticed CPU's reaction and gave Barth a look of confusion. "What's up with CPU?"

"He's embarrassed," Barth said with a grin. "His eyes are getting so sharp; he thinks he can see right through clothes."

Emma and Mya's mouths dropped open, and they rushed over to their blankets to cover up.

Barth laughed, and CPU peered around anxiously. When CPU saw the Emma and Mya wrapping themselves like mummies, he waved his hands around and shouted, "No, it's not like that. I can't see your skin. I only see a faint outline of your bones, like an X-ray. Nothing else."

Mya turned her back to CPU. "Even so, keep your eyes pointed the other direction, thank you."

CPU did as Mya ordered. She and Emma wrapped themselves tightly in blankets and sat down beside Barth.

"You missed out yesterday," Mya said, staring at Barth without appearing to see him clearly. "Tarian showed us how they make their cakes and the fairy juice. I couldn't see, but Emma described it all for me. They have gardens of grapes and huge fields of grain in the middle of the forest."

"Tarian?" Barth asked.

"The blue fairy," Mya said, nibbling on her bottom lip. "Sirie's friend. The one who beat Sirie in the silence glove game."

"Oh, yeah, the quiet one."

"He's not that quiet," Mya said. "He's talkative, and his English is good, better than Sirie's or Theralin's. He promised to show us how they make their colorful gowns today."

Barth turned to CPU. "Did you hear that, CPU?" he shouted. "The blue fairy will show them how they make their thermochromic clothes. We should check it out."

"Yeah, okay," CPU said, without turning his head toward the other kids.

235

"The thermo what?" Mya asked, her brow creasing.

"Thermochromic," Barth said. "Tell her, CPU."

"It's when the color of something changes because of a difference in temperature," CPU said.

Mya's eyebrows drew together. "How does that happen?"

"I don't know," CPU said. "Some laboratories have shown it's possible, but I've never seen it actually done. Maybe the fairies can tell us."

Ted dropped his hands, and the music fell silent. He peered at the girls. "So, is ol' silver beard coming to visit you two today?"

Mya crossed her arms. "If you mean Theralin, I hope so. He's really sweet."

Ted chuckled. "He's sweet on you girls. But he ignores us, boys."

"Actually, it's Emma he likes," Mya said turning toward her sister, who gave a slight shrug. "He talks to me, but he's always watching her. It was strange talking to him at first, but he's nice, like a kind old uncle."

"What does he talk about?"

"He asks about our home, our parents, our school… things like that. Yesterday, I told him about the state parks and historical sites around Annaberry."

"That must have been fascinating," Barth snickered.

"Actually, it was. You'd be surprised. Theralin asked a bunch of questions. He's more cultured than some people I know," Mya said, frowning in Barth and CPU's general direction.

"Yeah, he's got culture. This place has culture," Ted said, looking around. "But ol' Theralin still prefers girls."

"Boys are boring." Mya chuckled. Then her gaze dropped to her hands. "Actually, he says Emma reminds him of his other daughter. He lost her and his wife in a war. Now, Sirie and Tarian are his only family."

The boys' smiles faded, and they became quiet. After a few moments, Ted said, "Those fairies get excited when he talks to you. They start whispering among themselves. Then when Emma does that thing with her hands to bend the light, they really flip out."

"I know," Emma said, blushing slightly. "I shouldn't do it, but it's fun, and I want to learn how to control it."

"Theralin says Emma is a light dancer," Mya said, glancing at her sister admiringly. "He says it's a rare gift."

Barth shook his head. He didn't want to hear any more about gifts and other loony stuff. He gritted his teeth and grabbed CPU's arm. "Come on, CPU. Let's get working on the roof."

In the woods, the boys found a grove of bamboo near their hideout and began pulling down stalks. They cut short and long pieces. Then they bound the long pieces with vines into a rectangular panel and used the shorter pieces to make a square panel. After that, they attached the square panel to the rectangular one so the square could swing freely. Then they laid the entire panel over the hole and spread leaves and dirt on top of it.

The sun was straight up in the sky when they finished. The boys returned to the clearing and devoured a dozen fruit and cakes, though Barth really longed for a hamburger, some French fries, and a soda.

"Hey, guys," Mya said, strolling up with Emma. "Tarian is going to show us how the fairies make their clothes. You wanna come?"

CPU had averted his eyes and didn't hear Mya, so Barth looked him in the face and repeated the question. CPU nodded excitedly. "Yes, count me in."

"Great! We'll see if Ted wants to come too," Mya said, glancing at her sister.

Barth groaned. "Do you have to? He'll keep waving his hands around and make that stupid music."

Mya stepped back. "What's wrong with his music? We love it," she said.

"Yeah, we do," Emma chimed in.

"But he's not playing instruments. He's making it out of thin air. Doesn't that bother you?"

"Well, Barth," Mya said, crossing her arms, "if you hadn't noticed, there's been a lot of crazy things happening lately. Besides, his music sounds nice." Emma nodded in agreement.

"Whatever," Barth said with an exasperated sigh. The girls looked at one another and headed away. They returned a few minutes later with Ted in tow.

"These boots are ready for walking," Ted said with a laugh. He swung his arms and produced a shower of sound, oblivious to Barth's displeasure.

Barth rubbed his brow and clenched his jaw.

At that moment, the blue fairy appeared out of the woods, gliding toward the kids with a band of copper sprites.

"I am Tarian," he said. "If you have an interest, I can take you to Fenietra, where you can learn some secrets of the Panishie. Do you wish to come?"

The kids all nodded eagerly, and the fairies led them into the woods.

Barth found himself walking beside Mya, as Emma led her by the hand. Barth remembered what Ted had said earlier about the old silver fairy and wondered why he was so interested in the girls.

"Did Theralin come to talk to you again today?" he asked.

"Yeah, he visited us this morning," Mya said, brushing loose hairs off her face. "He asked us a strange question. He wanted to know when we were born. We told him the month and day, but he also wanted to know the time: morning, afternoon or evening. He said it was important for fairies and said all copper sprites are born at night and in the winter."

Barth snorted. "Sounds like some astrology nonsense." He didn't have faith in that zodiac stuff. He believed in science.

As they passed through the woods, bugs of various colors and shapes hovered in the air, and forest creatures peered out from behind bushes and trees. Barth hoped there weren't any bears or mountain lions nearby. He liked the cool animals but didn't want any of them to eat him.

After a half hour, they came to a grassy clearing some fifty yards across. Several abandoned buildings made of white stone rose near the center of the clearing. An empty canal ran to the buildings from a dried-up creek bed on the far side of the glade. Near one of the stone buildings, a fallen statue lay partially embedded in the ground. The statue was of a bearded man dressed in a long gown and holding a peach-sized object in his hands. Barth judged the figure would stand two stories high if propped upright.

"What is this place?" he asked.

"It is what you see," Tarian replied, his expression blank.

"Oh, that clears things up," Barth said sarcastically.

Tarian didn't answer. Barth gave CPU a look

They skirted the edge of the clearing and re-entered the woods. They walked for about twenty more minutes before the fairies called a halt. Tarian told the children they had come to a secret place and must be blindfolded to go any further. The copper sprites brought out pieces of soft red cloth to cover the children's eyes.

Ted raised his hands in front of his face. "I don't want to go anywhere I can't see."

"Well, then you must wait here until we return," Tarian said matter-of-factly.

Ted became quiet and then grumbled, "Alright, go ahead and play your clandestine game."

Barth and CPU laughed. Barth didn't mind wearing a blindfold. The walk had begun to bore him, and this secrecy stirred his curiosity.

Barth adjusted the blindfold, so it was comfortable and waited.

CPU murmured, "Hey, I can see through this thing."

"Good," Barth whispered back. "Tell me what you saw later on."

"Huh?" CPU replied.

Barth didn't answer, knowing CPU wouldn't hear him anyway.

The fairies asked the children to hold hands and walk single file. Barth took Mya's and CPU's hands, and they started forward.

Barth expected to run into a tree or bush at any moment, but to his surprise, he stumbled only a couple of times, and the fairies caught him each time.

After a few minutes, he heard falling water in the distance and felt a cool mist on his skin. The sound grew louder until it seemed to thunder all around him. Mya asked if they were by a waterfall. Tarian said they were. Barth walked slowly, assuming the ground was wet and slippery.

The sound of falling water faded into the distance, and Barth bumped against something hard. He let go of CPU's hand for a moment and reached out, feeling the smooth surface of a stone wall.

"Are we in a cave?" he asked.

CPU didn't hear him, but Mya said, "I think so."

They made their way forward until the only sound was their footsteps. A scent like seawater filled the air and Tarian called a halt. He told the children to remove their blindfolds. Barth tugged his down and blinked in the dim light.

They were standing on a platform about ten feet across and three feet wide. The platform jutted out from the wall of a cave made of crystalline rock running off to the right and left as far as he could see. At the edge of the platform, a stone barrier rose waist high. Candles burned in crevices along the walls, filling the cave with a warm, flickering light.

Barth stepped to the edge of the platform and peered over the stone barrier. Below, fairies hovered around hundreds of snail-like creatures moving slowly across a flat stone surface carved into the cave floor. The fairies poured a clear liquid onto the stone from pitchers. The snails moved toward the liquid, consuming it as they passed and leaving behind glowing strands of a thread-like material.

"What're those?" Barth asked.

Tarian hovered at Barth's side. "They are eanies. They feed on a liquid called ilisey. As they eat and move along the rock, they leave a thread for their young to follow. We collect the thread and weave it into a fabric."

"You make clothes out of snail slime?" Ted said, scrunching up his nose.

Tarian nodded slowly. "Come this way." He led them through a narrow tunnel away from the platform to a room where hundreds of fairies washed and dried strands of the eanie thread. In a second room, the fairies worked on tiny looms whirling and weaving the strands into a shimmering silver fabric.

Emma stroked a piece of the fabric. "It feels like silk," she murmured.

Barth asked how the fairies made it into different colors.

"We don't," Tarian said. "The wearer causes the color. Each wearer's nature has its own hue, and the fabric reveals that."

Barth wasn't clear what Tarian meant, but he assumed that different body temperatures caused different colors.

When the tour was finished, they were blindfolded again and led out. The fairies guided them past the thundering waterfall and through the misty woods until Tarian told them to remove the blindfolds. Barth pulled his down and found they were standing before a large wooden structure.

Several copper sprites glided to a door and pushed it open. The fairies led the children inside, where they found a circular walled pen containing hundreds of small furry creatures moving together in a flowing mound. The creatures scurried about excitedly, climbing over one another as the mound swept in circles around the pen.

"What are they?" Emma asked. "They're cute."

"They are wadri," Tarian said. "They make their home in the forests of Hevelen."

"Why do they pile on top of each other like that?" CPU asked. "The ones at the bottom must get squished."

Tarian shook his head. "That is how they move in the forests. Underneath their fur, they have a hard shell which protects them. They move in large mounds through the woods, living on nuts, roots, and insects."

Several of the copper sprites floated to a small door at the side of the pen. They opened it and coaxed out one of the furry creatures, which was about the size of a kitten but the shape of a furry turtle. The children gathered around, taking turns holding and stroking the wadri. Barth pointed to a black spot of a nose at one end and a slit for its mouth. The animal's eyes remained nearly closed.

"I wish Annie and Celia were here," Mya said, rocking the wadri gently in her arms. "They'd love this little guy."

Mya handed the wadri to Barth. He held it hesitantly, anxious that he might do something wrong. The creature rolled from side to side in his hands, squeaking softly.

"It likes you," CPU said, slapping his forehead in feigned disbelief.

"All animals like Barth." Mya declared.

"Not true." Barth objected. "Even my dogs growl at me."

"The wadri are friendly creatures," Tarian said, "but be gentle. If they sense danger, they can bite with their needle-like teeth."

Barth stiffened and slowly set the furry creature on the floor. Several of the copper sprites hovered over the animal, stroking it until it squeaked again contentedly.

"The Panishe make blankets from the wadri's fur," Tarian said. "We shave them each spring, and the fur grows back before winter."

"Like sheep," Mya said with a laugh. "Tiny turtle sheep."

The fairies returned the wadri to the pen, and Tarian led the children outside. As the copper sprites began tying blindfolds back over their eyes, Tarian spun and gave a sharp command. Several of the sprites shot off while others assumed a defensive posture. Barth pulled down his blindfold.

"Danger has found us," Tarian said. "You must hide."

"What danger?" Ted asked.

"Rarewar."

Barth groaned. He caught CPU's eye, and they both knew what the other was thinking—they were too far from the hideout.

242

Tarian led the children into the trees and guided them to a thicket. There the copper sprites hovered in the branches with bows drawn. The children waited without moving for so long that Barth's left foot fell asleep, but he didn't dare shift his weight for fear of making a sound in the leaves.

Finally, Tarian and the sprites seemed to relax. Barth sighed and shook his foot to get the blood flowing. He nodded to CPU, who waggled his shoulders to release the tension. Then a sound reached Barth's ears—a beautiful sound that reminded him of a soft bed or a steamy bath. It filled his body with a soothing feeling that transfixed him. He couldn't move. The sprites dropped out of the air and landed motionless in the leaves.

"What happened?" CPU cried, hurrying to the fallen fairies. He spun and glanced at the other kids. "Hey guys, come help!"

No one moved. CPU cocked his head. "I hear something. What's that?" His frown softened to a slight smile. "It's faint but beautiful."

CPU's voice reached Barth's ears, but the words meant nothing. A feeling of serenity and peace enveloped Barth. The beautiful sound washed through his body like a river, drowning out all his worries and cares.

CPU grabbed Barth's arm and pulled. "Come on, we got to help!" he shouted. But CPU's tugging felt faint and distant to Barth.

CPU scanned the kids. "Snap out of it, guys! You're scaring me." His hands trembled, and he shouted again, his voice rising high and shrill. CPU's fear sliced through the beautiful sound. It touched Barth. He sensed something was wrong. It cleared his mind, but the exquisite resonance held his body fast.

CPU rushed over to Ted and then to Mya. "Wake up, wake up! Are you guys hypnotized? Come on, wake up!"

A noise joined the beautiful sound—the beating of heavy wings. Branches shattered and crashed to the ground. Something dropped from above, landing on the forest floor in a cloud of dust and leaves. Out of the cloud emerged a black-winged creature, its yellow eyes swirling.

A second winged beast tumbled through the canopy, landing near the first, then a third arrived. The birds stalked, circling the children. CPU froze, wide-eyed with fear. A bird swept at him, grasping his midsection in its powerful talons.

Barth wanted to shout, to help his friend, but the exquisite sound held him fast. Then Ted's hand moved a fraction. A discordant note sounded, cutting through the beautiful resonance. Barth blinked. Ted's hand moved again, bringing out another note. Barth tilted his head.

More notes rang out, and the fairies stirred. They leaped into the air and reached for their bows. Birds dove toward the children. One grabbed Ted and lifted him skyward. He swung his arms frenetically. Chaotic notes poured into the air, slicing through the hypnotic sound, and breaking it into jagged pieces.

Barth leaped, swinging his arms to grasp Ted's foot before the bird carried him away. He missed. Mya screamed, and Emma pulled her sister back. The girls dashed out of the thicket.

Tarian and the copper sprites shot at the birds. The winged beasts rose away from the fairies, gripping CPU and Ted in their great talons.

There was terror in CPU's eyes. Barth's anger swelled. His hands tightened into fists, and he shook with rage.

"Nooooo!"

A pounding grew in his head, and his mind went dark. A roar filled the air. The ground slid and rocked. Cracks split the earth, running through the forest like wildfire. Trees swayed and fell. The ground fractured.

Moments passed, and Barth's anger eased. The pounding quieted. Darkness faded from his mind. The earth grew still, and he opened his eyes. The beautiful sound was silent.

The copper sprites attacked again, but the birds rose away, lifting CPU and Ted into the sky.

Anger and frustration gripped Barth. His mind went dark. The earth shook, and the ground cracked. He stumbled forward. Talons closed around him, lifting him skyward. The thunder faded, and he opened his eyes.

244

Below, Mya and Emma were dashing through the trees away from the thicket. A winged beast pursued them. Emma spun and whirled her arms. The light warped and buckled. The girls disappeared. The bird squawked in confusion. Barth exhaled, a glimmer of hope stirring in him.

Mya and Emma reappeared some distance away. The black bird swept toward them. Emma swung her arms again, and the light twisted and bent. The girls vanished a second time.

Copper sprites buzzed by Barth's face, attacking the bird holding him in its grasp. The winged beast swung at the fairies with its oily-black wings, slapping them away. Then it powered upward.

The wind rushed by Barth's ears. He turned his head, searching for the fairies. Tarian and the copper sprites raced after his captor.

"Help," he cried. But as he watched, another bird dove down, colliding with the fairies and knocking them spinning away. His heart sank.

He searched the horizon. To the left, two birds were bearing CPU and Ted northward. Off to the right in the distance, a massive flock of the black birds hovered above Oriafen. Something caught his eye, a small figure riding on the back of a great winged beast as it circled above the great crystal stone. He squinted. Blond hair gleamed in the sunlight. He wondered who that was.

Then the beautiful sound swept through the atmosphere like a wave, washing through his senses. His fears and cares faded. The great bird spread its wings and soared skyward, carrying him into the north.

Chapter 17:
Wings and Snow

The morning light forced open Josh's eyes. He rolled over and peered around the clearing. He yawned, wishing he could sleep for a couple more hours, but he knew they had a long day ahead and needed to get an early start.

Dylan and Bobby lay beside him, snoring like little fire engines. Josh watched the younger boys, wondering for the umpteenth time if he'd done the right thing. Ted had said they could be attacked out here, and he was right. Back at Oriafen, at least the Panishie could defend them.

Josh shrugged and gazed up at the Anolari perched in the trees. Some seemed asleep, while others were keeping watch. He heard footsteps. Celia stepped out of the trees with a mound of fruit in her arms. Wesley came up behind her holding another armful.

"Breakfast," Celia cried, letting her fruit roll down onto her blanket. "We found oranges and peaches. We picked a whole bunch."

Josh peered up at Wesley. "How'd you sleep, bro?"

"I didn't, but Annie taught me something which helped. I feel better today."

Josh noticed color in Wesley's cheeks for the first time in days. He started to ask him about it when Sirie glided out of the woods. She buzzed up to his face.

"Good morning Josh," she said, her eyes twinkling.

"Good morning," he replied, leaning back to look at her. "You're in a good mood."

"Yes, I happy see you," Sirie said, tilting her head and smiling impishly.

"Me too," Josh said, reddening slightly. His eyes darted, and he caught Celia grinning. "What?"

"Nothing," Celia said with a giggle.

The other kids soon awoke. After eating breakfast, they packed their bags, and the party started out, heading southwest along the perimeter of the lake. They kept just inside the trees. Near mid-morning, the shore curved east, and they headed away from the water, hiking south through the woods.

With the mountains looming ahead, the land began to rise, breaking into ravines that rose and fell out of the valley. The tree cover thinned, but Leoku found a path through the woods that kept them well hidden.

By late morning, they were climbing straight up the mountainside. At noon, the party reached a wooded plateau some thousand feet above the valley floor. The air felt cool, and the sky was crystal clear.

Leoku called a halt, and the children gratefully dropped their packs, plopping down on the leaf-blanketed ground. Josh sipped from his water bottle and munched on a cake. Some of the kids complained of sore feet and aching muscles, but most seemed in a good mood.

Dylan produced a deck of cards and started playing a game of Crazy Eights with Celia, Annie, and Bobby. Josh eyed them for a moment and then rose and ambled back through the woods to the edge of the plateau.

He stared down at the valley spreading out like a carpet toward distant mountains. He wondered where they were. The forest reminded him of places he'd visited two summers ago when his dad took Dylan and him on a road trip through Vermont and Maine. But he hadn't seen any fairies, talking fish, or giant birds on that trip. Was this a different world? Was it like their home, only magical? Was it far away? And, how would they get home?

He shook his head. He knew he shouldn't think about it. There was no answer, and he had real-world problems – like getting all the kids to a safe place.

When he rejoined the others, Wesley was leaning back and laughing loudly as Dylan did a handstand on one arm and gripped the waist of his pants with the other.

The dark rings under Wesley's eyes had faded, and his skin showed a healthy glow. Josh knelt beside Annie, setting his hand on her shoulder. "Whatever you did, it worked. Our boy looks great."

Annie inclined her head. "I taught him how to meditate. My mom swears by it. I thought it would help."

"It did," Josh said, nodding. "How do you do it?

Annie repeated what she had told Wesley.

"Interesting," Josh murmured when she finished. "Maybe, I should try it."

Annie grinned.

After the kids finished lunch, Leoku led them through the woods to a waterfall pouring down from a gap high on the mountainside. A ledge passed behind the waterfall. They followed this to a wall carved into the cliff face.

Leoku spoke to Sirie, and she flew to the wall. She studied it, then nodded and darted to a spot on the lower right. She pressed her fingers against the stone, and then glided up to a spot on the top left. She pressed her fingers to the rock again and floated down to the center of the wall. There she pressed a third time.

The stone groaned, and an opening emerged in the rock just wide enough for the kids to pass through. Leoku waved to follow him. They entered a narrow tunnel. With everyone inside, Sirie pressed on the interior wall, and the stone closed behind them.

"How did you do that?" Josh asked.

"Feeling," Sirie said with a mischievous grin. "A Panishie door."

Josh nodded in realization.

The tunnel was dark except for a faint light off in the distance. Leoku led them to an enormous chamber with a soaring roof of translucent rock. Sunlight poured down through the rock, filling the room with a silvery light.

A stone path wound through the chamber, skirting crystalline pools laid amidst lush greenery. Around the pools hovered fairies in black gowns, tending to a myriad of plants and flowers growing in and around the water.

As the party moved through the chamber, fairies bowed to Sirie and stared solemnly at the children.

"What is this place?" Josh asked in a hushed voice.

"Panishie home long ago," Sirie replied.

"Before the Oriafar stone fell from the sky, the Panishie lived in these caves," Leoku said. "Now only a few Panishie remain to care for the flora and tend to the burial chambers within."

"They bury Panishie here?"

"They once did, before the Panishie made Oriafen their home."

The party followed the path to another tunnel that led to a second enormous chamber, this one filled with crystalline stalactites extending down from the ceiling toward stalagmites reaching up from the floor. The party made their way through the second chamber and to another tunnel that climbed steadily through the rock through several smaller rooms. Finally, it ended at a high stone wall.

Josh turned to Leoku. "What now?"

Leoku spoke to Sirie, and she glided to the wall. She pressed her fingers to the stone again, and the rock shifted, opening with a quiet groan. An icy breeze whipped in through the gap. Josh drew his coat close. He led the kids out onto the mountainside.

Out in the open air, Dylan shivered. "It's colder than a refrigerator in Alaska."

Gabrielle smirked. "Refrigerators aren't colder in Alaska."

"Yes, they are. If they weren't, food would warm up inside them."

Gabrielle rolled her eyes.

Leoku gathered the children around him. "Now the dangerous part of our journey begins," he said gravely. "We don't have the forest or caves to conceal us anymore. Use your Panishie blankets to cover yourselves. They will keep out the cold and hide you from unwelcome eyes."

Josh wasn't sure what Leoku meant by hiding from unwelcome eyes, but he – and the other kids – did as Leoku instructed. Then they made their way along a narrow footpath winding up the mountain slope.

Soon, Josh noticed his blanket was changing color as he moved through the landscape, blending in with the green of the wild grass at his feet, the brown dirt of the hillside, and the gray rocks scattered along the slope.

"This is camouflage," Dylan shouted.

Josh sighed in wonder.

The trail rose and fell, descending into ravines and then climbing out and continuing an upward ascent. As the party made their way up the mountainside, the temperature continued to fall. Josh spotted patches of snow around them. Gabrielle darted away from the trail. She glided up the slope to a patch of the white stuff. She grabbed a handful and squeezed it in her palms. Then she tossed the snowball at Dylan, who leaped to avoid it, letting off a loud fart.

Josh led the way for some time, but as the climb steepened and the children tired, he slowed to take up the rear, where he could catch stragglers. Sirie glided along beside him chattering happily in Panishie. Josh listened but understood little of what she said.

At the front of the troop, Bobby walked with several of the Anolari. He chatted with the ranger fairies in his cheerful, singsong voice, telling them about Annaberry and his dog, Willow. The ranger fairies listened attentively, bobbing their heads as he talked. Josh sensed they were warming to the boy.

At midafternoon, the party came to a rock wall and overhang that provided shelter from the wind. Leoku called a halt, and the kids gratefully dropped their packs. They plopped to the ground and began pulling food from their bags.

As Josh bit into an apple, he saw Leoku huddle with several of the ranger fairies. One of the fairies flew off.

Josh finished his apple and leaned back, resting his head against the rock wall. He closed his eyes. When he opened them, a white butterfly fluttered past his nose. He watched the delicate creature glide along until it disappeared beyond the rock wall. Then another appeared and another. Soon a dozen butterflies were quivering in the air beneath the overhang. More of the tiny creatures materialized until they filled the air like a white cloud.

"Where did all the butterflies come from?" Celia cried; her hands pressed to her chest so as not to accidentally hit one.

"We called them," Leoku said. "They are the asaria and live in the snow lands of Eelena. They will accompany us up the mountainside to provide more protection from unwelcome eyes."

"So rad," Gabrielle cried, stepping onto her board. She glided into the fluttering whiteness, sending butterflies tumbling away from her.

Dylan bounded after Gabrielle, clutching at his pants. "It's a butterfly blizzard," he cried, disappearing into the whiteness.

"Watch out for rocks," Josh yelled.

A moment later, he heard a thump and Dylan's laughter. Gabrielle appeared out of the cloud rubbing her forehead.

Leoku gazed at the children solemnly. "The winds have calmed, but as the evening nears, they will rise again, so we must move while we can. We cannot delay."

The kids groaned but gathered their stuff and followed Leoku into the whiteness.

As Josh made his way up the hillside in the cloud of butterflies, their tiny wings filled the air with a soft pulsating sound. He could see little. Annie and Celia were walking just ahead but kept disappearing and reappearing in the whiteness.

The party slowly ascended the mountainside. From time to time, the wind gusted, sending the butterflies tumbling around them and opening gaps in the whiteness, revealing blue sky and a gray landscape.

Late in the afternoon, the party reached a ledge backed by a shallow cave. Leoku called a halt for the day, and the kids let out a chorus of sighs. Josh parked himself on a large rock at the cave mouth and watched the butterflies disperse into the late afternoon air. He was tired, and the other kids looked exhausted – everyone except Wesley, who kept pacing around, his hands clenching and unclenching anxiously.

Josh pulled a peach out of his bag but decided he was tired of fruit and grabbed several cakes instead. Sirie landed on a ridge in the rock. She gazed out across the valley. Suddenly, her eyes narrowed, and her mouth tightened. She leaped into the air and darted over to the copper sprites. She spoke to them in a hurried and agitated voice. Leoku strode over and joined the conversation.

Sirie spun toward Josh, her body as tense as a cat on a burning roof. She cried, "*Ana grea*," and leaped off the ledge, winging north at high speed. The four copper sprites flashed into the air and raced after her.

Leoku gathered the ranger fairies around him and spoke in a grim voice. Then he too flew off the ledge, soaring in the direction Sirie had gone. Six of the Anolari followed him, while the other ranger fairies remained at the cave mouth.

Annie rushed over to Josh, her brows knitted with worry. "What's going on?"

"I don't know."

Gabrielle craned her neck, watching the fairies as they shrank into the blue. "I'd go after them," she said, "but we're so high up, I'm sure I'd freak out and have a nonsurvivable wipeout."

Josh walked over to a ranger fairy perched on a rock. He tried to talk to the creature, but the fairy just shrugged and gave a look of confusion. Annie talked to other ranger fairies and learned that a great flock of birds were flying toward Oriafen. Sirie and Leoku had flown off to help defend the Panishie homeland.

Josh's heart pounded. Five of his friends were still at Oriafen. They were in danger, and there was nothing he could do. Anger and frustration filled him.

The ranger fairies motioned for the kids to retreat into the cave. Josh crouched behind the rock he had been sitting on. From there, he had a good view of the valley. He squinted, searching the sky, and spotted a great dark mass moving south above the forest toward the center of the valley.

"Birds many," a ranger fairy murmured.

"Are they big, black ones?" Josh asked, but the fairy didn't reply. Josh leaned toward the little guy. The ranger fairy stood motionless a sweet smile on his face. Josh waited. He asked again. The ranger fairy still didn't reply. Josh swept his hand in front of the fairy's face. There was no reaction.

"What's wrong with him?" Dylan asked.

"It seems like he's in a trance," Josh said, frowning. Josh glanced around and noticed all the fairies were motionless.

"Something's wrong," he said, turning toward Bobby. "Do you feel it?"

Bobby rolled his eyes up in their sockets, so Josh could only see the whites. Bobby exhaled and his pupils became visible again. He peered into the distance. "Itt noot huurt."

Josh huffed in relief. "Alright," he said. "That's a good sign."

Josh picked up the stationary ranger fairy and carried him to the rear of the cave. He set the fairy down on a blanket, then he leaned close and listened to his chest. "He's breathing," Josh said. One by one, Josh laid each of the ranger fairies on the blanket beside the first.

The kids gathered around unmoving fairies. "What's wrong with them?" Celia asked.

"I don't know," Josh said, shaking his head. "It's like they're hypnotized."

"They look happy," Celia said.

Josh smiled and nodded.

The floor of the cave suddenly shuddered. Josh spread his arms to keep his balance, then he grabbed Celia to prevent her from falling. The cave jolted again, and a roar filled the air. The ranger fairies lying on the blanket suddenly sprang to life. They darted up and flew to the ledge, hovering there and talking loudly among themselves.

The mountain lurched again. Children screamed. Josh fell forward. Jagged cracks opened in the rock. He stumbled to his feet and staggered through the mouth of the cave. Bobby followed him out. Turning, Josh saw a snow bank some fifty yards to the left of them break free from the mountainside and slide down the slope.

Far below in the valley, the Fiali Peonie rocked and swayed, sending waves crashing into the woods along its shore.

The shaking swelled. Josh grabbed Bobby and crouched, expecting the mountain to collapse around them. Then everything quieted. He held his breath and stared at the younger boy. Bobby grinned like he'd just jumped off a rollercoaster.

"Is that it?" Josh asked anxiously.

"Sooo fuun!" Bobby cried, throwing up his arms.

A ripple of anger crossed Josh's face. "This isn't a game, Bobby." He swung toward one of the ranger fairies. "What happened?"

The fairy blinked and wobbled slightly. "Beautiful sound," he murmured, then he froze again.

Josh groaned and raised his hands to his forehead. "What's going on?"

Josh scanned the mountainside and the valley, his heart pounding. Long moments passed. The ranger fairy sprang back to life. It darted over to the other Anolari. They all began chattering and motioning excitedly.

Josh crouched again and peered into the distance. Far off, he saw the black mass hovering above the forest. Several birds seemed to leave the mass and wing north toward the mountains. Others left the main flock and glided above the trees, as if searching for something. What's going on? Josh said quietly.

He tried to talk to the ranger fairies, but they all seemed just as confused.

Then the main flock of birds started north, moving above the forest in a great black mass. The flock reached the hills and crossed over a pass, disappearing behind the mountains.

Josh studied the kids. Most looked bewildered and scared, talking in hushed, anxious voices and huddling under their blankets.

As the sun slowly sank in the west, a low rumble sounded. Josh turned left and saw a fireball thundering over the western mountains. The fiery object roared across the valley, turning the forest green into a brilliant wash of red, orange, and yellow. The fireball hurtled east, disappearing over the horizon. Quiet returned to the valley.

The sky grew dark. Bobby and Celia's owli rings began to glow, emitting a soft blue light. Josh worried the light could be seen. He asked the kids to hide the rings in their blankets.

Sitting in the darkness, apprehension and self-doubt filled Josh. He believed it was his fault that his friends were in danger. They had stayed behind in Oriafen because he hadn't persuaded them to leave. Leoku had warned that enemies would return. He was right. The question was if the Panishie could protect them.

Josh waited impatiently for any sign of Sirie or the other fairies who had flown away. There was none.

Josh sighed and looked over his shoulder. Wesley sat cross-legged a few feet away, his eyes closed and his back straight. Something about Wesley's position brought back a distant memory. Josh remembered his mom sitting up in a hospital bed. He and his dad had come to visit her. She looked thin and pale. Josh climbed onto the bed and curled up beside her. She held him close. They talked quietly for some minutes. Then her words drifted off. He tipped his head to see her face. Her eyes were closed, and her chin rested on her chest. He could hear her soft breathing.

Josh's dad gave him a kind smile and raised a finger to his lips. He helped Josh off the bed. They said goodbye and left the room. Josh didn't talk on the way home. That was the last time his saw his mom alive.

He often missed her. He missed his dad too. He missed his dad's deep, calm voice, and their talks on the backyard deck in the evenings.

But he didn't miss his stepmom, Teresa. Dylan did. Dylan was her son. Josh wasn't. Last summer, Josh had come home in the afternoon to find Teresa and Dylan on the bench in the garden. Teresa was tickling Dylan as he giggled and squirmed in her arms. Josh watched them from the window, smiling at their happiness. Then Teresa turned her head and noticed him through the glass. Her face hardened and she gave him a strained smile.

Josh ran to his room. He pulled an old photo album out from under his bed. It had pictures of his mom. He loved her smile and her gentle mahogany eyes. He thumbed through the pages and paused at a photo on a winter's day. He was walking with her through a park. Snowflakes were tumbling down.

"Come with me," his mom said. They strolled to a shop filled with wooden toys. He played with the toys for hours and took home a train set.

Come with me.

He wished he could hear her voice again.

Josh cleared his throat and opened his eyes. Quiet snoring echoed through the cave. The kids lay against one another like a row of sandbags on a levy.

The children clutched their blankets against the cold. Josh quietly made his way to the cave mouth and stared out at the stars twinkling in the moonless sky. The wind gusted, and he shivered. He returned to his blanket and curled up beneath it.

Josh awoke in the night to voices. He peered through the darkness. Sirie and Leoku were silhouetted at the cave mouth. He sensed other things there – larger things. He stood up.

"What happened?" he called out.

Sirie glided over. "You sleep now," she said in a weary voice.

"What happenned at Oriafen?"

Sirie shook her head. "We talk later. You sleep now."

"No, I want to know."

Sirie hesitated. "They gone," she finally murmured. "The Panishie search... I don't know."

Josh froze. Sirie kept speaking, but he couldn't hear her words. Leoku had been right. They weren't safe at Oriafen. The kids were gone, and it was all his fault.

Josh's shoulders slumped. "What happened?" he asked in a hollow voice.

"I don't know," Sirie said bitterly. "Will go back in morning."

Josh pressed his hands to his face. He felt weak and empty inside. He became still, not knowing what to do. Then determination returned. He took a deep breath and his hands closed. His eyes focused. He squinted, sensing strange objects on the ledge – towering objects. He drew back a step.

"What are those things?" he asked.

"Leoku call them," Sirie said. "They protect you. Now sleep."

Josh peered at the nearest object. It was about two feet wide at its base and rising straight up into the air before arching out in great arms.

"It's a tree," he murmured. He touched the object. The surface felt smooth and hard.

"Yes," Sirie said, tugging on his shirt. "It friend, but you sleep. Tomorrow we journey far."

Josh sighed. He nodded. "Okay... okay."

He stumbled back to his blanket and curled up beneath it but kept an eye on the towering objects filling the ledge.

When he awoke, his cheeks were numb, and ice covered the tips of his shoes. He peered at the cave mouth, where a half-dozen massive trees filled the ledge.

Josh sat up and threw off his blanket. He made his way through the sleeping kids to the cave mouth. There he stared up. Several strange monkey-like creatures sat in the branches of the trees. The monkey creatures had long, snow-white fur, dark, beady eyes, and bright orange lips.

A ranger fairy sat perched on a branch near two of the monkey creatures. He was talking to the furry monkeys in a language Josh didn't recognize.

The conversation stopped, and the monkeys gazed down. One barked an order, and a huge limb descended. Josh stumbled back in surprise. The limb slowed to a stop near the ground. The monkey creature eyed Josh and motioned. Josh's brow furrowed with uncertainty. He pointed at the limb. The fairy nodded. Josh swallowed and stepped forward. He cautiously sat down on the limb with his legs straddling each side. The limb slowly rose upward, lifting Josh into the leafy foliage.

"Brave boy," the monkey said with a grin that Josh didn't quite trust. The monkey seemed to sense Josh's doubt. It mumbled something to the ranger fairy and shook with laughter.

Josh peered warily at the furry creature. "Who are you?"

"I am a mountain ghost," the monkey said, with a cackle.

Josh suspected the creature was taunting him. His face heated with irritation.

The monkey blinked. Its mouth twitched nervously. The other monkeys began to twitter. Then one of the monkeys shouted, and another tree started to move. A section of the trunk lifted off the ground, trailing a string of roots that swung out over the hillside. The roots came down, gripped the slope, and lifted the rest of the tree off the ledge. The tree continued this maneuver in a clockwise motion, throwing out roots and gripping the ground before pulling itself upward and onward until it passed out of view.

Josh heard his brother's voice. "Whoa, it's a forest!"

Dylan was peering out of the cave mouth. He tilted his head and rubbed his eyes. Then he spotted Josh in the branches.

"How'd you get up there?"

Before Josh could answer, Dylan grabbed his pants with his left hand and let out a stinker that shot him into the air. He grabbed a branch of the tree with his right hand and swung himself up and onto Josh's limb.

The monkeys burst into loud chattering and swung here and there through the branches. One paused close to Dylan and peered at the boy, extending a furry hand toward his face.

Dylan drew away and leaped to another branch. "What are those things, Josh?" he cried.

"I don't know, but they can talk."

Josh caught the eye of the nearest monkey and pointed to the ground. "Down please."

"Not so brave," the creature said grinning.

The limb descended. When the branch neared the ground, Josh jumped off. Dylan dropped out of the tree and landed beside him.

Within the cave, most of the kids were still asleep. Wesley was sitting upright and cross-legged, with his eyes closed and his head bent forward.

Josh heard a faint buzzing. He turned and saw Sirie gliding up through the trees, her face red and tear stained.

"Did you go back?" he asked, extending his hand. She landed on his palm.

"Yes, they destroy so much," Sirie said, anger simmering in her eyes.

Leoku glided up and landed beside the nearest tree.

"The Panishie have suffered," he said shaking his head wearily. "The rarewar came for your friends. The Panishie fought, but the rarewar brought a gifted one, a child with golden hair and a voice of exquisite beauty. The child sang, and all who heard the sound were frozen in wonder. As we flew to Oriafen, the sound reached our ears. It entranced us. We fell out of the sky. I thought our lives were ended, but the earth shook, and thunder rolled the valley. It drowned out the beautiful sound. We awoke from the trance and rushed to Oriafen but were too late. The earth had been split, trees ripped from the ground, boulders tossed through the woods, water drained from the pools, and your friends gone."

"What happened to them?" Josh cried.

The anxiety in his voice awoke several other kids. Footsteps sounded. Wesley, Annie, and Gabrielle stepped out of the cave. They stood near Josh.

"Your friends have been taken to Sidtarr, the usurper of Risrean," Leoku said solemnly.

Josh remembered that name. Leoku had talked about him at Oriafen. Josh's eyes grew steely. "Who is this Sidtarr?"

"He is a tyrant. He lusts for power. He rules a land to the north but seeks to conquer all Hevelen. He hopes to use your friends' gifts for this purpose. He is ruthless and cruel but can appear kind to those he is using."

"What should we do?" Wesley asked.

The ranger fairy grimaced. "As I have said, you must go to the Silver City. There you will find the silver cat. Only he can help your friends."

"Who is this silver cat you keep talking about?" Dylan asked.

"He is a gifted one like you, but very powerful."

"Is he a cat?"

Hyena-like laughter broke out among the monkey creatures.

A sudden fury seized Josh. "Why are you laughing? This isn't funny! Shut up!"

The monkeys fell silent but stared icily at Josh. He ignored their gaze. Anguish swelled in him. His friends had been taken to someplace – he didn't know where - and he couldn't help them. He had to find some cat, who could. None of it made sense. He raised his hands to his face and closed his eyes. The world seemed to spin. He felt dizzy. He sat back on a rock and leaned forward resting his elbows on his knees. He felt a hand on his shoulder.

"You tried," Wesley said. "You tried to get them to come, but they wanted to stay."

"I didn't try hard enough," Josh said wearily.

"You didn't know. How could you? None of us did."

Tears rolled down Annie's cheeks. She sat beside Josh and wrapped her arm around his waist. "What should we do? How can we help them?"

"I don't know," Josh said, "but we'll find out."

Dylan leaped over and grabbed Josh's arm. He pulled himself close and burrowed his face into Josh's side. Josh hugged Dylan and exhaled. He had messed up, but he could still get these kids to a safe place. He couldn't quit now.

"We'll go to the Silver City," he said. "Then we'll see if that silver cat can help us. If he can – or even if he can't – we'll find the other kids and bring them there too."

Celia stepped out of the cave. She tiptoed over, rubbing her eyes. "Why is everyone hugging?"

"Because we need to," Annie said, smiling through her tears. "Do you want one too?"

"Uh-huh."

Annie spread her arms and grabbed Celia, lifting her off her feet. Annie plopped back down on the rock with Celia in her lap. Celia glanced over her shoulder. "Where did all the trees come from?" she asked.

Before anyone could answer, Celia glanced up and caught her breath. "Monkeys! Monkeys in the trees!"

"They are called the *mio eno*," Leoku said, "They live in these mountains. Mio eno means 'snow monkey'. They are masters of the tolepar, the walking trees of the highlands."

Celia blinked. "Walking trees? What trees?"

"Those," Leoku said, pointing to the towering objects on the ledge."

Celia's eyes widened. "They can walk?"

Leoku nodded.

Celia cautiously reached out and touched the tree closest to her.

"The mio eno live in ice cities high in these mountains. They use tolepar to build their cities. In return, the snow monkeys take care of the trees, keeping them healthy and strong."

Celia gazed up into the branches, her mouth open in astonishment.

Leoku turned to Josh. "You must leave this place. You cannot delay. Sidtarr will soon learn that gifted ones remain in Hevelen. He will send his servants to find you."

Josh understood. He returned to the cave and woke the remaining kids. As they ate a quick breakfast, he told them what had happened at Oriafen. Bobby and Celia began to cry. The other kids became quiet, looking at one another anxiously.

After they had finished eating, the children packed up their stuff. Several snow monkeys bellowed at the tolepar, and each tree lowered a great limb to the ground. Josh showed the kids how to sit on the limbs. They followed his example, then the enormous branches slowly rose back into the foliage with the kids astride them.

Once everyone was comfortably settled in the foliage, the snow monkeys shouted again, and the tolepar began moving off the ledge. Each tree threw out great roots that gripped the hillside and lifted its main trunk up the mountain slope in a turning manner so that each tree made a complete rotation every thirty feet or so.

After ten minutes of climbing, Josh stretched his arms and leaned back, nestling comfortably between the tree trunk and a limb to the right of the one on which he sat. He felt safe there, well hidden in the foliage. The other kids were concealed too, and he relaxed for the first time since the afternoon before.

The tolepar climbed the hillside steadily, moving through groves of pine and cypress, interrupted now and then by large fields of meadow grass. Josh spotted other trees moving along the hillside. Some joined their party, while others passed on and disappeared into the thick woods.

By midmorning, Josh had begun to dislike the snow monkeys. There was something sly, tricky about them that he didn't trust, and they had the annoying habit of yelling at the tolepar trees for no apparent reason. The yelling continued on and off throughout the morning, though the trees seemed to be doing everything fine.

At one point, several of the mio eno began harranging one of the trees. Josh glanced at Annie, who shook her head and rolled her eyes. On the far side of Annie, Rhea sat frowning with her arms folded tightly on her stomach. Rhea took a deep breath and suddenly shouted, "What's wrong with you idiots? The trees are great! Just shut up already!"

Annie and Josh laughed quietly, but the snow monkeys ignored Rhea and continued berating the tree.

Only Bobby seemed to like the mio eno, happily chatting with the furry creatures and asking them a constant stream of questions. The snow monkeys listened to Bobby patiently and replied to his questions, but Josh could tell their answers were vague and meaningless.

At one point, Josh climbed over to Bobby's branch. "So, what do you think of these guys?" he asked, pointing toward several of the snow monkeys.

"Theey smart!" Bobby said, his eyes twinkling. "Ii liikee eem."

"Huh..." Josh said, doubtfully. "Doesn't their yelling bother you?"

"Nooo," Bobby said. "Thaat juust waay theey aare."

Josh eyed the snow monkeys, wondering if Bobby saw something in them that he had missed.

By late morning, the trees were moving through a barren landscape blanketed in deep drifts of snow. Sirie sat silently on a small branch nearby Josh. He tried to talk to her several times, but she stared back at him silently, her face a mixture of grief and fury.

263

After another snow monkey tirade at the tolepar, Josh decided to probe Sirie. "The Panishie must love the mio eno," he said.

"No," Sirie replied with a hard glare. "Panishie not love mio eno."

"Why?" Josh asked feigning surprise.

Sirie hovered close to his ear and whispered in a stream of words, many of which he couldn't understand. But he made out something about the Panishie discovering precious stones in the Elena caverns, and the mio eno claiming the stones for themselves. Then some kind of conflict happened which didn't end until the Panishie left for Oriafen.

Josh eyed the snow monkeys, wondering if they still harbored bad feelings toward the Panishie.

Early in the afternoon, the tolepar reached a wall of ice rising more than a hundred feet into the mountain air. Without slowing, the trees started up the sheer wall, their great roots gripping the ice firmly. The trees climbed rapidly to the top, then crossed over and descended to a flat plain which spread toward distant ice structures.

"This mio eno home," Sirie said gloomily.

The trees advanced across the plain. As they neared the ice structures, Josh spotted immense tolepar trees standing beside the buildings as if on guard. Adult mio eno scurried along the icy ground from one building to another carrying baskets of food and goods, while young snow monkeys played together in narrow alleys between the structures.

As the trees passed between the ice structures, Josh peered into the windows, seeing vast rooms with floors covered in plush rugs of brown and orange. Food was laid out on low tables at the center of each room, and pillows surrounded each table.

"Can we stop here for the night?" Josh asked.

Sirie shook her head. "Mio eno not let outsiders stay in their land."

Josh sighed. It would be nice to sleep with a pillow on a soft rug. He imagined warming himself by a roaring fire but then realized these buildings couldn't have fires because they were made of ice.

The tolepars left the ice structures behind and headed toward an immense staircase that rose from the rear of the plain. The trees ascended the stairs to another ice wall rising as high as the first. They scaled this easily and continued up the mountainside.

As the temperatures plummeted, the kids wrapped themselves tightly in their blankets, but Josh found that even the wonderfully warm Panishie fabric couldn't keep out the bitter mountain cold.

By midafternoon, the ridge of the mountain came into view, and the tolepar began the final ascent. Near the crest, winds rose to gale force, pounding the trees and the children within the branches. But the cold didn't bother the snow monkeys, who chattered noisily among themselves and swung around in the branches as if it were a warm spring day.

The tolepar halted at the peak. Josh looked down the far side, seeing woods that began some distance below sweeping down to the lower reaches of the mountain. Beyond the woods, golden plains spread south as far as he could see. To the east, the forest ran along the slope of the mountain to a distant range marching south and shrouded in fog. To the west, the hillside dropped precipitously to a sea curling along the coast.

A snow monkey swung off a branch and cried, "From here you see all land and sky."

Not quite, Josh thought. He peered into the distance. There was no sign of the Silver City. No sign of any city. He twisted and scrutinized the distant mountains rising north of the valley. Beyond that range, a barren land stretched to the horizon.

Dylan shivered in his blanket. "Can we go?" he pleaded. "I feel like an ice cube on the moon."

Josh caught the eye of a snow monkey and waved forward. The creature grinned and bellowed. The trees shifted and began the descent into lands unknown.

Chapter 18:
Tumbling Light

"R un!" Emma cried, her heart pounding in her chest.

"Come on," She pulled Mya toward the undergrowth. The great bird swept down, its head bobbing and its yellow eyes swirling. Emma had no time to think. She whirled and swung her arms, warping and bending the light. The bird and everything beyond disappeared into a chaos of colors. She spun back, hearing the creature squawk in confusion. She grabbed Mya's hand and dashed forward frantically, stumbling through the trees to escape before the light refocused. She ducked behind some bushes and yanked Mya down beside her, then twisted, searching for the bird.

"Where is it? I can't see," Mya whispered forlornly.

"I know," Emma said in a hushed voice. "Just stay with me."

The light slowly coalesced, and the winged creature came into view, gliding low, hunting for its prey. The bird arced left and swept toward the bushes. Emma rose and swung her arms again, shattering the light into a thousand tiny shards as a roar filled the air. The ground shook, and the trees swayed. Cracks split the earth.

Emma grabbed Mya's wrist and tugged her along, staggering over the rolling ground. They stumbled through the woods until they found a thicket. Emma pulled her sister into the foliage, thorns, and twigs scratching their arms and faces as they pushed deeper.

At the center of the thicket, the girls squatted, breath coming in rapid gasps. Emma peered back through the bushes, searching for any sign of the winged beast. The ground rocked and slid. She tipped forward onto her knees, then back up into a squatting position. The shaking stopped, and everything fell quiet. Emma glanced at Mya and raised a finger to her lips. Mya nodded. The girls waited breathlessly.

There was a thump, and a creature landed in the forest. The bird moved through the woods sniffing the air and tearing at the ground. Then a squawk shattered the stillness, and the beast dove into the thicket, lunging toward the girls. Emma swung her arms again, and the light whirled and scattered. She grabbed Mya's hand and pulled her through the foliage behind them. They broke into the open. Emma pulled Mya along and gradually sped up until they were sprinting through the woods, dodging in and out of trees. Then Mya stumbled and fell headlong. Emma pulled up and ran back.

"You okay," she asked, helping her sister to her feet.

"Yeah, but I can't breathe," Mya said, gasping, one hand pressed to her chest. "I need to stop."

"Yeah, okay," Emma said, also out of breath. She looked back anxiously. "Let's stop here."

The girls ducked behind an elm tree and squatted. Emma leaned against the trunk, resting her hands on her knees. Mya squatted beside her. Emma scanned the woods around them. Every now and then, she ducked her head around the tree to look back the way they'd come. There was no sign of the bird. Minutes passed, and their breathing slowed.

Emma had no idea where they were, but she believed Oriafen was behind them. She took Mya's hand and cautiously led her back the way they'd come. Several minutes went by. She heard a flapping and ducked under the branches of a spruce, pulling Mya with her. They huddled together. Emma was thankful she wasn't alone.

The flapping grew louder, then faded. Silence returned. The girls continued through the woods until they came to a grassy field dotted with purple larkspurs and yellow daisies. They paused at the tree line. Emma stared up at the sky for a moment, then back at the field. "It looks about fifty yards to the other side," she said. "And I don't see any birds."

"So, do we cross?" Mya asked.

"Yes. But let's hurry."

Emma pulled her sister forward. The girls loped through the grass. Emma kept her eyes on the distant trees. She felt hopeful. They couldn't be far from Oriafen. The fairies should find them soon.

A breeze gusted, and the smell of meadow grass and wildflowers filled her senses. Then a flapping stirred a sudden terror. A dark shape plunged out of the sky, landing in the field ahead. Emma let out a scream and skidded to a stop, pulling Mya with her.

"What is it, Em?" Mya cried in panic.

"A bird."

Emma's eyes darted. There was nowhere to hide.

The creature angled its nasty head and peered at the girls through swirling yellow eyes. Emma pushed Mya behind her. Then she dipped her head and whirled her hands, bending and twisting the light. The view fractured and fragmented, breaking into a thousand colors, like strange paintings she had seen at a modern art museum. She stepped sideways, motioning for Mya to follow. She continued swinging her arms, manipulating the light. The bird squawked and crashed here and there through the grass, searching blindly for the girls.

Emma circled the creature, again and again, whirling her arms until the bird's cries weakened and morphed into forlorn screeches that eventually fell silent.

Emma took Mya's hand and quietly, but hurriedly, led her to the woods, ignoring the swirling colors behind them. They rushed through the trees, running until they could barely breathe. Finally, Mya pulled her to a stop. Both girls' chests were heaving and their bodies shaking.

"Do you know where we are?" Mya asked.

Emma glanced around and shook her head. She leaned over, pressing her hands to her knees. She believed Oriafen was ahead of them. "Let's keep going this way," she said, pointing. "Maybe we'll find the wooden building with the little furry animals."

"What about the boys?" Mya asked.

Emma blinked, and her heart thumped. She had forgotten about them in the rush to escape the birds. "I don't know," she said, her voice cracking. "I hope the fairies rescued them."

Then the awful realization hit her. She'd seen Ted and CPU carried into the sky. Taken away by the terrible birds to some horrible place. What would happen to them? Tears filled her eyes. She leaned forward and covered her face with her hands.

Mya's arms came around her, and she started to cry too. They held each other tight and let their emotions pour out until finally, they grew quiet.

Emma cleared her throat. "I hate this place, Mya. Why are we here? And why didn't I listen to Josh?" She wiped her cheeks. "He told us this place wasn't safe, and I didn't believe him."

Mya shook her head. "It doesn't matter now, Em. We didn't know. We just have to find the fairies again and hope the boys are okay."

Emma nodded tightly, and they rose, walking hand in hand. Emma's breathing slowed, and she felt calm. A thought came to her.

"Do you remember the sound when the birds came?" she asked. "That beautiful, pure sound? It was so wonderful… I didn't want to move. I couldn't move."

"Me either," Mya said, staring off at nothing. "It felt like a dream or like heaven. Where did it come from?"

Emma shrugged. "It was beautiful, I wasn't scared. Even when the birds came, I wasn't afraid. I just wanted to listen." She raised her hand and rubbed at her dry lips. "But I don't think CPU could hear it. You remember? He kept asking what was wrong when none of us could move."

"Yeah... Something's wrong with his hearing—like my eyes."

"Uh huh... But when the earthquake started, the music stopped. Do you remember?"

Mya gave a slow nod.

A distant flapping interrupted the conversation. Sudden panic filled Emma. She pushed Mya toward a grove of ash trees. They crawled under the lowest branches of a tree and huddled together.

Emma raised her eyes but could see nothing. The flapping grew louder and then faded. Quiet returned to the forest. She exhaled, feeling a wave of exhaustion. "I'm tired," she said, closing her eyes. "Let's stay here for a while."

"Okay. I'm tired too."

Emma put her palms together and lay them flat on the leafy ground. Then she rested her head on her hands and closed her eyes, quickly sinking into sleep.

When she awoke, it was dark. She sat up and squinted but could see nothing. She heard her sister snoring softly and reached out, finding Mya beside her. Emma listened to the night sounds— crickets chirping and a faint buzzing. A breeze rustled the branches. She leaned against the tree, wishing she was home in her bed. She missed her safe room and her mom's food. She decided to stay awake until morning.

She awoke with light streaming down through the branches, making pretty patterns on her clothes and skin. So much for staying awake. She rolled over and shook Mya. "Hey, it's morning."

Mya rubbed her eyes. "Huh?"

Emma knocked several leaves out of Mya's hair. Then she sighed. "I'm starved."

"Me too," Mya said. "Do you think the birds are gone?"

"Probably, we slept all night."

"Good. I'm thirsty. Maybe we can find some water."

Emma crawled out from under the tree. She brushed the dirt and leaves off her clothes. Mya scrambled out behind her.

"Which way?" Mya asked.

Emma rubbed her forehead. "I don't know, but let's keep going that way," she said, pointing in the direction they had been walking the day before. Mya nodded with little enthusiasm.

As they made their way through the woods, the ache in Emma's belly grew, and she began to feel light-headed.

Mya tugged her to a stop. "Do you hear that?"

"Hear what?"

"Water, I think. Over there," Mya said, pointing off to the right.

Emma listened, angling her head. "Yeah, I do hear something."

The sound seemed to come from thick underbrush. The girls headed toward it. They pushed their way through the bushes and found themselves at the bank of a creek several feet wide.

The girls bent down and drank eagerly. After satisfying her thirst, Emma strolled along the bank, wondering if she could find any fruit, but didn't. She returned to her sister and sat, drawing her knees to her chest and wrapping her arms around them.

"I wonder what Mom is doing?" she said, tipping her head.

Mya wiped her mouth and winced. "I don't want to think about it. She must be going nuts. We've been gone for a week. She probably thinks we've been kidnapped or something."

"Yeah, and I bet she's cleaned the house ten times. I wonder if Dad is back from his business trip?"

Mya folded her arms. "I'm sure he is."

Emma rested her chin on her hands. "I miss Mom but... not Dad so much."

"Yeah, well... you're still mad at him," Mya said with a slight frown. "But it's not just Dad's fault you know. Mom can be difficult."

Emma pursed her lips. Difficult was a nice way to put it. Her mom could be maddening. She was a neat freak who constantly nagged after them to clean their rooms, fold their clothes, and wash their dishes. She also nitpicked how they dressed, how they talked, their posture, and their manners.

But what Emma hated most was when her mom would say, "If you loved me, you'd do (something) for me." Emma loved her mom and hated feeling she needed to prove it. But even so, she blamed her dad. If he wasn't away all the time, her mom would be happier and wouldn't be so frustrating.

"Why does Dad need to go on all those trips? He comes back for a day or two, and then he's gone again."

"It's his job," Mya replied. "He's the top salesman at his company. That's why we have a nice house and a new car."

"Remember when we were little, and we'd go on picnics or to drive-in movies in the old station wagon? We used to go camping too. We never do that anymore, because he's always away."

Mya shrugged. "Yeah, he works too much, but something else has changed. When he's home, he and Mom don't talk much. The only time Mom speaks to him is when she wants him to do a chore or go to the store. He does what she asks and doesn't complain, but something's wrong. I don't know what, but—"

"I hate it," Emma cried, clenching her hands.

Mya's arms came around her in a warm embrace. "It's okay, Em," Mya said. "At least they don't yell at each other like the Leebers across the street and aren't divorcing like Annie's parents or uncle Julius and Aunt Marian. They love each other. You can tell. I think it'll get better."

Emma sighed. She hoped Mya was right.

Mya unwrapped her arms and sat back. Then she began to hum softly.

Emma eyed her with slight irritation. "Why are you doing that?"

"Remember when I sang in the woods and all the animals came? I promised I wouldn't do it with any other kids around, but now it's just you and me, so I'm wondering if it will happen again."

She paused, giving a mischievous grin. "You wouldn't eat them, would you?"

Emma rolled her eyes. "Yuck! They're covered in fur and feathers."

Mya resumed her humming. Emma recognized the song. It was one their grandfather used to play for them, but she didn't remember the words. She raised her eyes and spotted a pair of blue jays alighting on a branch above them.

Then several gray mice hopped out of the underbrush on the far side of the creek. The mice paused, their little ears wiggling nervously as they listened. Behind them, a raccoon poked its head out from behind an alder bush. It raised its nose and sniffed the air.

A thrill coursed through Emma. She glanced to her right as a large gray rabbit, and several baby ones hopped out from behind an elm tree. The baby rabbits tipped their heads from side to side as they listened to the tune. Emma laughed. "Look," she said pointing.

"What?" Mya asked.

"Rabbits."

Mya peered in the direction Emma pointed. "I can't see. How many?

"A momma and three little ones."

Mya smiled. "Are there any other animals?"

"Yes," Emma said and described each of the creatures she could see.

Mya sighed and continued humming.

A squirrel with a hazelnut in its teeth hopped onto a stump to their left. The squirrel took the nut in its paws and bit down, cracking the shell. It immediately swallowed the kernel and dropped the shell pieces into the leaves. It listened for a moment and then scampered away. The squirrel soon returned with its cheeks puffed out like two golf balls. It opened its mouth and dropped five more hazelnuts onto the stump.

The squirrel ate one of the nuts. Emma's stomach ached from hunger. She mustered up her nerve and stepped toward the little creature.

The squirrel's eyes grew wide, and it readied to flee. But Emma knelt and smiled gently. She stuck out her hand, palm up, hoping the creature would understand. The squirrel cocked its head back and forth, then it grabbed a hazelnut, broke the shell, and scurried forward, dropping the kernel into Emma's outstretched palm.

"Thank you," she said, beaming.

The squirrel sat upright and blinked as Emma popped the nut into her mouth. It wasn't much, but she chewed slowly, savoring the flavor before swallowing. Emma smiled again at the squirrel and sat back down beside Mya.

A moment later, a chipmunk scurried forward and dropped a walnut on the ground beside the girls. Then the raccoon on the far side of the creek waddled over to the bank with a bright red apple in one paw. It set the fruit down at the edge of the water and waddled away.

"Look!" Emma exclaimed, using a large rock as a steppingstone to hop across the creek. "They know we're hungry."

She picked up the apple and took a bite. The sweetness burst into her mouth. "Mmm." She stepped back over the creek and handed the apple to Mya, who took a bite.

They shared the apple with Mya humming intermittently. A pair of squirrels appeared and dropped more nuts at their feet. Then an opossum left a pear. A dozen small gray birds landed on the bank each holding a plump grape in its beak.

Mya squinted. "I think those birds are vireos."

The little birds dropped the fruit and flew off.

"This is wonderful," Emma cried, picking up a grape and washing it off before popping it into her mouth. "Really crazy, but wonderful."

The forest creatures brought more food, including berries, peaches, and a variety of nuts, many of which Emma had never seen. They also left roots, worms and a few dead insects, which the girls avoided.

So long as Mya hummed, the food kept coming. When the girls were full, Mya grew quiet, and the animals slowly drifted away. The girls drank again from the creek, then Emma led Mya back out through the bushes, and they continued walking in the direction they had been going earlier, hoping to find the fairies before dark.

After a half hour, Emma began to miss the animals and asked Mya to hum again.

"I think I'll do a different song," Mya replied. "I wonder if they'll still come. What should I sing?"

"I don't know. How about 'Twinkle, Twinkle Little Star'?"

Mya chuckled and began singing the lullaby. Soon, a menagerie of scampering, hopping, trotting, and flying creatures had joined the girls as they walked through the woods.

By mid-afternoon, Emma's hunger had returned. She spotted a creek, and they stopped there to rest. The animals brought more food.

After filling her stomach, Emma lay back and stared at blue sky peeking through the branches. Her thoughts drifted to the kids who had left with the ranger fairies. "I hope Josh and the others are okay."

"Yeah," Mya said. "They've probably reached the mountains by now."

"Wesley didn't look happy when they left."

"Uh huh. Maybe because you weren't going," Mya said, with a sly grin.

"Shush," Emma said, slapping the air. "That's not true. Something was bothering him."

"Sarah."

Emma nodded slowly. She wondered what had happened to Sarah and Timmy. Theralin said they had a protector, but who was that? She wished she and Mya had a protector.

After a short rest, the girls started out again. Emma led Mya by the hand. They walked for several hours but didn't see any sign of the fairies. Emma began to worry they would have to spend another night in the forest. Then the woods abruptly ended, and a stunning sight rose before them.

From the tree line, the ground climbed gradually for some fifty feet to the top of the incline, where a white stone wall towered into the air and ran several hundred yards to the right and left before disappearing around the curve of the hilltop.

"What is this?" Mya said, shading her eyes from the sun.

"A wall. Maybe there's a city inside—with people." Emma clapped her hands in excitement. "Look, there's a gate over there." She pointed some distance to the right, where a wrought-iron gate stood in the stone wall. The girls hurried along the base of the hill, keeping just inside the trees until they reached a set of white stone stairs leading up to the black gate.

"I don't hear anything," Mya said with her hand to her ear. "Why is it so quiet?"

Emma scanned the wall. "Should we go to the gate? We could see what's inside, but we'll be out in the open. Those black birds might see us."

Mya bit her lip. "Yeah, but if there're people, they can help us."

Emma nodded and led Mya up the stairs, nervously checking the sky for any sign of black birds. When she reached the gate, Emma peered through the bars, viewing an empty courtyard. On the far side of the courtyard, stone houses lined a pathway that appeared to run toward the center of a town. The place looked abandoned.

"Where is everyone?" Emma said half to herself.

Mya tipped her head back and listened. "I don't hear anything."

"Let's go inside," Emma said quietly. She gently pushed on the iron bars, and the gate swung in.

Emma led Mya across the courtyard, avoiding clumps of leaves and dirt scattered over the ground. Patches of grass grew in cracks between the stones.

At the first house, they stopped before a beautiful arched doorway that rose high above their heads. They passed under the archway and entered a hall that led to a room with an enormous wooden table surrounded by half a dozen chairs. The table was eye level, and the seats rose above Emma's waist.

"Everything is huge," she whispered. "Like it was made for giants." She ran her hand across the seat of a chair. When she lifted it away, a layer of dust covered her palm. Cobwebs fluttered in the corners of the ceiling. "It's so dirty. As if no one has cleaned this place in a long time."

Emma led Mya into a second room, which appeared to be a kitchen with cabinets and a fireplace. They continued to a third room with large black-rimmed windows and a thick woven mat covering the floor. They explored the rest of the house and found a chamber with a bathtub the size of a small pool, along with two other empty rooms.

Disappointed, Emma led Mya back outside. When she passed through the archway, she stopped to look around. The silence was eerie.

Mya came up beside her. "Where is everyone?"

Emma shook her head. "Why would they build a beautiful town like this and not live in it?" Hands on her hips, she turned from side to side.

"Let's go further into town," Mya suggested. "Maybe there are people there."

Emma was starting to feel weird about the place but agreed to go.

They walked down the stone path toward the center of town, passing house after house, with the only sound their footsteps and the wind scattering dry leaves. The path ended at a large dome-shaped stone building with a glittering roof that rose higher than a church steeple.

They entered and found themselves in a cavernous hall, empty except for a fountain at its center. The floor was covered in concentric rings of stone surrounding the fountain, and the roof was a honeycomb of windows through which sunlight poured into the vast room.

Emma cleared her dry throat and grabbed Mya's hand tugging her forward. Mya followed unhurriedly, tipping her head from side to side and sniffing the air. "It smells minty."

Emma was too thirsty to care about the smell. She went straight to the fountain. A low stone wall surrounded the fountain enclosing a pool that shimmered in the sunlight. Emma leaned down, cupping her hands, and scooped up the water. It tasted cold and sweet. She drank eagerly. Mya knelt beside her, sniffing the water for a moment, then drinking some herself.

Emma wiped her mouth and exhaled. Then she plopped down on the low wall. Mya sat beside her.

Emma peered at the back of the hall. "There's a door over there," she said, pointing. "Do you want to see where it goes?"

Mya nodded. They headed to the rear of the hall but found the door led to an empty room. They stepped back into the large chamber.

Emma gazed up at the windows in the ceiling and noticed they were set in a series of rings. Those in the outermost sphere were triangles, while those in the second ring were rectangles, and the third, pentagons. They continued this way to the innermost ring, which was a series of octagons. At the center of the sphere was a single nine-sided window as wide as the dome-shaped monkey bars in their playground back at school.

"This place is so beautiful. I wonder what happened to the people who lived here," Emma said, half to herself.

Mya shrugged.

"I'm hungry," Emma said, "Let's go back outside and see if the animals will bring us more food?"

Mya nodded, and Emma led her out of the hall and down the stone path to the iron gate. They sat down at the top of the stairs, and Mya began to hum "Row, Row, Row Your Boat" in a clear voice. Animals of every size and shape soon appeared out of the forest, scurrying and scampering up the slope, while birds circled overhead and landed on the wall and hillside.

The forest creatures brought more nuts and fruits, and the girls ate hungrily. As Emma bit into her second apple, a deep growl rose from the woods. The animals suddenly scattered, and the girls were left alone on the hilltop. Emma peered into the trees and gasped as a massive wolf creature padded out of the forest.

Mya stopped humming. "What is it?" she asked anxiously. But Emma couldn't speak. She could hardly breathe.

The wolf moved onto the slope, its great back rising as high as a horse, and its sinews rippling like a lion. The creature fixed its steely gaze on the girls, its amber eyes shining like golden pools. Black speckles dotted its thick gray coat, and enormous teeth shown beneath its long snout.

Two more wolves appeared out of the trees, following the first up the slope. Emma's heart pounded. "It's wo-o-olves, Mya," she stammered. "S-s-sing."

Mya tried to hum, but only heavy, awkward breaths came out.

Emma gulped and raised her trembling hands to warp the light. Then a squeak pierced the air. Emma looked down. A ground squirrel quivered at her feet. The little creature sprang forward. It scampered down the slope, chattering excitedly in high-pitched squeaks that sounded faintly like the fairy language.

The squirrel scurried to the first wolf, its body trembling as it bounced around like a baby kangaroo on a mattress. The wolf ignored the squirrel, and Emma's hands began to whirl, twisting and turning the light. Then Mya's voice returned and the first notes of "Across the Universe" filled the air. Emma's hands grew still, and she waited for the light to reform.

The wolves came into view, standing motionless on the hillside. Then they gently lay their massive bodies down. Emma glanced at her sister with a trembling smile creeping across her face. "They like it."

Mya blinked and wiped strands of hair out of her eyes. The squirrel scampered back to the girls and nuzzled Mya's leg. Emma became still, listening to her sister hum the beautiful melody. Other animals returned cautiously, some bringing food. They gathered near the top of the stairs, keeping a wary eye on the wolves.

Emma ate until she was full. Then she stuffed more food in her pockets for later. The wolves listened peacefully as the sun sank low in the sky. The ground began to tremble, and a rumble filled the air. The wolves raised their heads. The noise swelled to a roar, drowning out Mya's voice. Emma scooted close and wrapped her arms around her sister. She knew what was coming.

The fireball appeared above the western mountains and hurtled across the valley, turning the sky into a blaze of yellow and orange. The wolves howled mournfully, then a wave of heat slammed the hill. Emma and Mya buried their faces against one another as the wind pounded the slope. Everything grew quiet.

Mya resumed her humming until darkness covered the land. When she grew quiet, the wolves rose and padded back into the woods.

"Okay," Emma said in a hushed voice. "What do we do now?"

"I don't know, but I'm exhausted," Mya said. She leaned forward and wiped her face with her hands.

Emma peered over her shoulder. "We could sleep in one of the houses."

Mya nodded. "It'll be creepy, but better than sleeping out here in the open."

"I remember a mat in one of the rooms. Let's go there."

Emma led Mya into the house and found the room with the mat. They lay down side by side. Starlight poured in through the windows casting shadows around them.

Mya quickly dozed off. Emma's eyes grew heavy, and she began to drift off, but then something triggered her instincts, and she came back to full wakefulness. A dark shape passed into the room. Her heart thumped. She heard the rise and fall of an animal's breath – a wolf. There was nowhere to hide. She readied her hands, but the creature lay down, curling its enormous body around her and Mya, its thick, soft fur pressing against them.

Emma's heartbeat slowed. The wolf wanted to protect them, to keep them warm. She eased back and slowly sank into sleep.

She awoke to the sound of soft fluttering and blinked in the bright morning light. Her eyes adjusted, and she found two copper sprites hovering beside her. The wolf was gone. She sat up with a start. One of the fairies signaled to the other and glided out of the room.

The second one said, "*Metoha*."

"Oh," Emma said, feeling a tingle of excitement run down her spine. "Hello." She tugged on her sister's arm. "Mya, Mya... the fairies are back!"

Her sister popped up and glanced around. "Where? What?"

"Right here," Emma said, pointing.

Mya squinted, and a thankful smile spread across her face. "Hello."

The copper sprite nodded its mouth a flat, expressionless line.

"There must be more. Let's go and see," Emma said, bounding off the mat. She paused at the doorway to smooth down her clothes and hurried to the entrance of the house. There a dozen fairies hovered near two massive wolves. One of the wolves was the gray one with black speckles in its coat she had seen the day before. It seemed to be listening as several of the fairies spoke.

At the head of the fairies was an older one in a long silver gown. Emma's heart leaped. "Theralin!"

"Is he here?" Mya asked squinting.

Theralin turned and glided toward the girls, his face softening into deep relief at the sight of them.

"I joy see you," he said. "You good health?"

"Yes, we're fine," Emma said. "But what about our friends? Are they okay?"

Theralin's eyes darkened. "They gone. Rarewar take them. Gifted one with sunlight voice make Panishie still. Cannot protect your friends."

Emma's worst fears were confirmed. She became weak in the legs, and her hands trembled.

"What going to happen to them?" Mya asked.

"They go to Rarewar master. He want them."

"What can we do?"

"You go Silver City. There you safe. Jianar take you." Theralin nodded toward the wolves.

"Are you coming?" Emma asked.

Theralin shook his head. "No, Oriafen suffer. Ground shake and break land. Much to heal. Tarian guide you."

Theralin turned and gazed down the stone path at several fairies gliding out of a house. Emma recognized the blue fairy among them. Her lips spread in a smile.

Tarian rushed toward her. "You are well?"

"Yes," Emma said, meeting his gentle gaze.

"Forgive us for not finding you sooner. We thought the rarewar had carried you away until animals of the forest told us you were at Giridin."

"Giridin?" Emma asked.

"This place is Giridin," Tarian said, glancing around. "A town of the Ancients."

"The who?"

Tarian waved off the question. "We will speak of this later."

Theralin glided over to the wolf with the black-speckled fur. He spoke to the massive creature in an unfamiliar language. The wolf growled, and the other wolf lay down before Emma.

Theralin turned. "Jianar bear you. Rarewar not steal you."

Emma wasn't sure what he meant. The wolf stretched its great neck forward so that its back dipped even lower. Emma gasped and spun toward her sister.

"They want us to ride, Mya. Ride on the wolves."

"What? No way. We'll fall off."

Emma gestured toward Theralin, who stared at the girls sternly. "You ride," he said. "Jianar bring you to Feriyan. You safe."

Emma assumed "jianar" meant the wolves, but she had no idea how she could ride something like that.

"We don't know how."

Theralin shook his head. "Try, and you learn."

Emma gulped and stepped closer to the enormous creature. She wondered how she could get onto its back. Then she heard Mya say, "Hey, that wasn't so hard."

Emma whirled. Mya was sitting upright on the black-speckled wolf.

"How did you do that?"

"I climbed on."

"How did you see?"

"It's a gray blob, but too big to miss."

Emma twisted back toward her wolf. She started forward and sprang, sliding her leg up and over the back of the enormous animal. To her amazement, Emma landed comfortably in its soft fur. She scooted forward, finding a dip behind the beast's shoulder blades, and leaned forward, grabbing chunks of its thick fur.

Tarian glided over. "Jianar are gentle. Do not fear."

Emma nodded. The wolf padded toward the gate. As it started down the hillside, she clenched her teeth and gripped the fur, afraid she would slide forward and tumble right off the animal.

The fairies flew alongside. When the wolves reached the trees, Theralin and most of the copper sprites stopped. Emma peered back. Theralin's hand rose, and he gave a slight wave before Emma lost sight of him. She felt a pang of loss. Her time with the fairies had been like a wonderful dream.

The wolves moved stealthily through the forest. Mya leaned into her beast's back and gripped fistfuls of fur at the base of its neck. Emma did the same, her legs pressing against the wolf's fluid sides, her body warm against the dense and constantly moving fur.

Other huge creatures joined the pack until a dozen great wolves moved soundlessly through the forest. Above, Tarian flew along with five copper sprites.

The wolves increased to a run and the ground rushed by. The forest became a blur. Emma closed her eyes and pressed her face into the thick hair, wondering what lay ahead.

Chapter 19:
The Pass

Sarah sat upright in the saddle and rubbed her neck. They had been riding for two days, heading in a north-westerly direction toward a pass in the mountains. That morning, they'd begun ascending the foothills that climbed out of the valley.

Sarah had been nervous riding a horse at first, but Marigo was gentle and good-natured, and Sarah soon found it easy. Timmy sat behind her and seemed comfortable too. He'd even nodded off more than once, leaning on her shoulder and almost tumbling off the horse.

Marigo seemed tireless and sometimes impatient, hurrying into a quick trot and passing by Osa and the ponies. Once she got ahead, she'd increase to a full gallop, causing Eredel to chase her down. When he caught Marigo, Eredel would scold the mare, but the horse didn't seem to mind.

It was fun traveling with Eredel. He was chatty and laid-back, recounting stories of the land he called Hevelen and the strange creatures that lived in Elderlan forest. He told them about colorful fairies who lived in the woods, bouncing bears that traveled in herds, and climbing rabbits that nested in the treetops. Sarah kept an eye out, but only spotted several deer and a beaver swimming in a creek.

To her relief, Eredel had stopped shooting off electricity. Color had returned to his face, and his skin lost some of its spooky transparency.

Gala trotted happily alongside the horses, occasionally growling or barking at something unseen in the woods. He'd disappear from time to time but always returned with his tail wagging.

Cenio sat perched on Eredel's shoulder, serenely watching the passing scenery and cawing on occasion for no apparent reason.

When they reached the foothills, the ascent was gradual. Sarah didn't realize how high they'd climbed until late in the morning when she peered back and saw the wooded valley stretching out a thousand feet below.

Eredel said the mountains beyond the foothills were called the Uelena Range. Beyond the mountains lay a dry, barren wasteland which they had to cross.

As the sun reached its high point on the second day, they came to a wooded plateau. Eredel led the children through the trees to a stream, where they halted for lunch. Sarah knelt on the bank, happy to dip her dry, chapped hands in the cold water.

As they ate, Eredel told them of travelers who journeyed to this plateau to see a rare flower named the deliena which bloomed once every twelve years. Pilgrims also came to pray and meditate. The plateau was high enough above the valley to stay cool in the summer but avoided the winter snows. Eredel said he'd spent a winter on the plateau when he was young and lived near a waterfall that cascaded down from high in the mountains.

After finishing his meal, Eredel's eyes drooped, and he lay back, resting his head on his pack. Soon he was quietly snoring. Sarah wasn't tired. Well, not sleepy tired. She needed to stretch. She asked Timmy if he wanted to explore the area. Timmy nodded, and

Gala joined them as they set out, following the stream through the woods.

When they heard a distant roar of water, they hurried toward the sound. The trees ended, and they stepped onto the bank of a wide pool surrounded on three sides by a gray rock wall. A light mist filled the air and on the far side of the pool water cascaded down the cliff face from a point high on the mountain slope.

The three of them plopped down on the bank. Sarah closed her eyes, enjoying the cool mist and the afternoon sun on her face. She leaned back, lacing her fingers behind her head, and breathed in slowly. It felt so peaceful.

After a few minutes, Timmy wanted to go back, so they followed the stream in the direction they'd come. As they rounded a bend, Sarah noticed movement at the edge of the trees ahead. She slowed and squinted. She spotted an animal that looked like a plump dog. When it hopped from its front to its back paws, she realized it was a bear—a baby bear. "Look," she said in a hushed voice.

Timmy peered in the direction she pointed. The cub bounded down to the stream and splashed into the water. It flopped around and scrambled back onto the bank, shaking its fur so that water sprayed everywhere. As the cub spun, it stumbled in excitement and bumped into several rocks, causing them to roll into the water.

The baby bear stopped suddenly; its eyes fixed on the tumbling rocks as they disappeared under the surface. The cub waited, as if expecting the rocks to reappear, then it bounced along the shore eagerly, bumping another large stone and causing several more rocks to roll into the water.

"It's so cute," Sarah whispered. "Let's get closer." She tugged on Timmy's arm, pulling him along.

Sarah ducked behind a tree, then hurried to the next one. She did this several times, inching closer to the baby bear. Gala panted quietly and stayed beside her, while Timmy followed reluctantly. Sarah found a large bush they could hide behind.

The cub bounded over to a rock in the shape of a lopsided bowling ball and bent its head, pushing against the rock with its shoulder until the stone came free and rolled down the bank into the stream. The baby bear hopped around excitedly; then it seemed to lose its balance and tipped forward, rolling headfirst into the water.

Sarah let out an involuntary laugh and then cupped her hand over her mouth. The cub's head popped up, and its ears perked, searching curiously. It scanned the bank until its gaze fell on the bush. It paused, staring intently. Then, it splashed out of the water and bounded to the right of the bush, where it could get a better view.

They had been discovered. Sarah stood up. The cub pogoed eagerly, swinging its head from side to side and growled mischievously. At least to Sarah, it seemed mischievous instead of angry. She turned to Timmy. "It wants to play."

"Playing is fine, but at the right time," Timmy replied, biting his lip.

Sarah turned to the baby bear and leaned forward. "Hello," she said, stretching out her hand. The cub swung around and gave a happy growl. Sarah cautiously stepped forward. She glanced over her shoulder and saw that Timmy wasn't following.

The cub bounced and swung around, then bounded down the bank and back into the water. Sarah straightened and hurried forward. She heard footsteps and turned. Timmy was behind her.

"It's so fun!" She laughed.

Timmy frowned.

The cub bounded out of the water and hopped on the bank shaking off its fur.

Sarah knelt. "Come here, cutie," she said. "Don't be afraid."

The cub sprang forward, then halted. Sarah heard a deep growl. The baby bear turned.

Sarah raised her eyes to see a full-grown brown bear pad out of the trees down the bank. The large bear snarled and charged. Gala yelped and sprang forward, coming between the children and the rushing beast. The dog planted his paws, bared its teeth and growled fiercely.

The bear slowed, eyeing Gala. Then it veered to the right and lunged, swinging a huge paw at the dog. Gala leaped away, avoiding the blow and dipped, nipping the beast on its underside. The bear swung again. Gala dashed toward the trees and spun back, barking fiercely. The bear bounded after the dog, but Gala bolted away and dodged behind a stump.

Sarah didn't know what to do. She didn't want Gala to get hurt but hoped he could keep distracting the bear. She glanced from side to side, wondering where to run. Then there was a buzzing sound and a flash lit up the air. The bear crashed to the ground and rolled forward, becoming still.

The cub bounded over to the bear and nuzzled its muzzle. Eredel stepped out of the woods, his jaw clenched and his eyes steely.

"That was foolish," he said as he strode up. "Where there is a cub, a mother is not far away. If a bear thinks her cub is in danger, she will protect it."

Sarah gapped at the motionless beast. "Is it dead?" she asked, her voice quivering.

Eredel gave a quick shake of his head. "Stunned. But she'll wake soon. We should go. Where's Timmy?"

Sarah suddenly realized he wasn't with her. She scanned the bank and trees but didn't see him. Then she walked over to the bush where they had hidden. He was sitting there, his eyes open, but not speaking or moving.

Sarah crouched beside him. "You okay?"

Timmy didn't answer. She turned to Eredel. "He must've sped up when the bear attacked us, and now he has slowed down. It'll take a couple of minutes for him to become normal again."

"We can't wait," Eredel said. He picked Timmy up under the boy's knees and back. "We must leave."

Gala barked and bounded past Sarah. They returned to the spot where they'd eaten lunch. Eredel set Timmy down, then readied the horses. Timmy stood up and shook himself, blinking several times.

"Are you okay?" Sarah asked.

Timmy nodded. "Yeah. I just feel kinda itchy every time after that happens," he said, scratching his neck and back.

"I'm sorry," Sarah said. "We should have left that club alone."

Timmy shrugged. "Everything slowed down, and I was going to carry you and Gala away, then Eredel appeared, so I sat down behind the bush to wait."

Eredel helped Sarah and Timmy back onto Marigo. They crossed the stream at a shallow spot and continued through the woods until the land began to climb. They rode through the afternoon, following a trail which ascended the hill in long arcing sweeps. As they rose up the mountainside, the trees thinned, and they often found themselves out in the open. Below, blue lakes dotted the green landscape, and rivers wound through the woods.

When the sun began to sink in the west, they made camp in a grove of pines. Eredel built a fire. Sarah plopped down on a fallen log and watched the dancing flames. The ground began to tremble, and a familiar rumble filled the air. She faced the west.

The orange light rose over the mountains. Eredel, who was preparing a stew, seemed undisturbed by the rising noise. An enormous fireball appeared on the horizon, hurtling toward the valley. The sound swelled, and the ball of flame thundered over the western mountains. Sarah ducked and covered her face as the fiery object roared across the sky. Then everything quieted. She straightened and stared at Eredel.

"It didn't feel hot."

"It's far away."

"You told us before it's dragon fire. Where does it come from?"

"Far from here is a great city," Eredel said grimly. "At the heart of the city is a stone tower as wide as a lake and as high as a mountain. In that tower live a thousand dragons. Each day the fire from those dragons fills a great furnace and burns until it's blasted from nine holes high in the tower. The fires soar over land and sea until they fall into distant oceans. One of the nine passes over Elderlan each day." He looked west. "As a reminder."

"A reminder of what?"

"Power. The dragon master. He is a gifted one, like you and me. He was once a friend, but his gift corrupted him."

Eredel's gaze clouded. He stirred the stew. Sarah met Timmy's eyes, then looked back at Eredel. "Have you seen a dragon?"

"Yes."

"What are they like?"

"They are giant lizards with wings and fire. Some are gentle. Others are fierce. Some are small. Others are immense. Most are proud, solitary creatures, but they all obey their master."

"The dragon master."

Eredel nodded.

As darkness fell, a breeze cooled the air. The children ate and huddled by the fire. Timmy whispered that it would be nice to have marshmallows. Sarah laughed. Eredel draped blankets over their shoulders, and Sarah gazed at the night sky.

"The stars are so bright," she said.

"Yes, they are closer," Eredel replied.

"But I don't see the moon. Where is it?"

"There is none."

"Huh?"

"We are far from your world. In this land, plants and creatures are like the ones you know, but different, and there is no moon."

"Why not?"

Eredel shook his head. He pointed to a constellation in the shape of a tree, rising from the western horizon. At the center of the tree, a star shone faintly blue and brighter than the rest.

"That's the sapphire star," he said. "It's said that if you follow the star west for a thousand leagues, you'll come to the sapphire island. But the island is impenetrable, with sheer cliffs rising a thousand feet. They say the Ancients sailed to the island and now make it their home."

Eredel pointed to other strange constellations and told stories for each. As he talked, Sarah's eyes drooped, and her mind became fuzzy. She drifted off to sleep. When she awoke, it was morning, and Eredel was tending the horses. Sarah rolled over and woke Timmy.

They ate the soft, pancake-like bread they had packed and strawberries from Eredel's garden. Eredel saddled the horses, and they continued the trek.

During the morning, Eredel taught them two songs. Sarah didn't understand the words, but the melodies sounded nice. The first one was a fun and happy song. Eredel said travelers sang it to pass the time and to keep up their spirits. The second song was beautiful but sad. Eredel told them it was about a prince and princess of neighboring kingdoms who fell in love. When a war started between the kingdoms, the princess secretly fled her land to be with the prince. But she was mistakenly killed by soldiers of her father, the king. When the prince learned of her death, he left his kingdom and lived the rest of his days as a hermit.

The beauty of the second song touched Sarah. She asked Eredel why he lived alone, and if he had lost a love. Eredel laughed. "No, that's not why I live in Elderlan. And I'm not alone. I have many companions – Gala, Lela, Cenio, Osa, Marigo, and the other animals of the farm."

"What about people?" Sarah said. "Don't you have friends?"

"Yes, but they live far away," Eredel said. "I will take you to meet one when we cross the mountains."

"Is he a gifted one?" Sarah asked.

"No, he was born in this land."

"Do you have gifted friends?"

"Yes."

"How many?"

Eredel frowned. Then he said, "Several."

"What are their gifts?"

"Maybe you will meet them someday, and they can show you."

"Why is it hard to find a sapphire fruit?" Sarah asked.

"They were destroyed."

"Why?"

"Long ago it was prophesied that a gifted one would end the age of dragons, so the dragon master destroyed all sapphire fruit and burned the trees."

"Since we're gifted ones, would he hurt us?"

"He doesn't know you are here. But if he did, he would seek out your gifts. There is only one he fears – the barren one."

"Who's that?"

"The prophecy tells of a gifted one with invulnerability to magic. He is called the barren one."

Sarah's brow creased. She wondered what it would be like to be invulnerable to magic.

They stopped for lunch in a wooded area and then resumed the ascent. Early in the afternoon, the ground steepened, so they dismounted and led the animals by the reins. Patches of snow appeared, becoming thicker as the afternoon progressed until they were walking through icy drifts that crunched beneath their feet.

With the sun sinking low in the sky, they reached a plateau barren of trees. With no shade, the snow had melted, and puffs of grass grew out of the moist soil. Eredel called a halt. Sarah stretched her arms and ambled across the plateau. She stared down the hillside and then turned, gazing at the mountains rising before them.

Suddenly, Cenio let out a shrill caw and flapped into the air.

Sarah hurried over. "What's wrong with her?"

Eredel shook his head and gazed east. Sarah followed his line of sight and saw a dark cloud passing over the mountains.

Cenio cawed again. Eredel squinted. Then his eyes widened. "That's not a cloud. Those are rarewar, a great flock passing into Elderlan." He wheeled. "You must hide."

He led Sarah and Timmy to a thicket at the western edge of the plateau, and they crawled into it. Gala knelt beside Sarah. She rubbed the dog's neck and waited.

Sarah peered out of the underbrush and watched the dark cloud pass down the mountain slope. It headed south over the forest. She squinted, making out dozens of birds moving in three wedge formations.

"So many," she murmured.

"Yeah, birds of danger cluster to ranger," Timmy said.

As usual, Sarah had no idea what he was saying.

The flock reached the midpoint of the valley and slowed there, hovering above the trees.

"They've gone to Oriafen," Eredel exclaimed.

"What?" Sarah asked.

"The home of the Panishie—a fairy people," he answered grimly. He paused as if thinking. "I've been a fool. Gifted ones— your friends—are there."

Sarah caught her breath. "Our friends? Where?"

"With the fairies—the Panishie."

"Our friends are with fairies? You mean little people?"

Eredel nodded and continued staring intensely at the dark flock.

"How do you know?"

"Sidtarr would only make war on the fairies if they had something he wanted. The Panishie are harboring your friends."

Fear swelled in Sarah's chest. She glanced at Timmy; her eyes wide. "Wesley and the others are there. They're in danger."

Timmy bobbed his head but looked confused.

Cenio cawed. Then the bird dropped out of the air and plopped onto a patch of grass. Eredel strode over and picked him up. He listened to the bird's chest.

"Her heart beats and her eyes shine, but she doesn't move," he said. He lay the crow down on the grass.

Sarah hugged her shoulders. She kept thinking about Wesley and the others, wondering what was happening to them.

The horses and ponies were still and quiet. Gala sat motionless, but his eyes gleamed. Sarah rubbed the dog's coat. He didn't respond.

"Something's wrong with Gala," she said.

The ground suddenly lurched. "Whoa!" Sarah cried, tipping forward. The hillside trembled and seemed to roll beneath her. A roar sounded, and snow crashed down the mountain slope several hundred yards to her right.

Cenio fluttered up into the air, squawking wildly. Gala came to life and barked excitedly. The horses neighed and stomped their hooves.

"They're awake!" Sarah said. "The animals are awake."

The ground shuddered, and cracks appeared in the earth. Eredel strode over to Cenio and waved to Sarah and Timmy. "Come to me. It's safer at the center of the plateau."

Sarah tried to stand and grabbed Timmy's hand as the earth juddered beneath her feet. She pushed her way through the underbrush. Then the shaking abruptly stopped, and everything went quiet. Sarah hurried across the plateau with Timmy jogging behind her.

Eredel's eyes were wide. "This is something new," he said, rubbing his brow. He called to Cenio. The crow landed on his shoulder. Then it made strange sounds as if talking to the man. Eredel turned to Sarah and Timmy.

"Cenio sees a child riding a rarewar. A young one with blond hair. A black cloth covers the child's eyes, and it sings with a voice of great beauty. Is that one of your friends?"

Sarah and Timmy looked at one another. "Maybe it's Mya," Sarah said. "She has blond hair and can sing really pretty. Remember all those animals followed her?"

Timmy nodded.

"The voice transfixed Cenio and the other creatures," Eredel said.

"But we didn't hear it," Sarah said.

"Neither did I. We are too far away. Animals' ears are more sensitive."

The ground jolted. Sarah stumbled and grabbed Timmy to stay upright. A roar filled the air, and the ground shook for several moments, then stopped, and everything quieted.

Cenio screeched and soared upward. The bird hovered for a long moment before returning to Eredel's shoulder. Eredel quirked an eyebrow and tapped his lips. "Cenio sees other children. Rarewar are carrying three away. One is larger than the others, and strange music fills the air around him."

"That must be Ted," Sarah cried. "He can make music with his hands. What do the other kids look like? Does one have a short ponytail?"

Eredel spoke to Cenio. The bird squawked, and Eredel frowned.

"They're too far off. Even a crow's sharp eyes can't see such detail." Eredel pointed east. "The rarewar are bearing them to the mountains."

Sarah squinted, sighting several black specks gliding over the forest. The birds rose, winging up the hillside and disappeared between the slopes.

"Where are they going?" Sarah asked.

"To Risrean. To their master."

"You mean Sidtarr?" Sarah asked.

Eredel gave a slight nod.

"What should we do?" Sarah said, her throat tightening.

Eredel's eyes met her. "We'll find your friends and bring them to a safe place."

The certainty in his voice eased Sarah's panic. She exhaled softly.

They resumed the ascent, determined to move quickly. They pitched camp beside a creek running through a grove of Aspens.

As the sun sank low, a fireball appeared and thundered across the valley. The flames no longer frightened Sarah, but she trembled at the thought that they came from dragons – real dragons!

Eredel built a fire and cooked dinner. Sarah wasn't hungry. After picking at her food, she wrapped a blanket over her shoulders. Exhaustion enveloped her, and she dozed off cuddling next to Gala.

The following day they climbed steadily until they reached the pass. To the north, a brown land spread to the horizon.

"That is the Netupana," Eredel said, pointing. "We must cross that barren wasteland to find your friends. But first, we'll journey along the lower slopes of the Uelena to the home of an old comrade who may help us."

Eredel spurred Osa forward, and the horse cantered down the rocky path winding along the northern slope of the mountain. Marigo and the ponies followed. Gala trotted at the rear.

As they descended, Sarah searched the sky for black birds. She saw nothing but pillowy clouds floating through the blue. Beneath the blue, a brown land spread endlessly, empty of trees, grass, and water. Sarah shuddered. She didn't know how they'd cross that wasteland, but they had to. They had no choice.

Chapter 20:
Golden Fields

Rhea brushed hair out of her eyes and shifted on the branch. Her butt and back were sore from the long hours of riding. As the trees descended the snow-covered slopes, the wind died away, and gray clouds parted, revealing a clear blue sky. She tipped her head back and closed her eyes, feeling the warm sunshine on her face.

The tolepar trees moved through scattered woods, the outliers of a forest blanketing the lower reaches of the mountain and extending out into the plain below. Beyond the woods, golden fields ran south to the horizon.

As they descended the mountain slope, the snow grew sparser, shrinking to scattered clumps. The tolepar passed through forests of pine and beach, finally slowing to a halt at a shallow cave protruding from the hillside. There, they lowered their branches, and the children climbed off.

Rhea took a deep breath and exhaled slowly. It felt good to be on firm ground. She shook out her legs and stretched her arms.

The snow monkeys shouted at the tolepars, and the trees started back up the hillside. Bobby waved goodbye, tears rolling down his cheeks. Rhea frowned. She liked the walking trees, but the snow monkeys gave her the creeps. She had almost smacked one when it slid too close and leered at her with its unblinking eyes.

So long snow pervs," Annie murmured.

Rhea shot a glance at Annie and chuckled, realizing Annie had got the same feeling from the snow monkeys.

Rhea bent over and touched her toes. She did some jumping jacks and hip twists to get her blood flowing, while the other kids explored the cave and the surrounding woods, uncorking some of the energy they'd bottled up during the long ride.

After finishing her warmups, Rhea plopped down on a rock and pulled some cakes and fruit out of her pack. She ate slowly and stared into the cave, which was low ceilinged and extended some fifteen feet into the mountainside. The walls were a smooth black stone, and the floor was covered in leaves.

The Anolari collected a pile of wood and started a fire just inside the cave mouth. The kids gathered around the flames, warming their hands.

Rhea gulped down the last of her water, then headed out to find more. She came upon a creek some fifty yards down the hillside and re-filled her bottle. She splashed water on her arms and face to wash off some of the dirt that had collected over the past couple of days.

On the way back to the cave, she spotted Wesley sitting by himself under a tree. He was cross-legged, with his back straight, and his eyes closed. He was meditating. She watched him for a moment. Meditating seemed weird to her, but if it helped him relax, she wasn't going to criticize.

She returned to the cave and knelt by the fire. The air was cooling, so she pulled out her blanket and wrapped it around her shoulders. She lay back, resting her feet close to the flames, and drifted off to sleep.

When she awoke, the fire had shrunken to red embers, and her feet were toasty. Bobby lay snoring beside her, and Dylan on the other side of him. She sat up and peered out the cave mouth. In the starlight, she glimpsed ranger fairies perched in the trees.

She heard wheezing like steam slipping out of a cracked teapot and smiled to herself, recognizing Annie's snoring. She gazed at Bobby. In the faint light, he looked so gentle and innocent. She sighed, remembering the day he got hurt.

She and Annie were walking through Newbury Park when they spotted Ted sitting under an old sycamore tree with a crowd of kids surrounding him. He was telling a silly story about a teddy bear who kept accidentally breaking playground equipment. As Rhea listened, a drop landed on her cheek. She raised her head. Dark clouds stretched to the horizon. More drops pattered her. She tugged on Annie's arm, and they ducked under the tree branches as rain began streaming out of the sky.

She peered across the field and spotted a boy with his dog. They were running together. The boy was laughing. Thunder sounded, and lightning lit up the sky. Then a flash streaked down from the clouds and hit the boy in a brilliant burst of white. He fell to the ground, and the dog yelped in fright. A woman screamed and ran to the boy. Rhea stepped out from under the tree and started to jog, accelerating across the field as water flew off her clothes and hair.

As she neared the boy, she recognized him. It was Bobby. He lay motionless in the grass, his eyes vacant, and a pink, feathered mark running from his neck to his forehead. She knelt and pressed her ear to his chest.

"Is he alive?" The woman asked through sobs. It was Bobby's mom.

Rhea grimaced. "He isn't breathing."

She straddled Bobby and placed the heel of her right hand at the center of his chest. Then she set her left hand on top of her right and began pushing rhythmically. After thirty seconds, she paused and turned to Bobby's mom.

"Blow into his mouth," she said. Ms. Forester leaned forward, took a deep breath and blew into Bobby's lungs.

"Someone call 911," Rhea shouted. A passerby pulled out his phone and tapped in a number.

Annie jogged up, her mouth hanging open and her face pale. She fell to her knees. "Oh no!" she cried, "It's Bobby. Poor Bobby!"

Rhea continued pumping. Ms. Forester blew into his mouth again. Bobby suddenly jerked and coughed hoarsely. Then he let out a moan and swung his head painfully from side to side.

A siren rang out. Rhea leaned back, and her hands dropped to her sides. She rose as the ambulance roared onto the grass. Paramedics leaped out and rushed to Bobby. They examined him, loaded him on a stretcher, and carried him away.

As the ambulance drove off, Annie stepped toward Rhea. "How did you do that?"

Rhea brought a shaky hand to her forehead and swept strands of hair off her face. "Girl Scouts – we learned CPR last summer." She stumbled away.

It was two months before Rhea saw Bobby again. He was standing in his yard and leaning on a metal walker like old people sometimes use. Bobby's mom was with him. At the sight of him, Rhea's stomach tightened, and her jaw clenched. She asked him how he was. Bobby said "good," but there was a vacantness in his eyes that disturbed her, and he stumbled over his words.

Bobby's mom thanked Rhea again and again, saying she had saved his life. Rhea glanced down in embarrassment and walked away feeling like she'd failed.

In the next several months, Bobby improved. He still talked funny, but Rhea began to see glimpses of the intelligence and cleverness she remembered so clearly. She kept her eye on him. She wasn't going to let something bad happen again.

Rhea listened to the night sounds. She pulled the blanket over her shoulders and closed her eyes. She awoke to voices. The other kids were up and moving about. Her back was stiff. She plucked a brush out of her bag and tugged it through her tangled hair.

She was hungry but tired of eating the fairy cakes and had only a few pieces of fruit left. Annie offered her an apple. Rhea took it and thanked Annie. As she bit into the fruit, Rhea stepped out of the cave and stared at the gray, morning sky, her arms pressed against her stomach. She heard voices. Josh and Wesley strode out of the trees, their hair wet and water dripping down their arms.

"Did you guys jump in the creek?" she asked.

"Yep," Wesley said, flashing a smile. "We followed it down to where it makes a pool, then took a dip there. It's cold but felt great!"

Rhea shivered. She'd like to take a bath but didn't dare undress with the other kids around.

Leoku asked the children to pack up their things. Ten minutes later, they headed out. They quickly reached the creek and traversed it where several large rocks stuck out from the current.

After an hour of walking, the hillside abruptly dropped off for several hundred yards in an almost vertical descent. To the left, a path wound down the slope in a series of zigzags. Rhea started toward the path, but several ranger fairies suddenly buzzed around her and herded her and the other kids into the trees.

"What's up?" Rhea asked in annoyance. The fairies signaled for quiet. Leoku hovered at the edge of the trees and pointed some distance down the cliff face where a huge bird sat perched on a rock. Rhea's heart thumped. It looked like the birds which had attacked them days before. The winged creature was alone and feeding on something it gripped in its talons.

Leoku frowned. "The creature cannot know you are here," he said. "It must be eliminated before it can fly back to its master."

Rhea nodded.

"But it's alone," Annie objected, "and far from home." She turned toward Bobby. "Does it scare you?"

Bobby's eyes rolled up in their sockets, so only the whites were visible. He leaned back slightly. "Nooo, iit noot scaaryy," he finally said, blinking in surprise.

"See... he knows when something is dangerous," Annie said. "Maybe this bird is okay."

"We don't know that," Josh replied sternly. "Just because it doesn't scare him doesn't mean it's safe. If it tells its master, we could have a hundred of those birds coming back for us." He turned to Leoku. "Do it."

The ranger fairy gave a slight nod.

While the children remained hidden in the trees, the Anolari crept along the cliff face, staying in the shadows. Sirie and the copper sprites followed close behind.

The fairies advanced to within fifteen yards of the bird and stopped there. Minutes passed. Rhea began to wonder what was going on. "Come on," she said in a hushed voice. "What are you waiting for?"

Sirie hovered close to Leoku and seemed to be saying something to him. The ranger fairy bobbed his head twice, then he glided into the open.

The black bird caught sight of the ranger fairy and swung around, its feathers rising in a defensive stance. Leoku hovered before the bird. Rhea heard strange chirping sounds from Leoku. The bird made some loud croaks. Leoku chirped again. The bird croaked. This conversation went on for some time until Leoku bowed and glided back to other fairies. The fairies huddled together, then Leoku led them all back toward the trees where the children remained hidden.

"What's going on?" Josh asked as the fairies glided into the woods.

"The bird is an outcast," Leoku said, with a sigh. "It cannot return to its home. Siriena recognized the creature. The bird agreed to help us if we promised to guide it to the southern mountains where others of its kind live. The Anolari can do this. You need not fear that bird. I will call it over."

Rhea eyes widened. "Are you crazy? It could attack us!"

"Then my companions will slay it. But the bird has no reason to harm you. It has no master now."

Celia began to tremble. Her fingers squeezed against her palms, and tears shimmered in her eyes. "I'm afraid," she said anxiously. "Please don't let it come."

Josh knelt and put his hands on the sides of Celia's waist. "Don't be scared," he said. "You're safe with us. We won't let it hurt you." He turned to Annie. "Can you take her into the woods for a minute?"

Annie nodded and grasped Celia's hand. "Come on, señorita. I saw a rabbit dart into a bush a little way back. Maybe we can find it."

Celia wiped her cheeks and left with Annie.

Leoku called to the rarewar. The creature rose into the air with a powerful beat of its wings. As it neared the trees, the bird caught sight of the children, and its head swung back in alarm. It stopped in mid-air, hovering there.

Leoku called again. The bird cautiously advanced and landed in a grassy area at the edge of the trees. It peered warily at the children, its yellow eyes swirling. When its eyes fell on Rhea, the bird drew back with a snort.

Sirie glided toward the rarewar. She pulled back her gray hood and loosened her golden locks, letting them fall about her shoulders. The bird froze. Fresh scars were visible along the creature's great talons. Sirie made several chirping sounds, then she bowed. What's she doing? Rhea wondered.

The bird's eyes softened, then it dipped its neck and emitted a gentle caw. Leoku stepped closer and chirped. The bird swayed its neck and answered with a croak. This went on for several minutes. When the exchange ended, the rarewar rose out of the grass and glided back to the rock it had been perched on along the cliff face.

Sirie glided over to Josh and whispered something in his ear. Josh's eyes widened. He turned to the other kids. "Guys, that's not just any bird. It's the one that carried Celia away!"

There was a moment of stunned silence, then Gabrielle lunged forward, her baseball cap tipping back. "Let's get it."

"No, no," Josh said, grabbing her. "The bird can help us get to the Silver City. It can be our lookout."

"But how can we trust it?" Rhea cried. 'It could carry one of us away at any moment."

"Yeah, it did that to Celia," Dylan cried, rising into the air with a fart like a bear after a bowl full of chili.

Leoku strode among the children. "It is a rarewar. Most of its kind live in the crags of southern Hevelen. Many years ago, Sidtarr captured some and took them to Risrean, where he bred them to do his bidding. They serve him well, but when they fail, Sidtarr shows no mercy. This one cannot return."

"Sidtarr?" Dylan said, blinking. "Is that the guy who's hunting us?"

"Yes," Leoku answered. "He covets your gifts and has sent his servants to capture you."

"He sounds like a real jerk-face," Rhea said, with a growl. "If I meet him, I'll show him my gift." She raised her hands and made a sizzling sound.

The other kids laughed uneasily.

Josh rubbed his forehead. "This bird can't go back to its master. But it can help us."

Rhea frowned. She didn't trust the bird. Why would it change so quickly? She sensed Dylan and Gabrielle didn't either, but the other kids believed Josh. She crossed her arms and didn't say anymore.

When Annie and Celia returned, Josh told them about the bird. Celia's face went white. "No, no, no," she murmured.

Sirie hovered close and stroked Celia's cheek with her tiny fingers. "Don't afraid," she said. "It not hurt you."

"But I am afraid," Celia protested, her eyes welling up with tears again. She covered her face with her hands.

Annie picked Celia up in her arms, then she sat down on a stump. "It's okay. It's okay," she said, rocking Celia gently.

Annie looked at the other kids. "Give her a minute. She needs to cry it out. Then she'll be okay."

Rhea stepped away. She thought they were all crazy. She huffed and strode into the woods. A sudden longing for home filled her. She missed her room. She missed her bed. She missed her mom's cooking. Her mom made the best shrimp gumbo and peach cobbler.

And, she missed her little sister, Niren. Although only seven, Niren could always make her laugh. Niren could also be annoying – like when she insisted that Rhea watch anime cartoons with her or played in Rhea's room when she was trying to get her homework done. But Niren could also be sweet and lovable. She liked to sit in Rhea's lap and wrap her arms around her big sister's neck. She was warm and affectionate, like their dad. That's what Rhea missed most about her dad – his warmth, his hugs, and his understanding smile.

A thump brought Rhea out of her thoughts. She turned to see Dylan bounding toward her, his hands gripping his baggy jeans.

"Do you trust that thing?" Dylan cried as he landed before her, his face flushed.

"What thing?"

"The bird."

Rhea shook her head. "But your brother does."

"I know. He's nuts."

"Maybe..."

As Dylan complained about Josh, she turned and started back.

The other kids came into view, and Rhea did a double take. The black bird had landed in the grass at the edge of the trees and was facing Celia. It dipped its head so that its beak almost touched the ground.

Leoku stood to the right of the winged creature. "It seeks forgiveness," he said. "And, it promises to be a faithful protector for you and your friends."

Celia wiped her cheeks, then stepped forward and knelt, extending her hand. The creature raised its beak and softly tapped Celia's palm. She smiled and looked around. "It wants to be my friend."

Josh squatted beside her. "Is that okay?"

Celia nodded, her eyes shining.

Josh smiled. Leoku made a chirping sound. The bird raised its neck and cawed several times.

"Its name is Heyolu," Leoku said. "It's a descendant of Dewlera, the mother of all rarewar."

"Happy to meet you, Heyolu," Celia replied, softly. She told the bird her name and the name of each of the kids, pointing to each one as she did. Leoku translated. The bird bobbed its head with each name. When Celia introduced Rhea, the red-headed girl stared into the bird's eyes, and for the first time, she felt no threat from it.

After the introductions, the bird stretched its wings and rose into the air, landing on a branch high in a tree above them. Leoku led the children down a narrow path descending the cliff face. At the bottom of the cliff, they plunged into thick forest. Rhea glanced over her shoulder and caught sight of the black bird gliding above the trees behind them.

The party trekked for several hours, stopping briefly at a creek to fill their water bottles, then continued to a grove of beech trees, where they rested and ate lunch. After they had eaten, Leoku led most of the kids away to find a patch of blackberries. Rhea and Celia stayed behind.

Rhea chose a sunny open spot between the trees to lay down and get some rays. Celia plunked down beside her and began humming. Rhea closed her eyes enjoying the sun on her skin. She heard a soft whooshing sound and sat up. Celia was pressing her forearms together and sticking them forward as a pink bubble expanded from her wrists. The sphere quickly swelled to the size of a balloon.

"That's so weird," Rhea murmured, her mouth twisting to one side.

Celia smiled. "But fun – I want to see how big it can get."

"Why?... You planning to float away?"

Celia giggled. "No, it'll only float a few feet off the ground. It won't go into the sky."

Rhea didn't understand how the bubble could float. It didn't have helium or another gas inside. And, even if it did, it should float straight up like a hot air balloon.

As the bubble swelled, it bumped against Rhea's arm. She scooted over and watched the sphere expand to the size of a beach ball.

There was rustling, and Dylan bounded into the glade. "Hot bananas," he cried, landing in front of Celia. Cherry alighted on his shoulder.

"Didn't you go look for blackberries?" Celia said.

"I did. We found a bush as big as a back yard. I ate some, but they didn't taste very good, so I came back. What're you doing with the bubble? Can I get inside, like the fairies did?"

Celia bit her lip, remembering the fairies flying around inside the bubble at Oriafen. That was okay, but Dylan was different. "You're too big. You'll pop it," she said.

"Aww… no, I'm not," Dylan said. "It won't pop. Even if it did, you could make another one."

Celia frowned and her eyes narrowed. She didn't say anything.

The bubble continued expanding until Rhea guessed it was over five feet across. A breeze picked up, and the sphere bumped against branches to the right of the kids. Celia moved away from the trees.

"Can I jump in now? It's so big. Please, please…" Dylan begged.

Celia pursed her lips. She seemed to think for a moment. "Okay," she finally said, "but be careful."

Dylan pumped his fist and let off a dozen quick farts like a line of firecrackers that lifted him into the air and suspended him there for some ten seconds.

Celia turned her arms, and a narrow gap appeared across the bubble. She twisted her arms again, and the gap widened.

Rhea blinked. "How do you do that?"

"When I turn my arms up, it opens, and when I turn them down, it closes," Celia said.

"But the air doesn't blow out."

Celia shrugged. Dylan stuck his hand through the gap. He fingered the bottom of the sphere and pushed on it. The bubble dipped slightly but bounced right back when he lifted his hand away.

"Ready?" Dylan asked.

"Guess so," Celia said, halfheartedly. Dylan lifted one foot and stuck it through the gap. Then he hopped inside. He stumbled around for a moment trying to get his balance, while Cherry glided in circles around him.

Dylan steadied himself and hopped, touching the roof of the bubble. He landed and plopped down, laying out spread eagle. "Everything looks pink in here," he said as the bubble bobbed gently.

The warbler landed on his stomach. Dylan lay there for a moment with a smile on his face, then he leaped up and bounced again, palming the roof. The bubble rocked and swayed, tugging on Celia's wrists.

"Stop it, Dylan," Celia said. "It's pulling on me."

"Sorry," the boy said. "This is more fun than a bouncy house!"

"Cool it," Rhea instructed, coming to her feet. She touched the surface of the sphere. It felt rubbery and soft like the spandex leggings her mom wore to the gym. She spread her arms and tried to grip the bubble, but it slipped out of her hands and bobbed away, pulling Celia along with it.

"I don't like this," Celia complained. "I'm gonna stop."

"No, no, don't," Dylan pleaded.

Celia ignored him and spread her arms. The bubble deflated. Dylan sprang through the gap with Cherry darting after him, as the sphere collapsed around them. Dylan landed in the dirt and staggered, then caught his balance. The goo shrank into a pink ball on Celia's wrists, then vanished like water down a pipe.

"You okay?" Rhea asked Celia in concern.

"I'm tired," Celia said. She leaned forward and rested her head on her folded arms. A moment later, she was snoring quietly.

Rhea glared at Dylan. "See what you did!"

Dylan's shoulders hunched. "I didn't mean to. It was just fun."

Rhea gave him a reproachful frown. Dylan had taken advantage of Celia, and she didn't like it.

The other kids returned minutes later, their bags stuffed with blackberries. Everyone packed up their things and readied to go. Rhea couldn't wake Celia, so she picked her up in her arms, and the party set out.

After a half hour, Celia awoke, and Rhea set her down to walk.

Late in the afternoon, they reached the end of the forest. At the last grove of trees, the ranger fairies called a halt. Ahead, golden fields stretched south to the horizon. Leoku said they would camp there. Rhea dropped her pack wearily and plopped down under a tree.

The other kids sat around her, talking and pulling food out of their packs. Rhea closed her eyes. She wanted to sleep. A sound of flapping wings reached her ears, and she opened her eyes. Above, a bird swooped out of the sky, landing on a branch high in the tree above her. It was Heyolu. She hadn't seen the rarewar for hours and was relieved it had returned. Someone tapped Rhea's shoulder. She turned and found Bobby kneeling beside her with a small pillow in his hands. "Thiis foor yoouu, Riiyaa."

Rhea's brow creased. "For me? Where'd you get it?"

"Maade iit," Bobby said with a grin.

"Huh?" Rhea replied, not understanding what he meant by "made it." She took the cushion in her hands. It was square-shaped and beautifully quilted. "You've been carrying this around?"

Bobby shook his head. "Noo, maakee iit… toodaay."

"What?"

Bobby's eyes twinkled.

Annie stepped over. "He gave Ted some kind of dog whistle before we left Oriafen. I don't know where he got that from, but he said he made that too."

Rhea's scrutinized Bobby, wondering what other treasures were hidden in his pack. She examined the pillow, running her fingers along its smooth fabric.

"Thank you. It's really nice. I can use it," she said, nodding.

Bobby grinned and sprang to his feet.

Rhea set the pillow behind her back and leaned against the tree. She pulled out her book, Grapes of Wrath, and found her place. She read until the light had faded. The air was getting chilly, but Leoku cautioned the children against building a fire for fear it would attract unwanted attention, so the kids wrapped themselves in their fairy blankets and huddled together.

In the darkness, fireflies emerged from the grass, sparkling in a menagerie of colors – yellow, red, green and purple. They swept between the trees and among the children, darting here and there. Celia and Bobby's rings glowed. The tiny creatures whirled about the blue lights in bands of shimmering color. But soon the kids grew tired of the buzzing and asked Bobby and Celia to hide the rings. They did, and the flies buzzed away.

Rhea lay back, resting her head on the pillow. She drifted off to sleep. She awoke with the morning light shining in her eyes. Her stomach ached. She sat up and grabbed a couple of cakes out of her bag.

Annie rolled over and surveyed the area with tired eyes. "I'm sick of walking. Can we just stay in one place for a day?"

"That would be nice," Rhea replied, "but our water won't last long, and there's none around here."

Josh came over and squatted beside the girls. "Leoku says we're starting the most dangerous part of the journey today. It's eight days walk to the Silver City. We'll be traveling over open ground. Heyolu will be our lookout, but if the black birds find us, there'll be no place to hide. We'll have to fight."

Annie shuddered.

"Okay by me," Rhea said defiantly, though Josh's words made her hands tremble.

"Let's hope not," Josh said.

After breakfast, the party started out. They hiked through the morning until they came to a shallow stream gurgling through a grassy field. They waded across the stream and stopped for lunch on the far side. By the time they finished eating, the sun was high in the sky. They re-filled their water bottles, packed up their things, and resumed the trek.

Late in the afternoon, a breeze picked up. Above, dark clouds flowed east at a rapid clip, passing across the sun and putting the field into shadow. A raindrop landed on Rhea's cheek. She felt another on her arm. Leoku had warned them of sudden thundershowers in the plain. She spotted a lone tree in the distance and hurried toward it. The others did the same.

More sprinkles pattered Rhea's arms and face. Celia began to fall behind, so Rhea picked her up and ran, reaching the tree just as the clouds opened and rain gushed out of the sky. The tree was an old hackberry with wide limbs and thick green foliage that provided shelter from the downpour.

Rhea set Celia down and brushed the water off her clothes, feeling lucky that they had escaped most of the deluge. Annie jogged up and came to a stop with an annoyed frown. "I'm soaked," she said and swung her head from side to side, sending a spray of water off her hair.

Bobby reached the tree last, his clothes completely drenched. He grinned and bounced lightly on his toes. Rhea nudged Annie. "He's in a good mood."

"Hey Bobby," Annie said. "You like rain?"

"Yees, iit woondeefuull," Bobby cried, sweeping his arms through the air for emphasis. "Mee moom noot leet mee plaay iin raaiin."

The girls nodded with slight frowns.

"She's probably worried you'll get sick," Annie said.

"Shee fraaiid ii huurt. Buut ii noo fraaiid."

The memory of Bobby running through Newbury Park on that rainy-day months ago came back to Rhea, and her smile disappeared.

311

Bobby's eyes twinkled. "Ii liikee raaiin," he cried. Then he turned and sprang into the field. A flash lit up the sky. "Liightniing," Bobby shouted, raising his arms and hopping through the grass. Another flash cut through the gray. Thunder pounded the air.

"Bobby," Rhea yelled. "Your mom is right. Get out of the rain."

Bobby ignored her and kicked at water drops falling all around him. Rhea tensed. Something felt wrong – terribly wrong. She sprang. Bobby saw her and froze. She grabbed him, and they fell together, tumbling through the wet grass. At that instant, a bolt of lightning slashed down from the sky and slammed into the field some twenty yards from where Bobby had been standing.

Rhea rolled onto her back and sat up on her elbows, watching smoke rise off the blackened grass.

"Whoa," she said. "That was close."

"Hooot! Yoouu hoot!" Bobby hollered, shoving her back. Bobby scrambled to his feet and dashed toward the tree. Rhea stumbled up and trotted after him.

Bobby came under the branches, and Annie grabbed him. "You okay?" she said, holding him there.

"Yeeaah, Rheeaa hoot aagaaiin, hoot!"

Rhea strode under the tree, her clothes soaked through. "That was a heart stopper," she said frowning.

"How'd you know?" Annie asked.

Rhea shrugged. "Intuition – but I guess I was off. It wouldn't have hit him."

"Better safe than a goner."

Rhea sighed and grabbed her bag. She sat down and pulled out her last pear. She held the fruit; her hand was trembling.

In the distance, a dark object soared through the downpour. It glided to the tree and landed on a high branch. Rhea tipped her head back. It was Heyolu. The bird shook off its thick plumage and brought its wings in, becoming still.

After a half hour, the rain died away, but the sun was low in the sky, so Leoku told them to make camp there.

Bobby sat down beside Rhea and gave her a lopsided grin.

"What do you want?" she asked, hearing the annoyance in her voice.

"Yoouu prooteect mee."

Rhea rolled her eyes. "Yeah, because you keep getting in trouble."

"Ii soorry," Bobby said, leaning close. "Youu liikee myy biig siisteer."

Rhea quirked an eyebrow. She hadn't thought of that before. She did feel sorta sisterly toward him. Her frown softened. She reached out her arm and wrapped it around his shoulder. "Okay, little bro. You listen to me from now on."

Bobby's eyes twinkled. "Okaayy, biig siis."

A breeze gusted, blowing Rhea's hair back. She stared off into the distance. It felt safe there, but they had far to go. She didn't know what lay ahead.

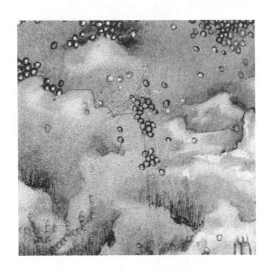

Chapter 21:
Betrayal

Bobby awoke and rolled over. Rhea lay beside him. Her cheeks twitched, and she exhaled noisily. Bobby grinned. She reminded him of Willow.

He peered up into the branches of the hackberry tree. Several ranger fairies were there, keeping watch. Bobby liked the ranger fairies, but they didn't talk much. He thought probably because they didn't know much English and he only knew a few words of the fairy language. He had tried to learn more, but he kept forgetting them. Josh and Annie were good at the fairy language. He wasn't. He frowned to himself in frustration, wishing he could learn easier.

He looked at his water bottle on the ground beside the blanket. It was empty. He had dreamt of a river and wondered if there was one nearby. He hopped to his feet and strolled into the tall grass. A breeze brushed his face. He shaded his eyes from the sun. The sky was clear except for a single white cloud.

He missed Willow. He wondered if she missed him. He knew she'd love it here, romping through the grass, chasing balls and searching for squirrels and rabbits. He missed her bark and how she liked to jump into his arms.

He gazed off, remembering the day he had played with Willow in Newbury Park. It was the start of summer. Clouds had appeared, and it began to rain. There was a flash, and suddenly he was looking down from high above.

A white light surrounded him. The light was like a tunnel leading away. He followed the light. It came to a meadow surrounded by tall, gray trees. The meadow was quiet and peaceful. He felt happy and free.

Five months later, the yellow beast drove into the same meadow. Bobby recognized it immediately and tried to tell Ben and the other kids. But they didn't understand.

When he came to the meadow the first time, he wanted to stay, but he heard a cry. It was his mom. She was screaming. He hurried back through the light and saw her far below in the park. She was kneeling beside him in the grass. Rhea was pushing on his chest.

Then a whooshing sensation passed through him, and he was back in his body. His skin burned and his muscles throbbed terribly. Everything went black.

He awoke in a hospital with tubes running from his arms and mouth to machines on the side of his bed. The pain was gone, but a floating, dizzy sensation made him feel like he would throw up. His mom and dad were there, beside the bed. They talked to him, but he couldn't understand what they said.

The days drifted by like clouds. Friends came and went – Wesley, Josh, Sarah, Annie, Barth, Dylan and Ted. Josh visited often.

After several weeks he went home, but he'd forgotten how to do many things. He couldn't tie his shoes anymore. He tried, but his fingers didn't do what they were supposed to do. When he walked, he kept tripping and falling. When he tried to use a spoon, the food fell into his lap or on the floor. It was annoying and frustrating. Sometimes it made him angry.

But learning how to talk again was the toughest thing. He could hear the words in his head, but when he tried to say them, they didn't come out right. He had thought talking was easy, but it was hard... really hard.

The wind gusted. Bobby tipped his head. He missed his mom. He'd seen her in his dream, and he'd talked to her. He told her that he'd danced in the rain and that Rhea had tackled him just before the lightning hit the ground. He liked dreams. He could see people he missed in them, like his mom and dad, and Willow.

A bird darted by his face, then another. The birds whirled in a corkscrew pattern. He recognized one was Dylan's bird. The other was pretty with blue feathers and a snow white breast. The two played together, twirling and dodging until they spied a swarm of gnats and dove toward the insects, catching many in their beaks.

Bobby ambled through the field until a green rise appeared ahead. He hurried and found a large mound covered in short, mossy grass. He clambered up the mound and discovered a spring bubbling out of the top. He squinted at the water, wondering why it was there. He crouched and cupped his hands. The water felt cold and tasted sweet. He drank several gulps, then re-filled his bottle.

After drinking his fill, he straightened and gazed around. He saw nothing but endless grass, so he tramped down the mound and started back toward the hackberry tree.

He hadn't walked fifty yards when a sharp pain bit into his left side. He bent over. Another sharp pain throbbed below his stomach. Then, another jabbed him on the right side. He hunched down. The pain eased. He tried to walk, but the pain returned. It hurt so much. He moaned and bent over. He dropped into the grass and curled up, his mind a fog of pain. Then he heard footsteps.

"Bobby, what's wrong?" Came a voice. "Are you okay?" It was Wesley. "We need to get back to the tree. Birds are coming – a whole bunch. Heyolu saw them and warned the fairies."

Bobby tried to sit up, but the pain throbbed intensely. He fell over. Wesley's arms came under him and lifted. Wesley hurried through the grass, carrying Bobby toward the tree. The pain gradually faded, and Bobby's mind cleared. He heard voices and looked ahead. The tree was close. The children were running around in a panic.

Wesley set Bobby down at the base of the tree. The pain was gone. He sat up and blinked. The ranger fairies had gathered in a circle. Sirie and the copper sprites joined them. Leoku spoke for several moments, and the fairies shot away, fanning out in a wide line.

Bobby peered into the sky and saw a dark cloud approaching from the north. As he watched, the cloud became clearer, and he saw it was birds – a huge flock of birds

Wesley strode over. "You feel better?"

"Yeees."

Wesley rubbed Bobby's shoulder, then he opened the gray sack at his belt and tugged out a silence glove. He pulled the glove onto his right hand. Josh and Annie stood a few feet away. Josh already wore his gloves and frowned at the sky with gritted teeth.

"There's a ton of them," Josh said. "Annie, wait until I give the signal, then scream your lungs out. Okay?"

She gave a quick nod.

"Maybe It'll help us even these odds out," Josh murmured.

Dylan bounded up, gripping his pants with one hand and letting off a low fart like a cast iron pot hitting the ground. "What do I do?"

"Stand there," Josh said, pointing to the right side of the tree. "When the birds get close, take off. Hopefully, some will follow you. You can keep them busy, while we try to handle the rest."

Dylan quivered, and his eyes gleamed.

Rhea strode over, her arms and face morphing red. She held a pouch with a silence glove pulled halfway out. "I can't wear these," she said, tossing the bag to the ground. "The silver stuff melts as soon as I touch it."

"Can I have 'em?" Dylan cried.

"Knock yourself out."

Dylan grabbed the pouch and squatted to keep his pants from sliding down. He pulled out the gloves and tugged one onto each hand. Then he bounded to where Josh had pointed and waited.

Bobby peered at the oncoming flock. There were dozens of the huge black birds flying among a swarm of small gray ones.

As the flock neared the line of fairies, a strange cawing rang out, and a single rarewar dropped down from above, diving between the onrushing birds and fairies. The lone black bird hung in the air for a moment. Then it let out a long guttural sound. Bobby recognized the sound. It was Heyolu!

The flock slowed before the lone rarewar, seeming mystified by the sight of it. Then the largest bird answered with a harsh croak, and three of the rarewar launched at Heyolu. The birds collided and cut with talon and beak. They tumbled through the air, and Heyolu fought fiercely.

Shouts rang out from the ranger fairies, and a spray of arrows soared toward the birds. Black and gray ones fell out of the sky. Two flights of gray birds split off from the rest, one arcing right and the other left. The gray birds swung around the line of fairies to attack from behind, but as they did, the Anolari whirled, shooting a cloud of arrows. Many of the little birds tumbled out of the air, but the rest set upon the fairies.

Something darted into Bobby's view. He turned to see a crouched figure racing across the sky toward the gray birds, attacking from behind. He gasped – it was Gabrielle. She was crouched, the brim of her hat tilted down, and one hand gripping the base of her board. She extended her other hand – which wore a silence glove glittering in the sunlight – and swept into the crowd of birds, knocking scores out of the air. The little creatures scattered but re-massed as Gabrielle arced around.

Meanwhile, the main flock closed on the fairies from the front. The Anolari pulled out their cleavers and hollered fiercely as they wielded their tiny axes. Sirie drew her silver blade and attacked like a tiny tornado as the four copper sprites defended her backside.

The agile gray birds darted and nipped at the fairies, while the larger rarewar swept past the defenders and dove toward the children gathered beneath the tree.

"Get ready," Josh shouted. "When I yell, Dylan, you go... Annie, wait for my signal, then scream like a wild child."

Josh became still, his eyes focused, knees bent and feet apart. He wore silver gloves on each hand. Wesley and Rhea waited beside him, while Annie crouched ten feet back, holding Bobby and Celia close to her. Some twenty feet to the right, Dylan squatted, ready to spring.

The thunder of wings swelled, and Bobby's heart pounded in his chest. Josh shouted, and Dylan vaulted some fifteen feet into the air with a fart like a missile launch. The birds winged toward the ground, and the thunder swelled to a crescendo. Josh gave Annie the signal, and her voice rang out, reverberating in a cry that froze everything in its path.

Tiny waves swept through the atmosphere like ripples on a pond. The world fell silent. All was still – all, except Josh. The boy moved swiftly through the flock, slapping the black birds with his silence gloves. The silence lasted for long moments, then the ripples faded, and motion returned. Sound thundered.

Bobby covered his ears and dipped his head as nine rarewar crashed to the ground in a cloud of dust. The birds lay where they'd fallen, their eyes open, but bodies immobilized. Josh and Wesley sprang among the birds, slapping them again and again with their silence gloves.

In the sky, the fairies formed into the shape of a ball to defend against the relentless attacks of the gray birds. Gabrielle swung her board around and shot toward birds massing around the fairies. She careened into the flock, scattering the winged creatures, but the board tipped, and she lost her balance. She fell. The deck whipped down as she dropped toward the ground. Gabrielle lunged for the board, but it was too late. Bobby heard the thump from forty yards away.

Dylan vaulted through the field, gripping his pants as stink bombs exploded into the morning air. Three rarewar hunted him. They nipped at his heels and snapped at his clothes. Cherry darted among the great birds, pecking at their eyes and wings.

Dylan bounded through the grass, then let off a loud stink bomb and shot high into the air and backward, soaring over the pursuing birds and landing behind them. The rarewar squawked and swung around, causing two to collide and tumble to the ground. But they were soon up again and hunting the boy.

Near the hackberry tree, a half dozen rarewar circled in the air. Josh and Wesley dashed back to the tree as several winged creatures dove toward them. A bird rushed at Wesley. He leaped aside, slapping the creature. The rarewar crashed into the grass, but a second bird came from the left, knocking Wesley off his feet. Rhea screamed and sprinted toward the winged beast. She threw her arms forward, and flames shot from her fingertips. The bird screeched and flapped in panic, rising away from the fire.

A rarewar plunged toward Annie as she hugged Celia and Bobby. The winged beast gripped Celia and tugged her upwards, but Annie held on. Rhea spun and dashed back. The bird lifted Annie and Celia into the air. Rhea leaped and grasped the rarewar's tail feathers. The oily plumage burst into flame. The bird squawked in fright, releasing the girls and fleeing into the sky. Annie dropped to the ground with Celia in her arms.

The fairies battled the throng of gray birds. They broke through the horde and sped toward the children.

Dylan bounded toward the tree with a winged beast in hot pursuit. He leaped past Rhea, and she raised her arms. Flames danced off her hands and jetted at the bird. The creature screeched and dodged the fire.

Sirie and the ranger fairies set upon the remaining birds. The winged creatures fought fiercely but fell one by one until the flock panicked and bolted. The fairies pursued, bringing down several more birds with their arrows, but couldn't match the speed of the winged beasts and gave up the hunt.

As the fleeing birds shrank into the distance, Dylan threw up his arms. "We did it!" he hollered.

Josh's eyes shown, and a rare smile appeared on lips. He grabbed Wesley and Annie. "You were awesome!" he said, hugging them both.

Bobby brushed off his pants and stood up. He scanned the area. Scores of birds lay strewn near the tree and in the field. The ranger fairies moved from one to another, finishing off those still alive. Bobby swallowed hard. The birds frightened him, but he didn't want them to die. A heaviness filled his chest.

"Hey, some help over here," came a cry. It was Gabrielle's voice.

Bobby glanced around but didn't see her. "Wheeree aaree yoouu?"

"Over here."

Bobby jogged toward the sound. Dylan bounded past him and came to a stop some forty yards from the tree. When Bobby reached Dylan, he found Gabrielle sitting in the grass with both legs sticking straight out in front of her. One leg was strangely bent.

Gabrielle leaned on an elbow, her hair tousled, and her baseball cap and black sneakers strewn about her. She grimaced at the boys. "I jacked up my leg."

Dylan shouted to Josh. Bobby squatted and frowned, not knowing what to do.

Josh strode over. "So, you had a fall," he said kneeling and feeling along Gabrielle's calf. "Tell me where it hurts."

When he reached her ankle, Gabrielle clenched her teeth in pain. "There."

Josh frowned. "It may be broken, or at least a bad sprain."

"If Sarah were here," Gabrielle muttered, "she'd use her electric tingles on it."

"Yeah," Josh said with a shrug. "Well, let's get you into the shade, so you can rest it." He put his arms under Gabrielle's back and thighs and gently lifted. Bobby and Dylan followed them to the tree.

Celia leaped to her feet as they neared. "What happened, Gabi?"

"I went gonzo and paid for it," Gabrielle said, wincing.

Josh set Gabrielle down, resting her back against the tree trunk. He scanned the area. "Where's Sirie?"

Bobby shrugged. Josh's brow knit and he started back into the field. Bobby trailed behind. Josh jogged, searching here and there for the fairy. Then, he slowed, resting his hands on his waist. Bobby followed his gaze and saw Sirie kneeling in trampled grass some ten feet away with a copper sprite kneeling beside her. Three fallen figures lay before them. Bobby squinted and saw they were the other copper sprites.

Sirie removed a white cloth from her bag. She and the kneeling copper sprite spread the cloth out. Together they lifted one of the fallen sprites onto the fabric. Sirie leaned close and set her hand on the top of the wounded fairy's head. A light pulsed from its forehead, passing up Sirie's arm, and the fallen sprite went limp.

Sirie raised her head. Tears shown in her eyes.

"Ohh Siirrii," Bobby murmured, his chest welling up with sadness.

Sirie covered the fallen sprite with the cloth. Then she moved to the next injured one. She set her hand on its forehead. A light passed up her arm again, and she wrapped a cloth around the now limp body. She did the same with the third fairy.

After each fallen sprite was wrapped in cloth, Sirie and the remaining copper fairy bore the bundles up into the hackberry tree, where they laid them out on branches. When all of the bundles were resting in the tree, Sirie and the copper sprite hovered before them with bowed their heads. Then, the golden fairy glided down and alighted softly on Josh's shoulder, tears streaking her cheeks and her face ashen.

Bobby tried to meet her eyes. "Ii soorry Siirri," he said with deep feeling. "Yoouu loose friieends."

Sirie nodded slightly, but didn't speak, and stared off into space.

Josh put his hand on Bobby's shoulder. "Come on. Let's go see about the Anolari."

Leoku and a crowd of ranger fairies were gathered on the far side of the tree. As they neared, Bobby gasped and Josh sighed in sadness. The ranger fairies were standing around six fallen comrades lying on the ground in a circle. Each of the standing Anolari moved from one fallen one to another and knelt with bowed head. They spoke in hushed voices and in a language that Bobby didn't understand.

After each Anolari completed the circle, Leoku placed his palm on the chest of the first fallen one. A pulse of light passed from the injured fairy up Leoku's arm. Leoku's body glowed for a moment, and then the light disappeared. Leoku did this with each of the fallen fairies, moving with increasing difficulty from one to the next as if carrying a mounting weight.

When he finished the circle, Leoku staggered over to the hackberry tree and hugged its wide trunk. A pulse of light glowed around him for a moment and then passed to the tree, spreading up through the branches and boughs until it lit up the entire hackberry in shimmering white light.

Leoku stepped away and stumbled back to his comrades. He dropped to the ground, his face pale and his head tipped forward. The other Anolari surrounded him and rested their hands on his back. Leoku leaned down, his forehead touching the ground and his breath coming out in heavy gasps.

After some moments, the ranger fairies rose and wrapped each of their fallen comrades in brown cloth and laid them side by side in a row on the ground. Then they and Leoku sat before the fallen fairies with folded arms and heads bowed.

Bobby heard a flapping noise and raised his eyes. Heyolu glided out of the sky and landed on a branch high in the tree. Bobby wondered what the rarewar thought of so many dead birds and fairies. He felt Heyolu must be sad.

Josh cleared his throat. "The fairies have suffered," he said, quietly. "It's terrible. But the birds will return. We can't stay here long." He eyed Sirie perched on his shoulder. "How soon can we leave?"

"Anolari need time," she said.

Josh nodded. "They died for us. But if we don't get to the Silver City, it'll be for nothing."

Sirie glided off Josh's shoulder and landed near Leoku. She stood beside the ranger fairy, her legs crossed, and her arms folded.

"Let's talk to the other kids," Josh said to Bobby. They headed to the far side of the tree where they found the children crowded around Gabrielle and chattering loudly.

Celia was seated in Annie's lap, while Dylan was hopping back and forth and describing his escape from the birds with quick moves and his rocket farts.

Josh knelt beside Gabrielle "How's your leg?"

She shook her head. "I can't stand. It hurts too much."

Josh grimaced. "I guess we'll need to carry you."

"What about a bubble?" Celia said. "She could ride inside one."

Josh quirked an eyebrow. "Ride? What do you mean?"

"The bubble's I make float. Dylan jumped around inside one."

Josh looked puzzled. "Dylan was in a bubble you made?"

Celia bobbed her head. "Yeah, yesterday, for a little bit, when we were in the forest."

"It was awesome," Dylan hollered.

"How did you get inside?" Josh asked in surprise.

"She opened it," Dylan said, staring at Celia. "Show him. Make another one."

Celia's eyes sparkled, and she rose out of Annie's lap. Celia planted her feet, took a deep breath and pressed her arms together. The goo oozed from her wrists, forming a bubble that expanded rapidly. Within thirty seconds it had swelled to the size of a beach ball.

The bubble continued to grow until it reached the width of a small wading pool. Bobby rubbed his eyes in amazement, guessing that Josh or Rhea could get inside now.

The bubble floated about a foot off the ground, while the top of it brushed against the lower branches of the hackberry tree.

"Let's move this into the field," Josh said. "We don't want it to pop."

Celia stepped backwards, tugging the bubble along with her until she stood some twenty feet from the outer edge of the tree. The other kids followed her.

"Open it," Dylan cried. "Show them."

Celia twisted her wrists, and a gap appeared in the sphere that ran halfway around the bubble and opened almost two feet at its widest.

"This is crazy," Josh said, tapping the surface of the sphere. "Why doesn't the air blow out?"

Celia shrugged. "Rhea asked the same thing. Maybe it's magic!"

"I'm going in," Dylan exclaimed and promptly sprang through the gap. Cherry darted in after him. Dylan landed inside the sphere and bounced off the bottom, swinging his arms as the warbler darted around him.

"See, it floats," Dylan hollered. "And it's big enough for all of us."

Josh rubbed his chin. "Can you get inside, Celia?"

The young girl blinked. "Huh?"

"Inside the bubble – can you climb in?"

"I don't know."

"Try, but don't let it collapse."

Celia stepped up to the opening. The pink elastic running from her wrists to the side of the sphere stretched out in a funnel shape as she moved, narrow at her wrists and wide at the sphere. She raised one leg and slipped it through the gap. Then she dipped her head and tumbled into the bubble. Dylan scrambled out of her way as she rolled to the bottom.

Celia lay there for a moment blinking, her arms pressed together and extended above her head. The bubble bobbed but continued to float. Celia rolled onto her stomach.

"Cool," Josh cried, punching the air. "You can ride inside. Now we just need to find something to pull it with."

Wesley fingered the pink surface. "So strange," he murmured.

Celia turned her wrists and the gap in the bubble closed. As it did, the funnel running from her wrists to the sphere shifted to the interior wall.

"Whoa," Wesley said, in surprise.

Josh smiled. "Can you make it bigger?"

"I think so," Celia said, pressing her arms together. The bubble expanded, swelling to some ten feet in diameter, and towering over the children. But as it grew, Celia's breathing became labored, and her face turned pale.

"Okay, that's enough," Josh said, with a worried look. "Are you alright?"

Celia nodded, but Bobby thought she appeared tired.

"Let's see if Gabi can get in there with you," Josh said.

"No way," Gabrielle cried, sliding backwards through the grass. "I'm not getting into that freaky thing. I'd rather crawl to the Silver City."

Josh shook his head. "Sorry, it's too far to crawl, and we can't carry you. Riding is the only option."

Josh squatted and picked up Gabrielle's hat. He stuck it on her head and raised her off the ground. Gabrielle gritted her teeth in pain.

Celia turned her wrists and the gap in the bubble reappeared. Josh leaned through the opening and gently set Gabrielle down at the bottom of the sphere. Gabrielle reclined and carefully stretched out her legs.

"Hoow dooees iit feeel?" Bobby asked.

Gabrielle touched her palms to the rubbery, pink surface. "I guess okay,... kinda squishy, but not as weird as I thought."

The wind gusted, jostling the bubble. Josh spread his arms and grabbed the sphere. "Let's move this further from the tree," he said. "I'm worried the wind will push it into the branches."

Wesley, Annie, and Rhea helped Josh push the bubble further into the field.

"Now we just need something to tie it with," Josh said, "so we can pull it."

"Maybe the ranger fairies have string or rope," Wesley said.

Josh nodded and started back toward the tree. Bobby hurried after him. They found the Anolari wrapping the last of their fallen comrades in white cloth.

Leoku turned as the boys strode up. He gave them a sad frown and said, "I'm sorry, we must leave you."

Bobby didn't understand.

Josh tipped his head and blinked. "What? Leave where?" he asked.

"We must honor our custom and bury our fallen comrades at Tolera Rius… the burial ground of our people."

"Where is that?"

"Many days east of here."

"We can go with you."

"I'm sorry, you cannot. It's not permitted. And, if you did, the rarewar would hunt you down. None of us would reach Tolera Rius."

Josh frowned. His brow creased. "What about us?"

"You must make your own way."

Josh tottered slightly, then steadied himself. "You're leaving? But you promised to take us to the Silver City. We know you've lost many of your friends. We feel terrible. But you're our only hope to get to a safe place. We thought you were fairies that cared for things?"

"We care for the land. We have no duty to the peoples of this or any other land."

Josh shook his head in disbelief. "Then why did you bring us here? We would have been better off with the Panishie."

"You must go to the Silver City, but we cannot take you further. Heyolu, the rarewar will come with us. You must make your own way."

Bobby felt dizzy. The ground beneath him seemed wobbly. He looked back. Rhea and Annie were hurrying toward them. They seemed to have heard the commotion.

"What's going on?" Annie asked as she jogged up.

Josh's eyes were bitter, and his face tense. "The Anolari are leaving."

"So? We're ready to go too."

"Leeaaviing uus," Bobby cried.

"They need to bury their dead," Josh said. "They're going a different way. We can't come with them. We're on our own."

Rhea's expression hardened and her face grew red. "Why? They can't do this."

Leoku bowed. "I'm sorry. We must."

"No . . . no," Rhea sputtered. "You're not leaving. We need you!"

Leoku turned away. Rhea stepped forward. "You brought us here. You have to finish what you started."

Leoku raised his hands in protest. "No, we can't. We have our duty."

"You must," Rhea yelled. She reached toward Leoku and small flames shot from her fingertips. Five of the ranger fairies shot into the air and drew their cleavers.

"Whoa, whoa," Josh yelled, stepping between Rhea and the fairies. He glared at Leoku. "She's angry. You need to keep your promises."

Leoku's jaw tightened. "Goodbye gifted ones. Good fortune to you."

"I knew it," Rhea shouted. "I knew they'd let us down. I knew it! You can't trust them. You can't trust anyone. They'll always betray you and leave you when you need them most."

Annie stepped in front of Rhea and met her gaze. "No, not everyone will let you down. You can count on me. You can count on Josh. You can count on Wesley, and Bobby, and Dylan, and Gabrielle, and Celia. We'll stick together. We'll do this together."

Annie took Rhea's hands in hers, then jerked away. "Ow! You're so hot! I forgot," she said, waving her fingers in the air to cool them off. "Ow, ow, ow!"

Rhea grit her teeth.

"Youu caan coouunt oon mee," Bobby said hopefully.

Rhea's expression softened.

Leoku tipped his head in embarrassment. "You have a long journey. You must leave. Time is precious."

"We know," Josh said. "We know, but which way to go?"

"South," Leoku replied, pointing. "You should reach the Garno River in two days. On the far side of the Garno, you'll find caves where you can rest. From there, will begin the most difficult part of your journey. It is four days on foot through the Besenon desert. You will find no food or water. At the end of the Besenon, you will come to the Folria River. The Folria marks the beginning of the Feriyan Valley. From there it is two days walk to the Silver City."

Josh nodded. He turned to Rhea. "Let's do this," he said, putting a hand on her shoulder

Rhea sucked in her cheeks and breathed out slowly. Bobby took her hand. It felt warm.

"I almost forgot," Josh said to Leoku. "We need some rope or string."

The ranger fairy's eyebrows rose.

"To tie around that bubble," Josh continued, pointing to the pink sphere floating in the distance.

Leoku stared silently for a moment. Then he flew off and returned a minute later with a ball of thread the size of a large peach. He handed this to Josh.

Josh fingered the hair-thin thread. "Is it strong?"

Leoku smiled. "Stronger than you or I. If you reach the Silver City, find the Silver Cat. He will protect you."

"Yeah, if," Rhea said, bitterly.

Josh put his arm over her shoulder and turned to Bobby and Annie. "Come on, you guys." The four headed toward the bubble.

"Eight days," Annie groaned. "That's forever. Those birds will be back long before that."

Josh shook his head. "It won't be eight days."

"Whyy?" Bobby asked.

Josh's eyes gleamed. "Because we won't walk – we'll run."

Chapter 22:
The Canyon

Wesley heard shouting from across the grove and craned his neck. Rhea was stomping her feet and shaking her fist. *Why is she so pissed off?* He wondered. A breeze gusted and nudged the bubble to the right. Wesley scooted over and spread his arms to keep it in place. Dylan bounded around the far side and gripped the sphere. They had to be careful. The bubble could easily be swept away in the wind, carrying Celia and Gabrielle off with it.

Wesley pressed his fingers into the pink surface. It felt soft but taut, like a giant balloon. He gazed at Celia and felt a tingle in his spine that it all came from her.

"You guys okay?" he asked.

"Yeah, sure…" Gabrielle said, with feigned indifference.

"It's nice," Celia replied, blinking and glancing around. "It's comfortable, but it makes me feel kinda dizzy."

"Take it easy," Wesley said. "Josh and those guys will be back soon." He glanced over his shoulder. The other kids were trudging over from the far side of the tree. He sensed something was wrong.

"What's going on?" Wesley asked as they neared.

"They're bailing on us," Josh said, anger flashing in his eyes.

"What?" Wesley asked in confusion.

"The ranger fairies. They're leaving."

Wesley tried to make sense of the words. "What? Why?"

Josh shook his head. "They say to bury their dead."

"But they brought us here? How can they leave us?"

"Because they're flakes," Rhea cried. "We don't need them."

"It's their tradition," Annie said. "We can't go with them."

"What are we supposed to do?"

"Find the Silver City," Josh said with a steely look. "We're on our own, but we can do it." He held up the ball of thread. "At least they gave us this. Help me tie it around the bubble."

Wesley took the end of the string and stumbled around the sphere, still in shock from the news. He brought the end of the string back to Josh. Together they made another loop over the top.

"I've been thinking," Josh said. "I believe I understand Celia's gift. This bubble is for carrying stuff. It floats even if someone's inside. And, the air doesn't blow out when it opens. It's crazy! But that's how it is, so we should use it."

Wesley frowned wondering what Josh meant. They wound the thread around the sphere firmly encasing it in a net of string and leaving ten feet of extra line at the end.

Josh waved the other kids over. "Okay, we're gonna take turns pulling this thing, but whoever pulls has to run – no walking. Everybody else rides inside. Who wants to pull first?"

"I'll go," Wesley said. He loved running and was sick of walking.

"Okay. When you need a break, let us know."

Wesley nodded and tied the end of the line around his waist.

Sirie glided over. Josh turned to her. "What're you gonna do?"

She raised her eyes, her face pale, and her golden tresses disheveled. "*Ana rea iwa feo tera ima.*"

Wesley didn't understand the words.

Josh began to translate, "To the end of ...." He hesitated, seeming startled.

"What'd she say?" Wesley asked.

Josh cleared his throat. "She's coming," he said, avoiding Wesley's eyes. Josh turned to Celia. "Can you open the bubble?"

Celia nodded and twisted her wrists. A gap appeared in the center of the sphere about five feet across and two feet high.

"Okay, everybody, get in," Josh said.

"Yaay," Bobby exclaimed. Wesley lifted Bobby inside. He clambered around until he found a comfortable spot and plopped down.

Annie stared at Wesley inquisitively. "You're gonna run?"

"Yeah," Wesley said bouncing lightly on his toes. "We can take turns."

Annie shook her head. "I hate to run. I couldn't go a hundred yards without stopping. If I had to pull this thing, I'd be walking all the way."

Wesley laughed, not sure if she was kidding.

Annie raised a foot to stick it through the opening in the bubble, but as she did, her heel caught the edge, and she stumbled forward, falling in face first.

"Yo!" Gabrielle hollered, yanking her injured leg out of Annie's path.

Annie planted her hands on the bottom of the bubble and steadied herself. "Well, that takes talent," she said sheepishly. She scooted over to Celia. Then she stared up through the pink elastic. "This is unreal. I can't believe you made it," she said smiling at the younger girl.

Celia laughed and leaned sideways, resting her head in Annie's lap.

Rhea dropped her backpack through the opening. Then she stepped away and stretched her arms. A broad smile spread across her face. The air around her seemed to lighten, and the sunlight glistened off her skin. Wesley blinked, thinking she was actually pretty when she wasn't frowning.

Rhea pulled a hairband out of her pocket and tied her wavy tresses back in a ponytail. Then she raised her arms. "Let's go."

"Aren't you getting in?" Wesley asked.

"No, I'll run with you. See if you can keep up."

Wesley grinned, but Josh shook his head.

"Unless you're pulling, you ride inside. If you run now, you'll only be tired later."

Rhea started to object, but Josh's expression hardened, and it was clear he wasn't going to budge. Rhea huffed and threw up her hands. She climbed inside. Then a look of concern appeared on Josh's face. "Where's Dylan?"

Wesley glanced around but didn't see Dylan.

"Heee geettiing waateer," Bobby exclaimed.

Where's water? Wesley wondered. Then a sound like a motor scooter backfiring rang out. He turned and saw Dylan leaping through the tall grass with a half-dozen bottles in his arms.

"Hot bananas, fuel for the run," Dylan cried as he bounded up. He pointed behind him. "Bobby told me about a little hill with water back there, so I took a bunch of the bottles from your bags to go find it. It was bubbling right out of the ground."

Dylan handed full bottles to Josh and Wesley. Then he bounded over to the sphere and leaped through the gap. He landed with a bounce inside the bubble, causing a pink wave to rush around the surface, and handed the remaining bottles to the other kids.

Josh stepped over to the bubble. "I'm getting in," he said, lifting one leg through the opening. But when his foot came down, it passed right through the pink surface as if it weren't there and landed on the ground below. The other kids gasped.

"Whoa!" Josh exclaimed, staring at his foot in bewilderment. He reached forward to touch the bubble, but his hand moved through the pink wall as if it were a wisp of smoke.

"What the?!" Josh said blinking in astonishment.

"Are you a ghost?" Dylan asked, his voice quivering.

Josh stepped back. "I can see the bubble, but I can't touch it or feel it."

"Someone's not getting a ride," Gabrielle said, shaking her head.

Sirie hovered close to Josh and peered at him through weary eyes. *"Feo anea awa."*

"What'd she say?" Wesley asked.

"Something about me being different," Josh said.

"Ba savi feo," Sirie continued.

"She says "it doesn't touch me" ... I don't know what that means. But it figures. Everything else is different for me."

Wesley's brain grew foggy. "What're you gonna do?" he asked.

Josh folded his arms. "Well, I can't ride, so I guess I'll have to run with you or whoever's pulling."

"Okay," Wesley said. "We can run together. See how long we can go."

Josh nodded.

Wesley guessed they could run for an hour or so, then both would be exhausted and need to stop.

"Let's get started," Josh said.

Wesley took a swig from his bottle and checked the string tied about his waist. He glanced at the other kids inside the bubble, then he started forward slowly, letting the pink sphere pick up speed gradually. It moved gently through the tall grass like a boat through water.

"It's a blimp, a mini-blimp," Annie said with a laugh.

Wesley raised his knees and began to jog. The bubble bobbed and swayed behind him. Inside, the kids pressed their hands against the elastic wall and grinned excitedly.

As they left the hackberry tree behind, Wesley glanced over his shoulder. Several ranger fairies stood at the edge of the tree watching them go. He sensed a melancholy in their expressions and wondered if they felt bad about what they'd done. Then he turned away. He didn't want to think about the ranger fairies anymore. He was done with them.

Josh ran about five feet to his right with Sirie and the copper sprite hovering just behind Josh. Wesley talked to him for a while, but then they both settled into a comfortable stride and fell quiet.

After some minutes, Wesley heard quacking and glanced up as a flock of geese passed overhead. He watched their wings gently rise and fall as they shrank into the distance.

A ground squirrel scurried across an open area ahead, causing Wesley to wonder what other creatures lived in this grassland. He passed through a swarm of tiny gnats, getting several in his mouth.

The numbness in his legs had receded to his ankles so that he couldn't feel his feet, but otherwise, he felt good.

He loved to run – just like his mom. For as long as he could remember, his mom had jogged every day. When he was little, his dad would take Sarah and him to watch her run in races.

He remembered the first time he jogged with his mom. He was nine years old, and it was Easter Sunday. That morning, he and Sarah had hunted for eggs in the backyard and eaten most of the candy they'd found in their Easter baskets.

After eating all the candy, Wesley's stomach felt weird, so he headed to his room to play some video games. He passed by his mom, who was sitting at the bottom of the stairs. She had on jogging shorts and was tying her running shoes.

"Where are you going?" he asked.

"To Newbury Park."

"Can I go?"

"I'm going on a run."

"I know." He had wanted to run with her for a while. "Can I go too?"

His mom hesitated, eyeing him skeptically. "Are you sure? It's over a mile."

"Yes," Wesley said eagerly. "I can do it."

His mom paused. Then her mouth formed a smile. "Okay," she said, "go get your sneakers."

Wesley rushed to his room and met his mom in the front yard. They jogged for several blocks. He liked the running, but the queasiness in his stomach got worse. They turned a corner, and the huge oak and elm trees of Newbury Park loomed ahead. Wesley jogged to the edge of the park. Then he stopped abruptly and leaned over. He threw up under some bushes.

His mom looked at him sympathetically. "Are you okay?"

"Yeah," Wesley said. "I think there was something wrong with that candy."

His mom laughed. "Any candy will do that if you eat too much of it."

Wesley's stomach felt better. They jogged around the park and headed back home.

When they reached their front yard, he was out of breath but happy and proud of himself. From then on, he ran with his mom several times a week.

One day she asked him if he wanted to do a three-mile race with her on Thanksgiving. It sounded fun, so he said he did. Wesley took third place for kids under ten. A couple of months later they signed up for a five-mile run. He and his mom ran side by side at first, but then a boy Wesley's age passed by them. Wesley wanted to keep up with the boy, so his mom told him to go on ahead. Wesley sped up and caught the kid. They ran together for the rest of the race and sprinted at the end. Wesley barely won.

"Are you getting tired?" Josh asked.

Wesley blinked, coming out of his thoughts. "No, I'm okay," he said, truthfully.

Josh raised his shirt and wiped his face with the bottom of it. His cheeks were pale and his breathing heavy. After several minutes, Josh said, "Actually, I need a break. Let's stop."

Josh slowed to a walk, and Wesley did too. Almost an hour had passed since they'd left the hackberry tree, and the green fields had given way to scrub grass.

Josh leaned forward, resting his hands on his knees and panting loudly. He peered into the bubble. "How're you guys doing?"

"Good," Dylan cried. "When do I get to pull?"

Josh straightened. "Patience, bro. You'll get your turn."

After a few minutes, Wesley and Josh resumed jogging. They hadn't gone far when Dylan hollered. "Hey, it's shrinking. Look out!"

Wesley glanced back and saw the bubble had contracted by a third. Wrinkles and creases crisscrossed its surface. "What's going on?" he yelled, slowing and spreading his arms to catch the shrunken bubble.

"Celia's asleep," Annie said. The younger girl's arms had moved apart. Annie pressed them together, and the bubble began re-expanding. Rhea scrounged in her pack and found a hairband. She slipped it over Celia's wrists; then she tied a scarf around Celia's forearms just below the elbow to hold her arms together.

The bubble swelled to its original size, and the kids settled back down. Wesley and Josh resumed running, but Josh soon fell back. Wesley slowed, letting the bubble glide along, while he waited for his friend.

"How do you do it?" Josh asked when he caught up. "We've been running for over an hour. I'm about dead, but you look like you just got started."

Wesley shrugged. "I'm not tired." He felt okay, though the numbness in his feet had moved up to his shins.

"You been sleeping at night?" Josh asked.

Wesley nodded. "A little. Meditating helps. It clears my head."

The boys resumed jogging. It was getting close to noon, and the air had warmed. As they loped through the scrub grass, Wesley wiped his face with his sleeve and stared up at a huge bank of gray and white clouds that covered much of the southern sky.

After a half hour, Rhea shouted that she wanted to pull, so Wesley stopped, and Rhea climbed out. He gave her the end of the string and got inside the bubble. As Rhea ran, he lay back, watching the beautiful, empty landscape. Far off to the east, he could faintly see snow-peaked mountains rising out of flatland. It seemed so peaceful and serene. He pinched himself to make sure he wasn't dreaming.

Rhea ran at a good clip, so Josh fell behind even quicker. Wesley watched as his friend shrank into the distance, wondering how much longer Josh could keep this up.

After some thirty minutes, Rhea slowed and began walking, her face red and her breathing heavy. A few minutes later, Josh caught up. Rhea stopped and rested her hands on her hips. "I'm done, guys. Someone else needs to carry the load."

"Let's stop here for a while," Josh said, glancing up at the sun which had reached the high point in the sky. "We can eat lunch."

Annie woke Celia. The younger girl moaned and opened her eyes. She sat up and coughed hoarsely.

"That doesn't sound good," Wesley said.

Annie frowned. "Making the bubble tires her out."

Celia twisted her arms and made a gap in the bubble. Everyone, except her and Gabrielle, climbed out. The kids sat around eating and talking. After lunch, Annie, Bobby, and Dylan walked off to explore the area, while Josh, Wesley, and Rhea rested.

My legs are dead," Josh said, rubbing his calves.

"We've run pretty far today. We could walk until it gets dark," Wesley suggested.

Josh shook his head. "If we walk, we'll never make it to the Silver City. We have to run."

Wesley grimaced. Rhea was silent.

When the other kids returned, Dylan asked if he could pull the bubble. Josh eyed his brother skeptically. "Yeah, but no jumping. We don't want the bubble bouncing around like a basketball."

Dylan frowned. "But jumping is the best part."

"Nope. Then you can't pull, bro."

"You're such a flat tire, Josh."

Josh rolled his eyes, and the other kids laughed.

"How about I pull, and you run with me?" Josh suggested. "Then you can jump all you want."

"Hot bananas," Dylan cried.

Josh tied the string around his waist and started out. Dylan ran alongside, shooting off regular stink bombs that kept launching him into the air as Cherry darted around.

Soon, the ground began to rise toward a wide hill. Josh leaned forward and pulled the bubble up the slope. When he reached the top, he slowed, taking in the view.

"Watch out," Wesley hollered.

Josh wheeled just as the bubble swung up behind him, hitting him in the chest and knocking him to the ground. Dylan leaped over and grabbed the strings encircling the bubble. He pulled. The threads tightened, and the sphere slowed, tipping downward. The kids inside tumbled forward.

"Owww! My fricken leg!" Gabrielle yelled.

Dylan strained, pulling the bubble to a stop just past where Josh lay sprawled on the ground, sweat dripping down his face.

Josh raised himself on his elbows and let out a deep breath. "Thanks, bro. I got a little distracted."

"It's cool," Dylan said proudly. "I've got you covered."

"You alright?" Wesley asked.

Josh stood up with an embarrassed grin. "Yeah," he said. He took a swig from his bottle. "Anyone else wants to pull this thing?"

Wesley said he did and climbed out of the bubble. Dylan hopped in. Wesley started down the hill with Josh jogging behind.

At the bottom of the hill, the terrain flattened, and Wesley ran at a steady pace. After thirty minutes, when he spotted something strange ahead. The land seemed to end about a hundred yards away. He slowed and waited for Josh. "You see that?" he asked.

Josh squinted. "Looks like the end of the earth."

The boys ambled forward, while the kids inside the bubble craned their necks to see better. As they drew near, a sheer cliff came into view descending to a green valley far below. The valley stretched for several hundred yards to a cliff that rose back up on the far side to another plateau level with them.

"It's a canyon," Josh said, gritting his teeth. "It's massive. The ranger fairies didn't tell us about this."

The boys treaded close. Wesley glanced right and saw the canyon ran north to the horizon. To the left, it continued in a southeasterly direction for some distance before angling west. He pointed. "If we follow it south, it turns, and we can get past it there."

Josh nodded and stepped to the cliff edge. He peered over. Wesley didn't like heights and held back a few feet.

In the canyon far below, a vast herd of animals moved south. The front of the herd neared a river.

"Those look like bison," Josh said. "Thousands of them."

Sirie landed on Josh's shoulder. *"Sevi anea Ea Emon."*

"What'd she say?" Wesley asked.

"Something about 'Ea Emon,'" Josh said. "I don't know."

In the canyon, the herd suddenly panicked. The lead animals bounded into the river, while those further back streamed to the right and left to reach the water quicker. The bison sprang into the current, splashing frantically toward the far bank. When they reached land, they shook off their hides and started back into a run.

"Something spooked them," Josh said.

Wesley looked north and spotted a pack of large creatures rushing down the canyon toward the herd. He hollered and pointed, counting fifteen animals in all. Tiny figures rode on two of the large animals.

"Hot bananas, those are wolves," Dylan cried, "and huge ones. They're hunting the bison."

"They jianar," Sirie said.

The lead wolf reached the water as the last of the bison clambered onto the far bank.

Just then, a breeze picked up. The bubble bumped Wesley from behind. He spun and stretched his arms to catch the sphere. Inside the kids shouted. Josh rushed over. The wind gusted and pushed the bubble around to Wesley's right, whirling it out over the precipice. Panicked cries erupted from inside.

Wesley clutched the string about his waist and braced his legs on a rocky outcrop. "Whoa, whoa," he shouted as the bubble dragged him toward the cliff's edge. He grasped at the ground, sinking fingers into crevices in the rock. Josh wrapped his arms around Wesley's and heaved, leaning back for leverage. The boys strained against the wind, inch by inch wrenching the pink sphere back onto the plateau.

They pulled the bubble over solid ground, and Wesley relaxed. Then the wind gusted, and the bubble careened back toward the precipice, yanking Wesley out of Josh's grip. Screams rang out from inside the sphere as it rushed into the open air above the canyon.

Wesley stumbled forward and fell off the cliff edge. He swung in the air helplessly with only the thin line of string keeping him from falling a thousand feet to the canyon floor.

Sirie and the copper sprite buzzed around him. They gripped his shirt and pants and strained against the wind, drawing him back to safety. As Wesley neared the rock face, Josh lunged and grabbed his hand, yanking him onto solid ground.

The wind died away, and Josh fell back. The bubble careened onto the plateau. Wesley landed on the rocky surface and bounced, banging his knees and elbows. The bubble sailed past him. Josh leaped up and chased the pink sphere as Wesley stumbled along behind, tangled in the string.

Josh caught the bubble and wrapped his arms through the threads. He dragged the sphere away from the precipice. The bubble bounced and swayed as the kids inside yelled and screamed. Wesley staggered along behind.

When they were some fifty feet from the cliff, Wesley shouted, and Josh came to a stop. Wesley bent over, resting his hands on his knees. He untangled himself from the string.

"Let's stay away from canyons," Josh said with a grin.

"Yeah, let's," Wesley said, closing his eyes in exhaustion.

They checked on the other kids. Everyone seemed okay, though frazzled and in shock. Wesley's heart was pounding like a tennis ball in a spinning clothes dryer. He pulled the bubble in a southeasterly direction. Josh ran alongside. They made their way through the empty scrubland until the canyon curved west. Then they angled south.

Glancing up, Wesley guessed it was near three in the afternoon. He wasn't tired yet, but the numbness in his legs had risen to his knees. Josh was struggling to keep up. Wesley slowed and waited. Then he started out again.

After some time, Wesley saw a shimmer in the distance. As he approached, he realized it was a river flowing west out of distant hills to the east. The river crossed the scrubland in the direction of the canyon.

Wesley stopped some thirty feet from the bank. Josh staggered up a few minutes later, his cheeks pale and his clothes soaked with sweat.

Wesley walked to the water's edge and knelt to drink. He washed his arms and face. Josh came up beside him, moving awkwardly as if his legs were about to crumple beneath him.

The river looked a hundred feet across. The water was ice cold. On the far shore, a rocky slope rose some thirty feet into the air and extended to the right and left as far as Wesley could see. Shallow caves and outcroppings pocked the rocky slope.

Josh plunged his head into the water and drank deeply. He leaned back. "This must be the Garno River," he said. "We're making good time. Leoku thought we wouldn't get here until tomorrow afternoon."

"How can we cross it?"

"Swim and pull the bubble with us."

"The current looks fast."

"Yeah, it'll probably carry us downstream a ways before we get to the other side. We can swim it, and it'll cool us off."

Wesley took a deep breath. He'd swum in rivers before, but not one as cold or as fast as this.

Josh told the other kids what he and Wesley were going to do.

"What if the bubble sinks?" Dylan asked.

"Why would it?" Josh said. "It'll just float over the water like it's floating now."

Dylan's eyes darted. He didn't seem convinced.

Wesley slid the string up around his chest and stepped into the current. Josh came up beside him. They slogged forward. With the numbness in his legs, Wesley didn't feel the cold until the water reached his thighs, then it momentarily locked up his muscles.

"Whoa, this is freezing!"

"It must be snowmelt," Josh said staring at the distant hills. "But after all that running, it feels good."

The boys made their way forward with the bubble floating a foot above the water behind them. The river was shallower than Wesley expected, rising to just above his waist. He and Josh swam part of the way and then trudged through the shallower areas. They finally climbed onto the far bank some fifty yards downstream with water pouring off their clothes.

Wesley pulled the bubble onto the bank and plopped down on a rock in exhaustion.

"Can we get out of here?" Annie asked.

"Yeah," Josh said, "You all can."

Annie woke Celia, and she opened the bubble. The kids started climbing out. Wesley helped Celia. When he set her down, she stood awkwardly, her forearms still tied together.

"Can I take these off?" she asked.

"Okay," Wesley said. He helped her remove the scarf and hairband.

Celia rubbed her eyes. "I'm tired. I'm going to let the bubble shrink."

She spread her arms, and the pink goo streamed back into her wrists like water into a drain. The bubble vanished, and the string fell to the ground.

Celia sighed and ambled over to Annie.

Wesley knelt at the water's edge and filled his bottle. Josh joined him there.

"How're you feeling?" Josh asked.

"Okay," Wesley said, "except for the numbness in my legs."

Josh studied him. "You look pale, and the dark spots are showing on your face again."

Wesley touched his cheek.

"You're pushing yourself hard," Josh said. "You don't know it, but you are. And, that numbness worries me. Still, you look better than you did a couple of days ago. Do you think you can run more today?"

Wesley shrugged. "Sure."

Josh rose and motioned for Wesley to follow him. They ambled down the bank out of earshot of the other kids. Josh found a wide rock shaded by a ledge and sat down. He patted the stone. Wesley took a seat beside him.

"You remember Leoku told us we have 'gifts'?" Josh said. "Dylan can jump high. Rhea gets hot. Annie can freeze everything. Celia can make the bubble."

Wesley nodded.

Josh rubbed his hands through his hair. "Well, I think I've figured out your gift and my gift."

"Oh… what are they?"

"You can run practically forever. You can pull that bubble for hours and hours and not get tired. I wish I could. It's an awesome gift. But remember Leoku said we have weaknesses? I think I know yours now. Although you don't feel tired, you really are. That's why you don't look good. So, be careful. Don't push yourself too hard."

Wesley bit his lip. "Okay. What about you?"

"My gift? It's kinda weird. Remember you said everything is different for me? Annie's scream doesn't affect me. The mist monster didn't freeze me. I can't feel Rhea's heat. And, I can't touch the bubble. Why? I think it's because those things are magic, and magic doesn't affect me. That's my gift."

Wesley's brow creased. "Is that why you could open the door of that giant cage we found? Because it was magic?"

"Probably," Josh said. He gazed at Wesley for a moment. "I need you to do something for me."

345

"Huh? What?"

"I want you to try to run with the bubble all the way to the Silver City. Can you?"

"I'll try."

"This is the beginning of the Besenon desert. Leoku said it would take us four days to walk across. I think you can run it in a day and a half. At the end of the Besenon is the Folria River. After the Folria, it's two days walk to the Silver City. If you run, you should make it in a day. Can you do that?"

"You mean run for two and a half days? I thought you said I shouldn't push myself?"

"I know," Josh said, his lips trembling slightly. "You shouldn't, but we need to get the kids to a safe place. I'm worried... I'm worried about you. I'm worried about them. I think your running is the only way we can get there before the rarewar come back. Don't push yourself too hard. If you're feeling drained, stop and rest. And, if that numbness gets worse – if it gets near your chest – your heart – stop, okay? Don't keep running."

Wesley stared at his hands. "Yeah, I'll try, but what about you? Can you run all the way to the Silver City?"

"No, I'm done," Josh said, shaking his head. "I can't go anymore."

"Then what's the point?"

"You can. I can't."

"What about you?"

"I'll wait here until the sun goes down. Then I'll move by dark."

Wesley stared at Josh. A fog filled into his brain. "You mean we leave you behind?"

"Yeah, it's the only way," Josh said firmly.

"But we can all move by dark."

"No, there won't be places to hide during the day. We'll be seen. If it's just me, I can find a rock or something to crawl under. We need to get the other kids to a safe place. It's the only way."

Wesley's jaw tightened. "I don't know," he said, choking up.

Josh put his arm around him and pulled him close. "Remember, back at Oriafen I told you I'd need you? I must have ESP or something," Josh said, smiling wistfully. "You're the only one who can do this."

Wesley raised his head. He could feel tears in the corners of his eyes.

"Okay," Josh said, his voice softening. "Let's keep it together. We need to be tough. The other kids are counting on us." He hugged Wesley.

Wesley wiped his cheeks. He didn't want to leave Josh, but he knew they had to get the other kids to a safe place. They didn't have much time. Josh was right. He and Josh headed back along the bank and found the kids sitting and chatting as they munched on cakes and fruit.

Rhea stood some distance from the others staring out at the river. Dylan bounded onto a boulder. "Look, guys," he shouted and leaped high over the water, wrapping his arms around his knees and pulling his legs to his chest. He landed with a splash that sprayed all the kids, especially Rhea.

Rhea dove into the river and swam to Dylan. She dunked him several times before swimming back to shore.

Josh laughed. He looked relaxed, almost relieved. He called the kids over and told them what he and Wesley were going to do.

Dylan stared at the ground and frowned. "No, we aren't leaving you."

"And, you can't expect Celia to make that bubble for three days," Annie said. "She's already exhausted."

"Yes, I can," Celia said firmly. She sat up straight. "I can, but Josh needs to come with us."

"I wish I could," Josh said, shaking his head.

Rhea let out a shrill cry. Everyone jumped. "No," she shouted, her face darkening. "We can't leave you behind. We need to stay together."

"It's impossible," Josh said. "I can't run like Wesley, and I can't ride in the bubble. You need to get to a safe place soon – before the birds come back. I'll get there, trust me. I'll meet you there in a couple of days."

"Ii beeliieeve Joosh. Hee bee okaayy," Bobby exclaimed, hopping over and wrapping his arms around the older boy.

Josh returned the hug. "Thanks, Bob. I'm counting on you."

"Ii knoow."

Sirie landed on Josh's shoulder. She peered at him with her clear brown eyes. *"Ana pitu iwa feo."*

Josh hesitated, then nodded.

"What'd she say?" Dylan asked.

"She's staying with me. But the rest of you have to go."

Tears trickled down Celia's cheeks. She touched the second finger on her right hand. "If you're going to walk at night, you'll need this," she said, tugging off the owli ring which the fairies had given her. She handed it to Josh. "You can use it to see your way."

"That's so kind," Josh said. "But you keep it. You may be traveling at night too."

"But you'll be alone," Celia said. "You'll need it more than us."

The determination in Josh's face weakened, and he accepted the ring. He slid it onto his little finger and held up his hand. "It fits," he said with obvious surprise. He glanced around. "Alright, everybody, grab your stuff and climb to the top of these rocks. Celia can make the bubble again up there."

Wesley made his way up the rocky slope. At the top, he saw a barren landscape stretching forward to the horizon. The other kids gathered there, gazing at the wasteland apprehensively. Celia tried to make another bubble. She had difficulty at first but finally got one to expand to slightly smaller than the original one.

"That's all I can do," Celia said, her shoulders drooping.

"That's fine," Josh replied, "It's big enough. Now everybody climb inside."

Wesley and Rhea wrapped the string around the sphere, while the other kids got in. When the bubble was fully encased in a net of string, Wesley tied the end around his waist. Rhea climbed in last, and Celia closed the bubble.

Josh stepped away, his jaw clenched and his eyes glistening. "Okay, see you all soon."

Wesley wanted to say something, but there was a lump in his throat. He hesitated. Josh frowned and waved him forward. Wesley took a deep breath and started out. The other kids waved and shouted goodbyes.

Wesley picked up speed. He glanced back. Josh grinned and pumped his fist. Wesley forced a smile, wondering when he would see his friend again. Then he turned and looked ahead, scanning the empty land. It seemed endless. He exhaled and stretched his legs, increasing his stride. The desert rushed by.

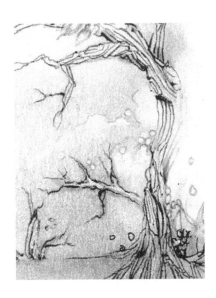

Chapter 23:
Besenon

Bobby listened to the rush of wind as the bubble moved through the dry air. He peered out at the landscape spreading off in every direction in a tan emptiness, only broken here and there by a withered tree, or a solitary boulder appearing out of nowhere as if dropped from the clouds by sky giants.

Wesley ran steadily through the afternoon heat, pulling the bubble along. Bobby leaned back, feeling the sphere quiver as it moved through the warm air. He tipped his head and watched puffs of dust shoot up each time Wesley's sneakers hit the chalky soil.

Beside him, Celia lay with her head in Annie's lap. Celia's arms were tied together, and her face pale. She seemed to drift in and out of sleep and moaned as if having a nightmare. Annie leaned close and whispered something in Celia's ear which quieted her.

Behind Annie, Dylan squatted with an impatient frown, while his hands fidgeted, and his feet tapped the bubble's rubbery surface. Cherry sat silently on Dylan's shoulder, observing the passing landscape like a monk on a mountain top.

Dylan shifted and sprang into the air, causing Bobby to laugh out loud and the other kids to yell at him. Dylan bounced around several times while Cherry glided in circles. Then he plopped back down where he'd been squatting, and the warbler landed back on his shoulder.

On the far side of the bubble, Rhea sat doing her stretching exercises; only pausing now and then to stare ahead or watch Wesley.

At the front of the sphere, Gabrielle lay with her head on her board. Her eyes shifted toward Bobby. "This is the way to travel."

Bobby smiled.

Wesley covered mile after mile until a hill loomed out of the emptiness. There was no way around it, so he headed straight up the slope, only slowing as the incline steepened severely. He swung his arms and struggled up the last stretch. At the top, he turned and caught the bubble, easing it to a stop. He bent forward – his breath coming in gasps – and rested his hands on his knees.

"Can we get out of here?" Annie said. "My legs are stiff and sore."

Wesley nodded. Celia opened the bubble. Everyone except Gabrielle and Celia climbed out.

Bobby strolled across the hilltop. It felt good to move around. He ambled to the far edge of the hill and stared down at the desert stretching into the distance. Annie and Rhea came up behind him.

"Does this ever end?" Rhea asked.

"Yeah, Wesley says if he keeps running, we'll get to the end tomorrow," Annie said, folding her arms. "Then one more day to the Silver City."

"Let's hope," Rhea said. "Our water won't last much longer."

The ground began to tremble. Orange and yellow colors rose into the western sky. The shaking swelled, and a red dot appeared on the western horizon.

Dylan bounded up. "It's a fireball!" he hollered. "Another one! Leoku said there were nine."

The dot swelled, racing east across the southern sky, a cloud of flame and smoke trailing in its wake. The fireball crossed the horizon and disappeared behind mountains to the east. Everything fell quiet.

"Hey, get back inside you guys," Wesley said. "We need to go further before it gets dark."

"Aren't you tired?" Annie asked.

"No," Wesley said matter-of-factly, but Bobby saw Wesley's skin had turned a grayish tone and his cheeks and eyes looked hollow.

The children climbed back into the bubble and Celia closed the gap. Wesley pulled the sphere to the far side of the hilltop and started down. As he descended the slope, his stride lengthened so that he bounded six to seven feet with each leap.

At the bottom of the hill, the ground leveled out, and Wesley settled into a comfortable pace. Bobby's eyes grew heavy, and he drifted off to sleep. A cry awoke him.

"What's that?" Dylan shouted, pointing ahead.

Bobby sat up and peered into the distance. An enormous dark cloud hovered above the desert there like smoke from an army of diesel trucks. He thought it was a rain cloud at first, but as they neared, he realized it was something else. A breeze gathered, and a pitter-patter sounded on the bubble's surface. Wesley twisted, his hair blowing around like threads of yarn in a fan. "It's sand," he shouted. "A sandstorm!"

The drumming grew louder as they passed into the dark cloud, and the light faded. Bobby could see nothing but Wesley's silhouette struggling against the wind and sand.

The darkness continued for long minutes, then the beating quieted, and sunlight reappeared. Wesley slowed and brushed sand off his face and arms. He stared into the bubble. "You guys okay?"

"Yeah," Annie said. "But we're inside. How about you?"

"I'm alright – just tons of sand down my shirt and pants."

Wesley tugged on his clothes in several places. Then he started to jog again.

He ran until the sun was low on the horizon. An immense boulder appeared ahead with a large outcrop jutting from its left side.

Wesley slowed. "Maybe we can sleep beside that," he said. "The ledge could protect us from the rain."

The kids agreed. Wesley pulled the bubble up to the boulder. Bobby and the other children climbed out. Bobby stretched his arms. He yawned, then a sharp pain stabbed into his right side. He bent over in agony.

"What's wrong?" Annie asked, crouching with her hand on his back.

"Someethiing baad," he moaned.

"What? What's bad?"

Pain filled Bobby's mind, blocking out all other thoughts. He fell to the ground and faintly heard Wesley's voice. "I see something. It looks like one of the black birds."

"Yeah, it's one," Gabrielle said. "Maybe a scout."

Bobby's eyes opened to slits, and he glimpsed an enormous bird in the distance winging toward them. The aching swelled. The rarewar passed overhead and circled twice above them. Then it turned and headed back the way it had come.

"What should we do?" Annie asked, watching the bird shrink into the distance.

"Nothing we can do," Rhea said. "It's gonna tell the others. They'll come for us. We'll never reach that Silver City."

"What if we don't stop tonight?" Wesley said, staring at the bubble. "What if I keep running until the morning?... Maybe we can still get there first."

"Can you?" Annie asked anxiously.

"Yeah, my legs feel okay," Wesley said rubbing his calves. "Let me eat, then we can go." He grabbed his bag and tugged out several cakes and an apple.

Bobby's pain faded, and he sat upright. He stared at the sun disappearing beneath the horizon. He wondered when the birds would come back, and if Wesley could keep running in the dark. He remembered the owli ring which the Panishie had given him. He scrounged around in his bag and pulled it out. The stone emitted a beautiful blue light. He handed it to Wesley.

"Ummm," Wesley said taking the ring as he swallowed a mouthful of cake. He slid the ring on his fourth finger. "Thank you, Bobby. This will help!"

After Wesley had finished eating, the kids climbed back into the bubble. Bobby settled down in his favorite spot, and Wesley started out, holding the owli ring up to light the way.

Even with the ring shining on Wesley's finger, Bobby could see little in the dark. He felt nervous, but the vibrations of the bubble gradually calmed him. He wrapped his blanket around his shoulders, curled up next to Celia, and drifted into sleep.

A jolt woke Bobby. He sat upright. Ahead, Wesley was stumbling in the dark, struggling to stay on his feet. He almost fell, but caught himself and slowed, turning to grab the bubble and bringing it to a stop.

"Are you okay?" Annie asked.

"Sorry," Wesley said. "I must have fallen asleep. I was running, and my eyes kept wanting to close. Then the bubble bumped into me. It almost knocked me down."

"You should rest," Annie said. "You need sleep."

"No, I'm okay," Wesley replied. "I can keep going."

"You sure?"

Wesley nodded firmly.

"Where's Bobby's ring?" Rhea asked in a sharp tone.

Bobby saw it wasn't on Wesley's finger.

"It's in my pocket," Wesley said. "The stars are so bright here; I can see without it." He tipped his head back. "And, I was afraid those birds might spot the light."

Wesley's voice had a strange hollow sound, and his face was bony and gaunt. Bobby sensed there was something wrong, and his heartbeat quickened. Wesley seemed to move around normally, but there was something different about him – like he wasn't all there. Bobby watched Wesley, a queasy feeling growing in his stomach. His hands began to twitch.

Wesley started out again. After some time, the soft vibrations of the bubble lulled Bobby, and he relaxed, slowly drifting into sleep.

He awoke with sunlight in his eyes. He sat up on his elbows and blinked. It was morning. Wesley was still running through the empty land.

"Heey," Bobby shouted.

Wesley glanced over his shoulder. His face looked pale and haggard, his eyes distant and misty.

"Hey," Wesley said back in a raspy voice.

"Hoow yoouu?"

"I'm okay," Wesley said. "Tired, but okay."

"Yoouu ruun aall niight?"

"Most of it. I walked a couple of times, but then I got antsy and started running again."

Dylan rolled over. "Where are we?"

"The Besenon desert," Wesley said.

"Still?" Dylan groaned. He lay back.

Wesley had run for another hour when Bobby noticed a sparkle ahead – a shimmering across the desert floor. "Loook," he cried, pointing.

Wesley squinted. "It's another river. It must be the Folria!"

As they drew near, Bobby saw the water ran east to west along a dip in the desert floor.

Wesley slowed. "It doesn't look as wide as the Garno. It shouldn't be hard to swim across."

He strolled to the river's edge and waded in. The water quickly deepened. He began to stroke. Bobby scrambled around excitedly in the bubble, watching as the current flowed by below.

The river carried Wesley almost a hundred yards downstream before he slogged onto the far bank. He plopped down in the sand and tugged the bubble onto the shore.

"Phew… Swimming wears me out more than running," he said. "I need a break. You guys can get out for a while."

Celia opened a gap, and Bobby climbed out. He stretched his arms. The air felt fresh. He took a deep breath and strolled along the bank. He climbed the rise of the land beyond the river and found golden fields swaying in the breeze. The change surprised him – one side of the river was desert and the other grassland.

He returned to the kids, who were eating and chatting on the bank. After some twenty minutes, Wesley was ready to run again.

Gabrielle stared at the bubble and scowled. "I'm done with that pink prison. I wanna ride my board."

"What about your leg?" Annie asked.

"If I sit, I can keep it straight. I just need to get my board into the air." Gabrielle raised her head, eyeing a boulder at the crest of the rise. "Maybe I can ride off that…. Can you help me up there?"

Annie and Rhea supported Gabrielle as she limped up to the boulder. Bobby and Dylan followed behind. On top of the boulder, it was flat and some twenty feet across. Gabrielle set her skateboard down at the near side. Then she sat on the board with her injured leg sticking out in front of her.

"Now, if you guys push me, I should be able to get enough speed to fly off this thing," she said.

Annie, Rhea, Dylan, and Bobby climbed onto the boulder. The four crouched behind Gabrielle, their hands pressed against her back and waist.

"When I say 'go', push as hard as you can," Gabrielle said. "Ready… Go!"

Bobby and the others scrambled forward, shoving Gabrielle and the skateboard across the stone. Gabrielle leaned down, gripping the sides of the deck. The board neared the end of the rock, and the kids pulled up. The skateboard shot off the boulder. It dipped slightly, then leveled out and glided smoothly above the waving grass.

"Waahooo," Gabrielle hollered. She made a wide arc and headed back toward the river, shooting out over the water.

The other kids strolled back down to the bubble and climbed in. Wesley pulled them up the bank and jogged into the field. Gabrielle glided up behind, riding just inches above the grass. Bobby watched her for a moment. Then he lay back, listening to the rushing air.

As Wesley ran through the morning, the land rose and fell. Hours passed, and the sun reached a high point in the sky.

Bobby peered ahead and spotted something in the distance off to the right. He squinted and blinked. It looked like a house.

"Heeey," he yelled, pointing. "Whaat's thaat?"

All heads turned. There was silence, then the kids began shouting. Wesley nodded; his eyes wide. He angled toward the house.

As they neared, Bobby saw it was a farm with several sheep and chickens roaming outside. No people were visible.

"Where is everyone?" Dylan asked as they neared the house.

"Let's stop and look around," Annie said. "We can find who lives here."

Wesley shook his head. "We can't stop. We need to keep going."

"But what if they can help us?" Annie objected.

"If the fairies couldn't protect us, I don't think some farmers can. Leoku told us the Silver City is the only safe place. We need to get there."

Annie's shoulders slumped, and the other kids frowned in disappointment. Bobby eyed Celia, who was still asleep. She looked pale. Bobby noticed dark spots on her skin.

As the farmhouse receded into the distance, Bobby felt a pang of hunger. He tugged a pear out of his bag and took a bite. The sweet flavor burst in his mouth, and he closed his eyes in enjoyment. When he opened his eyes, he blinked in surprise at the sight of two figures stepping out from behind a tree some distance ahead and to the left. It was a boy and a girl. "Heeyy, loook…," he shouted, pointing at the children.

"Whoa!" Dylan cried. "It's kids! They must live on the farm."

Gabrielle glided up beside Wesley. "Let's go talk to them."

Wesley squinted, seeming to think it over for a moment.

The boy looked nine or ten, with short, blonde hair and a serious, though curious expression. He wore a blue shirt and brown trousers. The girl was dressed in a pretty white frock and was almost a head shorter than the boy, with straight, brown hair that fell to her shoulders, and eyes that twinkled in the sunlight.

"No, we can't stop," Wesley finally said. "We don't have time. We need to get to the Silver City today."

Gabrielle glanced at the other kids open-mouthed. She rolled her eyes and swung around to the far side of the bubble, twirling a finger by her ear to indicate Wesley was crazy. Dylan and Bobby nodded.

The bubble passed some fifty yards from the tree. The little girl suddenly cried out and scrambled forward. But the boy leaped and grabbed her before she got far, holding her tightly.

Bobby stared crestfallen. Across the distance, his eyes met those of the boy. Bobby smiled wistfully. The boy stared back, then he raised one hand and gave a slight wave, still holding the girl with his other arm.

"You see that?" Dylan hollered. "He waved at us!"

Dylan raised his arms and waved both back at the kids, shouting, "Hey, Hey, we're friends!"

Bobby glared at Wesley as the children by the tree receded into the distance. Bobby wanted to meet them, to talk to them. The kids looked nice. He wondered if they could speak English. He was sure Josh would have stopped. Bobby crossed his arms in frustration and frowned.

The children shrunk from view. Bobby sat and let out a deep sigh.

As the afternoon passed, the golden fields thinned to scattered clumps of grass sprouting from dry, rocky soil. The land sloped upwards for some time, then leveled out and began a gradual descent into a wide green valley. Wesley slowed to a stop, and they all stared in wonder. Small villages dotted the valley. A dark forest ran along its eastern edge. To the west, a shoreline arched inward and then veered back out to mountains rising out of the sea.

At the far end of the valley, a great silver wall stretched between mountain cliffs rising in the west and east. Beyond the wall, ruby, sapphire, and emerald towers glittered in the afternoon sun.

"We made it!" Annie cried. "It's the Silver City."

"That's a wide valley," Rhea said, her brow creasing. "I doubt we can reach the other side by dark."

"But we're close..." Annie sighed. "And it's so beautiful."

Wesley trotted down the slope, picking up speed as he descended through the knee-high grass. Gabrielle whipped by on her board. Above, blue sky with a sprinkling of puffy white clouds spread to the horizon. A breeze pushed the bubble leftward. Wesley angled his stride to stay in front of the sphere.

Bobby gazed at the silver wall and the towers sparkling beyond it. His heart quickened, and he couldn't stop grinning. Annie cradled Celia in her lap. Bobby scooted over to Annie and touched Celia's cheek. Her skin felt cold and damp.

"Iis shee siick?" Bobby asked.

Annie shrugged. "I don't know. The bubble seems to tire her out. She's getting weak."

Bobby grimaced. Celia and Wesley were doing wonderful things, but it seemed to hurt them. He didn't understand why.

As they descended the hillside, villagers could be seen in the fields and the roads. Some stared in amazement at the boy pulling the enormous pink bubble. Others shouted and waved. The children waved back, but Wesley didn't slow or stop for anyone.

To the west, a cobblestone road wound down into the valley, on which horses pulled carts of grain and farmers drove flocks of sheep.

Bobby pointed to the road. "Wee goo theeree?"

Wesley stared for a moment. Then he shook his head. "Too crowded. It'll slow us down. We can move faster through the fields."

Bobby's shoulders sagged. He wanted to go to the road, to meet the people and see the animals. He wanted to talk to them and learn more about them.

By mid-afternoon, they reached the base of the valley. Ahead, a rushing river cut through the land, turning and swirling through giant boulders and pools before dropping in a series of waterfalls toward the sea.

Far off to the left, the cobblestone road reached a stone bridge spanning the river. A crowd of carts, villagers, and animals were massed there, waiting to cross.

Wesley gazed at the bridge, his brows drawing together. He seemed unsure of what to do. The river looked swift and treacherous, but it could take hours to get through the crowd waiting at the crossing.

Bobby scanned the countryside. Then he spotted something some distance upstream. It looked like another bridge though smaller and made of wood. No one was waiting there. He shouted and pointed.

Wesley squinted. "Wow..." Wesley said, starting forward. "Let's check that out."

As they neared the wooden bridge, the roar of water rushing by beneath it filled Bobby's ears. The bridge looked dilapidated, with many broken planks and cracked beams.

Wesley slowed to a stop at the edge of the structure. Gabrielle glided up. "You gonna try it?"

"I don't know," Wesley said. "What do you think?"

"Go for it! It look's rundown but it should be okay for a bunch of kids."

Wesley took a deep breath and stepped onto the planks. They buckled slightly but held.

An enormous black bird suddenly dropped out of the sky and landed on the rail on the left side of the bridge. It was a rarewar.

"Whoa!" Wesley cried, abruptly stepping back.

"Where did that come from?" Dylan shouted.

Bobby glanced around. He didn't see any other birds.

"I think it's alone," Wesley muttered. "What does it want?"

The bird eyed the children mildly and began preening its feathers.

Bobby rested his hand on his stomach. It didn't hurt. He told the other kids. Wesley stared at the bird; his gaze cloudy. Then his eyes cleared. "Hey, it must be Heyolu!"

Bobby let out a cry of realization.

"What's he doing here?" Rhea asked. "I thought he went away with those stupid ranger fairies."

"Maybe he missed us," Dylan said.

Rhea frowned doubtfully.

Wesley stepped onto the bridge. "Hello," he said to the bird.

The rarewar eyed him, then croaked softly. It returned to its preening.

"It's definitely Heyolu," Annie said. "He must have missed us." She stared at Wesley. "Are you gonna try this bridge or go back to the stone one with all the people and animals?"

"This bridge looks rickety," Wesley said, "but I think if I go carefully, I can get across it."

Gabrielle glided up. "I'll ride beside you. If you start to fall, grab onto me."

Wesley rolled his eyes. "Yeah, and we'll both end up in the river."

Gabrielle grinned. "I don't mind a little water."

Wesley took another step. The planks creaked but didn't break. He cautiously advanced, gripping the right-hand rail firmly. Gabrielle glided along beside him.

After several minutes of slow, careful steps, Wesley reached the mid-point of the bridge. He glanced back. Bobby smiled and gave a thumbs up. Wesley took another step. The plank beneath his right foot suddenly snapped, and several pieces fell toward the water. Wesley stumbled, his right leg dropping through the hole. His hands caught his fall at the base of the bridge. The planks beneath them held.

For a moment, the only sound was the rushing water.

"Are you okay?" Annie asked anxiously.

"Yes... I think so," Wesley said. He cautiously raised his leg out of the hole. He sat there for a moment and took a deep breath.

"Do you wanna go back?" Dylan asked.

Wesley shook his head. He rose and stepped over the broken plank. He cautiously made his way forward.

After several more nervous minutes, he reached the far bank and stepped off the bridge. He pulled the bubble up behind him and leaned forward, resting his hands on his knees.

"Yoouu diid iit," Bobby hollered. The other kids yelled and cheered.

Wesley nodded and wiped sweat off his forehead. He straightened and gazed up the hillside. An old dirt road overgrown with weeds led away from the bridge. He started up the road, tugging the bubble along behind him.

Back at the bridge, Heyolu spread his great wings and rose into the air. He glided toward the children, passing above them. Wesley increased his pace. Bobby watched for a moment, feeling safe again. He leaned back and sank into the bubble's rubbery surface.

Wesley shook his head. He rose and stepped over the broken plank. He cautiously made his way forward.

After several more nervous minutes, he reached the far bank and stepped off the bridge. He pulled the bubble up behind him and leaned forward, resting his hands on his knees.

"Yoouu diid iit," Bobby hollered. The other kids yelled and cheered.

Wesley nodded and wiped sweat off his forehead. He straightened and gazed up the hillside. An old dirt road overgrown with weeds led away from the bridge. He started up the road, tugging the bubble along behind him.

Back at the bridge, Heyolu spread his great wings and rose into the air. He glided toward the children, passing above them. Wesley increased his pace. Bobby watched for a moment, feeling safe again. He leaned back and sank into the bubble's rubbery surface.

Chapter 24:
The Cat

The world swam before Wesley's eyes as he struggled up the dirt trail. Objects moved in and out of focus, seeming to disappear and reappear, then disappear again. He felt hollow inside, empty – like a barrel drained of all its water. He had run since the wooden bridge. Hours had passed. He'd lost all sense of time. Sometimes he forgot where he was or why he was even running, but then it all came flooding back. He had to get to the Silver City, to get the kids to a safe place. He had to do it… he'd promised Josh.

Sweat dripped down his face. It soaked his shirt and pants. His throat was dry, and his voice was hoarse. He glanced at the bottle in his hand – empty. He closed his eyes, trying to forget the pain and exhaustion. The world spun slowly.

The numbness advanced toward his chest. In the morning, it had reached his waist, and he'd lost all feeling in his legs. He didn't know how he could still run, but his legs kept moving. The numbness continued creeping upward. Josh had warned him to stop if it got near his chest... his heart. But Wesley couldn't stop. He was too close.

Wesley peered up the hillside. How much further? He couldn't tell. The rising land kept curving out of view. Occasionally, he spotted villagers in the fields to the right or left, or cottages in the distance, but he ignored them. He needed to get to the Silver City.

He glanced over his shoulder. Celia and Bobby were sleeping on either side of Annie, with Celia's head resting in Annie's lap. To the right of them, Rhea lay stretched out the length of the bubble, gazing west. Dylan sat a few feet behind Annie playing solitaire and shouting in frustration each time the bubble bumped suddenly and scrambled his cards.

Annie caught Wesley's eye, and her brow creased. "You need to take a break, Wes. You should stop."

He shook his head. "No, I'm okay."

"But you don't look good," Annie said, frowning.

"I know," Wesley answered, tottering slightly in his stride. "I pretty tired, but I can't stop yet."

Wesley wiped his face with the end of his shirt. Gabrielle glided up beside him, coasting smoothly through the warm afternoon air. Wesley eyed her with a tinge of envy. It looked easy riding on her board... But from her drooping eyes and occasional painful winces, he knew she was tired, and her leg hurt.

"How much further?" Gabrielle asked.

Wesley shrugged.

Ahead, the slope steepened. He lowered his chin and swung his arms. His heart pounded, and his breath came in heavy gasps as he struggled up the sharp incline.

Then the slope tapered, and to his surprise, he came out over the top. He slowed and blinked in amazement. Ahead, a grassy plain spread out for hundreds of yards toward a massive silver wall rising high into the sky. He scanned from right to left. The wall ran in either direction as far as he could see.

As he stood there, the bubble came up from behind and bumped him, almost knocking him down. He caught his balance and turned, facing the other kids with a lopsided grin. "We made it."

"You did it!" Annie cried. "We've reached the Silver City!"

Dylan whooped and bounced upward, sending his cards flying and waking Bobby and Celia. Rhea stretched her arms, her eyes gleaming.

Wesley peered hard at the wall. Tiny figures moved along the battlements. To the right, two circular white towers rose at the wall's center. Between the towers, an enormous black draw bridge extended across a wide moat. Crowds of people and animals moved across the bridge, passing in and out of the city.

Wesley wondered what they would find in the city. Leoku said a silver cat lived there who could help them. Wesley started to jog, forgetting his fatigue and worries. A euphoria filled him. They had done it! Josh had said they would, and he was right.

Wesley lengthened his stride and loped comfortably, pulling the bubble along above the knee-high grass. He felt peaceful and serene for the first time in many days. Then a cry broke through his tranquility. He glanced back. Bobby lay curled up at the bottom of the bubble. Annie and Rhea were leaning over him.

"Something's wrong," Rhea said. She turned and stared at the sky behind them. Wesley looked, but his eyes were too tired to focus.

"Where does it hurt?" Annie asked.

"Stoomaach," Bobby moaned. "Soomeethiing baad. Soomeethiing coomiing."

"I don't see anything…," Rhea said. Then she went silent. "Wait… No… Oh no… Wesley, go. Hurry, go! The birds. They're coming back."

Fear rippled through Wesley, and he accelerated to a full sprint. Wind rushed by his ears. Moments passed. The gate still seemed far off. He glanced back; a darkness covered part of the sky.

"Man… tons of them," Dylan shouted. "Clouds of them."

Gabrielle darted up on her board, gliding alongside Wesley. "Faster. Faster, Wes. You got to get there."

"I know," he gasped. "You go on ahead. Don't wait for me. Tell them at the gate we need help."

"You sure?"

"Yeah, go. Go!"

Gabrielle grimaced and leaned forward. The board dipped and accelerated, pulling away. Wesley stared into the bubble. Annie had one arm wrapped around Bobby and the other cradling Celia.

"Hundreds of them," Dylan shouted. "And a giant bird at the front. Something is riding it – a monkey or something."

"Get on your gloves," Rhea shouted. "We're gonna fight."

"I wish Josh were here," Dylan said, his voice cracking.

"He's not!" Rhea cried. "It's just us... Annie, you take care of Celia and Bobby. Dylan, you and I will handle these freaking birds."

Rhea yanked on her silence gloves. She raised her hands, almost touching the roof of the bubble. Then she spread her arms wide as the birds descended out of the sky.

A thunder of wings filled Wesley's ears. He glanced over his shoulder. The birds darkened the blue, hundreds of them. A giant rarewar – twice the size of the others – led the flock. And, a furry creature rode on the giant bird.

Wesley squinted. The furry creature looked like one of the snow monkeys, only brown colored. It held something in its' small, furry hand – a metal object, like a baton. *What's that?* He wondered.

"You ready?" Rhea shouted.

"Uh-huh," Dylan said with a gulp.

Wesley looked ahead. His eyes focused on the draw bridge, still far away. The crowd there had begun to scatter. He strained, sprinting with every trace of strength. His heart pounded, his lungs burned, and the numbness in his chest inched relentlessly upward.

The thunder of wings swelled, drowning out all other sound. A shadow passed overhead. The flock swept by in a great wave, and the sky went dark.

In the blackness, a bird descended, its powerful talons outstretched. The creature sank its long claws into the pink sphere.

367

There was a ripping, and Annie screamed. Her voice reverberated through the atmosphere. The world became still and silent. Wesley couldn't move. He couldn't speak, but he could think. He readied himself.

The moments drew out in a long hush. Then Annie's voice faded, and the thunder roared back. The sphere burst, hurling Wesley forward. He hit the ground and rolled, as other kids tumbled around him.

Rhea bumped into Bobby, and Bobby cried out in pain. Rhea somersaulted to a stop and sprang to her feet, her skin glistening red.

Annie rolled with Celia in her arms. She tumbled to a stop near Bobby, and turned, facing the dark sky.

Wesley lay face down in the grass. He tried to lift himself, but he had no strength and collapsed back into the field.

Birds swept down from the sky – dozens of rarewars and countless small gray ones. Dylan sprang to his feet and released a noisy stink bomb that propelled him into the air. He touched down some ten yards away and dashed off as the winged beasts pursued.

Dylan raced in the direction of the gate, running in a zigzag fashion to avoid the clutches of the birds. But the rarewars closed on him. One reached out to snatch him and Dylan spun, letting off a fart like a Cadillac backfire, and launched between the bird and another, slapping them both with his gloves as he passed. The winged creatures crashed to the ground, tumbling through the grass in a cloud of dust.

Rhea sprang toward Annie, who screamed "Watch out!" as five rarewars dove toward her. The red-headed girl whirled and slapped at the winged beasts, knocking three out of the air. The other birds fled.

Rhea tilted her head and eyed the flock darkening the sky. "Stop this," she yelled, tiny flames flickering from the edges of her eyes. "Go away. Leave us alone."

The birds watched her mutely. Rhea screamed and tugged off her gloves, exposing her hands that glistened red. She raised them. Bright flames shot from her fingertips at several of the birds.

The winged creatures squawked in fright and retreated, exposing a patch of blue sky.

"Leave us," Rhea yelled, "or I'll have to hurt you!"

The monkey creature shouted in a strange language, and two rarewars swept toward Wesley. Rhea swung her arms and lines of flame flashed through the air, striking the descending birds. The winged creatures screeched in terror as their plumage burst into flame.

Rhea knelt beside Bobby, Annie, and Celia. "I'll stay here with the girls," she said to Bobby. "You get Wes and bring him over. I'll keep the birds away."

Bobby nodded and started toward Wesley. Three rarewars descended. Rhea yelled and flames shot from her hands, striking the birds. The winged creatures shrieked and fled back into the sky.

Bobby reached Wesley and grabbed him by the arms. He tried to help him up, but Wesley couldn't get off the ground. Bobby squatted and locked his hands under Wesley's upper arms. He strained. Wesley came to his knees.

Then a voice filled the air. "Gifted ones, do not fear. Do not flee. I am the envoy of Sidtarr, the Ruler of Risrean. He is a friend to gifted ones. He welcomes you to his realm. He will teach you. He will guide you. You will learn to master your gifts."

Wesley pivoted toward the sound – which strangely reminded him of a pirate in an old movie. He gasped. It was the monkey creature who was talking.

"Who are you?" Rhea shouted. "Why are you hunting us? We know who our friends are, and you aren't one. Go away, or I'll turn you all into flying barbecues."

The monkey frowned coldly. "Be careful, gifted one. My master is generous and will help you, but his anger is to be feared. Do not defy him."

Rhea laughed. "We don't need your master's help," she said, raising her arms. Tiny flames shot from her fingertips like arrows of heat, heading straight toward the monkey. The bird beat its great wings and rose out of the path of the fire. Rhea swung around and shot flames at the other birds, forcing much of the flock into retreat.

Wesley came to his feet and stumbled with Bobby toward the other kids.

A lone rarewar descended out of the sky. The bird glided over to Annie and hovered before her – its' great wings pulsing the air and stirring up a cloud of dust.

Rhea spun and threw her arms out toward the winged beast, but Annie cried, "No, Rhea! It's Heyolu!"

In the chaos, Wesley had forgotten about the lone rarewar. His eyes went to the creature's talons, recognizing the ugly scars.

Annie gazed at Celia, lying unconscious in her lap. She lifted the young girl, offering her to the great bird. Heyolu beat its wings and edged closer, gently taking Celia in its strong talons.

The flock seemed confused, thinking Heyolu was one of them. The lone rarewar rotated and beat its wings, starting toward the city. The monkey realized their mistake and shouted fiercely. A half dozen rarewars gave chase as Heyolu winged across the field.

Peering into the distance, Wesley spotted Gabrielle gliding near the gate.

"Watch out!" Rhea screamed.

Wesley ducked and flames shot over his head. He heard terrified squawks and spun. Three rarewars fled with their plumage ablaze.

"Over here," Rhea yelled. Wesley and Bobby stumbled over and crouched beside Annie.

Rhea whirled, eyeing the huge flock, hovering in a wide circle around the children. She started toward the largest bird carrying the monkey. "It's time for you to leave," she hollered and extended her arms, fingers spread wide. Lines of flame shot from each fingertip. Pandemonium erupted as the birds dodged the fire, and the flock drew back further.

"You will regret this," the monkey bellowed. He yelled and rarewars dove toward the children from all directions. A sense of hopelessness filled Wesley. There were too many birds. Rhea couldn't fight them all. He leaned against Annie and raised his hands in self-defense. The thunder of wings swelled.

Then a roar broke through the thunder – a roar that seemed to freeze the world. The roar came again. The birds faltered. Another roar sounded, louder still. Then a creature bounded through the gate and across the drawbridge – a sight which would forever remain burned in Wesley's memory.

It was an enormous cat with long, flowing silver fur that shimmered like water in a spring breeze.

The cat vaulted across the bridge and bounded into the field. It reminded Wesley of a Bengal tiger he'd seen once, but many times larger. It moved powerfully and gracefully, with an aristocratic bearing. The cat turned toward the children, and its eyes sparkled in the sunlight.

The cat roared again and leaped into the field. Behind it, Gabrielle glided out of the gate as horns filled the air. A throng of soldiers rushed through the gate and across the draw bridge. The soldiers poured into the field with drums beating and armor clanking.

The cat raced toward the children, the wind flowing through its long silver fur. The soldiers swept into the plain following the great feline.

The monkey shouted and dozens of rarewars, along with an uncounted number of gray birds, launched at the cat, while the remaining rarewars dove at the children.

"Get down!" Rhea shouted as she rushed back to the other kids. Wesley ducked his head. Rhea stopped beside them and raised her arms; then she began to spin. Flames shot out from her fingertips, forming a ring in the air. She spun faster, her arms rising and falling. The ring became a funnel of flame widest near the ground and narrowest at the top, encircling the four children.

The air within the funnel grew hot, and Wesley had difficulty breathing. The flames sparked and crackled, while the sound of horns and drums carried across the field, and the ground trembled under a thousand charging feet.

The rarewars recoiled from the fire. The monkey hollered again, and dozens of small gray birds dove at the children. The little birds dodged the flames and slipped into the funnel. They attacked the kids, pecking and scratching mercilessly with beak and claw.

Wesley swung at the small birds with the little strength he had. But they were quicker than his tired arms and easily dodged his blows.

Rhea slapped at the little birds with her fiery hands, but this interrupted her spinning and gaps formed in the funnel, allowing more birds to sweep in.

As the funnel collapsed, Annie tugged on her silence gloves and sprang to her feet. She swung right and left, slapping everywhere. Dozens of little birds fell out of the air.

Across the field, the great flock hurtled toward the cat. They collided with the feline at the midpoint of the grassy plain, swarming and attacking with talon and beak. The cat dipped and dodged with wonderful agility, leaping away from the birds and striking back with its powerful paws, swatting the winged creatures out of the air. But the birds besieged the cat again and again.

As the winged creatures teemed around the cat, the feline leaped, rolling its enormous body and striking out with all four paws, tearing at feather and cracking bone. Winged creatures dropped to earth in crumpled heaps, and the cat landed back on its feet, resuming its race toward the children.

Dozens of gray birds lay strewn around Annie. She dropped her arms in exhaustion and slowed to catch her breath. Rhea smiled admiringly and resumed spinning, rebuilding the funnel of fire. Annie ducked inside and crouched next to Wesley and Bobby.

The furry monkey yelled at the rarewars, pointing at the children, but the winged beasts recoiled from the gauntlet of fire. The monkey's face twisted in fury, and the creature raised the metal baton, pointing it at Rhea. A blue light shot from the tip of the baton, hitting Rhea just above the waist. She screamed and fell back. The funnel of fire faded away.

"What was that?" Rhea screamed, staring at her waist. "It hurts like hell!"

Wesley and Annie scrambled over to Rhea. Her lower shirt was burnt black, and blood seeped from a wound at the center of the blackness.

"He shot me with something!" Rhea cried.

"It's not my wish to hurt you," the monkey cried, "but you must obey." He yelled at the rarewars again, and they swept down.

"Hot bananas," a voice hollered. A booming fart rang out, and Dylan launched over the kids' heads, rocketing straight into the descending cluster of birds. He slapped everywhere with his silence gloves, and three rarewar fell to earth, while the other birds were thrown into confusion.

Rhea raised one hand, the other clutching her bleeding waist. She shot flames at the birds, and several of the creatures caught fire.

Dylan landed and launched skyward again, slapping more of the birds.

Rhea straightened; her jaw clenched in pain. She threw out both arms toward the monkey. "That was wrong. This is for you."

Flames burst from Rhea's fingertips. The bird carrying the monkey rose away, but the flames grazed its wings. The rarewar squawked in alarm as its feathers caught fire.

"You will regret this, child," the monkey cried, his mouth curled in fury. He pointed the baton, and another blue light shot out, this time striking Rhea in the shoulder. She screamed in agony and fell back, landing in the grass as blood seeped from a second puncture wound.

Dylan bounded over Wesley's head, shooting off a pair of farts like popping tires and slapped several more birds. Three rarewars fell out of the air. Dylan bolted away.

Wesley turned. The silver cat approached swiftly as dozens of birds swarmed and besieged it. The feline swatted at the winged creatures, knocking some away, but the rest continued to assail the cat.

The legion of soldiers followed some distance behind, charging across the field with Gabrielle gliding along nearby.

Gabrielle accelerated and darted ahead of the soldiers, increasing her speed and gaining on the cat. As she neared the feline, Gabrielle ducked, shooting through the crowd of birds, briefly distracting the attackers, and giving the cat some momentary relief.

Gabrielle darted away, and several of the rarewars chased her. Gabrielle headed back toward the charging legion. The soldiers shot a cloud of arrows into the air, forcing the oncoming birds to abandon the pursuit.

Wesley turned his attention to the flock surrounding him, Rhea, Annie and Bobby. Almost two dozen rarewars remained. The monkey shouted again. Half of the birds swept down. Rhea raised her good arm unsteadily. She shot lines of flame, but the winged beasts dodged the fire and plunged toward the children.

Wesley stumbled back as talons closed around his shoulders and waist. A bird lifted him off the ground. Another winged creature gripped Annie, but she slapped the rarewar with her silence gloves. The bird fell forward, landing on Annie and knocking her to the ground. As Annie struggled to extricate herself from beneath the unconscious bird, another winged beast came upon her. Annie slapped that one too, and it fell beside the other.

The rarewar clutching Wesley beat its wings and rose skyward. Another bird caught Bobby and lifted him away from the ground. Rhea swung around, shooting fire randomly but missing everything. Her head tipped sideways, and her eyes stared unfocused as blood seeped from the wounds at her waist and shoulder. She clenched her teeth and raised her good arm; flames shot from her fingertips. Bobby's bird dodged the fire, but the blaze scorched Wesley's winged creature, and the rarewar shrieked in terror, releasing its prize. Wesley plummeted toward the ground.

Annie screamed. Everything froze – the birds, the cat, the soldiers, and the children. All became motionless and silent. Long moments of quiet passed with Wesley poised some twenty feet above the hard ground.

Finally, Annie's scream faded, and motion returned. Wesley plunged toward the ground. Then a silver blur swallowed him in a cushion of soft fur. They tumbled together. The fur opened, and

Wesley's feet touched the ground. He raised his head. The enormous cat towered above him.

The cat wheeled around and bounded toward the flock. It leaped, slapping right and left at the remaining birds. The winged creatures scattered. The cat pivoted and rushed toward the enormous bird bearing the furry monkey. The cat sprang and grasped the rarewar, dragging the bird to earth. The force of their landing crumpled the winged creature and pitched the monkey into the field.

The furry monkey tumbled head over heals, then rolled to a stop and scrambled to its feet, still gripping the metal baton in its furry hand. The monkey spun and pointed the baton at the cat. A blue light shot out from the metal tip, but the feline seemed to know the danger and sprang out of the way with astonishing quickness.

Rhea shouted in fury and flung her good arm forward. Flames burst forth, racing above the grass and hitting the monkey square in the chest. The furry creature fell back with a scream as its fur erupted in fire.

The cat wheeled and bounded over the heads of the children. It twisted and turned in the air, swatting birds out of the sky.

The monkey rolled on the ground, extinguishing the fire. Then it leaped to its feet. A rarewar dove and clutched the monkey, carrying it away.

The thunder of the legion swelled to a crescendo. The earth shook, and arrows whistled through the air, striking the winged beasts. Gabrielle shot by Wesley with a cry and whipped around, while Dylan bounded overhead with a stink bomb like a boulder landing in a pool of mud.

Cries rang out among the rarewars, and the flock retreated. The bird holding Bobby beat its wings and moved north with the others. The cat bounded in pursuit of the flock.

Wesley stumbled to his feet. The legion swept around him, swallowing him in a great moving mass. Rhea dropped her arms in exhaustion and gazed despondently as Bobby shrank into the distance.

Soldiers wearing shiny silver armor and leather jerkins stopped to gaze wide-eyed at the children. They offered bandages and ointment to Rhea for her wounds, but she screamed and pushed them away, her hot skin burning all she touched.

The soldiers drew back in fear, and Rhea strode through the crowd, her eyes fixed on the birds fleeing north. Wesley followed, stumbling with the little strength left in his legs.

* * * *

Bobby strained against the bird's firm grasp. He watched despairingly as his friends shrank into the distance. The flock soared northward until out of arrow range. They slowed, seeming confused. The furry monkey yelled, his small fists flailing and his voice shrill. He pointed toward the children left behind and shouted in a berating tone. The winged beasts' heads bobbed, and their eyes darted – uncertain, unsure.

Below, the plain spread out like a vast, green blanket. The cat raced across the expanse, its muscles turning under its flowing silver fur, while the legion receded in its wake.

A low rumble reached Bobby's ears, a familiar sound. He twisted and scanned the sky. An orange glow rose in the west, swallowing the blue. A dot appeared on the horizon – a red dot. The dot swelled rapidly into a twisting, turning ball of fire, hurtling toward the plain. Bobby knew what it was.

The monkey barked in a trembling voice; the imperiousness suddenly gone. The flock dove. Bobby's bird descended with the others, but the cat had closed the gap with the birds. Bobby's bird eyed the feline and squawked in realization that it was the object of the cat's pursuit. The rarewar beat its wings and rose skyward.

The fireball thundered out of the west, its roar drowning out all other sounds. Bobby twisted, struggling desperately in the bird's grip. His heart pounded, and he screamed, but the roar swallowed his cry. He turned toward the oncoming fire and froze, rigid with fear.

All at once the roar faded, and light surrounded him. A soft white light like a cloud of tranquility. Images passed before his eyes – his home, his mom, his dad, and Willow. A wonderful peace filled him, washing through him.

In the swelling roar and blinding light, he closed his eyes and leaned back. His arms fell to his side.

* * * *

Wesley stumbled after Rhea as she shoved her way through the crowd. She screamed at the soldiers in her way and shot flames into the air while her gaze remained fixed on the birds and Bobby.

The fireball thundered out of the west, growing rapidly as it neared the plain. Wesley sensed it was flying lower than the one they'd seen back at the forest, hurtling through the air almost level with the wall. The ground shook, and the soldiers slowed to watch in wonder.

The bird gripping Bobby plunged with the flock, then rose back into the sky alone. Wesley slowed and brought his hands to his mouth.

The cat neared the end of the plain where the land swept up in a final rise. The bird hovered there just beyond the rise as Bobby struggled in its grip.

The fireball swelled, its flowing molten flame seeming to fill half the sky. Bobby became still. Then he leaned back, and his body went limp.

Wesley gasped, and Rhea dropped to her knees. The cat hurtled up the rise, its muscles heaving.

* * * *

The white light cushioned Bobby like a cloud. He felt at peace and happy. Then something stirred in him and the light faded. Life surged through his body, forcing air into his lungs – he didn't want to die! He twisted against the talons.

Below the cat lowered its head and vaulted off the rise of the land. For an instant, Bobby saw the great creature's silver face. Then the cat crashed into him, knocking away the winged beast, and pulling the boy into its embrace. The impact stunned Bobby, knocking the air from his chest and drowning him in a silvery softness.

The cat's momentum carried them upward, its thick fur muffling the rising thunder. Then the fur turned suffocatingly hot – hotter Bobby thought than his mom's car on a summer afternoon.

The cat's momentum slowed. It hung for an instant in the air, then it fell, tumbling down, down, down.

* * * *

Wesley gasped as the cat vaulted off the rise, rising higher and higher into the air. The cat swatted the bird away and swallowed Bobby in its silvery embrace, then both vanished into the roaring flames at the bottom edge of the fireball.

Rhea bent forward, and Wesley went numb. The ball of fire streaked across the sky, and a small burning object fell in its wake, tumbling over and over, and disappearing beyond the rise of the plain.

A hurricane wind slammed into the field, knocking Wesley, Rhea, and everyone around them to the ground. Rhea struggled to her feet, tears streaming down her face. Wesley lay still, in stunned shock. Then he clambered up and stumbled forward, following Rhea as she limped through the grass, her left arm cradling her waist and her right arm hanging useless.

* * * *

The cat slammed into the ground and rolled, tumbling over and over until it came to a stop in a shallow dip in the hillside. Bobby remained still and waited. The creature didn't move. Finally,

Bobby pushed on the great paw pressing against him and edged it outward. He slid to the ground and tried to stand, stumbling before he came to his feet. He squinted and gazed up the slope. They were some fifty yards down from the peak. Black marks streaked the grass for some half of that distance where the cat had tumbled.

Much of the creature's fur was burned away, and its flesh shone black, red and blistered. Bobby knelt beside the great cat, sadness swelling inside him.

"Iii soorryy," he said, tears trickling down his cheeks.

One eye of the cat cracked open a sliver and sparkled like a brilliant emerald. The creature's mouth moved, and it emitted a painful groan. The cat made a rough, grating sound and its body rippled and throbbed. The charred fur constricted and twisted, morphing into the blackened, blistered skin of a man, but a man unlike any which Bobby had ever seen. He was enormous, stretching out along the ground like a twisted, fallen tree. Little remained of his silver hair and beard, but what did, shimmered in the sun, while blisters and gashes covered his blackened skin.

Bobby leaned forward. "Yoouu aaliivee?"

The enormous man groaned. "Yes, I believe I am," he said and paused. "But don't let me do such a foolish thing again." He let out a deep, pure, warm laugh. The laugh was cut short by a painful grimace.

"Itt huurt?" Bobby asked.

"Yes... and I think it will hurt for a long time."

The man raised himself on one elbow and gazed down at his blackened, blistered body. He winced and gritted his teeth. "At least I have a good story for my old friend, Eredel."

The man sat upright with a groan. His body towered over Bobby. The man closed his eyes and let out a deep sigh. He raised his hands and brought them together before his chin, interlacing his fingers, as if he were praying. He became still. Then he peered down at Bobby. "Tell me your name young one, so that I may know for whom I have done such a foolish thing."

"Ii... Ii aam Boobbyy," Bobby stammered.

"Ah... that is a good name," the man replied, wincing as he shifted his body slightly. "I have a friend – an old friend – with that name. I am Trethian, though most call me the Silver Cat."

A commotion arose at that moment, and Bobby gazed up the hillside. A crowd of soldiers appeared over the rise and rushed down toward them, shouting in a language that sounded to Bobby like that of the Panishie.

The soldiers hurried to Trethian, and a female one pulled out medical supplies from her pack. She handed ointment to the others, and together they spread it on Trethian's blackened skin. The female soldier paused in her work and studied Bobby. She sighed and gave him a relieved smile, apparently realizing that he wasn't hurt.

As the soldiers rubbed ointment on Trethian, he flinched and grumbled, but the soldiers ignored this. A younger one stood behind the rest, carrying an enormous silver cloak in his arms. Bobby caught his eye. The young soldier stared back, then winked as if to say everything would be okay.

When the soldiers finished spreading ointment on Trethian, the young one lay the cloak over the shoulders of the enormous man. Trethian rose, and Bobby saw he towered over the others. The soldiers bowed before the huge man as if he were their king, and Bobby suspected he was.

The female soldier spoke. Trethian and the others laughed, but Trethian's laugh was cut short by a painful grimace. He looked down at Bobby. "My comrade thinks it's humorous that I am grievously wounded, while you are unscathed. She tells me I should spend less time protecting others, and more time guarding myself." He laughed again in a deep voice.

* * * *

Wesley followed Rhea through the crowd. They reached the open field, and Rhea tried to run, but after several strides she groaned and leaned forward, clutching her side. She slowed to a walk. Wesley stumbled after her.

In the distance, soldiers disappeared over the rise of the hill. Wesley wondered what they would find on the other side. He tried not to think of Bobby, but the terrible sight of the burning cat falling out of the sky had etched in his mind. He had little hope that either of them had survived the fall.

As he and Rhea neared the rise of the plain, a band of soldiers came over from the far side. An enormous figure strode among them – a man who towered like a giant over the others. The gigantic man wore a long, shimmering silver cloak. His skin was blackened, and much of his hair and beard was patchy and bedraggled.

Wesley slowed to stare. Then he heard a cry, "Rheeaa! Weesleeyy!"

The band of soldiers parted, and Bobby came sprinting out, his arms swinging joyfully. Rhea leaped forward, tears flowing down her cheeks. She ran to Bobby and took him in her arms. She squeezed, then grimaced and let him go. Bobby's gaze dropped to the wounds at her shoulder and waist. "Yoouu huurt."

"Yeah," Rhea said, through clenched teeth, "But I'll be okay... And you're alive!"

"Yeees," Bobby said, drawing his arms in and glancing over his shoulder. "Thee Siilveer Caat saavee mee! Coomee meeet hiim."

Bobby took Rhea and Wesley's hands in his own and pulled them toward the soldiers. As they neared the towering stranger, Wesley saw the man's blackened skin was covered in blisters, scratches, and cuts. Much of his hair and beard had burned away, but what remained shimmered in the sunlight.

"Hello, young ones," the man said. His eyes went to Rhea. "You are injured, child."

"Yes," she said. "So are you."

The man grimaced and smiled. "Yes, come with me to the Silver City, and we shall heal together."

He reached down and took Rhea's hand. Then he took Bobby's. Bobby grinned at Wesley and grasped his hand too. The man smiled at each of them, his emerald eyes glinting in the sunlight.

The four strolled down the rise of the hill and into the plain.

Ahead, Gabrielle was gliding over the grass with Dylan bounding along beside her. In the distance, Annie stood among a crowd of soldiers. Her eyes met Wesley's, and he sensed joy and relief in her face.

* * * *

Many leagues to the north, an ebony-skinned boy stepped out from under a lonely stone in the empty desert. He brushed dust off his shirt and out of his short curly black hair. A golden-haired fairy hovered in the air beside him, staring up at the sky.

"You saw the birds coming back?" Josh asked. "How many?"

Sirie folded her arms. "They not many and have no gifted ones... They fail."

A smile of relief spread across Josh's face. "They did it," he murmured. "They made it to the Silver City." He glanced at Sirie. "When the sun sets, let's get moving."

She nodded.

* * * *

To the west, a band of jianar padded swiftly over the rocky red earth of the Eo Canyon, moving quietly in the afternoon shadows. Above the lead wolf, a blue fairy and four copper sprites glided in the warm breeze.

Emma sat upright and gazed at the canyon wall soaring skyward. "It's so peaceful here, Mya. And, it seems to go on forever."

"I wish it would," Mya murmured. "It's so calm and beautiful."

Emma nodded.

* * * *

Many leagues to the north beyond the Eelena and Uelena ranges, three riders and a dog made their way west along the roots of the mountains.

"How much farther?" Sarah asked.

"Not far," Eredel answered. He pointed ahead. "Our destination."

Sarah peered across the rolling land to where the mountainside swung out into the plain. There, a high stone wall rose, arcing out and around the base of a hill.

"What is that?"

"The Benapara Outpost – the watchman of the north," Eredel said. "An old friend is the overseer there. We will seek his help."

"But will the help be help we need?" Timmy murmured.

Eredel gave the boy a hard look. "You say the oddest things young Tim, but we will see what help there is."

* * * *

Far across the brown lands stretching league after league northward from the Benapara Outpost, the castle of Risrean rose dark and ominous along the white cliffs and crashing sea of Yiliar. In a dungeon, deep beneath the castle, three boys sat in the dim light of a walled room.

"Did you hear that beautiful sound earlier?" Ted asked. "It woke me. It was faint but wonderful. I just wanted to keep listening."

"I didn't hear it," CPU said, shaking his head. "But I don't hear much now. If it was the same sound you heard before the birds carried us away, I know who's making it. I saw him. It was a boy. He had blonde hair and a blindfold over his eyes. His voice hypnotized you, but not me. I could barely hear it."

"He's in this castle," Barth said, sitting upright. "I wonder why? And, why are they keeping us down here? What do they want? We've been in this dungeon for days. They feed us, then go away. It makes no sense!"

"Stay cool, man," CPU said. "Don't get upset. We don't want things to start shaking and this castle to come crashing down on us."

"I know, I know," Barth said with a grunt. "When I get frustrated, I try to think of something that makes me feel better, like my go-carts, my treehouse, and drones. It helps me cool down."

Ted swept his hands through the air. Delicate notes like the plucking of violin strings poured out. The other boys listened silently.

"I'm beginning to like that," Barth said finally.

"I'm glad," Ted laughed. "But I'd make it anyway."

"I know. It's getting better. It breaks up the boredom."

Ted's hands moved again. The sound carried through the dungeon walls, echoing down passageways and into dark rooms in the great labyrinth of stone. It reached the ears of creatures large and small – some that welcomed the sound, and others that didn't.

Appendix I:
Abbreviated Dictionary of the Iapar Dialect
(spoken by the people and creatures of Hevelin)

ama	ancient/old/primeval	dia	law/rule/commandment
anea	is/are	dio	glove
anolar	ranger/roamer/nomad	dima	will/intend
ana	I/me	doth	violate/break/breach
ara	outpost	duali	magic
ava	too	emon	canyon
awa	special/unique	eno	monkey
ba	no/not	eori	wrong
baesa	dry	ere	light
beao	they/them	cril	leader/chief
beala	wander/roam/journey	ewar	mammoth/huge/enormous
beile	understand/know/realize	far	stone/rock/gem
		fen	glade
beles	to master/to learn	feo	you/yourself
beo	he/she	feri	silver
cenarri	sapphire	fiali	south/southern
cien	and	filia	silence
cirel	dragon	gadre	black
criel	should	geo	to want
cyano	different	grea	to go
danu	boy	hanu	girl
dar	shore	heri	hide/conceal
dath	angry/furious	hin	cat
del	wielder/controller/user	hithe	release/liberate/free

honna	please	metoha	hello
humi	must/require/ necessary	mette	welcome/greetings
		mi	do/did/done
iapar	east/eastern	mia	flee/run away
ima	end	mio	snow
ineo	common/ordinary	moni	fruit
ipa	but/however	mora	language/tongue/ speech
ita	or		
iwa	with	movae	serene/patient/ tolerant
jeon	quickly/ rapidly		
jien	hurt	moya	here/at this place
jui	find	mulah	way/direction
kella	hear	nari	pretty/lovely
kio	appear/seem	nea	there
lar	ruin	netalu	nice/sweet/ charming
len	island		
lena	mountain/ range	netu	brown
lene	move/take action	namo	stream/creek/river
luma	creature/animal	non	quiet
mana	say/speak	onno	above/beyond
maya	okay/all right	oria	light, illumination
mea	us/we	osa	sea/ocean
meandu	friend/pal/comrade	ose	soon
mealo	danger/peril/ threat/ risk	owali	together
		owli	lantern
meau	their	palon	betrayal
mele	crag/cliff/ridge	pana	land
mello	from	pani	prism
meo	happy/glad	pena	fate/destiny/doom
methe	further/farther	peonie	mirror
metia	because	pitu	stay/remain

plena	guest	sienn	water
qui	have/had	sirie	golden
quon	voice/voices	suena	home/house
rarei	crag/cliff/bluff	sye	crystal
rea	go/depart	tea	yes
risir	north/northern	tera	earth/world
rius	field/meadow	tra	cavern
roya	assume	tria	end
runi	why	une	and
runos	violators/transgressors	vothe	forgive/pardon/excuse
savi	touch/contact	verana	show/reveal
seta	leave/withdraw	wanna	now/at this point
setha	what	wenna	follow/pursue/chase
sette	where		
seva	that	wente	vigilance/watchfulness
seve	speak/talk/converse	yan	realm/kingdom
sevi	this	yon	fire/flame
shie	fairies/fairies	zum	war

Appendix II:
Abbreviated List of People, Places, Creatures and Objects of Hevelin

Anolari	winged rangers
asaria	white butterflies of Eelena
Benapara Ara	Benapara Outpost
Besenon Pana	a desert land in Hevelen
Celione	a Sienshie princess; Wife of Theralin; Mother of Siriena and Fioena
cenarri moni	a sapphire fruit
Cendri	a Panishie fairy
Cenio	Eredel's crow
Cirelyon Zum	Dragon Fire Wars
deliena	A flower that blooms once every twelve years
Dewlera	mother of all rarewar
Ea Emon	Ea Canyon
eanies	snail-like creatures
Eelena	the southern mountain range bordering Elderlan
Eanimus	a river that passes under Eelena
Elderlan	a forest between the Eelena and Uelena mountain ranges
Eredel	the light wielder
Esante Trea	the Pool of Esante
Fenietra	the glade caverns
Feralon	a Sienshie prince; brother of Celione
ferihin	silver cat
Feriyan	Silver Realm

Fiali Peonie	Southern Mirror Lake
filia dio	silence gloves
Fioena	a Panishie princess; daughter of Theralin and Celione; sister of Siriena
Folria Namo	a river of Hevelen in the southern Besenon Pana
Gadreshie	black fairies
Gala	Eredel's male dog
Garno Namo	a river of Hevelen in the northern Besenon Pana
Giridin	a town in Elderlan built by the Ancients.
Hevelen	the sister island
Heyolu	a rarewar bird
Hiapana Mele	Hiapana Crags
Hiapana Lena	Hiapana Mountains
ilisey	a clear liquid made from the phimea fruit
immi	the bouncing bears
jianar	the great wolves of Hevelen
Lela	Eredel's female dog
Malon	Sienshie prince; brother of Celione
Marigo	Eredel's gray mare
Meosey	Happy Dip Pass
mio eno	the snow monkeys
Netupana	the brown land
Opal	iron structure built to protect the seeli moni trees of Elderlan
Onil	a trail leading east to west through Elderlan
Oriafar	light stone
Oriafen	light glade (home of Panishie)

Osa	Eredel's golden colored horse
Owli far	lantern stone
Palon Zum	the war of betrayals
Panishie	the prism fairies
phimea	a grape-like fruit
rarewar	the crag mammoth
Risrean	a kingdom of northern Hevelen
Sienshie	the water fairies
Sidtarr	ruler of Risrean
Siriena (Sirie)	a fairy princess of the Panishie (daughter of Theralin)
sieli moni	the crystal fruit
Tarian	a Sienshie prince; the son of Malon, and the cousin of Siriena
Theralin	the chief of the Panishie tribe (father of Siriena)
tolepar	a species of tree
Tolera Rius	the fields of Tolera
Trethian	king of the Silver City
Teralar Zum	war that destroyed much of the ancient world
Uelena	the northern mountains bordering Elderlan
wadri	small furry animals that live in the forests of Elderlan and move in large mounds
Yiliar	the Northern Shore

For further information on the Kingdom of the Silver Cat
and the Sapphire Fruit Chronicles, please visit
www.sapphirefruit.com

ABOUT THE AUTHOR

Thomas (Tom) Carroll fell in love with fantasy adventure stories as a child. He read all types of imaginary stories from folk tales to epic adventures to ancient myths. The idea for Kingdom of the Silver Cat first came to him while he was riding on a bus to school in the fourth grade. He wrote early chapters over the next several years but eventually became interested in other things and put it aside.

As an adult, with children of his own, Mr. Carroll returned to the story and decided to finish it. The tale grew in the writing until it would no longer fit into a single book. Kingdom of the Silver Cat is the first book in the series called the Sapphire Fruit Chronicles.

Mr. Carroll lives in Northern California.

CPSIA information can be obtained
at www.ICGtesting.com
Printed in the USA
FSHW011506300420
69796FS